W9-BUF-720

The Creative Collection of American Short Stories

CREATIVE EDITIONS

The Creative Collection of American Short Stories

Illustrated by Yan Nascimbene

Introduction by Ray Bradbury

CONTENTS

INTRODUCTION by RAY BRADBURY

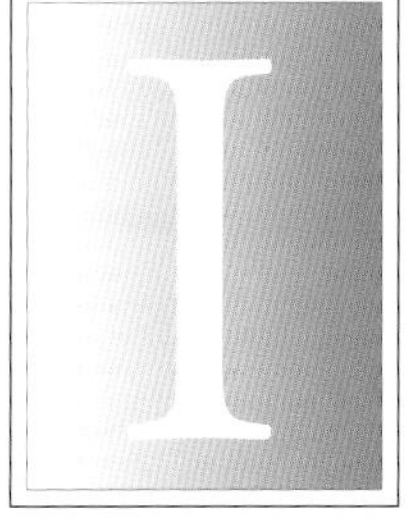

In your hands are 272 pages containing 17 superb short stories. You may choose, as I do, to look upon this collection as one might an emerald. This is a fitting metaphor, I think, for a couple of reasons. First, writing a short story masterpiece is not unlike cutting and polishing a gemstone—both tasks require a keen eye, practiced technique, and a confident hand. Second, reading this anthology is akin to examining a cut emerald with many surfaces: depending on how you hold and look at it, you'll see many different facets. In short stories, each of these facets can reflect its own truths about life.

I gained this outlook long ago. When I was 18 years old, I found myself freshly graduated from high school but lacking the means to go on to college. Circumstances being what they were, I did a very wise thing: I decided that I would walk down to the library and educate myself. And so I did. I went to the library 3 days a week for 10 years and graduated from its towering stacks and quiet aisles at the age of 28.

Somewhere along my path, either during those library years or after, each of the stories within this volume came into my life and helped bring my gaze onto certain facets of the human condition. I believe in reading this sort of collection as a means of both improving oneself and making discoveries about others. Each of these writers—Twain, Hughes, and the rest—holds up a piece of his or her life and shows it to you and says, "How's this? This moment is about loving or appreciating a certain incident, and here it is."

I can't really pick out any one particular story here that is my super-favorite, but if forced to do so, I'd probably have to say "The Chrysanthemums," by John Steinbeck. I first read this story of flowers and loneliness when I was 21, and it helped me to see a different way of writing on a subject and doing so objectively. The story also led me to pick up and read Steinbeck's classic novel *The Grapes of Wrath* and educated me in the means of writing prose poetry, which influenced the writing of my own story collection, *The Martian Chronicles.*

You'll find in this anthology writers who achieved triumph with a single brilliant tale. "The Lottery," by Shirley Jackson, brought in a flood of praise from all over America and beyond in the late 1940s, but she never wrote another thing that really equaled it. She penned many other stories and novels, but "The Lottery" was the one work that forever after was mentioned any time and anywhere she was introduced.

Another writer to get acquainted with here, especially if you are drawn to humor, is James Thurber. "The Secret Life of Walter Mitty" became an obsession of mine when I was living in Ireland in 1953, writing the screenplay for John Huston's *Moby Dick.* I ran out to the nearest bookstore and bought 12 books by Thurber because this story of imagination so sparked *my* imagination, making me want to learn more about the total arc of his work.

I'd like to remark specifically on one more story: "The Black Cat," by Edgar Allan Poe. I read this dark tale when I was nine years old, and it changed my life. I went on to devour the complete works of Poe, and when I set a personal course as a young writer in my 20s, he told me the direction to go. All my friends told me not to write weird stories, but Mr. Poe told me to not listen to them—to go ahead and write stories as weird as I wanted and send them to *Weird Tales.*

These are the short stories whose facets gleam most brightly to me. Each of these authors was a teacher to me at one time or another. I took from their works lessons, encouragement, and career guidance. And so they became, for me, not just authors but—in a sense—kin. Aunts, uncles, cousins, and honorary fathers and mothers.

I could comment on more of these great American tales—on Ambrose Bierce's "An Occurrence at Owl Creek Bridge," Alice Walker's "Everyday Use," and Wallace Stegner's "In the Twilight." But I won't. I will instead open the door and invite you inside. I will wish you well in finding a story that may end up being your own special love or inspiration—an experience in reading and truth that you may someday share with another at the dinner table or on a plane ride.

So enjoy these stories … and the education along the way.

Ray Bradbury

June 2009

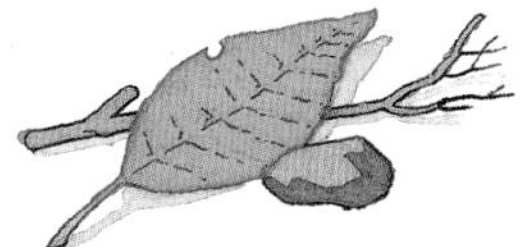

Edgar Allan Poe

The Black Cat

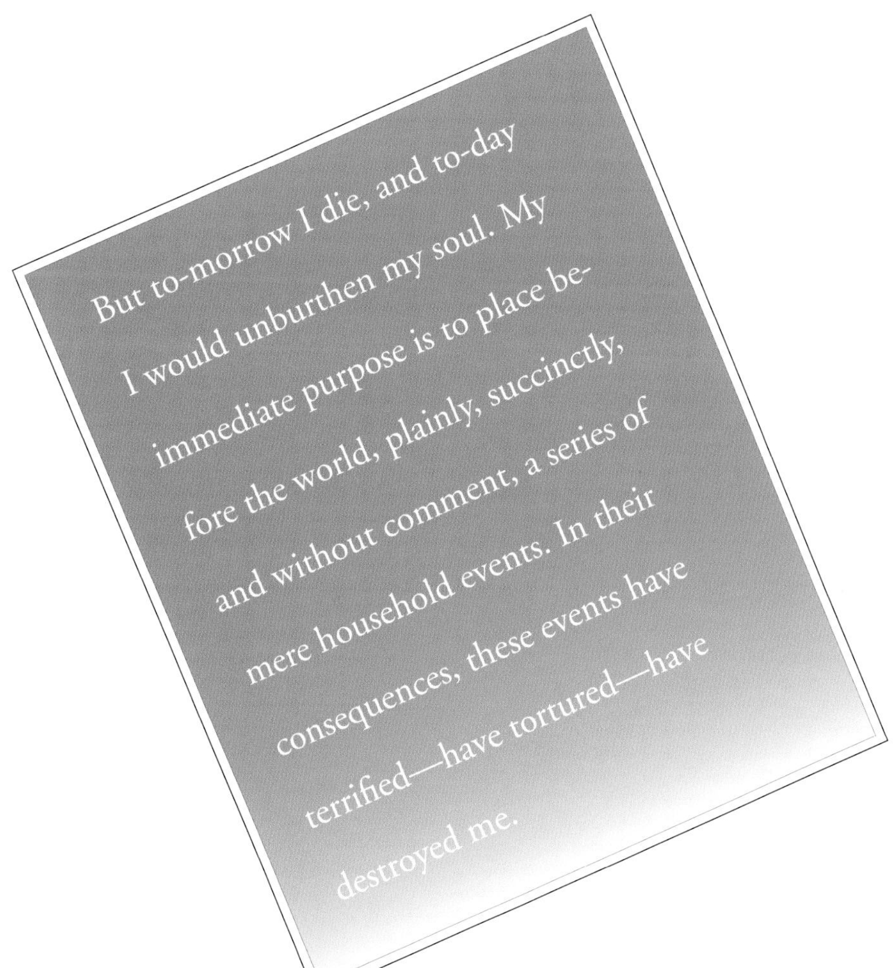

or the most wild, yet most homely narrative which I am about to pen, I neither expect nor solicit belief. Mad indeed would I be to expect it, in a case where my very senses reject their own evidence. Yet, mad am I not—and very surely do I not dream. But to-morrow I die, and to-day I would unburthen my soul. My immediate purpose is to place before the world, plainly, succinctly, and without comment, a series of mere household events. In their consequences, these events have terrified—have tortured—have destroyed me. Yet I will not attempt to expound them. To me, they have presented little but Horror—to many they will seem less terrible than *baroques*. Hereafter, perhaps, some intellect may be found which will reduce my phantasm to the common-place—some intellect more calm, more logical, and far less excitable than my own, which will perceive, in the circumstances I detail with awe, nothing more than an ordinary succession of very natural causes and effects.

From my infancy I was noted for the docility and humanity of my disposition. My tenderness of heart was even so conspicuous as to make me the jest of my companions. I was especially fond of animals, and was indulged by my parents with a great variety of pets. With these I spent most of my time, and never was so happy as when feeding and caressing them. This peculiarity of character grew with my growth, and in my manhood, I derived from it one of my principal sources of pleasure. To those who have cherished an affection for a faithful and sagacious dog, I need hardly be at the trouble of explaining the nature or the intensity of the gratification thus derivable. There is something in the unselfish and self-sacrificing love of a brute, which goes directly to the heart of him who has had

frequent occasion to test the paltry friendship and gossamer fidelity of mere *Man*.

I married early, and was happy to find in my wife a disposition not uncongenial with my own. Observing my partiality for domestic pets, she lost no opportunity of procuring those of the most agreeable kind. We had birds, goldfish, a fine dog, rabbits, a small monkey, and *a cat*.

This latter was a remarkably large and beautiful animal, entirely black, and sagacious to an astonishing degree. In speaking of his intelligence, my wife, who at heart was not a little tinctured with superstition, made frequent allusion to the ancient popular notion, which regarded all black cats as witches in disguise. Not that she was ever *serious* upon this point—and I mention the matter at all for no better reason than that it happens, just now, to be remembered.

> I took from my waistcoat-pocket a pen-knife, opened it, grasped the poor beast by the throat, and deliberately cut one of its eyes from the socket! I blush, I burn, I shudder, while I pen the damnable atrocity.

Pluto—this was the cat's name—was my favorite pet and playmate. I alone fed him, and he attended me wherever I went about the house. It was even with difficulty that I could prevent him from following me through the streets.

Our friendship lasted, in this manner, for several years, during which my general temperament and character—through the instrumentality of the Fiend Intemperance—had (I blush to confess it) experienced a radical alteration for the worse. I grew, day by day, more moody, more irritable, more regardless of the feelings of others. I suffered myself to use intemperate language to my wife. At length, I even offered her personal violence. My pets, of course, were made to feel the change in my disposition. I not only neglected, but ill-used them. For Pluto, however, I still retained sufficient regard to restrain me from maltreating him, as I made no scruple of maltreating the rabbits, the monkey, or even the dog, when by accident, or through affection, they came in my way. But my disease grew upon me—for what disease is like Alcohol!—and at length even Pluto, who was now becoming old, and consequently somewhat peevish—even Pluto began to experience the effects of my ill temper.

One night, returning home, much intoxicated, from one of my haunts about town, I fancied that the cat avoided my presence. I seized him; when, in his fright at my violence, he inflicted a slight wound upon my hand with his teeth. The fury of a demon instantly possessed me. I knew myself no longer. My original soul seemed, at once, to take its flight from my body and a more than fiendish malevolence, gin-nurtured, thrilled every fibre of my frame. I took from my waistcoat-pocket a pen-knife, opened it, grasped the poor beast by the throat, and deliberately cut one of its eyes from the socket! I blush, I burn, I shudder, while I pen the damnable atrocity.

When reason returned with the morning—when I had slept off the fumes of the night's debauch—I experienced a sentiment half of horror, half of remorse, for the crime of which I had been guilty; but it was, at best, a feeble and equivocal feeling, and the soul remained untouched. I again plunged into excess, and soon drowned in wine all memory of the deed.

In the meantime the cat slowly recovered. The socket of the lost eye presented, it is true, a frightful appearance, but he no longer appeared to suffer any pain. He went about the house as usual, but, as might be expected, fled in extreme terror at my approach. I had so much of my old heart left, as to be at first grieved by this evident dislike on the part of a creature which had once so loved me. But this feeling soon gave place to irritation. And then came, as if to my final and irrevocable overthrow, the spirit of PERVERSENESS. Of this spirit philosophy takes no account. Yet I am not more sure that my soul lives, than I am that perverseness is one of the primitive impulses of the human heart—one of the indivisible primary faculties, or sentiments, which give direction to the character of Man. Who has not, a hundred times, found himself committing a vile or a silly action, for no other reason than because he knows he should *not*? Have we not a perpetual inclination, in the teeth of our best judgment, to violate that which is *Law*, merely because we understand it to be such? This spirit of perverseness, I say, came to my final overthrow. It was this unfathomable longing of the soul *to vex itself*—to offer violence to its own nature—to do wrong for the wrong's sake only—that urged me to continue and finally to consummate the injury I had inflicted upon the unoffending brute. One morning, in cool blood, I slipped a noose about its neck and hung it to the limb of a tree;—hung it with the tears streaming from my eyes, and with the bitterest remorse at my heart;—hung it *because* I knew that it had loved me, and because I felt it had given me no reason of offence;—hung it *because* I knew that in so doing I was committing a sin—a deadly sin that would so jeopardize my immortal soul as to place it—if such a thing were possible—even beyond the reach of the infinite mercy of the Most Merciful and Most Terrible God.

For months I could not rid myself of the phantasm of the cat; and, during this period, there came back into my spirit a half-sentiment that seemed, but was not, remorse.

On the night of the day on which this cruel deed was done, I was aroused from sleep by the cry of fire. The curtains of my bed were in flames. The whole house was blazing. It was with great difficulty that my wife, a servant, and myself, made our escape from the conflagration. The destruction was complete. My entire worldly wealth was swallowed up, and I resigned myself thenceforward to despair.

I am above the weakness of seeking to establish a sequence of cause and effect, between the disaster and the atrocity. But I am detailing a chain of facts—and wish not to leave even a possible link imperfect. On the day succeeding the fire, I visited the ruins. The walls, with one exception, had fallen in. This exception was found in a compartment wall, not very thick, which stood about the middle of the house, and against which had rested the head of my bed. The plastering had here, in great measure, resisted the action of the fire—a fact which I attributed to its having been recently spread. About this wall a dense crowd were collected, and many persons seemed to be examining a particular portion of it with very minute and eager attention. The words "strange!" "singular!" and other similar expressions, excited my curiosity. I approached and saw, as if graven in *bas relief* upon the white surface, the figure of a gigantic *cat*. The impression was given with an accuracy truly marvellous. There was a rope about the animal's neck.

When I first beheld this apparition—for I could scarcely regard it as less—my wonder and my terror were extreme. But at length reflection came to my aid. The cat, I remembered, had been hung in a garden adjacent to the house. Upon the alarm of fire, this garden had been immediately filled by the crowd—by some one of whom the animal must have been cut from the tree and thrown, through an open window, into my chamber. This had probably been done with the view of arousing me from sleep. The falling of other walls had compressed the victim of my cruelty into the substance of the freshly-spread plaster; the lime of which, with the flames, and the *ammonia* from the carcass, had then accomplished the portraiture as I saw it.

Although I thus readily accounted to my reason, if not altogether to my conscience, for the startling fact just detailed, it did not the less fail to make a deep impression upon my fancy. For months I could not rid myself of the phantasm of the cat; and, during this period, there came back into my spirit a half-sentiment that seemed, but was not, remorse. I went so far as to regret the loss of the animal, and to look about me, among the vile haunts which I now habitually frequented, for another pet of the same species, and of somewhat similar appearance, with which to supply its place.

One night as I sat, half stupefied, in a den of more than infamy, my attention was suddenly drawn to some black object, reposing upon the head of one of the immense hogsheads of Gin, or of Rum, which constituted the chief furniture of the apartment. I had been looking steadily at the top of this hogshead for some minutes, and what now caused me surprise was the fact that I had not sooner perceived the object thereupon. I approached it, and touched it with my hand. It was a black cat—a very large one—fully as large as Pluto, and closely resembling him in every respect but one. Pluto had not a white hair upon any portion of his body; but this cat had a large, although indefinite splotch of white, covering nearly the whole region of the breast.

Upon my touching him, he immediately arose, purred loudly, rubbed against my hand, and appeared delighted with my notice. This, then, was the very creature of which I was in search. I at once offered to purchase it of the landlord; but this person made no claim to it—knew nothing of it—had never seen it before.

I continued my caresses, and, when I prepared to go home, the animal evinced a disposition to accompany me. I permitted it to do so; occasionally stooping and patting it as I proceeded. When it reached the house it domesticated itself at once, and became immediately a great favorite with my wife.

For my own part, I soon found a dislike to it arising within me. This was just the reverse of what I had anticipated; but—I know not how or why it was—its evident fondness for myself rather disgusted and annoyed. By slow degrees, these feelings of disgust and annoyance rose into the bitterness of hatred. I avoided the creature; a certain sense of shame, and the remembrance of my former deed of cruelty, preventing me from physically abusing it. I did not, for some weeks, strike, or otherwise violently ill use it; but gradually—very gradually—I came to look upon it with unutterable loathing, and to flee silently from its odious presence, as from the breath of a pestilence.

What added, no doubt, to my hatred of the beast, was the discovery, on the morning after I brought it home, that, like Pluto, it also had been deprived of one of its eyes. This circumstance, however, only endeared it to my wife, who, as I have already said, possessed, in a high degree, that humanity of feeling which had once been my distinguishing trait, and the source of many of my simplest and purest pleasures.

With my aversion to this cat, however, its partiality for myself seemed to increase. It followed my footsteps with a pertinacity which it would be difficult to make the reader comprehend. Whenever I sat, it would crouch beneath my chair, or spring upon my knees, covering me with its loathsome caresses. If I arose to walk it would get between my feet and thus nearly throw me down, or, fastening its long and sharp claws in my dress, clamber, in this manner, to my breast. At such times, although I longed to destroy it with a blow, I was yet withheld from so doing, partly by a memory of my former crime, but chiefly—let me confess it at once—by absolute *dread* of the beast.

> With my aversion to this cat, however, its partiality for myself seemed to increase.

This dread was not exactly a dread of physical evil—and yet I should be at a loss how otherwise to define it. I am almost ashamed to own—yes, even in this felon's cell, I am almost ashamed to own—that the terror and horror with which the animal inspired me, had been heightened by one of the merest chimaeras it would be possible to conceive. My wife had called my attention, more than once, to the character of the mark of white hair, of which I have spoken, and which constituted the sole visible difference between the strange beast and the one I had destroyed. The reader will remember that this mark, although large, had been originally very indefinite; but, by slow degrees—degrees nearly imperceptible, and which for a long time my Reason struggled to reject as fanciful—it had, at length, assumed a rigorous distinctness of outline. It was now the representation of an object that I shudder to name—and for this, above all, I loathed, and dreaded, and would have rid myself of the monster *had I dared*—it was now, I say, the image of a hideous—of a ghastly thing—of the GALLOWS!—oh, mournful and terrible engine of Horror and of Crime—of Agony and of Death!

And now was I indeed wretched beyond the wretchedness of mere Humanity. And *a brute beast*—whose fellow I had contemptuously destroyed—*a brute beast* to work out for *me*—for me a man, fashioned in the image of the High God—so much of insufferable wo! Alas! neither by day nor by night knew I the blessing of Rest any more! During the former the creature left me no moment alone; and, in the latter, I started, hourly, from dreams of unutterable fear, to find the hot breath of the thing upon my face, and its vast weight—an incarnate Night-Mare that I had no power to shake off—incumbent eternally upon my *heart!*

Beneath the pressure of torments such as these, the feeble remnant of the good within me succumbed. Evil thoughts became my sole intimates—the darkest and most evil of thoughts. The moodiness of my usual temper increased to hatred of all things and of all mankind; while, from the sudden, frequent, and ungovernable outbursts of a fury to which I now blindly abandoned myself, my uncomplaining wife, alas! was the most usual and the most patient of sufferers.

One day she accompanied me, upon some household errand, into the cellar of the old building which our poverty compelled us to inhabit. The cat followed me down the steep stairs, and, nearly throwing me headlong, exasperated me to madness. Uplifting an axe, and forgetting, in my wrath, the childish dread which had hitherto stayed my hand, I aimed a blow at the animal which, of course, would have proved instantly fatal had it descended as I wished. But this blow was arrested by the hand of my wife. Goaded, by the interference, into a rage more than demoniacal, I withdrew my arm from her grasp and buried the axe in her brain. She fell dead upon the spot, without a groan.

This hideous murder accomplished, I set myself forthwith, and with entire deliberation, to the task of concealing the body. I knew that I could not remove it from the house, either by day or by night, without the risk of being observed by the neighbors. Many projects entered my mind. At one period I thought of cutting the corpse into minute fragments, and destroying them by fire. At another, I resolved to dig a grave for it in the floor of the cellar. Again, I deliberated about casting it in the well in the yard—about packing it in a box, as if merchandize, with the usual arrangements, and so getting a porter to take it from the house. Finally I hit upon what I considered a far better expedient than either of these. I determined to wall it up in the cellar—as the monks of the middle ages are recorded to have walled up their victims.

Uplifting an axe, and forgetting, in my wrath, the child-ish dread which had hitherto stayed my hand, I aimed a blow at the animal which, of course, would have proved instantly fatal had it descended as I wished.

For a purpose such as this the cellar was well adapted. Its walls were loosely constructed, and had lately been plastered throughout with a rough plaster, which the dampness of the atmosphere had prevented from hardening. Moreover, in one of the walls was a projection, caused by a false chimney, or fireplace, that had been filled up, and made to resemble the red of the cellar. I made no doubt that I could readily displace the bricks at this point, insert the corpse, and wall the whole up as before, so that no eye could detect anything suspicious.

And in this calculation I was not deceived. By means of a crow-bar I easily dislodged the bricks, and, having carefully deposited the body against the inner wall, I propped it in that position, while, with little trouble, I re-laid the whole structure as it originally stood. Having procured mortar, sand, and hair, with every possible precaution, I prepared a plaster which could not be distinguished from the old, and with this I very carefully went over the new brick-work. When I had finished, I felt satisfied that all was right. The wall did not present the slightest appearance of having been disturbed. The rubbish on the floor was picked up with the minutest care. I looked around triumphantly, and said to myself—"Here at least, then, my labor has not been in vain."

My next step was to look for the beast which had been the cause of so much wretchedness; for I had, at length, firmly resolved to put it to death. Had I been able to meet with it, at the moment, there could have been no doubt of its fate; but it appeared that the crafty animal had been alarmed at the violence of my previous anger, and forebore to present itself in my present mood. It is impossible to describe, or to imagine, the deep, the blissful sense of relief which the absence of the detested creature occasioned in my bosom. It did not make its appearance during the night—and thus for one night at least, since its introduction into the house, I soundly and tranquilly slept; aye, *slept* even with the burden of murder upon my soul!

The second and the third day passed, and still my tormentor came not. Once again I breathed as a freeman. The monster, in terror, had fled the premises forever! I should behold it no more! My happiness was supreme! The guilt of my dark deed disturbed me but little. Some few inquiries had been made, but these had been readily answered. Even a search had been instituted—but of course nothing was to be discovered. I looked upon my future felicity as secured.

Upon the fourth day of the assassination, a party of the police came, very unexpectedly, into the house, and proceeded again to make rigorous investigation of the premises. Secure, however, in the inscrutability of my place of concealment, I felt no embarrassment whatever. The officers bade me accompany them in their

The officers bade me accompany them in their search. They left no nook or corner unexplored. At length, for the third or fourth time, they descended into the cellar. I quivered not in a muscle. My heart beat calmly as that of one who slumbers in innocence.

search. They left no nook or corner unexplored. At length, for the third or fourth time, they descended into the cellar. I quivered not in a muscle. My heart beat calmly as that of one who slumbers in innocence. I walked the cellar from end to end. I folded my arms upon my bosom, and roamed easily to and fro. The police were thoroughly satisfied and prepared to depart. The glee at my heart was too strong to be restrained. I burned to say if but one word, by way of triumph, and to render doubly sure their assurance of my guiltlessness.

"Gentlemen," I said at last, as the party ascended the steps, "I delight to have allayed your suspicions. I wish you all health, and a little more courtesy. By the bye, gentlemen, this—this is a very well constructed house." [In the rabid desire to say something easily, I scarcely knew what I uttered at all.]—"I may say an *excellently* well constructed house. These walls—are you going, gentlemen?—these walls are solidly put together;" and here, through the mere phrenzy of bravado, I rapped heavily, with a cane which I held in my hand, upon that very portion of the brick-work behind which stood the corpse of the wife of my bosom.

But may God shield and deliver me from the fangs of the Arch-Fiend! No sooner had the reverberation of my blows sunk into silence, than I was answered by a voice from within the tomb!—by a cry, at first muffled and broken, like the sobbing of a child, and then quickly swelling into one long, loud, and continuous scream, utterly anomalous and inhuman—a howl—a wailing shriek, half of horror and half of triumph, such as might have arisen only out of hell, conjointly from the throats of the damned in their agony and of the demons that exult in the damnation.

Of my own thoughts it is folly to speak. Swooning, I staggered to the opposite wall. For one instant the party upon the stairs remained motionless, through extremity of terror and of awe. In the next, a dozen stout arms were toiling at the wall. It fell bodily. The corpse, already greatly decayed and clotted with gore, stood erect before the eyes of the spectators. Upon its head, with red extended mouth and solitary eye of fire, sat the hideous beast whose craft had seduced me into murder, and whose informing voice had consigned me to the hangman. I had walled the monster up within the tomb!

MARK TWAIN

The Celebrated Jumping Frog of Calaveras County

You never see a frog so modest and straightfor'ard as he was, for all he was so gifted. And when it come to fair and square jumping on a dead level, he could get over more ground at one straddle than any animal of his breed you ever see.

HOTEL
Eve's
SALOON

In compliance with the request of a friend of mine, who wrote me from the East, I called on good-natured, garrulous old Simon Wheeler, and inquired after my friend's friend, Leonidas W. Smiley, as requested to do, and I hereunto append the result. I have a lurking suspicion that *Leonidas W.* Smiley is a myth; that my friend never knew such a personage; and that he only conjectured that if I asked old Wheeler about him, it would remind him of his infamous *Jim* Smiley, and he would go to work and bore me to death with some exasperating reminiscence of him as long and tedious as it should be useless to me. If that was the design, it succeeded.

I found Simon Wheeler dozing comfortably by the bar-room stove of the old, dilapidated tavern in the decayed mining camp of Angel's, and I noticed that he was fat and bald-headed, and had an expression of winning gentleness and simplicity upon his tranquil countenance. He roused up, and gave me good-day. I told him that a friend of mine had commissioned me to make some inquiries about a cherished companion of his boyhood named *Leonidas W.* Smiley—*Rev. Leonidas W.* Smiley—a young minister of the Gospel, who he had heard was at one time a resident of Angel's Camp. I added that if Mr. Wheeler could tell me anything about this Rev. Leonidas W. Smiley, I would feel under many obligations to him.

Simon Wheeler backed me into a corner and blockaded me there with his chair, and then sat me down and reeled off the monotonous narrative which follows this paragraph. He never smiled, he never frowned, he never changed his voice from the gentle-flowing key to which he tuned his initial sentence, he never betrayed the slightest suspicion of enthusiasm; but all through the interminable narrative there ran a vein of impressive earnestness and sincerity, which showed me plainly that, so far from his imagining that there was anything ridiculous or funny about his story, he regarded it as a really important matter, and admired its two heroes as men of transcendent genius in *finesse*. To me, the spectacle of a man drifting serenely along through such a queer yarn without ever smiling, was exquisitely absurd. As I said before, I asked him to tell me what he knew of Rev. Leonidas W. Smiley, and he replied as follows. I let him go on in his own way, and never interrupted him once:

"There was a feller here once by the name of *Jim* Smiley, in the winter of '49—or maybe it was the spring of '50—I don't recollect exactly, somehow, though what makes me think it was one or the other is because I remember the big flume wasn't finished when he first came to the camp; but anyway, he was the curiousest man about always betting on anything that turned up you ever see, if he could get anybody to bet on the other side; and if he couldn't, he'd change sides. Any way that suited the other man would suit *him*—any way just so's he got a bet, *he* was satisfied. But still he was lucky, uncommon lucky; he most always come out winner. He was always ready and laying for a chance; there couldn't be no solit'ry thing mentioned but that feller'd offer to bet on it, and take ary side you please, as I was just telling you. If there was a horse-race, you'd find him flush or you'd find him busted at the end of it; if there was a dog-fight, he'd bet on it; if there was a cat-fight, he'd bet on it; if there was a chicken-fight, he'd bet on it; why, if there was two birds setting on a fence, he would bet you which one would fly first; or if there was a camp-meeting, he would be there reg'lar to bet on Parson Walker, which he judged to be the best exhorter about here, and so he was too, and a good man. If he even seen a straddle-bug start to go anywheres, he would bet you how long it would take him to get to—to wherever he was going to, and if you took him up, he would foller that

He was always ready and laying for a chance; there couldn't be no solit'ry thing mentioned but that feller'd offer to bet on it, and take any side you please, as I was just telling you.

straddle-bug to Mexico but what he would find out where he was bound for and how long he was on the road. Lots of the boys here has seen that Smiley, and can tell you about him. Why, it never made no difference to *him*—he'd bet on *any* thing—the dangdest feller. Parson Walker's wife laid very sick once, for a good while, and it seemed as if they warn't going to save her; but one morning he come in, and Smiley asked how she was, and he said she was considerable better—thank the Lord for his inf'nite mercy—and coming on so smart that with the blessing of Prov'dence, she'd get well yet; and Smiley, before he thought, says, "Well, I'll risk two-and-a-half that she don't, anyway."

"Thish-yer Smiley had a mare—the boys called her the fifteen-minute nag, but that was only in fun, you know, because of course she was faster than that—and he used to win money on that horse, for all she was so slow and always had the asthma, or the distemper, or the consumption, or something of that kind. They used to give her two or three hundred yards' start, and then pass her under way; but always at the fag end of the race she'd get excited and desperate-like, and come cavorting and straddling up, and scattering her legs around limber, sometimes in the air, and sometimes out to one side among the fences, and kicking up m-o-r-e dust, and raising m-o-r-e racket with her coughing and sneezing and blowing her nose—and always fetch up at the stand just about a neck ahead, as near as you could cipher it down.

"And he had a little small bull-pup, that to look at him you'd think he warn't worth a cent but to set around and look ornery and lay for a chance to steal something. But as soon as money was up on him he was a different dog; his under-jaw'd begin to stick out like the fo'castle of a steamboat, and his teeth would uncover, and shine savage like the furnaces. And a dog might tackle him, and bully-rag him, and bite him, and throw him over his shoulder two or three times, and Andrew Jackson—which was the name of the pup—Andrew Jackson would never let on but what *he* was satisfied, and hadn't expected nothing else—and the bets being doubled and doubled on the other side all the time, till the money was all up; and then all of a sudden he would grab that other dog jest by the j'int of his hind leg and freeze to it—not chaw, you understand, but only jest grip and hang on till they throwed up the sponge, if it was a year. Smiley always come out winner on that pup, till he harnessed a dog once that didn't have no hind legs, because they'd been sawed off by a circular saw, and when the thing had gone along far enough, and the money was all up, and he come to make a snatch for his pet holt, he see in a minute how he'd been imposed on, and how the other dog had him in the door, so to speak, and he 'peared surprised, and then he looked sorter

He ketched a frog one day, and took him home and said he cal'lated to edercate him; and so he never done nothing for three months but set in his back yard and learn that frog to jump. and you bet you he *did* learn him, too.

discouraged-like, and didn't try no more to win the fight, and so he got shucked out bad. He give Smiley a look, as much as to say his heart was broke, and it was *his* fault, for putting up a dog that hadn't no hind legs for him to take holt of, which was his main dependence in a fight, and then he limped off a piece and laid down and died. It was a good pup, was that Andrew Jackson, and would have made a name for hisself if he'd lived, for the stuff was in him and he had genius—I know it, because he hadn't had no opportunities to speak of, and it don't stand to reason that a dog could make such a fight as he could under them circumstances, if he hadn't no talent. It always makes me feel sorry when I think of that last fight of his'n, and the way it turned out.

"Well, thish-yer Smiley had rat-tarriers, and chicken cocks, and tomcats, and all them kind of things, till you couldn't rest, and you couldn't fetch nothing for him to bet on but he'd match you. He ketched a frog one day, and took him home, and said he cal'lated to edercate him; and so he never done nothing for three months but set in his back yard and learn that frog to jump. And you bet you he *did* learn him, too. He'd give him a little punch behind, and the next minute you'd see that frog whirling in the air like a doughnut—see him turn one summerset, or maybe a couple, if he got a good start, and come down flat-footed and all right, like a cat. He got him up so in the matter of ketching flies, and kep' him in practice so constant, that he'd nail a fly every time as fur as he could see him. Smiley said all a frog wanted was education, and he could do 'most anything—and I believe him. Why, I've seen him set Dan'l Webster down here on this floor—Dan'l Webster was the name of the frog—and sing out, 'Flies, Dan'l, flies!' and quicker'n you could wink he'd spring straight up and snake a fly off'n the counter there, and flop down on the floor again as solid as a gob of mud, and fall to scratching the side of his head with his hind foot as indifferent as if he hadn't no idea he'd been doin' any more'n any frog might do. You never see a frog so modest and straightfor'ard as he was, for all he was so gifted. And when it come to fair and square jumping on a dead level, he could get over more ground at one straddle than any animal of his breed you ever see. Jumping on a dead level was his strong suit, you understand; and when it come to that, Smiley would ante up money on him as long as he had a red. Smiley was monstrous proud of his frog, and well he might be, for fellers that had traveled and been everywheres all said he laid over any frog that ever *they* see.

Smiley was monstrous proud of his frog, and well he might be, for fellers that had traveled and been everywheres all said he laid over any frog that ever *they* see.

"Well, Smiley kep' the beast in a little lattice box, and he used to fetch him down-town sometimes and lay for a bet. One day a feller—a stranger in the camp, he was—come acrost him with his box, and says:

"'What might it be that you've got in the box?'

"And Smiley says, sorter indifferent-like, 'It might be a parrot, or it might be a canary, maybe, but it ain't—it's only just a frog.'

"And the feller took it, and looked at it careful, and turned it round this way and that, and says, 'H'm—so 'tis. Well, what's he good for?'

"'Well,' Smiley says, easy and careless, 'he's good enough for *one* thing, I should judge—he can outjump any frog in Calaveras County.'

"The feller took the box again, and took another long, particular look, and give it back to Smiley, and says, very deliberate, 'Well,' he says, 'I don't see no p'ints about that frog that's any better'n any other frog.'

"'Maybe you don't,' Smiley says. 'Maybe you understand frogs, and maybe you don't understand 'em; maybe you've had experience, and maybe you ain't only a amature, as it were. Anyways, I've got *my* opinion, and I'll resk forty dollars that he can outjump any frog in Calaveras County.'

"And the feller studied a minute, and then says, kinder sad-like, 'Well, I'm only a stranger here, and I ain't got no frog; but if I had a frog, I'd bet you.'

"And then Smiley says, 'That's all right—that's all right—if you'll hold my box a minute, I'll go and get you a frog.' And so the feller took the box, and put up his forty dollars along with Smiley's, and set down to wait.

"So he set there a good while thinking and thinking to himself, and then he got the frog out and prized his mouth open and took a teaspoon and filled him full of quail-shot—filled him pretty near up to his chin—and set him on the floor. Smiley he went to the swamp and slopped around in the mud for a long time, and finally he ketched a frog, and fetched him in, and give him to this feller, and says:

"'Now, if you're ready, set him alongside of Dan'l, with his fore paws just even with Dan'l's and I'll give the word.' Then he says, 'One—two—three—*git*!' and him and the feller touched up the frogs from behind, and the new frog hopped off lively, but Dan'l give a heave, and hysted up his shoulders—so—like a Frenchman, but it warn't no use—he couldn't budge; he was planted as solid as a church, and he couldn't no more stir than if he was anchored out. Smiley was a good deal surprised, and he was disgusted too, but he didn't have no idea what the matter was, of course.

"The feller took the money and started away; and when he was going out at the door, he sorter jerked his thumb over his shoulder—so—at Dan'l, and says again, very deliberate, 'Well,' he says, 'I don't see no p'nts about that frog that's any better'n any other frog.'

"Smiley he stood scratching his head and looking down at Dan'l a long time, and at last he says, 'I do wonder what in the nation that frog throw'd off for—I wonder if there an't something the matter with him—he 'pears to look mighty baggy, somehow.' And he ketched Dan'l by the nap of the neck, and lifted him up and says, 'Why, blame my cats if he don't weigh five pound!' and turned him upside down, and he belched out a double handful of shot. And then he see how it was, and he was the maddest man—he set the frog down and took out after that feller, but he never ketched him. And—"

[Here Simon Wheeler heard his name called from the front yard, and got up to see what was wanted.] And turning to me as he moved away, he said: "Just set where you are, stranger, and rest easy—I ain't going to be gone a second."

But, by your leave, I did not think that a continuation of the history of the enterprising vagabond *Jim* Smiley would be likely to afford me much information concerning the Rev. *Leonidas W.* Smiley, and so I started away.

At the door I met the sociable Wheeler returning, and he buttonholed me and recommenced:

"Well, thish-yer Smiley had a yaller one-eyed cow that didn't have no tail, only just a short stump like a bannanner, and—"

"Oh, hang Smiley and his afflicted cow!" I muttered good-naturedly, and bidding the old gentleman good-day, I departed.

AMBROSE BIERCE

An Occurrence at Owl Creek Bridge

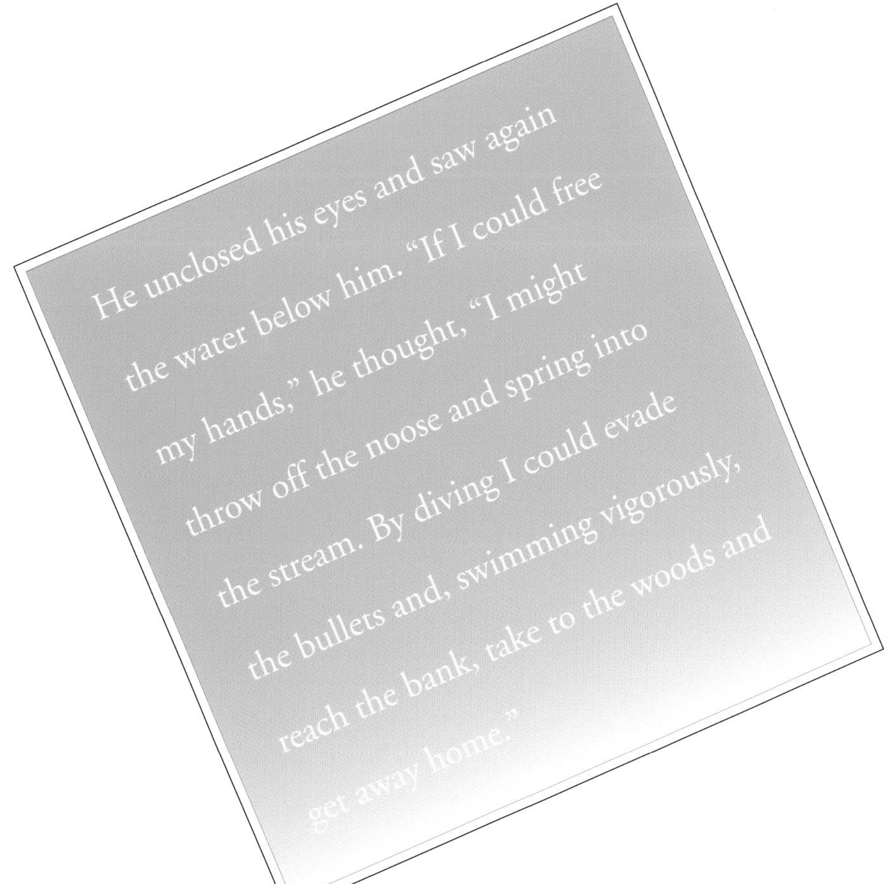

I

A man stood upon a railroad bridge in northern Alabama, looking down into the swift water twenty feet below. The man's hands were behind his back, the wrists bound with a cord. A rope closely encircled his neck. It was attached to a stout cross-timber above his head and the slack fell to the level of his knees. Some loose boards laid upon the sleepers supporting the metals of the railway supplied a footing for him and his executioners—two private soldiers of the Federal army, directed by a sergeant who in civil life may have been a deputy sheriff. At a short remove upon the same temporary platform was an officer in the uniform of his rank, armed. He was a captain. A sentinel at each end of the bridge stood with his rifle in the position known as "support," that is to say, vertical in front of the left shoulder, the hammer resting on the forearm thrown straight across the chest—a formal and unnatural position, enforcing an erect carriage of the body. It did not appear to be the duty of these two men to know what was occurring at the center of the bridge; they merely blockaded the two ends of the foot planking that traversed it.

Beyond one of the sentinels nobody was in sight; the railroad ran straight away into a forest for a hundred yards, then, curving, was lost to view. Doubtless there was an outpost farther along. The other bank of the stream was open ground—a gentle acclivity topped with a stockade of vertical tree trunks, loop-holed for rifles, with a single embrasure through which protruded the muzzle of a brass cannon commanding the bridge. Midway of the slope between the bridge and fort were the spectators—a single company of infantry in line, at "parade rest," the butts of the rifles on the ground, the barrels inclining slightly backward against the right shoulder, the hands crossed upon the stock. A lieutenant stood at the right of the line, the point of his sword upon the ground, his left hand resting upon his right. Excepting the group of four at the center of the bridge, not a man moved. The company faced the bridge, staring stonily, motionless. The sentinels, facing the banks of the stream, might have been statues to adorn the bridge. The captain stood with folded arms, silent, observing the work of his subordinates, but making no sign. Death is a dignitary who when he comes announced is to be received with formal manifestations of respect, even by those most familiar with him. In the code of military etiquette silence and fixity are forms of deference.

The man who was engaged in being hanged was apparently about thirty-five years of age. He was a civilian, if one might judge from his habit, which was that of a planter. His features were good—a straight nose, firm mouth, broad forehead, from which his long, dark hair was combed straight back, falling behind his ears to the collar of his well-fitting frock-coat. He wore a mustache and pointed beard, but no whiskers; his eyes were large and dark gray, and had a kindly expression which one would hardly have expected in one whose neck was in the hemp. Evidently this was no vulgar assassin. The liberal military code makes provision for hanging many kinds of persons, and gentlemen are not excluded.

The preparations being complete, the two private soldiers stepped aside and each drew away the plank upon which he had been standing. The sergeant turned to the captain, saluted and placed himself immediately behind that officer, who in turn moved apart one pace. These movements left the condemned man and the sergeant standing on the two ends of the same plank, which spanned three of the cross-ties of the bridge. The end upon which the civilian stood almost, but not quite, reached a fourth. This plank had been held in place by the weight of the captain; it was now held by that of the sergeant. At a signal from the former the latter would step aside, the plank

The man who was engaged in being hanged was apparently about thirty-five years of age. He was a civilian, if one might judge from his habit, which was that of a planter.

would tilt and the condemned man go down between two ties. The arrangement commended itself to his judgment as simple and effective. His face had not been covered nor his eyes bandaged. He looked a moment at his "unsteadfast footing," then let his gaze wander to the swirling water of the stream racing madly beneath his feet. A piece of dancing driftwood caught his attention and his eyes followed it down the current. How slowly it appeared to move! What a sluggish stream!

He closed his eyes in order to fix his last thoughts upon his wife and children. The water, touched to gold by the early sun, the brooding mists under the banks at some distance down the stream, the fort, the soldiers, the piece of drift—all had distracted him. And now he became conscious of a new disturbance. Striking through the thought of his dear ones was a sound which he could neither ignore nor understand, a sharp, distinct, metallic percussion like the stroke of a blacksmith's hammer upon the anvil; it had the same ringing quality. He wondered what it was, and whether immeasurably distant or near by—it seemed both. Its recurrence was regular, but as slow as the tolling of a death knell. He awaited each stroke with impatience and—he knew not why—apprehension. The intervals of silence grew progressively longer, the delays became maddening. With their greater infrequency the sounds increased in strength and sharpness. They hurt his ear like the thrust of a knife; he feared he would shriek. What he heard was the ticking of his watch.

He unclosed his eyes and saw again the water below him. "If I could free my hands," he thought, "I might throw off the noose and spring into the stream. By diving I could evade the bullets and, swimming vigorously, reach the bank, take to the woods and get away home. My home, thank God, is as yet outside their lines; my wife and little ones are still beyond the invader's farthest advance."

As these thoughts, which have here to be set down in words, were flashed into the doomed man's brain rather than evolved from it the captain nodded to the sergeant. The sergeant stepped aside.

II

Peyton Farquhar was a well-to-do planter, of an old and highly respected Alabama family. Being a slave owner and like other slave owners a politician he was naturally an original secessionist and ardently devoted to the Southern cause. Circumstances of an imperious nature, which it is unnecessary to relate here, had prevented him from taking service with the gallant army that had fought the disastrous campaigns ending with the fall of Corinth, and he chafed under the inglorious restraint, longing for the release of his energies, the larger life of the soldier, the opportunity for distinction. That opportunity, he felt, would come, as it comes to all in war time. Meanwhile he did what he could. No service was too humble for him to perform in aid of the South, no adventure too perilous for him to undertake if consistent with the character of a civilian who was at heart a soldier, and who in good faith and without too much qualification assented to at least a part of the frankly villainous dictum that all is fair in love and war.

One evening while Farquhar and his wife were sitting on a rustic bench near the entrance to his grounds, a gray-clad soldier rode up to the gate and asked for a drink of water. Mrs. Farquhar was only too happy to serve him with her own white hands. While she was fetching the water her husband approached the dusty horseman and inquired eagerly for news from the front.

"The Yanks are repairing the railroads," said the man, "and are getting ready for another advance. They have reached the Owl Creek bridge, put it in order and built a stockade on the north bank. The commandant has issued an order, which is posted everywhere, declaring that any civilian caught interfering with the railroad, its bridges, tunnels or trains will be summarily hanged. I saw the order."

"How far is it to the Owl Creek bridge?" Farquhar asked.

"About thirty miles."

"Is there no force on this side the creek?"

"Only a picket post half a mile out, on the railroad, and a single sentinel at this end of the bridge."

"Suppose a man—a civilian and student of hanging—should elude the picket post and perhaps get the better of the sentinel," said Farquhar, smiling, "what could he accomplish?"

The soldier reflected. "I was there a month ago," he replied. "I observed that the flood of last winter had lodged a great quantity of driftwood against the wooden pier at this end of the bridge. It is now dry and would burn like tow."

The lady had now brought the water, which the soldier drank. He thanked her ceremoniously, bowed to her husband and rode away. An hour later, after nightfall, he repassed the plantation, going northward in the direction from which he had come. He was a Federal scout.

> "Suppose a man—a civilian and student of hanging—should elude the picket post and perhaps get the better of the sentinel," said Farquhar, smiling, "what could he accomplish?"

III

As Peyton Farquhar fell straight downward through the bridge he lost consciousness and was as one already dead. From this state he was awakened—ages later, it seemed to him—by the pain of a sharp pressure upon his throat, followed by a sense of suffocation. Keen, poignant agonies seemed to shoot from his neck downward through every fiber of his body and limbs. These pains appeared to flash along well-defined lines of ramification and to beat with an inconceivably rapid periodicity. They seemed like streams of pulsating fire heating him to an intolerable temperature. As to his head, he was conscious of nothing but a feeling of fullness—of congestion. These sensations were unaccompanied by thought. The intellectual part of his nature was already effaced; he had power only to feel, and feeling was torment. He was conscious of motion. Encompassed in a luminous cloud, of which he was now merely the fiery heart, without material substance, he swung through unthinkable arcs of oscillation, like a vast pendulum. Then all at once, with terrible suddenness, the light about him shot upward with the noise of a loud plash; a frightful roaring was in his ears, and all was cold and dark. The power of thought was restored; he knew that the rope had broken and he had fallen into the stream. There was no additional strangulation; the noose about his neck was already suffocating him and kept the water from his lungs. To die of hanging at the bottom of a river!—the idea seemed to him ludicrous. He opened his eyes in the darkness and saw above him a gleam of light, but how distant, how inaccessible! He was still sinking, for the light became fainter and fainter until it was a mere glimmer. Then it began to grow and brighten, and he knew that he was rising toward the surface—knew it with reluctance, for he was now very comfortable. "To be hanged and drowned," he thought, "that is not so bad; but I do not wish to be shot. No; I will not be shot; that is not fair."

He was not conscious of an effort, but a sharp pain in his wrist apprised him that he was trying to free his hands. He gave the struggle his attention, as an idler might observe the feat of a juggler, without interest in the outcome. What splendid effort!—what magnificent, what superhuman strength! Ah, that was a fine endeavor! Bravo! The cord fell away; his arms parted and floated upward, the hands dimly seen on each side in the growing light. He watched them with a new interest as first one and then the other pounced upon the noose at his neck. They tore it away and thrust it fiercely aside, its undulations resembling those of a water snake. "Put it back, put it back!" He thought he shouted these words to his hands, for the undoing of the noose had been succeeded by the direst pang that he had yet experienced. His neck ached horribly; his brain was on fire; his heart, which had been fluttering faintly, gave a great leap, trying to force itself out at his mouth. His whole body was racked and wrenched with an insupportable anguish! But his disobedient hands gave no heed to the command. They beat the water vigorously with quick, downward strokes, forcing him to the surface. He felt his head emerge; his eyes were blinded by the sunlight; his chest expanded convulsively, and with a supreme and crowning agony his lungs engulfed a great draught of air, which instantly he expelled in a shriek!

He was now in full possession of his physical senses. They were, indeed, preternaturally keen and alert. Something in the awful disturbance of his organic system had so exalted and refined them that they made record of things never before perceived. He felt the ripples upon his face and heard their separate sounds as they struck. He looked at the forest on the bank of the stream, saw the individual trees, the leaves and the veining of each leaf—saw the very insects upon them: the locusts, the brilliant-bodied flies, the gray spiders stretching their webs from twig to twig. He noted the prismatic colors in all the dewdrops upon a million blades of grass. The humming of the gnats that danced above the eddies of the stream, the beating of the dragon-flies' wings, the strokes of the water-spiders' legs, like oars which had lifted their boat—all these made audible music. A fish slid along beneath his eyes and he heard the rush of its body parting the water.

He had come to the surface facing down the stream; in a moment the visible world seemed to wheel slowly round, himself the pivotal point, and he saw the bridge, the fort, the soldiers upon the bridge, the captain, the sergeant, the two privates, his executioners.

He had come to the surface facing down the stream; in a moment the visible world seemed to wheel slowly round, himself the pivotal point, and he saw the bridge, the fort, the soldiers upon the bridge, the captain, the sergeant, the two privates, his executioners. They were in silhouette against the blue sky. They shouted and gesticulated, pointing at him. The captain had drawn his pistol, but did not fire; the others were unarmed. Their movements were grotesque and horrible, their forms gigantic.

Suddenly he heard a sharp report and something struck the water smartly within a few inches of his head, spattering his face with spray. He heard a second report, and saw one of the sentinels with his rifle at his shoulder, a light cloud of blue smoke rising from the muzzle. The man in the water saw the eye of the man on the bridge gazing into his own through the sights of the rifle. He observed that

His brain was as energetic as his arms and legs; he thought with the rapidity of lightning.

it was a gray eye and remembered having read that gray eyes were keenest, and that all famous marksmen had them. Nevertheless, this one had missed.

A counter-swirl had caught Farquhar and turned him half round; he was again looking into the forest on the bank opposite the fort. The sound of a clear, high voice in a monotonous singsong now rang out behind him and came across the water with a distinctness that pierced and subdued all other sounds, even the beating of the ripples in his ears. Although no soldier, he had frequented camps enough to know the dread significance of that deliberate, drawling, aspirated chant; the lieutenant on shore was taking a part in the morning's work. How coldly and pitilessly—with what an even, calm intonation, presaging, and enforcing tranquility in the men—with what accurately measured intervals fell those cruel words:

"Attention, company! . . . Shoulder arms! . . . Ready! . . . Aim! . . . Fire!"

Farquhar dived—dived as deeply as he could. The water roared in his ears like the voice of Niagara, yet he heard the dulled thunder of the volley and, rising again toward the surface, met shining bits of metal, singularly flattened, oscillating slowly downward. Some of them touched him on the face and hands, then fell away, continuing their descent. One lodged between his collar and neck; it was uncomfortably warm and he snatched it out.

As he rose to the surface, gasping for breath, he saw that he had been a long time under water; he was perceptibly farther down stream—nearer to safety. The soldiers had almost finished reloading; the metal ramrods flashed all at once in the sunshine as they were drawn from the barrels, turned in the air, and thrust into their sockets. The two sentinels fired again, independently and ineffectually.

The hunted man saw all this over his shoulder; he was now swimming vigorously with the current. His brain was as energetic as his arms and legs; he thought with the rapidity of lightning.

"The officer," he reasoned, "will not make that martinet's error a second time. It is as easy to dodge a volley as a single shot. He has probably already given the command to fire at will. God help me, I cannot dodge them all!"

An appalling plash within two yards of him was followed by a loud, rushing sound, *diminuendo*, which seemed to travel back through the air to the fort and died in an explosion which stirred the very river to its deeps! A rising sheet of water curved over him, fell down upon him, blinded him, strangled him! The cannon had taken a hand in the game. As he shook his head free from the commotion of the smitten water he heard the deflected shot humming through the air ahead, and in an instant it was cracking and smashing the branches in the forest beyond.

"They will not do that again," he thought; "the next time they will use a charge of grape. I must keep my eye upon the gun; the smoke will apprise me—the report arrives too late; it lags behind the missile. That is a good gun."

Suddenly he felt himself whirled round and round—spinning like a top. The water, the banks, the forests, the now distant bridge, fort and men—all were commingled and blurred. Objects were represented by their colors only; circular horizontal streaks of color—that was all he saw. He had been caught in a vortex and was being whirled on with a velocity of advance and gyration that made him giddy and sick. In a few moments he was flung upon the gravel at the foot of the left bank of the stream—the southern bank—and behind a projecting point which concealed him from his enemies. The sudden arrest of his motion, the abrasion of one of his hands on the gravel, restored him, and he wept with delight. He dug his fingers into the sand, threw it over himself in handfuls and audibly blessed it. It looked like diamonds, rubies, emeralds; he could think of nothing beautiful which it did not resemble. The trees upon the bank were giant garden plants; he noted a definite order in their arrangement, inhaled the fragrance of their blooms. A strange, roseate light shone through the spaces among their trunks and the wind made in their branches the music of aeolian harps. He had no wish to perfect his escape—was content to remain in that enchanting spot until retaken.

At last he found a road which led him in what he knew to be the right direction. It was as wide and straight as a city street, yet it seemed untraveled. No fields bordered it, no dwelling anywhere.

A whiz and rattle of grapeshot among the branches high above his head roused him from his dream. The baffled cannoneer had fired him a random farewell. He sprang to his feet, rushed up the sloping bank, and plunged into the forest.

All that day he traveled, laying his course by the rounding sun. The forest seemed interminable; nowhere did he discover a break in it, not even a woodman's road. He had not known that he lived in so wild a region. There was something uncanny in the revelation.

By nightfall he was fatigued, footsore, famishing. The thought of his wife and children urged him on. At last he found a road which led him in what he knew to be the right direction. It was as wide and straight as a city street, yet it seemed untraveled. No fields bordered it, no dwelling anywhere. Not so much as the barking of a dog suggested human habitation. The black bodies of the trees formed a straight wall on both sides, terminating on the horizon in a point, like a diagram in a lesson in perspective. Overhead, as he looked up through this rift in the wood, shone great golden stars looking unfamiliar and grouped in strange constellations. He was sure they were arranged in some order which had a secret and malign significance. The wood on either side was full of singular noises, among which—once, twice, and again—he distinctly heard whispers in an unknown tongue.

His neck was in pain and lifting his hand to it found it horribly swollen. He knew that it had a circle of black where the rope had bruised it. His eyes felt congested; he could no longer close them. His tongue was swollen with thirst; he relieved its fever by thrusting it forward from between his teeth into the cold air. How softly the turf had carpeted the untraveled avenue—he could no longer feel the roadway beneath his feet!

Doubtless, despite his suffering, he had fallen asleep while walking, for now he sees another scene—perhaps he has merely recovered from a delirium. He stands at the gate of his own home. All is as he left it, and all bright and beautiful in the morning sunshine. He must have traveled the entire night. As he pushes open the gate and passes up the wide white walk, he sees a flutter of female garments; his wife, looking fresh and cool and sweet, steps down from the veranda to meet him. At the bottom of the steps she stands waiting, with a smile of ineffable joy, an attitude of matchless grace and dignity. Ah, how beautiful she is! He springs forward with extended arms. As he is about to clasp her he feels a stunning blow upon the back of the neck; a blinding white light blazes all about him with a sound like the shock of a cannon—then all is darkness and silence!

Peyton Farquhar was dead; his body, with a broken neck, swung gently from side to side beneath the timbers of the Owl Creek bridge.

STEPHEN CRANE

The Open Boat

A tale intended to be after the fact:
Being the experience of four men from the
sunk steamer *Commodore*

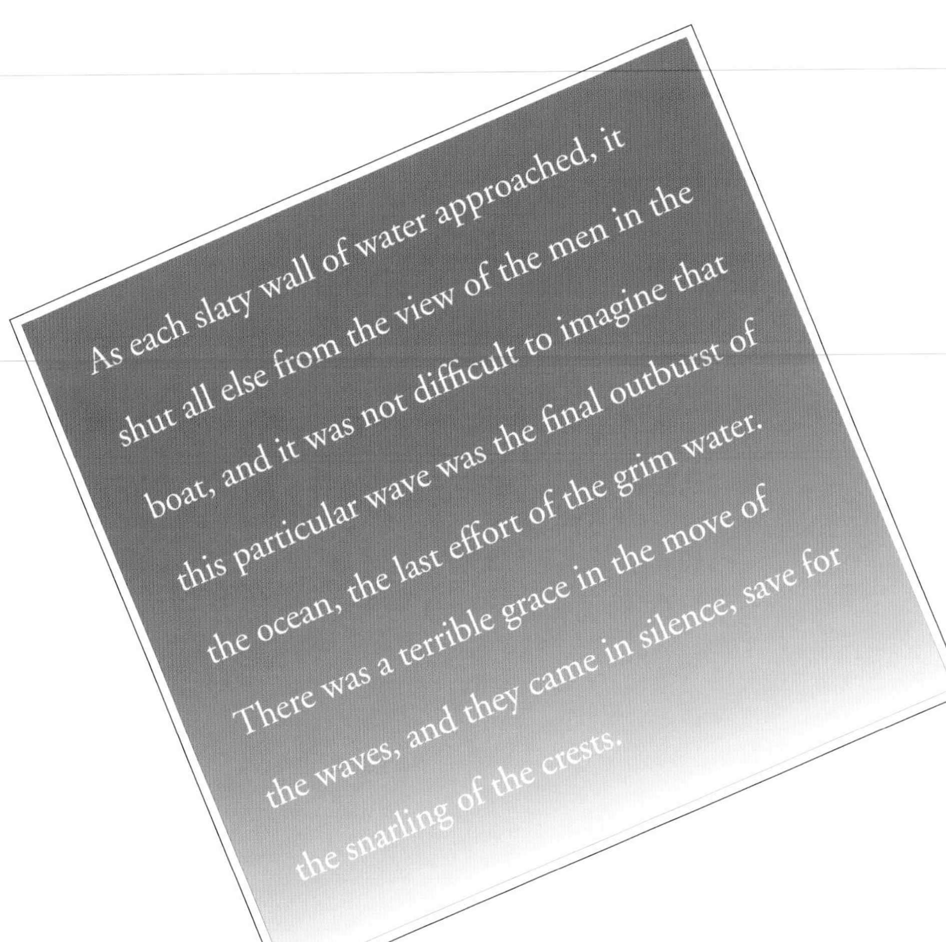

I

None of them knew the color of the sky. Their eyes glanced level and were fastened upon the waves that swept toward them. These waves were of the hue of slate, save for the tops, which were of foaming white, and all of the men knew the colors of the sea. The horizon narrowed and widened, and dipped and rose, and at all times its edge was jagged with waves that seemed thrust up in points like rocks.

Many a man ought to have a bathtub larger than the boat which here rode upon the sea. These waves were most wrongfully and barbarously abrupt and tall, and each froth-top was a problem in small-boat navigation.

The cook squatted in the bottom, and looked with both eyes at the six inches of gunwale which separated him from the ocean. His sleeves were rolled over his fat forearms, and the two flaps of his unbuttoned vest dangled as he bent to bail out the boat. Often he said, "Gawd! that was a narrow clip." As he remarked it he invariably gazed eastward over the broken sea.

The oiler, steering with one of the two oars in the boat, sometimes raised himself suddenly to keep clear of water that swirled in over the stern. It was a thin little oar, and it seemed often ready to snap.

The correspondent, pulling at the other oar, watched the waves and wondered why he was there.

The injured captain, lying in the bow, was at this time buried in that profound dejection and indifference which comes, temporarily at least, to even the bravest and most enduring when, willy-nilly, the firm fails, the army loses, the ship goes down. The mind of the master of a vessel is rooted deep in the timbers of her, though he commanded for a day or a decade; and this captain had on him the stern impression of a scene in the grays of dawn of seven turned faces, and later a stump of a topmast with a white ball on it, that slashed to and fro at the waves, went low and lower, and down. Thereafter there was something strange in his voice. Although steady, it was deep with mourning, and of a quality beyond oration or tears.

"Keep 'er a little more south, Billie," said he.

"A little more south, sir," said the oiler in the stern.

A seat in this boat was not unlike a seat upon a bucking broncho, and by the same token a broncho is not much smaller. The craft pranced and reared and plunged like an animal. As each wave came, and she rose for it, she seemed like a horse making at a fence outrageously high. The manner of her scramble over these walls of water is a mystic thing, and, moreover, at the top of them were ordinarily these problems in white water, the foam racing down from the summit of each wave requiring a new leap, and a leap from the air. Then, after scornfully bumping a crest, she would slide and race and splash down a long incline, and arrive bobbing and nodding in front of the next menace.

A singular disadvantage of the sea lies in the fact that after successfully surmounting one wave you discover that there is another behind it just as important and just as nervously anxious to do something effective in the way of swamping boats. In a ten-foot dinghy one can get an idea of the resources of the sea in the line of waves that is not probable to the average experience, which is never at sea in a dinghy. As each slaty wall of water approached, it shut all else from the view of the men in the boat, and it was not difficult to imagine that this particular wave was the final outburst of the ocean, the last effort of the grim water. There was a terrible grace in the move of the waves, and they came in silence, save for the snarling of the crests.

In the wan light the faces of the men must have been gray. Their eyes must

The crest of each of these waves was a hill, from the top of which the men surveyed for a moment a broad tumultuous expanse, shining and wind-riven.

have glinted in strange ways as they gazed steadily astern. Viewed from a balcony, the whole thing would, doubtless, have been weirdly picturesque. But the men in the boat had no time to see it, and if they had had leisure, there were other things to occupy their minds. The sun swung steadily up the sky, and they knew it was broad day because the color of the sea changed from slate to emerald-green streaked with amber lights, and the foam was like tumbling snow. The process of the breaking day was unknown to them. They were aware only of this effect upon the color of the waves that rolled toward them.

In disjointed sentences the cook and the correspondent argued as to the difference between a life-saving station and a house of refuge. The cook had said: "There's a house of refuge just north of the Mosquito Inlet Light, and as soon as they see us they'll come off in their boat and pick us up."

"As soon as who see us?" said the correspondent.

"The crew," said the cook.

"Houses of refuge don't have crews," said the correspondent. "As I understand them, they are only places where clothes and grub are stored for the benefit of shipwrecked people. They don't carry crews."

"Oh, yes, they do," said the cook.

"No, they don't," said the correspondent.

"Well, we're not there yet, anyhow," said the oiler, in the stern.

"Well," said the cook, "perhaps it's not a house of refuge that I'm thinking of as being near Mosquito Inlet Light; perhaps it's a life-saving station."

"We're not there yet," said the oiler in the stern.

II

As the boat bounced from the top of each wave the wind tore through the hair of the hatless men, and as the craft plopped her stern down again the spray slashed past them. The crest of each of these waves was a hill, from the top of which the men surveyed for a moment a broad tumultuous expanse, shining and wind-riven. It was probably splendid, it was probably glorious, this play of the free sea, wild with lights of emerald and white and amber.

"Bully good thing it's an on-shore wind," said the cook. "If not, where would we be? Wouldn't have a show."

"That's right," said the correspondent.

The busy oiler nodded his assent.

Then the captain, in the bow, chuckled in a way that expressed humor, contempt, tragedy, all in one. "Do you think we've got much of a show now, boys?" said he.

Whereupon the three were silent, save for a trifle of hemming and hawing. To express any particular optimism at this time they felt to be childish and stupid, but they all doubtless possessed this sense of the situation in their minds. A young man thinks doggedly at such times. On the other hand, the ethics of their condition was decidedly against any open suggestion of hopelessness. So they were silent.

"Oh, well," said the captain, soothing his children, "we'll get ashore all right."

But there was that in his tone which made them think; so the oiler quoth, "Yes! if this wind holds!"

The cook was bailing. "Yes! if we don't catch hell in the surf."

Canton-flannel gulls flew near and far. Sometimes they sat down on the sea, near patches of brown seaweed that rolled over the waves with a movement like carpets on a line in a gale. The birds sat comfortably in groups, and they were envied by some in the dinghy, for the wrath of the sea was no more to them than it was to a covey of prairie chickens a thousand miles inland. Often they came very close and stared at the men with black bead-like eyes. At these times they were uncanny and sinister in their unblinking scrutiny, and the men hooted angrily at them, telling them to be gone. One came, and evidently decided to alight on the top of the captain's head. The bird flew parallel to the boat and did not circle, but made short sidelong jumps in the air in chicken fashion. His black eyes were wistfully fixed upon the captain's head. "Ugly brute," said the oiler to the bird. "You look as if you were made with a jackknife." The cook and the correspondent swore darkly at the creature. The captain naturally wished to knock it away with the end of the heavy painter; but he did not dare do it, because anything resembling an emphatic gesture would have capsized this freighted boat; and so, with his open hand, the captain gently and carefully waved the gull away. After it had been discouraged from the pursuit the captain breathed easier on account of his hair, and others breathed easier because the bird struck their minds at this time as being somehow gruesome and ominous.

In the meantime the oiler and the correspondent rowed; and also they rowed. They sat together in the same seat, and each rowed an oar. Then the oiler took both oars; then the correspondent took both oars, then the oiler; then the correspondent. They rowed and they rowed. The very ticklish part of the business was when the time came for the reclining one in the stern to take his turn at the oars. By the very last star of truth, it is easier to steal eggs from under a hen than it was to change seats in the dinghy. First the man in the stern slid his hand along the thwart and moved with care, as if he were of Sèvres. Then the man in the rowing-seat slid his hand along the other thwart. It was all done with most extraordinary care. As the two sidled past each other, the whole party kept watchful eyes on the coming wave, and the captain cried: "Look out, now! Steady, there!"

The brown mats of seaweed that appeared from time to time were like islands, bits of earth. They were traveling, apparently, neither one way nor the other. They were, to all intents, stationary. They informed the men in the boat that it was making progress slowly toward the land.

The captain, rearing cautiously in the bow after the dinghy soared on a great swell, said that he had seen the lighthouse at Mosquito Inlet. Presently the cook remarked that he had seen it. The correspondent was at the oars then, and for some reason he too wished to look at the lighthouse; but his back was toward the far shore, and the waves were important, and for some time he could not seize an opportunity to turn his head. But at last there came a wave more gentle than the others, and when at the crest of it he swiftly scoured the western horizon.

"See it?" said the captain.

"No," said the correspondent, slowly; "I didn't see anything."

"Look again," said the captain. He pointed. "It's exactly in that direction."

At the top of another wave the correspondent did as he was bid, and this time his eyes chanced on a small, still thing on the edge of the swaying horizon. It was precisely like the point of a pin. It took an anxious eye to find a lighthouse so tiny.

"Think we'll make it, Captain?"

"If this wind holds and the boat don't swamp, we can't do much else," said the captain.

The little boat, lifted by each towering sea and splashed viciously by the crests, made progress that in the absence of seaweed was not apparent to those in her.

They sat together in the same seat, and each rowed an oar. Then the oiler took both oars; then the correspondent took both oars, then the oiler; then the correspondent. They rowed and they rowed.

She seemed just a wee thing wallowing, miraculously top up, at the mercy of five oceans. Occasionally a great spread of water, like white flames, swarmed into her.

"Bail her, cook," said the captain, serenely.

"All right, Captain," said the cheerful cook.

"That's the house of refuge, sure," said the cook. "They'll see us before long, and come out after us."

III

It would be difficult to describe the subtle brotherhood of men that was here established on the seas. No one said that it was so. No one mentioned it. But it dwelt in the boat, and each man felt it warm him. They were a captain, an oiler, a cook, and a correspondent, and they were friends—friends in a more curiously iron-bound degree than may be common. The hurt captain, lying against the water-jar in the bow, spoke always in a low voice and calmly; but he could never command a more ready and swiftly obedient crew than the motley three of the dinghy. It was more than a mere recognition of what was best for the common safety. There was surely in it a quality that was personal and heart-felt. And after this devotion to the commander of the boat, there was this comradeship that the correspondent, for instance, who had been taught to be cynical of men, knew even at the time was the best experience of his life. But no one said that it was so. No one mentioned it.

"I wish we had a sail," remarked the captain. "We might try my overcoat on the end of an oar, and give you two boys a chance to rest." So the cook and the correspondent held the mast and spread wide the overcoat. The oiler steered; and the little boat made good way with her new rig. Sometimes the oiler had to scull sharply to keep a sea from breaking into the boat, but otherwise sailing was a success.

Meanwhile the lighthouse had been growing slowly larger. It had now almost assumed color, and appeared like a little gray shadow on the sky. The man at the oars could not be prevented from turning his head rather often to try for a glimpse of this little gray shadow.

At last, from the top of each wave, the men in the tossing boat could see land. Even as the lighthouse was an upright shadow on the sky, this land seemed but a long black shadow on the sea. It certainly was thinner than paper. "We must be about opposite New Smyrna," said the cook, who had coasted this shore often in schooners. "Captain, by the way, I believe they abandoned that life-saving station there about a year ago."

"Did they?" said the captain.

The wind slowly died away. The cook and the correspondent were not now obliged to slave in order to hold high the oar. But the waves continued their old impetuous swooping at the dinghy, and the little craft, no longer underway, struggled woundily over them. The oiler or the correspondent took the oars again.

Shipwrecks are *apropos* of nothing. If men could only train for them and have them occur when the men had reached pink condition, there would be less drowning at sea. Of the four in the dinghy none had slept any time worth mentioning for two days and two nights previous to embarking in the dinghy, and in the excitement of clambering about the deck of a foundering ship they had also forgotten to eat heartily.

For these reasons, and for others, neither the oiler nor the correspondent was fond of rowing at this time. The correspondent wondered ingenuously how in the name of all that was sane could there be people who thought it amusing to row a boat. It was not an amusement; it was a diabolical punishment, and even a genius of mental aberrations could never conclude that it was anything but a horror to the muscles and a crime against the back. He mentioned to the boat in general how the amusement of rowing struck him, and the weary-faced oiler smiled in full sympathy. Previously to the foundering, by the way, the oiler had worked a double watch in the engine-room of the ship.

"Take her easy now, boys," said the captain. "Don't spend yourselves. If we have to run a surf you'll need all your strength, because we'll sure have to swim for it. Take your time."

Slowly the land arose from the sea. From a black line it became a line of black and a line of white—trees and sand. Finally the captain said that he could make out a house on the shore. "That's the house of refuge, sure," said the cook. "They'll see us before long, and come out after us."

The distant lighthouse reared high. "The keeper ought to be able to make us out now, if he's looking through a glass," said the captain. "He'll notify the life-saving people."

Their backbones had become thoroughly used to balancing in the boat, and they now rode this wild colt of a dinghy like circus men.

"None of those other boats could have got ashore to give word of this wreck," said the oiler, in a low voice, "else the life-boat would be out hunting us."

Slowly and beautifully the land loomed out of the sea. The wind came again. It had veered from the northeast to the southeast. Finally a new sound struck the ears of the men in the boat. It was the low thunder of the surf on the shore. "We'll never be able to make the lighthouse now," said the captain. "Swing her head a little more north, Billie."

"A little more north, sir," said the oiler.

Whereupon the little boat turned her nose once more down the wind, and all but the oarsman watched the shore grow. Under the influence of this expansion doubt and direful apprehension was leaving the minds of the men. The management of the boat was still most absorbing, but it could not prevent a quiet cheerfulness. In an hour, perhaps, they would be ashore.

Their backbones had become thoroughly used to balancing in the boat, and they now rode this wild colt of a dinghy like circus men. The correspondent thought that he had been drenched to the skin, but happening to feel in the top pocket of his coat, he found therein eight cigars. Four of them were soaked with sea-water; four were perfectly scatheless. After a search, somebody produced three dry matches; and thereupon the four waifs rode impudently in their little boat, and with an assurance of an impending rescue shining in their eyes, puffed at the big cigars, and judged well and ill of all men. Everybody took a drink of water.

IV

"Cook," remarked the captain, "there don't seem to be any signs of life about your house of refuge."

"No," replied the cook. "Funny they don't see us!"

A broad stretch of lowly coast lay before the eyes of the men. It was of low dunes topped with dark vegetation. The roar of the surf was plain, and sometimes they could see the white lip of a wave as it spun up the beach. A tiny house was blocked out black upon the sky. Southward, the slim lighthouse lifted its little gray length.

Tide, wind, and waves were swinging the dinghy northward. "Funny they don't see us," said the men.

The surf's roar was here dulled, but its tone was nevertheless thunderous and mighty. As the boat swam over the great rollers the men sat listening to this roar. "We'll swamp sure," said everybody.

It is fair to say here that there was not a life-saving station within twenty miles in either direction; but the men did not know this fact, and in consequence they made dark and opprobrious remarks concerning the eyesight of the nation's life-savers. Four scowling men sat in the dinghy and surpassed records in the invention of epithets.

"Funny they don't see us."

The light-heartedness of a former time had completely faded. To their sharpened minds it was easy to conjure pictures of all kinds of incompetency and blindness and, indeed, cowardice. There was the shore of the populous land, and it was bitter and bitter to them that from it came no sign.

"Well," said the captain, ultimately, "I suppose we'll have to make a try for ourselves. If we stay out here too long, we'll none of us have strength left to swim after the boat swamps."

And so the oiler, who was at the oars, turned the boat straight for the shore. There was a sudden tightening of muscles. There was some thinking.

"If we don't all get ashore," said the captain—"if we don't all get ashore, I suppose you fellows know where to send news of my finish?"

They then briefly exchanged some addresses and admonitions. As for the reflections of the men, there was a great deal of rage in them. Perchance they might be formulated thus: "If I am going to be drowned—if I am going to be drowned—if I am going to be drowned, why, in the name of the seven mad gods who rule the sea, was I allowed to come thus far and contemplate sand and trees? Was I brought here merely to have my nose dragged away as I was about to nibble the sacred cheese of life? It is preposterous. If this old ninny-woman, Fate, cannot do better than this, she should be deprived of the management of men's fortunes. She is an old hen who knows not her intention. If she has decided to drown me, why did she not do it in the beginning and save me all this trouble? The whole affair is absurd. . . . But no, she cannot mean to drown me. She dare not drown me. She cannot drown me. Not after all this work." Afterward the man might have had an impulse to shake his fist at the clouds. "Just you drown me, now, and then hear what I call you!"

The billows that came at this time were more formidable. They seemed always just about to break and roll over the little boat in a turmoil of foam. There was a preparatory and long growl in the speech of them. No mind unused to the sea would have concluded that the dinghy could ascend these sheer heights in time. The shore was still afar. The oiler was a wily surfman. "Boys," he said swiftly, "she won't live three minutes more, and we're too far out to swim. Shall I take her to sea again, Captain?"

"Yes; go ahead!" said the captain.

This oiler, by a series of quick miracles and fast and steady oarsmanship, turned the boat in the middle of the surf and took her safely to sea again.

There was a considerable silence as the boat bumped over the furrowed sea to deeper water. Then somebody in gloom spoke. "Well, anyhow, they must have seen us from the shore by now."

The gulls went in slanting flight up the wind toward the gray, desolate east. A squall, marked by dingy clouds and clouds brick-red, like smoke from a burning building, appeared from the southeast.

"What do you think of those life-saving people? Ain't they peaches?"

"Funny they haven't seen us."

"Maybe they think we're out here for sport! Maybe they think we're fishin'. Maybe they think we're damned fools."

It was a long afternoon. A changed tide tried to force them southward, but the wind and wave said northward. Far ahead, where coast-line, sea, and sky formed their mighty angle, there were little dots which seemed to indicate a city on the shore.

"St. Augustine?"

The captain shook his head. "Too near Mosquito Inlet."

And the oiler rowed, and then the correspondent rowed. Then the oiler rowed. It was a weary business. The human back can become the seat of more aches and pains than are registered in books for the composite anatomy of a regiment. It is a limited area, but it can become the theater of innumerable muscular conflicts, tangles, wrenches, knots, and other comforts.

"Did you ever like to row, Billie?" asked the correspondent.

"No," said the oiler; "hang it!"

When one exchanged the rowing-seat for a place in the bottom of the boat, he suffered a bodily depression that caused him to be careless of everything save an obligation to wiggle one finger. There was cold sea-water swashing to and fro in the boat, and he lay in it. His head, pillowed on a thwart, was within an inch of the swirl of a wave-crest, and sometimes a particularly obstreperous sea came inboard and drenched him once more. But these matters did not annoy him. It is almost certain that if the boat had capsized he would have tumbled comfortably out upon the ocean as if he felt sure that it was a great soft mattress.

"What do you think of those life-saving people? Ain't they peaches?" "Funny they haven't seen us."

"Look! There's a man on the shore!"

"Where?"

"There! See 'im? See 'im?"

"Yes, sure! He's walking along."

"Now he's stopped. Look! He's facing us!"

"He's waving at us!"

"So he is! By thunder!"

"Ah, now we're all right! Now we're all right! There'll be a boat out here for us in half an hour."

"He's going on. He's running. He's going up to that house there."

The remote beach seemed lower than the sea, and it required a searching glance to discern the little black figure. The captain saw a floating stick and they rowed to it. A bath towel was by some weird chance in the boat, and, tying this on the stick, the captain waved it. The oarsman did not dare turn his head, so he was obliged to ask questions.

The remote beach seemed lower than the sea, and it required a searching glance to discern the little black figure.

"What's he doing now?"

"He's standing still again. He's looking, I think. . . . There he goes again. Toward the house. . . . Now he's stopped again."

"Is he waving at us?"

"No, not now; he was, though."

"Look! There comes another man!"

"He's running."

"Look at him go, would you!"

"Why, he's on a bicycle. Now he's met the other man. They're both waving at us. Look!"

"There comes something up the beach."

"What the devil is that thing?"

"Why, it looks like a boat."

"Why, certainly, it's a boat."

"No; it's on wheels."

"Yes, so it is. Well, that must be the life-boat. They drag them along shore on a wagon."

"That's the life-boat, sure."

"No, by God, it's—it's an omnibus."

"I tell you it's a life-boat."

"It is not! It's an omnibus. I can see it plain. See? One of these big hotel omnibuses."

"By thunder, you're right. It's an omnibus, sure as fate. What do you suppose they are doing with an omnibus? Maybe they are going around collecting the life-crew, hey?"

"That's it, likely. Look! There's a fellow waving a little black flag. He's standing on the steps of the omnibus. There come those other two fellows. Now they're all talking together. Look at the fellow with the flag. Maybe he ain't waving it!"

"That ain't a flag, is it? That's his coat. Why, certainly, that's his coat."

"So it is; it's his coat. He's taken it off and is waving it around his head. But would you look at him swing it!"

"Oh, say, there isn't any life-saving station there. That's just a winter-resort hotel omnibus that has brought over some of the boarders to see us drown."

"What's that idiot with the coat mean? What's he signaling, anyhow?"

"It looks as if he were trying to tell us to go north. There must be a life-saving station up there."

"No; he thinks we're fishing. Just giving us a merry hand. See? Ah, there, Willie!"

"Well, I wish I could make something out of those signals. What do you suppose he means?"

"He don't mean anything; he's just playing."

"Well, if he'd just signal us to try the surf again, or to go to sea and wait, or go north, or go south, or go to hell—there would be some reason in it. But look at him! He just stands there and keeps his coat revolving like a wheel. The ass!"

"There come more people."

"Now there's quite a mob. Look! Isn't that a boat?"

"Where? Oh, I see where you mean. No, that's no boat."

"That fellow is still waving his coat."

"He must think we like to see him do that. Why don't he quit it? It don't mean anything."

"I don't know. I think he is trying to make us go north. It must be that there's a life-saving station there somewhere."

"Say, he ain't tired yet. Look at 'im wave."

"Wonder how long he can keep that up. He's been revolving his coat ever since he caught sight of us. He's an idiot. Why aren't they getting men to bring a boat out? A fishing-boat—one of those big yawls—could come out here all right. Why don't he do something?"

"Oh, it's all right now."

"They'll have a boat out here for us in less than no time, now that they've seen us."

A faint yellow tone came into the sky over the low land. The shadows on the sea slowly deepened. The wind bore coldness with it, and the men began to shiver.

"Holy smoke!" said one, allowing his voice to express his impious mood, "if we keep on monkeying out here! If we've got to flounder out here all night!"

"Oh, we'll never have to stay here all night! Don't you worry. They've seen us now, and it won't be long before they'll come chasing out after us."

The shore grew dusky. The man waving a coat blended gradually into this gloom, and it swallowed in the same manner the omnibus and the group of people. The spray, when it dashed uproariously over the side, made the voyagers shrink and swear like men who were being branded.

"I'd like to catch the chump who waved the coat. I feel like socking him one, just for luck."

"Why? What did he do?"

"Oh, nothing, but then he seemed so damned cheerful."

In the meantime the oiler rowed, and then the correspondent rowed, and then the oiler rowed. Gray-faced and bowed forward, they mechanically, turn by turn, plied the leaden oars. The form of the lighthouse had vanished from the southern

"If I am going to be drowned—if I am going to be drowned—if I am going to be drowned, why, in the name of the seven mad gods who rule the sea, was I allowed to come thus far and contemplate sand and trees?"

horizon, but finally a pale star appeared, just lifting from the sea. The streaked saffron in the west passed before the all-merging darkness, and the sea to the east was black. The land had vanished, and was expressed only by the low and drear thunder of the surf.

"If I am going to be drowned—if I am going to be drowned—if I am going to be drowned, why, in the name of the seven mad gods who rule the sea, was I allowed to come thus far and contemplate sand and trees? Was I brought here merely to have my nose dragged away as I was about to nibble the sacred cheese of life?"

The patient captain, drooped over the water-jar, was sometimes obliged to speak to the oarsman.

"Keep her head up! Keep her head up!"

"Keep her head up, sir." The voices were weary and low.

This was surely a quiet evening. All save the oarsman lay heavily and listlessly in the boat's bottom. As for him, his eyes were just capable of noting the tall black waves that swept forward in a most sinister silence, save for an occasional subdued growl of a crest.

The cook's head was on a thwart, and he looked without interest at the water under his nose. He was deep in other scenes. Finally he spoke. "Billie," he murmured, dreamfully, "what kind of pie do you like best?"

V

"Pie!" said the oiler and the correspondent, agitatedly. "Don't talk about those things, blast you!"

"Well," said the cook, "I was just thinking about ham sandwiches, and—"

A night on the sea in an open boat is a long night. As darkness settled finally, the shine of the light, lifting from the sea in the south, changed to full gold. On the northern horizon a new light appeared, a small bluish gleam on the edge of the waters. These two lights were the furniture of the world. Otherwise there was nothing but waves.

Two men huddled in the stern, and distances were so magnificent in the dinghy that the rower was enabled to keep his feet partly warmed by thrusting them under his companions. Their legs indeed extended far under the rowing-seat until they touched the feet of the captain forward. Sometimes, despite the efforts of the tired oarsman, a wave came piling into the boat, an icy wave of the night, and the chilling water soaked them anew. They would twist their bodies for a moment and groan, and sleep the dead sleep once more, while the water in the boat gurgled about them as the craft rocked.

The plan of the oiler and the correspondent was for one to row until he lost the ability, and then arouse the other from his sea-water couch in the bottom of the boat.

The oiler plied the oars until his head drooped forward and the overpowering sleep blinded him; and he rowed yet afterward. Then he touched a man in the bottom of the boat, and called his name. "Will you spell me for a little while?" he said meekly.

"Sure, Billie," said the correspondent, awaking and dragging himself to a sitting position. They exchanged places carefully, and the oiler, cuddling down in the sea-water at the cook's side, seemed to go to sleep instantly.

The particular violence of the sea had ceased. The waves came without snarling. The obligation of the man at the oars was to keep the boat headed so that the tilt of the rollers would not capsize her, and to preserve her from filling when the crests rushed past. The black waves were silent and hard to be seen in the darkness. Often one was almost upon the boat before the oarsman was aware.

In a low voice the correspondent addressed the captain. He was not sure that the captain was awake, although this iron man seemed to be always awake. "Captain, shall I keep her making for that light north, sir?"

The same steady voice answered him. "Yes. Keep it about two points off the port bow."

The cook had tied a life-belt around himself in order to get even the warmth which this clumsy cork contrivance could donate, and he seemed almost stove-like when a rower, whose teeth invariably chattered wildly as soon as he ceased his labor, dropped down to sleep.

The correspondent, as he rowed, looked down at the two men sleeping underfoot. The cook's arm was around the oiler's shoulders, and, with their fragmentary clothing and haggard faces, they were the babes of the sea—a grotesque rendering of the old babes in the wood.

Later he must have grown stupid at his work, for suddenly there was a growling of water, and a crest came with a roar and a swash into the boat, and it was a wonder that it did not set the cook afloat in his life-belt. The cook continued to sleep, but the oiler sat up, blinking his eyes and shaking with the new cold.

"Oh, I'm awful sorry, Billie," said the correspondent contritely.

"That's all right, old boy," said the oiler, and lay down again and was asleep.

Presently it seemed that even the captain dozed, and the correspondent thought that he was the one man afloat on all the ocean. The wind had a voice as it came over the waves, and it was sadder than the end.

The wind had a voice as it came over the waves, and it was sadder than the end.

There was a long, loud swishing astern of the boat, and a gleaming trail of phosphorescence, like blue flame, was furrowed on the black waters. It might have been made by a monstrous knife.

Then there came a stillness, while the correspondent breathed with open mouth and looked at the sea.

There was seldom any expression upon their faces save the general one of complete weariness. Speech was devoted to the business of the boat.

Suddenly there was another swish and another long flash of bluish light, and this time it was alongside the boat, and might almost have been reached with an oar. The correspondent saw an enormous fin speed like a shadow through the water, hurling the crystalline spray and leaving the long glowing trail.

The correspondent looked over his shoulder at the captain. His face was hidden, and he seemed to be asleep. He looked at the babes of the sea. They certainly were asleep. So, being bereft of sympathy, he leaned a little way to one side and swore softly into the sea.

But the thing did not then leave the vicinity of the boat. Ahead or astern, on one side or the other, at intervals long or short, fled the long sparkling streak, and there was to be heard the *whirroo* of the dark fin. The speed and power of the thing was greatly to be admired. It cut the water like a gigantic and keen projectile.

The presence of this biding thing did not affect the man with the same horror that it would if he had been a picnicker. He simply looked at the sea dully and swore in an undertone.

Nevertheless, it is true that he did not wish to be alone with the thing. He wished one of his companions to awake by chance and keep him company with it. But the captain hung motionless over the water-jar, and the oiler and the cook in the bottom of the boat were plunged in slumber.

VI

"If I am going to be drowned—if I am going to be drowned—if I am going to be drowned, why, in the name of the seven mad gods who rule the sea, was I allowed to come thus far and contemplate sand and trees?"

During this dismal night, it may be remarked that a man would conclude that it was really the intention of the seven mad gods to drown him, despite the abominable injustice of it. For it was certainly an abominable injustice to drown a man who had worked so hard, so hard. The man felt it would be a crime most unnatural. Other people had drowned at sea since galleys swarmed with painted sails, but still—

When it occurs to a man that nature does not regard him as important, and that she feels she would not maim the universe by disposing of him, he at first wishes to throw bricks at the temple, and he hates deeply the fact that there are no bricks and no temples. Any visible expression of nature would surely be pelleted with his jeers.

Then, if there be no tangible thing to hoot, he feels, perhaps, the desire to confront a personification and indulge in pleas, bowed to one knee, and with hands supplicant, saying, "Yes, but I love myself."

A high cold star on a winter's night is the word he feels that she says to him. Thereafter he knows the pathos of his situation.

The men in the dinghy had not discussed these matters, but each had, no doubt, reflected upon them in silence and according to his mind. There was seldom any expression upon their faces save the general one of complete weariness. Speech was devoted to the business of the boat.

To chime the notes of his emotion, a verse mysteriously entered the correspondent's head. He had even forgotten that he had forgotten this verse, but it suddenly was in his mind.

A soldier of the Legion lay dying in Algiers;
There was a lack of woman's nursing,
there was dearth of woman's tears;
But a comrade stood beside him,
and he took that comrade's hand,
And he said: "I never more shall see
my own, my native land."

In his childhood, the correspondent had been made acquainted with the fact that a soldier of the Legion lay dying in Algiers, but he had never regarded it as important. Myriads of his schoolfellows had informed him of the soldier's plight, but the dinning had naturally ended by making him perfectly indifferent. He had never considered it his affair that a soldier of the Legion lay dying in Algiers, nor had it appeared to him as a matter for sorrow. It was less to him than the breaking of a pencil's point.

Now, however, it quaintly came to him as a human, living thing. It was no longer merely a picture of a few throes in the breast of a poet, meanwhile drinking tea and warming his feet at the grate; it was an actuality—stern, mournful, and fine.

The correspondent plainly saw the soldier. He lay on the sand with his feet out straight and still. While his pale left hand was upon his chest in an attempt to thwart the going of his life, the blood came between his fingers. In the far Algerian distance, a city of low square forms was set against a sky that was faint with the last sunset hues. The correspondent, plying the oars and dreaming of the slow and slower movements of the lips of the soldier, was moved by a profound and perfectly impersonal comprehension. He was sorry for the soldier of the Legion who lay dying in Algiers.

The thing which had followed the boat and waited had evidently grown bored at the delay. There was no longer to be heard the slash of the cutwater, and there was no longer the flame of the long trail. The light in the north still glimmered, but it was apparently no nearer to the boat. Sometimes the boom of the surf rang in the correspondent's ears, and he turned the craft seaward then and rowed harder. Southward, some one had evidently built a watch-fire on the beach. It was too low and too far to be seen, but it made a shimmering, roseate reflection upon the bluff back of it, and this could be discerned from the boat. The wind came stronger, and sometimes a wave suddenly raged out like a mountain-cat, and there was to be seen the sheen and sparkle of a broken crest.

The captain, in the bow, moved on his water-jar and sat erect. "Pretty long night," he observed to the correspondent. He looked at the shore. "Those life-saving people take their time."

"Did you see that shark playing around?"

"Yes, I saw him. He was a big fellow, all right."

"Wish I had known you were awake."

Later the correspondent spoke into the bottom of the boat. "Billie!" There was a slow and gradual disentanglement. "Billie, will you spell me?"

"Sure," said the oiler.

As soon as the correspondent touched the cold, comfortable sea-water in the bottom of the boat and had huddled close to the cook's life-belt he was deep in sleep, despite the fact that his teeth played all the popular airs. This sleep was so good to him that it was but a moment before he heard a voice call his name in a tone that demonstrated the last stages of exhaustion. "Will you spell me?"

"Sure, Billie."

The light in the north had mysteriously vanished, but the correspondent took his course from the wide-awake captain.

Later in the night they took the boat farther out to sea, and the captain directed the cook to take one oar at the stern and keep the boat facing the seas. He was to call out if he should hear the thunder of the surf. This plan enabled the oiler and the correspondent to get respite together. "We'll give those boys a chance to get into shape again," said the captain. They curled down and, after a few preliminary chatterings and trembles, slept once more the dead sleep. Neither knew they had bequeathed to the cook the company of another shark, or perhaps the same shark.

As the boat caroused on the waves, spray occasionally bumped over the side and gave them a fresh soaking, but this had no power to break their repose. The ominous slash of the wind and the water affected them as it would have affected mummies.

"Boys," said the cook, with the notes of every reluctance in his voice, "she's drifted in pretty close. I guess one of you had better take her to sea again." The correspondent, aroused, heard the crash of the toppled crests.

As he was rowing, the captain gave him some whisky-and-water, and this steadied the chills out of him. "If I ever get ashore and anybody shows me even a photograph of an oar—"

At last there was a short conversation.

"Billie! . . . Billie, will you spell me?"

"Sure," said the oiler.

VII

When the correspondent again opened his eyes, the sea and the sky were each of the gray hue of the dawning. Later, carmine and gold was painted upon the waters. The morning appeared finally, in its splendor, with a sky of pure blue, and the sunlight flamed on the tips of the waves.

On the distant dunes were set many little black cottages, and a tall white windmill reared above them. No man, nor dog, nor bicycle appeared on the beach. The cottages might have formed a deserted village.

The voyagers scanned the shore. A conference was held in the boat. "Well," said the captain, "if no help is coming, we might better try a run through the surf right away. If we stay out here much longer we will be too weak to do anything for ourselves at all." The others silently acquiesced in this reasoning. The boat was headed for the beach. The correspondent wondered if none ever ascended the tall wind-tower, and if then they never looked seaward. This tower was a giant, standing with its back to the plight of the ants. It represented in a degree, to the correspondent, the serenity of nature amid the struggles of the individual—nature in the wind, and nature in the vision of men. She did not seem cruel to him then, nor beneficent, nor treacherous, nor wise. But she was indifferent, flatly indifferent. It is, perhaps, plausible that a man in this situation, impressed with the unconcern of the universe, should see the innumerable flaws of his life, and have them taste wickedly in his mind, and wish for another chance. A distinction between right and wrong seems absurdly clear to him, then, in this new ignorance of the grave-edge, and he understands that if he were given another opportunity he would mend his conduct and his words, and be better and brighter during an introduction or at a tea.

"Now, boys," said the captain, "she is going to swamp sure. All we can do is to work her in as far as possible, and then when she swamps, pile out and scramble for the beach. Keep cool now, and don't jump until she swamps sure."

The oiler took the oars. Over his shoulders he scanned the surf. "Captain," he said, "I think I'd better bring her about and keep her head-on to the seas and back her in."

"Now, boys," said the captain, "she is going to swamp sure. All we can do is to work her in as far as possible, and then when she swamps, pile out and scramble for the beach. Keep cool now, and don't jump until she swamps sure."

"All right, Billie," said the captain. "Back her in." The oiler swung the boat then, and, seated in the stern, the cook and the correspondent were obliged to look over their shoulders to contemplate the lonely and indifferent shore.

The monstrous inshore rollers heaved the boat high until the men were again enabled to see the white sheets of water scudding up the slanted beach. "We won't get in very close," said the captain. Each time a man could wrest his attention from the rollers, he turned his glance toward the shore, and in the expression of the eyes during this contemplation there was a singular quality. The correspondent, observing the others, knew that they were not afraid, but the full meaning of their glances was shrouded.

As for himself, he was too tired to grapple fundamentally with the fact. He tried to coerce his mind into thinking of it, but the mind was dominated at this time by the muscles, and the muscles said they did not care. It merely occurred to him that if he should drown it would be a shame.

There were no hurried words, no pallor, no plain agitation. The men simply looked at the shore. "Now, remember to get well clear of the boat when you jump," said the captain.

Seaward the crest of a roller suddenly fell with a thunderous crash, and the long white comber came roaring down upon the boat.

"Steady now," said the captain. The men were silent. They turned their eyes from the shore to the comber and waited. The boat slid up the incline, leaped at the furious top, bounced over it, and swung down the long back of the wave. Some water had been shipped, and the cook bailed it out.

The third wave moved forward, huge, furious, implacable. It fairly swallowed the dinghy, and almost simultaneously the men tumbled into the sea.

But the next crest crashed also. The tumbling, boiling flood of white water caught the boat and whirled it almost perpendicular. Water swarmed in from all sides. The correspondent had his hands on the gunwale at this time, and when the water entered at that place he swiftly withdrew his fingers, as if he objected to wetting them.

The little boat, drunken with this weight of water, reeled and snuggled deeper into the sea.

"Bail her out, cook! Bail her out!" said the captain.

"All right, Captain," said the cook.

"Now, boys, the next one will do for us sure," said the oiler. "Mind to jump clear of the boat."

The third wave moved forward, huge, furious, implacable. It fairly swallowed the dinghy, and almost simultaneously the men tumbled into the sea. A piece of life-belt had lain in the bottom of the boat, and as the correspondent went overboard he held this to his chest with his left hand.

The January water was icy, and he reflected immediately that it was colder than he had expected to find it on the coast of Florida. This appeared to his dazed mind as a fact important enough to be noted at the time. The coldness of the water was sad; it was tragic. This fact was somehow mixed and confused with his opinion of his own situation, so that it seemed almost a proper reason for tears. The water was cold.

When he came to the surface he was conscious of little but the noisy water. Afterward he saw his companions in the sea. The oiler was ahead in the race. He was swimming strongly and rapidly. Off to the correspondent's left, the cook's great white and corked back bulged out of the water, and in the rear the captain was hanging with his one good hand to the keel of the overturned dinghy.

There is a certain immovable quality to a shore, and the correspondent wondered at it amid the confusion of the sea.

It seemed also very attractive; but the correspondent knew that it was a long journey, and he paddled leisurely. The piece of life-preserver lay under him, and sometimes he whirled down the incline of a wave as if he were on a hand-sled.

But finally he arrived at a place in the sea where travel was beset with difficulty. He did not pause swimming to inquire what manner of current had caught him, but there his progress ceased. The shore was set before him like a bit of scenery on a stage, and he looked at it and understood with his eyes each detail of it.

As the cook passed, much farther to the left, the captain was calling to him, "Turn over on your back, cook! Turn over on your back and use the oar."

"All right, sir." The cook turned on his back, and, paddling with an oar, went ahead as if he were a canoe.

Presently the boat also passed to the left of the correspondent with the captain clinging with one hand to the keel. He would have appeared like a man raising himself to look over a board fence if it were not for the extraordinary gymnastics of the boat. The correspondent marvelled that the captain could still hold to it.

They passed on, nearer to shore—the oiler, the cook, the captain—and following them went the water-jar, bouncing gaily over the seas.

The correspondent remained in the grip of this strange new enemy, a current. The shore, with its white slope of sand and its green bluff topped with little silent cottages, was spread like a picture before him. It was very near to him then, but he was impressed as one who, in a gallery, looks at a scene from Brittany or Holland.

He thought: "I am going to drown? Can it be possible? Can it be possible? Can it be possible?" Perhaps an individual must consider his own death to be the final phenomenon of nature.

But later a wave perhaps whirled him out of this small deadly current, for he found suddenly that he could again make progress toward the shore. Later still he was aware that the captain, clinging with one hand to the keel of the dinghy, had his face turned away from the shore and toward him, and was calling his name. "Come to the boat! Come to the boat!"

In his struggle to reach the captain and the boat, he reflected that when one gets properly wearied drowning must really be a comfortable arrangement—a cessation of hostilities accompanied by a large degree of relief; and he was glad of it, for the main thing in his mind for some moments had been horror of the temporary agony; he did not wish to be hurt.

Presently he saw a man running along the shore. He was undressing with most remarkable speed. Coat, trousers, shirt, everything flew magically off him.

"Come to the boat!" called the captain.

"All right, Captain." As the correspondent paddled, he saw the captain let himself down to bottom and leave the boat. Then the correspondent performed his one little marvel of the voyage. A large wave caught him and flung him with ease and supreme speed completely over the boat and far beyond it. It struck him even then as an event in gymnastics and a true miracle of the sea. An overturned boat in the surf is not a plaything to a swimming man.

The correspondent arrived in water that reached only to his waist, but his condition did not enable him to stand for more than a moment. Each wave knocked him into a heap, and the undertow pulled at him.

Then he saw the man who had been running and undressing, and undressing and running, come bounding into the water. He dragged ashore the cook, and then waded toward the captain; but the captain waved him away and sent him to the correspondent. He was naked—naked as a tree in winter; but a halo was about his head, and he shone like a saint. He gave a strong pull, and a long drag, and a bully heave at the correspondent's hand. The correspondent, schooled in minor formulae, said: "Thanks, old man." But suddenly the man cried, "What's that?" He pointed a swift finger. The correspondent said, "Go."

In the shallows, face downward, lay the oiler. His forehead touched sand that was periodically, between each wave, clear of the sea.

The correspondent did not know all that transpired afterward. When he achieved safe ground he fell, striking the sand with each particular part of his body. It was as if he had dropped from a roof, but the thud was grateful to him.

It seems that instantly the beach was populated with men with blankets, clothes, and flasks, and women with coffee-pots and all the remedies sacred to their minds. The welcome of the land to the men from the sea was warm and generous; but a still and dripping shape was carried slowly up the beach, and the land's welcome for it could only be the different and sinister hospitality of the grave.

When it came night, the white waves paced to and fro in the moonlight, and the wind brought the sound of the great sea's voice to the men on shore, and they felt that they could then be interpreters.

WILLA CATHER

Paul's Case

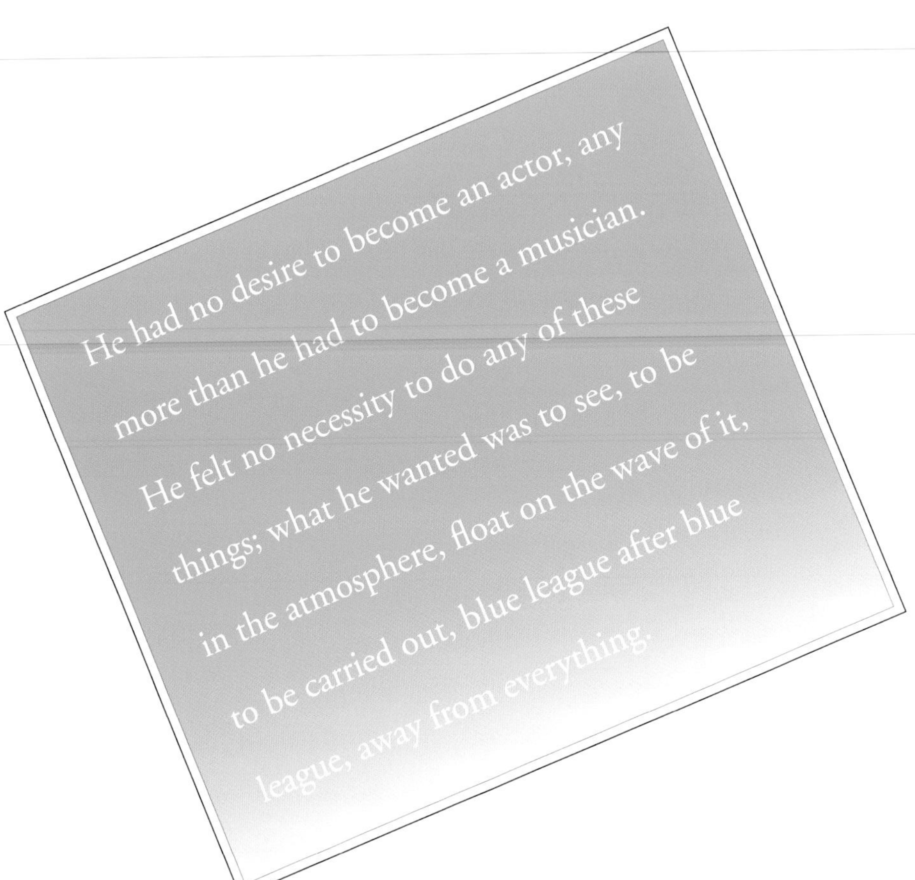

It was Paul's afternoon to appear before the faculty of the Pittsburgh High School to account for his various misdemeanors. He had been suspended a week ago, and his father had called at the Principal's office and confessed his perplexity about his son. Paul entered the faculty-room suave and smiling. His clothes were a trifle outgrown, and the tan velvet on the collar of his open overcoat was frayed and worn; but for all that there was something of the dandy about him, and he wore an opal pin in his neatly knotted black four-in-hand, and a red carnation in his buttonhole. This latter adornment the faculty somehow felt was not properly significant of the contrite spirit befitting a boy under the ban of suspension.

Paul was tall for his age and very thin, with high, cramped shoulders and a narrow chest. His eyes were remarkable for a certain hysterical brilliancy, and he continually used them in a conscious, theatrical sort of way, peculiarly offensive in a boy. The pupils were abnormally large, as though he were addicted to belladonna, but there was a glassy glitter about them which that drug does not produce.

When questioned by the Principal as to why he was there, Paul stated, politely enough, that he wanted to come back to school. This was a lie, but Paul was quite accustomed to lying; found it, indeed, indispensable for overcoming friction. His teachers were asked to state their respective charges against him, which they did with such a rancor and aggrievedness as evinced that this was not a usual case. Disorder and impertinence were among the offenses named, yet each of his instructors felt that it was scarcely possible to put into words the real cause of the trouble, which lay in a sort of hysterically defiant manner of the boy's; in the contempt which they all knew he felt for them, and which he seemingly made not the least effort to conceal. Once, when he had been making a synopsis of a paragraph at the blackboard, his English teacher had stepped to his side and attempted to guide his hand. Paul had started back with a shudder and thrust his hands violently behind him. The astonished woman could scarcely have been more hurt and embarrassed had he struck at her. The insult was so involuntary and definitely personal as to be unforgettable. In one way and another, he had made all his teachers, men and women alike, conscious of the same feeling of physical aversion. In one class he habitually sat with his hand shading his eyes; in another he always looked out of the window during the recitation; in another he made a running commentary on the lecture, with humorous intent.

His teachers felt this afternoon that his whole attitude was symbolized by his shrug and his flippantly red carnation flower, and they fell upon him without mercy, his English teacher leading the pack. He stood through it smiling, his pale lips parted over his white teeth. (His lips were continually twitching, and he had a habit of raising his eyebrows that was contemptuous and irritating to the last degree.) Older boys than Paul had broken down and shed tears under that ordeal, but his set smile did not once desert him, and his only sign of discomfort was the nervous trembling of the fingers that toyed with the buttons of his overcoat, and an occasional jerking of the other hand which held his hat. Paul was always smiling, always glancing about him, seeming to feel that people might be watching him and trying to detect something. This conscious expression, since it was so far as possible from boyish mirthfulness, was usually attributed to insolence or "smartness."

As the inquisition proceeded one of his instructors repeated an impertinent remark of the boy's, and the Principal asked him whether he thought that a courteous speech to make to a woman. Paul shrugged his shoulders slightly and his eyebrows twitched.

His eyes were remarkable for a certain hysterical brilliancy, and he continually used them in a conscious, theatrical sort of way, peculiarly offensive in a boy.

"I don't know," he replied. "I didn't mean to be polite or impolite, either. I guess it's a sort of way I have, of saying things regardless."

The Principal asked him whether he didn't think that a way it would be well to get rid of. Paul grinned and said he guessed so. When he was told that he could go, he bowed gracefully and went out. His bow was like a repetition of the scandalous red carnation.

His teachers were in despair, and his drawing master voiced the feeling of them all when he declared there was something about the boy which none of them understood. He added: "I don't really believe that smile of his comes altogether from insolence; there's something sort of haunted about it. The boy is not strong, for one thing. There is something wrong about the fellow."

"I don't really believe that smile of his comes altogether from insolence; there's something sort of haunted about it. The boy is not strong, for one thing. There is something wrong about the fellow."

The drawing master had come to realize that, in looking at Paul, one saw only his white teeth and the forced animation of his eyes. One warm afternoon the boy had gone to sleep at his drawing-board, and his master had noted with amazement what a white, blue-veined face it was; drawn and wrinkled like an old man's about the eyes, the lips twitching even in his sleep.

His teachers left the building dissatisfied and unhappy; humiliated to have felt so vindictive towards a mere boy, to have uttered this feeling in cutting terms, and to have set each other on, as it were, in the gruesome game of intemperate reproach. Some of them remembered having seen a miserable street cat set at bay by a ring of tormentors.

As for Paul, he ran down the hill whistling the Soldiers' Chorus from *Faust*, looking wildly behind him now and then to see whether some of his teachers were not there to witness his lightheartedness. As it was now late in the afternoon and

Paul was on duty that evening as usher at Carnegie Hall, he decided that he would not go home to supper.

When he reached the concert hall the doors were not yet open. It was chilly outside, and he decided to go up into the picture gallery—always deserted at this hour—where there were some of Raffelli's gay studies of Paris streets and an airy blue Venetian scene or two that always exhilarated him. He was delighted to find no one in the gallery but the old guard, who sat in the corner, a newspaper on his knee, a black patch over one eye and the other closed. Paul possessed himself of the place and walked confidently up and down, whistling under his breath. After a while he sat down before a blue Rico and lost himself. When he bethought him to look at his watch, it was after seven o'clock, and he rose with a start and ran downstairs, making a face at Augustus Caesar, peering out from the east-room, and an evil gesture at the Venus of Milo as he passed her on the stairway.

When Paul reached the ushers' dressing-room half a dozen boys were there already, and he began excitedly to tumble into his uniform. It was one of the few that at all approached fitting, and Paul thought it very becoming—though he knew the tight, straight coat accentuated his narrow chest, about which he was exceedingly sensitive. He was always excited while he dressed, twanging all over to the tuning of the strings and the preliminary flourishes of the horns in the music-room; but tonight he seemed quite beside himself, and he teased and plagued the boys until, telling him that he was crazy, they put him down on the floor and sat on him.

Somewhat calmed by his suppression, Paul dashed out to the front of the house to seat the early comers. He was a model usher. Gracious and smiling he ran up and down the aisles. Nothing was too much trouble for him; he carried messages and brought programs as though it were his greatest pleasure in life, and all the people in his section thought him a charming boy, feeling that he remembered and admired them. As the house filled, he grew more and more vivacious and animated, and the color came to his cheeks and lips. It was very much as though this were a great reception and Paul were the host. Just as the musicians came out to take their place, his English teacher arrived with checks for the seats which a prominent manufacturer had taken for the season. She betrayed some embarrassment when she handed Paul the tickets, and a *hauteur* which subsequently made her feel very foolish. Paul was startled for a moment, and had the feeling of wanting to put her out; what business had she here among all these fine people and gay colors? He looked her over and decided that she was not appropriately dressed and must be a fool to sit downstairs in such togs. The tickets had probably been sent her out of kindness, he reflected, as he put down a seat for her, and she had about as much right to sit there as he had.

When the symphony began Paul sank into one of the rear seats with a long sigh of relief, and lost himself as he had done before the Rico. It was not that symphonies, as such, meant anything in particular to Paul, but the first sigh of the instruments seemed to free some hilarious and potent spirit within him; something that struggled there like the Genius in the bottle found by the Arab fisherman. He felt a sudden zest of life; the lights danced before his eyes and the concert hall blazed into unimaginable splendor. When the soprano soloist came on, Paul forgot even the nastiness of his teacher's being there, and gave himself up to the peculiar intoxication such personages always had for him. The soloist chanced to be a German woman, by no means in her first youth, and the mother of many children; but she wore a satin gown and a tiara, and she had that indefinable air of achievement, that world-shine upon her, which always blinded Paul to any possible defects.

After a concert was over, Paul was often irritable and wretched until he got to sleep,—and tonight he was even more than usually restless. He had the feeling of not being able to let down; of its being impossible to give up this delicious excitement which was the only thing that could be called living at all. During the last number he withdrew and, after hastily changing his clothes in the dressing-room, slipped out to the side door where the singer's carriage stood. Here he began pacing rapidly up and down the walk, waiting to see her come out.

Over yonder, the Schenley, in its vacant stretch, loomed big and square through the fine rain, the windows of its twelve stories glowing like those of a lighted cardboard house under a Christmas tree. All the actors and singers of any importance stayed there when they were in the city, and a number of the big manufacturers of the place lived there in the winter. Paul had often hung about the hotel, watching the people go in and out, longing to enter and leave schoolmasters and dull care behind him forever.

At last the singer came out, accompanied by the conductor, who helped her into her carriage and closed the door with a cordial *auf wiedersehen*,—which set Paul to wondering whether she were not an old sweetheart of his. Paul followed the carriage over to the hotel, walking so rapidly as not to be far from the entrance when the singer alighted and disappeared behind the swinging glass doors which were opened by a negro in a tall hat and a long coat. In the moment that the door was ajar, it seemed to Paul that he, too, entered. He seemed to feel himself go after her up the steps, into the warm, lighted building, into an exotic, tropical world of shiny, glistening surfaces and basking ease. He reflected upon the mysterious dishes that were brought into the dining-room, the green bottles in buckets of ice, as he had seen them in the supper party pictures of the Sunday supplement. A quick gust of wind brought the rain down with sudden vehemence, and Paul was startled to find that he was still outside in the slush of the gravel driveway; that his boots were letting in the water and his scanty overcoat was clinging wet about him; that the lights in front of the concert hall were out, and that the rain was driving

It was not that symphonies, as such, meant anything in particular to Paul, but the first sigh of the instruments seemed to free some hilarious and potent spirit within him; something that struggled there like the Genius in the bottle found by the Arab fisherman.

in sheets between him and the orange glow of the windows above him. There it was, what he wanted—tangibly before him, like the fairy world of a Christmas pantomime; as the rain beat in his face, Paul wondered whether he were destined always to shiver in the black night outside, looking up at it.

He turned and walked reluctantly toward the car tracks. The end had to come sometime; his father in his nightclothes at the top of the stairs, explanations that did not explain, hastily improvised fictions that were forever tripping him up, his upstairs room and its horrible yellow wallpaper, the creaking bureau with the greasy plush collar-box, and over his painted wooden bed the pictures of George Washington and John Calvin, and the framed motto, "Feed my Lambs," which had been worked in red worsted by his mother, whom Paul could not remember.

Half an hour later, Paul alighted from the Negley Avenue car and went slowly down one of the side streets off the main thoroughfare. It was a highly respectable street, where all the houses were exactly alike, and where business men of moderate means begot and reared large families of children, all of whom went to Sabbath-school and learned the shorter catechism, and were interested in arithmetic; all of whom were as exactly alike as their homes, and of a piece with the monotony in which they lived. Paul never went up Cordelia Street without a shudder of loathing. His home was next to the house of the Cumberland minister. He approached it tonight with the nerveless sense of defeat, the hopeless feeling of sinking back forever into ugliness and commonness that he had always had when he came home. The moment he turned into Cordelia Street he felt the waters close above his head. After each of these orgies of living, he experienced all the physical depression which follows a debauch; the loathing of respectable beds, of common food, of a house permeated by kitchen odors; a shuddering repulsion for the flavorless, colorless mass of everyday existence; a morbid desire for cool things and soft lights and fresh flowers.

The nearer he approached the house, the more absolutely unequal Paul felt to the sight of it all; his ugly sleeping chamber; the cold bathroom with the grimy

He felt that he could not be accosted by his father tonight; that he could not toss again on that miserable bed.

zinc tub, the cracked mirror, the dripping spiggots; his father, at the top of the stairs, his hairy legs sticking out from his nightshirt, his feet thrust into carpet slippers. He was so much later than usual that there would certainly be inquiries and reproaches. Paul stopped short before the door. He felt that he could not be accosted by his father tonight; that he could not toss again on that miserable bed. He would not go in. He would tell his father that he had no car-fare, and it was raining so hard that he had gone home with one of the boys and stayed all night.

Meanwhile, he was wet and cold. He went around to the back of the house and tried one of the basement windows, found it open, raised it cautiously, and scrambled down the cellar wall to the floor. There he stood, holding his breath, terrified by the noise he had made; but the floor above him was silent, and there was no creak on the stairs. He found a soap-box, and carried it over to the soft ring of light that streamed from the furnace door, and sat down. He was terribly afraid of rats, so he did not try to sleep, but sat looking distrustfully at the dark, still terrified lest he might have awakened his father. In such reactions, after one of the experiences which made days and nights out of the dreary blanks of the calendar, when his senses were deadened, Paul's head was always singularly clear. Suppose his father had heard him getting in at the window and had come down and shot him for a burglar? Then, again, suppose his father had come down, pistol in hand, and he had cried out in time to save himself, and his father had been horrified to think how nearly he had killed him? Then, again, suppose a day should come when his father would remember that night, and wish there had been no warning cry to stay his hand? With this last supposition Paul entertained himself until daybreak.

The following Sunday was fine; the sodden November chill was broken by the last flash of autumnal summer. In the morning Paul had to go to church and Sabbath-school, as always. On seasonable Sunday afternoons the burghers of Cordelia Street usually sat out on their front "stoops," and talked to their neighbors on the next stoop, or called to those across the street in neighborly fashion. The men sat placidly on gay cushions upon the steps that led down to the sidewalk, while the women, in their Sunday "waists," sat in rockers on the cramped porches, pretending to be greatly at their ease. The children played in the streets; there were so many of them that the place resembled the recreation grounds of a kindergarten. The men on the steps—all in their shirt sleeves, their vests unbuttoned—sat with their legs well apart, their stomachs comfortably protruding, and talked of the prices of things, or told anecdotes of the sagacity of their various chiefs and overlords. They occasionally looked over the multitude of squabbling children, listened affectionately to their high-pitched, nasal voices, smiling to see their own proclivities reproduced in their offspring, and interspersed their legends of the iron kings with remarks about their sons' progress at school, their grades in arithmetic, and the amounts they had saved in their toy banks.

On this last Sunday of November, Paul sat all the afternoon on the lowest step of his "stoop," staring into the street, while his sisters, in their rockers, were talking to the minister's daughters next door about how many shirtwaists they had made in the last week, and how many waffles someone had eaten at the last church supper. When the weather was warm, and his father was in a particularly jovial frame of mind, the girls made lemonade, which was always brought out in a red-glass pitcher, ornamented with forget-me-nots in blue enamel. This the girls thought very fine, and the neighbors joked about the suspicious color of the pitcher.

Today Paul's father, on the top step, was talking to a young man who shifted a restless baby from knee to knee. He happened to be the young

On seasonable Sunday afternoons the burghers of Cordelia Street usually sat out on their front "stoops," and talked to their neighbors on the next stoop, or called to those across the street in neighborly fashion.

man who was daily held up to Paul as a model, and after whom it was his father's dearest hope that he would pattern. This young man was of a ruddy complexion, with a compressed, red mouth, and faded, near-sighted eyes, over which he wore thick spectacles, with gold bows that curved about his ears. He was clerk to one of the magnates of a great steel corporation, and was looked upon in Cordelia Street as a young man with a future. There was a story that, some five years ago—he was now barely twenty-six—he had been a trifle "dissipated," but in order to curb his appetites and save the loss of time and strength that a sowing of wild oats might have entailed, he had taken his chief's advice, oft reiterated to his employees, and at twenty-one had married the first woman whom he could persuade to share his fortunes. She happened to be an angular schoolmistress, much older than he, who also wore thick glasses, and who had now borne him four children, all near-sighted, like herself.

The young man was relating how his chief, now cruising in the Mediterranean, kept in touch with all the details of the business, arranging his office hours on his yacht just as though he were at home, and "knocking off work enough to keep two stenographers busy." His father told, in turn, the plan his corporation was considering, of putting in an electric railway plant at Cairo. Paul snapped his teeth; he had an awful apprehension that they might spoil it all before he got there. Yet he rather liked to hear these legends of the iron kings, that were told and retold on Sundays and holidays; these stories of palaces in Venice, yachts on the Mediterranean, and high play at Monte Carlo appealed to his fancy, and he was interested in the triumphs of these cash boys who had become famous, though he had no mind for the cash-boy stage.

After supper was over and he had helped to dry the dishes, Paul nervously asked his father whether he could go to George's to get some help in his geometry, and still more nervously asked for car-fare. This latter request he had to repeat, as his father, on principle, did not like to hear requests for money, whether much or little. He asked Paul whether he could not go to some boy who lived nearer, and told him that he ought not to leave his schoolwork until Sunday; but he gave him the dime. He was not a poor man, but he had a worthy ambition to come up in the world. His only reason for allowing Paul to usher was that he thought a boy ought to be earning a little.

Paul bounded upstairs, scrubbed the greasy odor of the dish-water from his hands with the ill-smelling soap he hated, and then shook over his fingers a few drops of violet water from the bottle he kept hidden in his drawer. He left the house with his geometry conspicuously under his arm, and the moment he got out of Cordelia Street and boarded a downtown car, he shook off the lethargy of two deadening days, and began to live again.

The leading juvenile of the permanent stock company which played at one of the downtown theaters was an acquaintance of Paul's, and the boy had been invited to drop in at the Sunday-night rehearsals whenever he could. For more than a year Paul had spent every available moment loitering about Charley Edwards's dressing-room. He had won a place among Edwards's following not only because the young actor, who could not afford to employ a dresser, often found him useful, but because he recognized in Paul something akin to what churchmen term "vocation."

It was at the theater and at Carnegie Hall that Paul really lived; the rest was but a sleep and a forgetting. This was Paul's fairy tale, and it had for him all the allurement of a secret love. The moment he inhaled the gassy, painty, dusty odor behind the scenes, he breathed like a prisoner set free, and felt within him the possibility of doing or saying splendid, brilliant things. The moment the cracked orchestra beat out the overture from *Martha,* or jerked at the serenade from *Rigoletto*, all stupid and ugly things slid from him, and his senses were deliciously, yet delicately fired.

Perhaps it was because, in Paul's world, the natural nearly always wore the guise of ugliness, that a certain element of artificiality seemed to him necessary in beauty. Perhaps it was because his experience of life elsewhere was so full of

Sabbath-school picnics, petty economies, wholesome advice as to how to succeed in life, and the unescapable odors of cooking, that he found this existence so alluring, these smartly clad men and women so attractive, that he was so moved by these starry apple orchards that bloomed perennially under the lime-light.

It would be difficult to put it strongly enough how convincingly the stage entrance of that theater was for Paul the actual portal of Romance. Certainly none of the company ever suspected it, least of all Charley Edwards. It was very like the old stories that used to float about London of fabulously rich Jews, who had subterranean halls, with palms, and fountains, and soft lamps and richly appareled women who never saw the disenchanting light of London day. So, in the midst of that smoke-palled city enamored of figures and grimy toil, Paul had his secret temple, his wishing-carpet, his bit of blue-and-white Mediterranean shore bathed in perpetual sunshine.

> It was at the theater and at Carnegie Hall that Paul really lived; the rest was but a sleep and a forgetting. This was Paul's fairy tale, and it had for him all the allurement of a secret love.

Several of Paul's teachers had a theory that his imagination had been perverted by garish fiction, but the truth was, he scarcely ever read at all. The books at home were not such as would either tempt or corrupt a youthful mind, and as for reading the novels that some of his friends urged upon him—well, he got what he wanted much more quickly from music; any sort of music, from an orchestra to a barrel organ. He needed only the spark, the indescribable thrill that made his imagination master of his senses, and he could make plots and pictures enough of his own. It was equally true that he was not stagestruck—not, at any rate, in the usual acceptance of that expression. He had no desire to become an actor, any more than he had to become a musician. He felt no necessity to do any of these things; what he wanted was to see, to be in the atmosphere, float on the wave of it, to be carried out, blue league after blue league, away from everything.

After a night behind the scenes, Paul found the schoolroom more than ever repulsive; the bare floors and naked walls; the prosy men who never wore frock coats, or violets in their buttonholes; the women with their dull gowns, shrill voices, and pitiful seriousness about prepositions that govern the dative. He could not bear to have the other pupils think, for a moment, that he took these people seriously; he must convey to them that he considered it all trivial, and was there only by way of a joke, anyway. He had autograph pictures of all the members of the stock company which he showed his classmates, telling them the most incredible stories of his familiarity with these people, of his acquaintance with the soloists who came to Carnegie Hall, his suppers with them and the flowers he sent them. When these stories lost their effect, and his audience grew listless, he would bid all the boys good-by, announcing that he was going to travel for a while; going to Naples, to California, to Egypt. Then, next Monday, he would slip back, conscious and nervously smiling; his sister was ill, and he would have to defer his voyage until spring.

He had autograph pictures of all the members of the stock company which he showed his classmates, telling them the most incredible stories of his familiarity with these people, of his acquaintance with the soloists who came to Carnegie Hall, his suppers with them and the flowers he sent them.

Matters went steadily worse with Paul at school. In the itch to let his instructors know how heartily he despised them, and how thoroughly he was appreciated elsewhere, he mentioned once or twice that he had no time to fool with theorems; adding—with a twitch of the eyebrows and a touch of that nervous bravado which so perplexed them—that he was helping the people down at the stock company; they were old friends of his.

The upshot of the matter was that the Principal went to Paul's father, and Paul was taken out of school and put to work. The manager at Carnegie Hall was told to get another usher in his stead; the doorkeeper at the theater was warned not to admit him to the house; and Charley Edwards remorsefully promised the boy's father not to see him again.

The members of the stock company were vastly amused when some of Paul's stories reached them—especially the women. They were hard-working women, most of them supporting indolent husbands or brothers, and they laughed rather bitterly at having stirred the boy to such fervid and florid inventions. They agreed with the faculty and with his father that Paul's was a bad case.

The east-bound train was plowing through a January snowstorm; the dull dawn was beginning to show gray when the engine whistled a mile out of Newark. Paul started up from the seat where he had lain curled in uneasy slumber, rubbed the breath-misted window glass with his hand, and peered out. The snow was whirling in curling eddies above the white bottom lands, and the drifts lay already deep in the fields and along the fences, while here and there the long dead grass and dried weed stalks protruded black above it. Lights shone from the scattered houses, and a gang of laborers who stood beside the track waved their lanterns.

Paul had slept very little, and he felt grimy and uncomfortable. He had made the all-night journey in a day coach because he was afraid if he took a Pullman he might be seen by some Pittsburgh business man who had noticed him in Denny & Carson's office. When the whistle woke him, he clutched quickly at his breast pocket, glancing about him with an uncertain smile. But the little, clay-bespattered Italians were still sleeping, the slatternly women across the aisle were in open-mouthed oblivion, and even the crumby, crying babies were for the nonce stilled. Paul settled back to struggle with his impatience as best he could.

When he arrived at the Jersey City station, he hurried through his breakfast, manifestly ill at ease and keeping a sharp eye about him. After he reached the Twenty-third Street station, he consulted a cabman, and had himself driven to a men's furnishing establishment which was just opening for the day. He spent upward of two hours there, buying with endless reconsidering and great care. His new street suit he put on in the fitting-room; the frock coat and dress clothes he had bundled into the cab with his new shirts. Then he drove to a hatter's and a shoe house. His next errand was at Tiffany's, where he selected silver mounted brushes and a scarf pin. He would not wait to have his silver marked, he said. Lastly, he stopped at a trunk shop on Broadway, and had his purchases packed into various traveling bags.

It was a little after one o'clock when he drove up to the Waldorf, and after settling with the cabman, went into the office. He registered from Washington; said his mother and father had been abroad, and that he had come down to await the arrival of their steamer. He told his story plausibly and had no trouble, since he offered to pay for them in advance, in engaging his rooms; a sleeping-room, sitting-room, and bath.

Not once, but a hundred times, Paul had planned this entry into New York. He had gone over every detail of it with Charley Edwards, and in his scrapbook at home there were pages of description about New York hotels, cut from the Sunday papers.

When he was shown to his sitting-room on the eighth floor, he saw at a glance that everything was as it should be; there was but one detail in his mental picture that the place did not realize, so he rang for the bellboy and sent him down for flowers. He moved about nervously until the boy returned, putting away his new linen and fingering it delightedly as he did so. When the flowers came, he put them hastily into water, and then tumbled into a hot bath. Presently he came out of his white bathroom, resplendent in his new silk underwear, and playing with the tassels of his red robe. The snow was whirling so fiercely outside his windows that he could scarcely see across the street, but within, the air was deliciously

Not once, but a hundred times, Paul had planned this entry into New York.

soft and fragrant. He put the violets and jonquils on the tabouret beside the couch, and threw himself down with a long sigh, covering himself with a Roman blanket. He was thoroughly tired; he had been in such haste, he had stood up to such a strain, covered so much ground in the last twenty-four hours, that he wanted to think how it had all come about. Lulled by the sound of the wind, the warm air, and the cool fragrance of the flowers, he sank into deep, drowsy retrospection.

It had been wonderfully simple; when they had shut him out of the theater and concert hall, when they had taken away his bone, the whole thing was virtually determined. The rest was a mere matter of opportunity. The only thing that at all surprised him was his own courage—for he realized well enough that he had always been tormented by fear, a sort of apprehensive dread that, of late years, as the meshes of the lies he had told closed about him, had been pulling the muscles of his body tighter and tighter. Until now, he could not remember the time when he had not been dreading something. Even when he was a little boy, it was always there—behind him, or before, or on either side. There had always been the shadowed corner, the dark place into which he dared not look, but from which something seemed always to be watching him—and Paul had done things that were not pretty to watch, he knew.

But now he had a curious sense of relief, as though he had at last thrown down the gauntlet to the thing in the corner.

Yet it was but a day since he had been sulking in the traces; but yesterday afternoon that he had been sent to the bank with Denny & Carson's deposit, as usual—but this time he was instructed to leave the book to be balanced. There was above two thousand dollars in checks, and nearly a thousand in the bank notes which he had taken from the book and quietly transferred to his pocket. At the bank he had made out a new deposit slip. His nerves had been steady enough to permit of his returning to the office, where he had finished his work and asked for a full day's holiday tomorrow, Saturday, giving a perfectly reasonable pretext. The bank book, be knew, would not be returned before Monday or Tuesday, and his father would be out of town for the next week. From the time he slipped the bank notes into his pocket until he boarded the night train for New York, he had not known a moment's hesitation.

How astonishingly easy it had all been; here he was, the thing done; and this time there would be no awakening, no figure at the top of the stairs. He watched the snowflakes whirling by his window until he fell asleep.

When he awoke, it was four o'clock in the afternoon. He bounded up with a start; one of his precious days gone already! He spent more than an hour in dressing, watching every stage of his toilet carefully in the mirror. Everything was quite perfect; he was exactly the kind of boy he had always wanted to be.

When he went downstairs, Paul took a carriage and drove up Fifth Avenue toward the Park. The snow had somewhat abated; carriages and tradesmen's wagons were hurrying soundlessly to and fro in the winter twilight; boys in woolen mufflers were shoveling off the doorsteps; the avenue stages made fine spots of color against the white street. Here and there on the corners were whole flower gardens blooming behind glass windows, against which the snowflakes stuck and melted; violets, roses, carnations, lilies of the valley—somehow vastly more lovely and alluring that they blossomed thus unnaturally in the snow. The Park itself was a wonderful stage winter-piece.

When he returned, the pause of the twilight had ceased, and the tune of the streets had changed. The snow was falling faster, lights streamed from the hotels that reared their many stories fearlessly up into the storm, defying the raging Atlantic winds. A long, black stream of carriages poured down the avenue, intersected here and there by other streams,

He spent more than an hour in dressing, watching every stage of his toilet carefully in the mirror. Everything was quite perfect; he was exactly the kind of boy he had always wanted to be.

tending horizontally. There were a score of cabs about the entrance of his hotel, and his driver had to wait. Boys in livery were running in and out of the awning stretched across the sidewalk, up and down the red velvet carpet laid from the door to the street. Above, about, within it all was the rumble and roar, the hurry and toss of thousands of human beings as hot for pleasure as himself, and on every side of him towered the glaring affirmation of the omnipotence of wealth.

The boy set his teeth and drew his shoulders together in a spasm of realization; the plot of all dramas, the text of all romances, the nerve-stuff of all sensations was whirling about him like the snowflakes. He burnt like a faggot in a tempest.

When Paul came down to dinner, the music of the orchestra floated up the elevator shaft to greet him. As he stepped into the thronged corridor, he sank back into one of the chairs against the wall to get his breath. The lights, the chatter, the perfumes, the bewildering medley of color—he had, for a moment, the feeling of not being able to stand it. But only for a moment; these were his own people, he told himself. He went slowly about the corridors, through the writing-rooms, smoking-rooms, reception-rooms, as though he were exploring the chambers of an enchanted palace, built and peopled for him alone.

When he reached the dining-room he sat down at a table near a window. The flowers, the white linen, the many-colored wineglasses, the gay toiletes of the women, the low popping of corks, the undulating repetitions of the *Blue Danube* from the orchestra, all flooded Paul's dream with bewildering radiance. When the roseate tinge of his champagne was added—that cold, precious, bubbling stuff that creamed and foamed in his glass— Paul wondered that there were honest men in the world at all. This was what all the world was fighting for, he reflected; this was what all the struggle was about. He doubted the reality of his past. Had he ever known a place called Cordelia Street, a place where fagged looking business men boarded the early car? Mere rivets in a machine they seemed to Paul,—sickening men, with combings of children's hair always hanging to their coats, and the smell of cooking in their clothes. Cordelia Street—Ah, that belonged to another time and country! Had he not always been thus, had he not sat here night after night, from as far back as he could remember, looking pensively over just such shimmering textures and slowly twirling the stem of a glass like this one between his thumb and middle finger? He rather thought he had.

He was not in the least abashed or lonely. He had no especial desire to meet or to know any of these people; all he demanded was the right to look on and conjecture, to watch the pageant. The mere stage properties were all he contended for. Nor was he lonely later in the evening, in his lodge at the Opera. He was entirely rid of his nervous misgivings, of his forced aggressiveness, of the imperative desire to show himself different from his surroundings. He felt now that his surroundings explained him. Nobody questioned the purple; he had only to wear it passively. He had only to glance down at his dress coat to reassure himself that here it would be impossible for anyone to humiliate him.

He found it hard to leave his beautiful sitting-room to go to bed that night, and sat long watching the raging storm from his turret window. When he went to sleep, it was with the lights turned on in his bedroom; partly because of his old timidity, and partly so that, if he should wake in the night, there would be no wretched moment of doubt, no horrible suspicion of yellow wallpaper, or of Washington and Calvin above his bed.

On Sunday morning the city was practically snowbound. Paul breakfasted late, and in the afternoon he fell in with a wild San Francisco boy, a freshman at Yale, who said he had run down for a "little flyer" over Sunday. The young man offered to show Paul the night side of the town, and the two boys went out together after dinner, not returning to the hotel until seven o'clock the next morning. They had started out in the confiding warmth of a champagne friendship, but their parting in the elevator was singularly cool. The freshman pulled himself together to make his train, and Paul went to bed. He awoke at two o'clock in the afternoon, very thirsty and dizzy, and rang for ice-water, coffee, and the Pittsburgh papers.

On the part of the hotel management, Paul excited no suspicion. There was

His dearest pleasures were the gray winter twilights in his sitting-room; his quiet enjoyment of his flowers, his clothes, his wide divan, his cigarette and his sense of power. He could not remember a time when he had felt so at peace with himself.

this to be said for him, that he wore his spoils with dignity and in no way made himself conspicuous. His chief greediness lay in his ears and eyes, and his excesses were not offensive ones. His dearest pleasures were the gray winter twilights in his sitting-room; his quiet enjoyment of his flowers, his clothes, his wide divan, his cigarette and his sense of power. He could not remember a time when he had felt so at peace with himself. The mere release from the necessity of petty lying, lying every day and every day, restored his self-respect. He had never lied for pleasure, even at school; but to make himself noticed and admired, to assert his difference from other Cordelia Street boys; and he felt a good deal more manly, more honest, even, now that he had no need for boastful pretensions, now that he could, as his actor friends used to say, "dress the part." It was characteristic that remorse did not occur to him. His golden days went by without a shadow, and he made each as perfect as he could.

On the eighth day after his arrival in New York he found the whole affair exploited in the Pittsburgh papers, exploited with a wealth of detail which indicated that local news of a sensational nature was at a low ebb. The firm of Denny & Carson announced that the boy's father had refunded the full amount of the theft and that they had no intention of prosecuting. The Cumberland minister had been interviewed, and expressed his hope of yet reclaiming the motherless lad, and Paul's Sabbath-school teacher declared that she would spare no effort to that end. The rumor had reached Pittsburgh that the boy had been seen in a New York hotel, and his father had gone East to find him and bring him home.

Paul had just come in to dress for dinner; he sank into a chair, weak to the

It was to be worse than jail, even; the tepid waters of Cordelia Street were to close over him finally and forever.

knees, and clasped his head in his hands. It was to be worse than jail, even; the tepid waters of Cordelia Street were to close over him finally and forever. The gray monotony stretched before him in hopeless, unrelieved years; Sabbath-school, Young People's Meeting, the yellow-papered room, the damp dish-towels; it all rushed back upon him with a sickening vividness. He had the old feeling that the orchestra had suddenly stopped, the sinking sensation that the play was over. The sweat broke out on his face, and he sprang to his feet, looked about him with his white, conscious smile, and winked at himself in the mirror. With something of the childish belief in miracles with which he had so often gone to class, all his lessons unlearned, Paul dressed and dashed whistling down the corridor to the elevator.

He had no sooner entered the dining-room and caught the measure of the music, than his remembrance was lightened by his old elastic power of claiming the moment, mounting with it, and finding it all sufficient. The glare and glitter about him, the mere scenic accessories had again, and for the last time, their old potency. He would show himself that he was game, he would finish the thing splendidly. He doubted, more than ever, the existence of Cordelia Street, and for the first time he drank his wine recklessly. Was he not, after all, one of these fortunate beings? Was he not still himself, and in his own place? He drummed a nervous accompaniment to the music and looked about him, telling himself over and over that it had paid.

He reflected drowsily, to the swell of the violin and the chill sweetness of his wine, that he might have done it more wisely. He might have caught an outbound steamer and been well out of their clutches before now. But the other side of the world had seemed too far away and too uncertain then; he could not have waited for it; his need had been too sharp. If he had to choose over again, he would do the same thing tomorrow. He looked affectionately about the dining-room, now gilded with a soft mist. Ah, it had paid indeed!

Paul was awakened next morning by a painful throbbing in his head and feet. He had thrown himself across the bed without undressing, and had slept with his shoes on. His limbs and hands were lead heavy, and his tongue and throat were parched. There came upon him one of those fateful attacks of clear-headedness that never occurred except when he was physically exhausted and his nerves hung loose. He lay still and closed his eyes and let the tide of realities wash over him.

His father was in New York; "stopping at some joint or other," he told himself. The memory of successive summers on the front stoop fell upon him like a weight of black water. He had not a hundred dollars left; and he knew now, more than ever, that money was everything, the wall that stood between all he loathed and all he wanted. The thing was winding itself up; he had thought of that on his first glorious day in New York, and had even provided a way to snap the thread. It lay on his dressing-table now; he had got it out last night when he came blindly up from dinner,—but the shiny metal hurt his eyes, and he disliked the look of it, anyway.

He rose and moved about with a painful effort, succumbing now and again to attacks of nausea. It was the old depression exaggerated; all the world had become Cordelia Street. Yet somehow he was not afraid of anything, was absolutely calm; perhaps because he had looked into the dark corner at last, and knew. It was bad enough, what he saw there; but somehow not so bad as his long fear of it had been. He saw everything clearly now. He had a feeling that he had made the best of it, that he had lived the sort of life he was meant to live, and for half an hour he sat staring at the revolver. But he told himself that was not the way, so he went downstairs and took a cab to the ferry.

When Paul arrived at Newark, he got off the train and took another cab, directing the driver to follow the Pennsylvania tracks out of the town. The snow lay heavy on the roadways and had drifted deep in the open fields. Only here and there the dead grass or dried weed stalks projected, singularly black, above it.

> He had a feeling that he had made the best of it, that he had lived the sort of life he was meant to live, and for half an hour he sat staring at the revolver.

Once well into the country, Paul dismissed the carriage and walked, floundering along the tracks, his mind a medley of irrelevant things. He seemed to hold in his brain an actual picture of everything he had seen that morning. He remembered every feature of both his drivers, of the toothless old woman from whom he had bought the red flowers in his coat, the agent from whom he had got his ticket, and all of his fellow passengers on the ferry. His mind, unable to cope with vital matters near at hand, worked feverishly and deftly at sorting and grouping these images. They made for him a part of the ugliness of the world, of the ache in his head, and the bitter burning on his tongue. He stooped and put a handful of snow into his mouth as he walked, but that, too, seemed hot. When he reached a little hillside, where the tracks ran through a cut some twenty feet below him, he stopped and sat down.

The carnations in his coat were drooping with the cold, he noticed, their red glory all over. It occurred to him that all the flowers he had seen in the show windows that first night must have gone the same way, long before this. It was only one splendid breath they had, in spite of their brave mockery at the winter outside the glass. It was a losing game in the end, it seemed, this revolt against the homilies by which the world is run. Paul took one of the blossoms carefully from his coat and scooped a little hole in the snow, where he covered it up. Then he dozed awhile, from his weak condition, seemingly insensible to the cold.

The sound of an approaching train awoke him, and he started to his feet, remembering only his resolution, and afraid lest he should be too late. He stood watching the approaching locomotive, his teeth chattering, his lips drawn away from them in a frightened smile; once or twice he glanced nervously sidewise, as though he were being watched. When the right moment came, he jumped. As he fell, the folly of his haste occurred to him with merciless clearness, the vastness of what he had left undone. There flashed through his brain, clearer than ever before, the blue of Adriatic water, the yellow of Algerian sands.

He felt something strike his chest,—his body was being thrown swiftly through the air, on and on, immeasurably far and fast, while his limbs gently relaxed. Then, because the picture-making mechanism was crushed, the disturbing visions flashed into black, and Paul dropped back into the immense design of things.

ERNEST HEMINGWAY

Hills Like White Elephants

The hills across the valley of the Ebro were long and white. On this side there was no shade and no trees and the station was between two lines of rails in the sun. Close against the side of the station there was the warm shadow of the building and a curtain, made of strings of bamboo beads, hung across the open door into the bar, to keep out flies. The American and the girl with him sat at a table in the shade, outside the building. It was very hot and the express from Barcelona would come in forty minutes. It stopped at this junction for two minutes and went on to Madrid.

"What should we drink?" the girl asked. She had taken off her hat and put it on the table.

"It's pretty hot," the man said.

"Let's drink beer."

"*Dos cervezas*," the man said into the curtain.

"Big ones?" a woman asked from the doorway.

"Yes. Two big ones."

The woman brought two glasses of beer and two felt pads. She put the felt pads and the beer glasses on the table and looked at the man and the girl. The girl was looking off at the line of hills. They were white in the sun and the country was brown and dry.

"They look like white elephants," she said.

"I've never seen one," the man drank his beer.

"No, you wouldn't have."

"I might have," the man said. "Just because you say I wouldn't have doesn't prove anything."

The girl looked at the bead curtain. "They've painted something on it," she said. "What does it say?"

"Anis del Toro. It's a drink."

"Could we try it?"

The man called "Listen" through the curtain. The woman came out from the bar.

"Four reales."

"We want two Anis del Toro."

"With water?"

"Do you want it with water?"

"I don't know," the girl said. "Is it good with water?"

"It's all right."

"You want them with water?" asked the woman.

"Yes, with water."

"It tastes like licorice," the girl said and put the glass down.

"That's the way with everything."

"Yes," said the girl. "Everything tastes of licorice. Especially all the things you've waited so long for, like absinthe."

"Oh, cut it out."

"You started it," the girl said. "I was being amused. I was having a fine time."

"Well, let's try and have a fine time."

"All right. I was trying. I said the mountains looked like white elephants. Wasn't that bright?"

"That was bright."

"I wanted to try this new drink. That's all we do, isn't it—look at things and try new drinks?"

"I guess so."

The girl looked across at the hills.

"They're lovely hills," she said. "They don't really look like white elephants. I just meant the coloring of their skin through the trees."

"Should we have another drink?"

"All right."

The warm wind blew the bead curtain against the table.

"The beer's nice and cool," the man said.

"It's lovely," the girl said.

"It's really an awfully simple operation, Jig," the man said. "It's not really an operation at all."

The girl looked at the ground the table legs rested on.

"I know you wouldn't mind it, Jig. It's really not anything. It's just to let the air in."

The girl did not say anything.

"I'll go with you and I'll stay with you all the time. They just let the air in and then it's all perfectly natural."

"Then what will we do afterwards?"

"We'll be fine afterwards. Just like we were before."

"What makes you think so?"

"That's the only thing that bothers us. It's the only thing that's made us unhappy."

The girl looked at the bead curtain, put her hand out and took hold of two of the strings of beads.

"And you think then we'll be all right and be happy."

"I know we will. You don't have to be afraid. I've known lots of people that have done it."

"So have I," said the girl. "And afterwards they were all so happy."

"Well," the man said, "if you don't want to you don't have to. I wouldn't have you do it if you didn't want to. But I know it's perfectly simple."

"And you really want to?"

"I think it's the best thing to do. But I don't want you to do it if you don't really want to."

"And if I do it you'll be happy and things will be like they were and you'll love me?"

"I love you now. You know I love you."

"I know. But if I do it, then it will be nice again if I say things are like white elephants, and you'll like it?"

"I'll love it. I love it now but I just can't think about it. You know how I get when I worry."

"If I do it you won't ever worry?"

"I won't worry about that because it's perfectly simple."

"Then I'll do it. Because I don't care about me."

The girl stood up and walked to the end of the station. Across, on the other side, were fields of grain and trees along the banks of the Ebro. Far away, beyond the river, were mountains.

"What do you mean?"

"I don't care about me."

"Well, I care about you."

"Oh, yes. But I don't care about me. And I'll do it and then everything will be fine."

"I don't want you to do it if you feel that way."

The girl stood up and walked to the end of the station. Across, on the other side, were fields of grain and trees along the banks of the Ebro. Far away, beyond the river, were mountains. The shadow of a cloud moved across the field of grain and she saw the river through the trees.

"And we could have all this," she said. "And we could have everything and every day we make it more impossible."

"What did you say?"

"I said we could have everything."

"No, we can't."

"We can have the whole world."

"No, we can't."

"We can go everywhere."

"No, we can't. It isn't ours any more."

"It's ours."

"No, it isn't. And once they take it away, you never get it back."

"But they haven't taken it away."

"We'll wait and see."

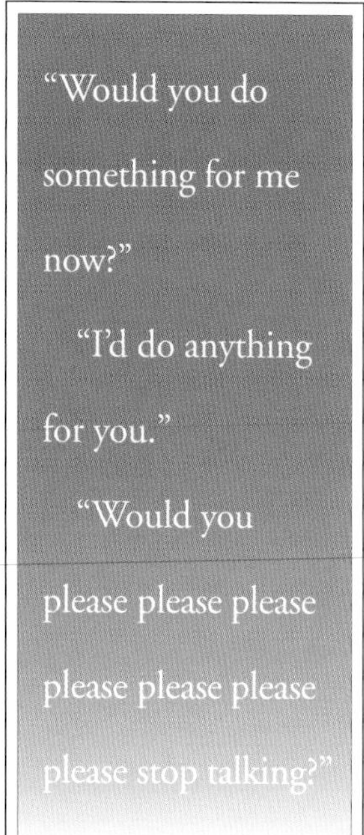

"Come on back in the shade," he said. "You mustn't feel that way."

"I don't feel any way," the girl said. "I just know things."

"I don't want you to do anything that you don't want to do—"

"Nor that isn't good for me," she said. "I know. Could we have another beer?"

"All right. But you've got to realize—"

"I realize," the girl said. "Can't we maybe stop talking?"

They sat down at the table and the girl looked across at the hills on the dry side of the valley and the man looked at her and at the table.

"You've got to realize," he said, "that I don't want you to do it if you don't want to. I'm perfectly willing to go through with it if it means anything to you."

"Doesn't it mean anything to you? We could get along."

"Of course it does. But I don't want anybody but you. I don't want anyone else. And I know it's perfectly simple."

"Yes, you know it's perfectly simple."

"It's all right for you to say that, but I do know it."

"Would you do something for me now?"

"I'd do anything for you."

"Would you please please please please please please please stop talking?"

He did not say anything but looked at the bags against the wall of the station. There were labels on them from all the hotels where they had spent nights.

"But I don't want you to," he said, "I don't care anything about it."

"I'll scream," the girl said.

The woman came out through the curtains with two glasses of beer and put them down on the damp felt pads. "The train comes in five minutes," she said.

"What did she say?" asked the girl.

"That the train is coming in five minutes."

The girl smiled brightly at the woman, to thank her.

"I'd better take the bags over to the other side of the station," the man said. She smiled at him.

"All right. Then come back and we'll finish the beer."

He picked up the two heavy bags and carried them around the station to the other tracks. He looked up the tracks but could not see the train. Coming back, he walked through the barroom, where people waiting for the train were drinking. He drank an Anis at the bar and looked at the people. They were all waiting reasonably for the train. He went out through the bead curtain. She was sitting at the table and smiled at him.

"Do you feel better?" he asked.

"I feel fine," she said. "There's nothing wrong with me. I feel fine."

KATHERINE ANNE PORTER

The Jilting of Granny Weatherall

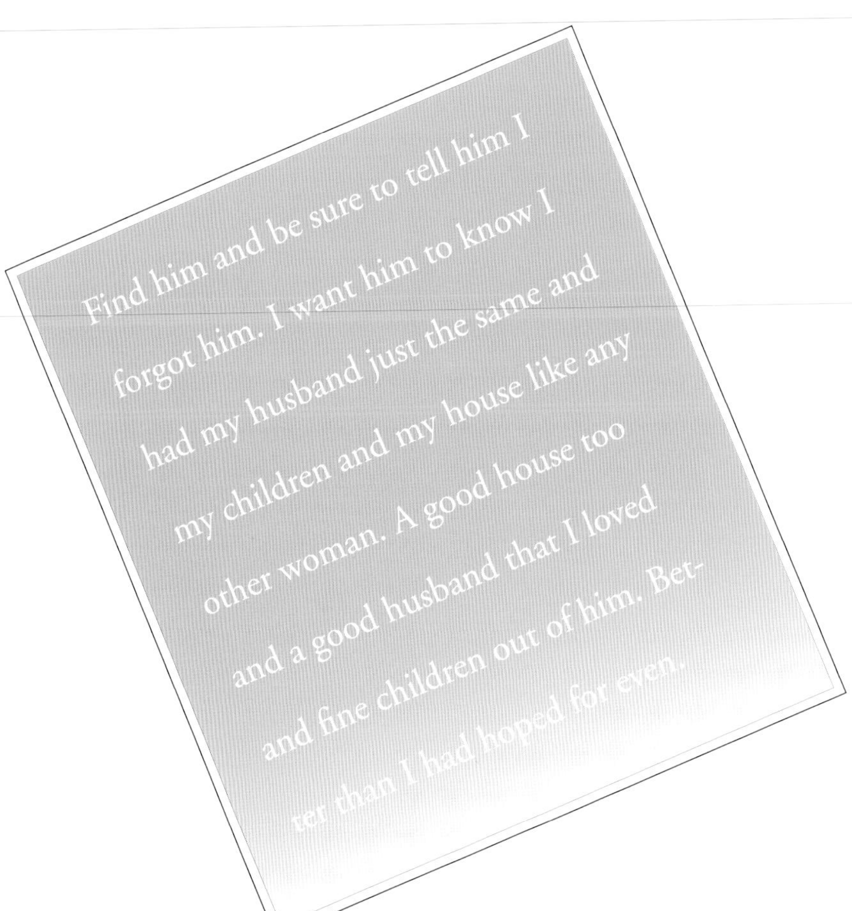

She flicked her wrist neatly out of Doctor Harry's pudgy careful fingers and pulled the sheet up to her chin. The brat ought to be in knee breeches. Doctoring around the country with spectacles on his nose! "Get along now, take your schoolbooks and go. There's nothing wrong with me."

Doctor Harry spread a warm paw like a cushion on her forehead where the forked green vein danced and made her eyelids twitch. "Now, now, be a good girl, and we'll have you up in no time."

"That's no way to speak to a woman nearly eighty years old just because she's down. I'd have you respect your elders, young man."

"Well, Missy, excuse me." Doctor Harry patted her cheek. "But I've got to warn you, haven't I? You're a marvel, but you must be careful or you're going to be good and sorry."

"Don't tell me what I'm going to be. I'm on my feet now, morally speaking. It's Cornelia. I had to go to bed to get rid of her."

Her bones felt loose, and floated around in her skin, and Doctor Harry floated like a balloon around the foot of the bed. He floated and pulled down his waistcoat and swung his glasses on a cord. "Well, stay where you are, it certainly can't hurt you."

"Get along and doctor your sick," said Granny Weatherall. "Leave a well woman alone. I'll call for you when I want you. . . . Where were you forty years ago when I pulled through milk-leg and double pneumonia? You weren't even born.

Don't let Cornelia lead you on," she shouted, because Doctor Harry appeared to float up to the ceiling and out. "I pay my own bills, and I don't throw my money away on nonsense!"

She meant to wave good-by, but it was too much trouble. Her eyes closed of themselves, it was like a dark curtain drawn around the bed. The pillow rose and floated under her, pleasant as a hammock in a light wind. She listened to the leaves rustling outside the window. No, somebody was swishing newspapers: no, Cornelia and Doctor Harry were whispering together. She leaped broad awake, thinking they whispered in her ear.

"She was never like this, *never* like this!" "Well, what can we expect?" "Yes, eighty years old. . . ."

Well, and what if she was? She still had ears. It was like Cornelia to whisper around doors. She always kept things secret in such a public way. She was always being tactful and kind. Cornelia was dutiful; that was the trouble with her. Dutiful and good: "So good and dutiful," said Granny, "that I'd like to spank her." She saw herself spanking Cornelia and making a fine job of it.

"What'd you say, Mother?"

Granny felt her face tying up in hard knots.

"Can't a body think, I'd like to know?"

"I thought you might want something."

"I do. I want a lot of things. First off, go away and don't whisper."

She lay and drowsed, hoping in her sleep that the children would keep out and let her rest a minute. It had been a long day. Not that she was tired. It was always pleasant to snatch a minute now and then. There was always so much to be done, let me see: tomorrow.

Tomorrow was far away and there was nothing to trouble about. Things were finished somehow when the time came; thank God there was always a little margin over for peace: then a person could spread out the plan of life and tuck in the edges orderly. It was good to have everything clean and folded away, with the hair brushes and tonic bottles sitting straight on the white embroidered linen: the day started without fuss and the pantry shelves laid out with rows of jelly glasses and brown jugs and white stone-china jars with blue whirligigs and words painted on them: coffee, tea, sugar, ginger, cinnamon, allspice: and the bronze clock with the lion on top nicely dusted off. The dust that lion could collect in twenty-four hours! The box in the attic with all those letters tied up, well, she'd have to go through that tomorrow. All those letters—George's letters and John's letters and her letters to them both—lying around for the children to find afterwards made her uneasy. Yes, that would be tomorrow's business. No use to let them know how silly she had been once.

While she was rummaging around she found death in her mind and it felt clammy and unfamiliar. She had spent so much time preparing for death there was no need for bringing it up again. Let it take care of itself for now. When she was sixty she had felt very old, finished, and went around making farewell trips to see her children and grandchildren, with a secret in her mind: This is the very last of your mother, children! Then she made her will and came down with a long fever. That was all just a notion like a lot of other things, but it was lucky too, for she had once and for all got over the idea of dying for a long time. Now she couldn't be worried. She hoped she had better sense now. Her father had lived to be one hundred and two years old and had drunk a noggin of strong hot toddy on his last birthday. He told the reporters it was his daily habit, and he owed his long life to that. He had made quite a scandal and was very pleased about it. She believed she'd just plague Cornelia a little.

"Cornelia! Cornelia!" No footsteps, but a sudden hand on her cheek. "Bless you, where have you been?"

"Here, Mother."

"Well, Cornelia, I want a noggin of hot toddy."

"Are you cold, darling?"

"I'm chilly, Cornelia. Lying in bed stops the circulation. I must have told you that a thousand times."

Well, she could just hear Cornelia telling her husband that Mother was getting a little childish and they'd have to humor her. The thing that most annoyed her was that Cornelia thought she was deaf, dumb, and blind. Little hasty glances and tiny gestures tossed around her and over her head saying, "Don't cross her, let her have her way, she's eighty years old," and she sitting there as if she lived in a thin glass cage. Sometimes Granny almost made up her mind to pack up and move back to her own house where nobody could remind her every minute that she was old. Wait, wait, Cornelia, till your own children whisper behind your back!

In her day she had kept a better house and had got more work done. She wasn't too old yet for Lydia to be driving eighty miles for advice when one of the children jumped the track, and Jimmy still dropped in and talked things over: "Now, Mammy, you've a good business head, I want to know what you think of this? . . ." Old. Cornelia couldn't change the furniture around without asking. Little things, little things! They had been so sweet when they were little. Granny wished the old days were back again with the children young and everything to be done over. It had been a hard pull, but not too much for her. When she thought of all the food she had cooked, and all the clothes she had cut and sewed, and all the gardens she had made—well, the children showed it. There they were, made out of her, and they couldn't get away from that. Sometimes she wanted to see John again and point to them and say, Well, I didn't do so badly, did I? But that would have to wait. That was for tomorrow. She used to think of him as a man, but now all the children were older than their father, and he would be a child beside her if she saw him now. It seemed strange and there was something wrong in the idea. Why, he couldn't possibly recognize her. She had fenced in a hundred acres once, digging the post holes herself and clamping the wires

Sometimes Granny almost made up her mind to pack up and move back to her own house where nobody could remind her every minute that she was old.

with just a negro boy to help. That changed a woman. John would be looking for a young woman with the peaked Spanish comb in her hair and the painted fan. Digging post holes changed a woman. Riding country roads in the winter when women had their babies was another thing: sitting up nights with sick horses and sick negroes and sick children and hardly ever losing one. John, I hardly ever lost one of them! John would see that in a minute, that would be something he could understand, she wouldn't have to explain anything!

> What does a woman do when she has put on the white veil and set out the white cake for a man and he doesn't come? She tried to remember.

It made her feel like rolling up her sleeves and putting the whole place to rights again. No matter if Cornelia was determined to be everywhere at once, there were a great many things left undone on this place. She would start tomorrow and do them. It was good to be strong enough for everything, even if all you made melted and changed and slipped under your hands, so that by the time you finished you almost forgot what you were working for. What was it I set out to do? she asked herself intently, but she could not remember. A fog rose over the valley, she saw it marching across the creek swallowing the trees and moving up the hill like an army of ghosts. Soon it would be at the near edge of the orchard, and then it was time to go in and light the lamps. Come in, children, don't stay out in the night air.

Lighting the lamps had been beautiful. The children huddled up to her and breathed like little calves waiting at the bars in the twilight. Their eyes followed the match and watched the flame rise and settle in a blue curve, then they moved away from her. The lamp was lit, they didn't have to be scared and hang on to mother any more. Never, never, never more. God, for all my life, I thank Thee. Without Thee, my God, I could never have done it. Hail, Mary, full of grace.

I want you to pick all the fruit this year and see nothing is wasted. There's always someone who can use it. Don't let good things rot for want of using. You waste life when you waste good food. Don't let things get lost. It's bitter to lose things. Now, don't let me get to thinking, not when I am tired and taking a little nap before supper. . . .

The pillow rose about her shoulders and pressed against her heart and the memory was being squeezed out of it: oh, push down the pillow, somebody: it would smother her if she tried to hold it. Such a fresh breeze blowing and such a green day with no threats in it. But he had not come, just the same. What does a woman do when she has put on the white veil and set out the white cake for a man and he doesn't come? She tried to remember. No, I swear he never harmed me but in that. He never harmed me but in that . . . and what if he did? There was the day, the day, but a whirl of dark smoke rose and covered it, crept up and over into the bright field where everything was planted so carefully in orderly rows. That was hell, she knew hell when she saw it. For sixty years she had prayed against remembering him and against losing her soul in the deep pit of hell, and now the two things were mingled in one and the thought of him was a smoky cloud from hell that moved and crept in her head when she had just got rid of Doctor Harry and was trying to rest a minute. Wounded vanity, Ellen, said a sharp voice in the top of her mind. Don't let your wounded vanity get the upper hand of you. Plenty of girls get jilted. You were jilted, weren't you? Then stand up to it. Her eyelids wavered and let in streamers of blue-gray light like tissue paper over her eyes. She must get up and pull the shades down or she'd never sleep. She was in bed again and the shades were not down. How could that happen? Better turn over, hide from the light, sleeping in the light gave you nightmares. "Mother, how do you feel now?" and a stinging wetness on her forehead. But I don't like having my face washed in cold water!

Hapsy? George? Lydia? Jimmy? No, Cornelia, and her features were swollen and full of little puddles. "They're coming, darling, they'll all be here soon." Go wash your face, child, you look funny.

Instead of obeying, Cornelia knelt down and put her head on the pillow. She seemed to be talking but there was no sound. "Well, are you tongue-tied? Whose birthday is it? Are you going to give a party?"

Cornelia's mouth moved urgently in strange shapes. "Don't do that, you bother me, daughter."

"Oh no, Mother. Oh, no. . . ."

Nonsense. It was strange about children. They disputed your every word. "No what, Cornelia?"

"Here's Doctor Harry."

"I won't see that boy again. He left just five minutes ago."

"That was this morning, Mother. It's night now. Here's the nurse."

"This is Doctor Harry, Mrs. Weatherall. I never saw you look so young and happy!"

"Ah, I'll never be young again—but I'd be happy if they'd let me lie in peace and get rested."

She thought she spoke up loudly, but no one answered. A warm weight on her forehead, a warm bracelet on her wrist, and a breeze went on whispering, trying to tell her something. A shuffle of leaves in the everlasting hand of God, He blew on them and they danced and rattled. "Mother, don't mind, we're going to give you a little hypodermic." "Look here, daughter, how do ants get in this bed? I saw sugar ants yesterday." Did you send for Hapsy too?

It was Hapsy she really wanted. She had to go a long way back through a great many rooms to find Hapsy standing with a baby on her arm. She seemed to herself to be Hapsy also, and the baby on Hapsy's arm was Hapsy and himself and herself, all at once, and there was no surprise in the meeting. Then Hapsy melted from within and turned flimsy as gray gauze and the baby was a gauzy shadow, and Hapsy came up close and said, "I thought you'd never come," and looked at her very searchingly and said, "You haven't changed a bit!" They leaned forward to kiss, when Cornelia began whispering from a long way off, "Oh, is there anything you want to tell me? Is there anything I can do for you?"

Yes, she had changed her mind after sixty years and she would like to see George. I want you to find George. Find him and be sure to tell him I forgot him. I want him to know I had my husband just the same and my children and my house like any other woman. A good house too and a good husband that I loved and fine children out of him. Better than I had hoped for even. Tell him I was given back everything he took away and more. Oh, no, oh, God, no, there was something else besides the house and the man and the children. Oh, surely they were not all? What was it? Something not given back.... Her breath crowded down under her ribs and grew into a monstrous frightening shape with cutting edges; it bored up into her head, and the agony was unbelievable: Yes, John, get the Doctor now, no more talk, the time has come.

> A shuffle of leaves in the everlasting hand of God, He blew on them and they danced and rattled.

When this one was born it should be the last. The last. It should have been born first, for it was the one she had truly wanted. Everything came in good time. Nothing left out, left over. She was strong, in three days she would be as well as ever. Better. A woman needed milk in her to have her full health.

"Mother, do you hear me?"

"I've been telling you—"

"Mother, Father Connolly's here."

"I went to Holy Communion only last week. Tell him I'm not so sinful as all that."

"Father just wants to speak with you."

He could speak as much as he pleased. It was like him to drop in and inquire about her soul as if it were a teething baby, and then stay on for a cup of tea and a round of cards and gossip. He always had a funny story of some sort, usually about an Irishman who made his little mistakes and confessed them, and the point lay in some absurd thing he would blurt out in the confessional showing his struggles

He had cursed like a sailor's parrot and said, "I'll kill him for you."

between native piety and original sin. Granny felt easy about her soul. Cornelia, where are your manners? Give Father Connolly a chair. She had her secret comfortable understanding with a few favorite saints who cleared a straight road to God for her. All as surely signed and sealed as the papers for the new Forty Acres. Forever . . . heirs and assigns forever. Since the day the wedding cake was not cut, but thrown out and wasted. The whole bottom dropped out of the world, and there she was blind and sweating with nothing under her feet and the walls falling away. His hand had caught her under the breast, she had not fallen, there was the freshly polished floor with the green rug on it, just as before. He had cursed like a sailor's parrot and said, "I'll kill him for you." Don't lay a hand on him, for my sake leave something to God. "Now, Ellen, you must believe what I tell you. . . ."

So there was nothing, nothing to worry about anymore, except sometimes in the night one of the children screamed in a nightmare, and they both hustled out shaking and hunting for the matches and calling, "There, wait a minute, here we are!" John, get the doctor now, Hapsy's time has come. But there was Hapsy standing by the bed in a white cap. "Cornelia, tell Hapsy to take off her cap. I can't see her plain."

Her eyes opened very wide and the room stood out like a picture she had seen somewhere. Dark colors with the shadows rising towards the ceiling in long angles. The tall black dresser gleamed with nothing on it but John's picture, enlarged from a little one, with John's eyes very black when they should have been blue. You never saw him, so how do you know how he looked? But the man insisted the copy was perfect, it was very rich and handsome. For a picture, yes, but it's not my husband. The table by the bed had a linen cover and a candle and a crucifix. The light was blue from Cornelia's silk lampshades. No sort of light at all, just frippery.

You had to live forty years with kerosene lamps to appreciate honest electricity. She felt very strong and she saw Doctor Harry with a rosy nimbus around him.

"You look like a saint, Doctor Harry, and I vow that's as near as you'll ever come to it."

"She's saying something."

"I heard you Cornelia. What's all this carrying on?"

"Father Connolly's saying—"

Cornelia's voice staggered and bumped like a cart in a bad road. It rounded corners and turned back again and arrived nowhere. Granny stepped up in the cart very lightly and reached for the reins, but a man sat beside her and she knew him by his hands, driving the cart. She did not look in his face, for she knew without seeing, but looked instead down the road where the trees leaned over and bowed to each other and a thousand birds were singing a Mass. She felt like singing too, but she put her hand in the bosom of her dress and pulled out a rosary, and Father Connolly murmured Latin in a very solemn voice and tickled her feet. My God, will you stop that nonsense? I'm a married woman. What if he did run away and leave me to face the priest by myself? I found another a whole world better. I wouldn't have exchanged my husband for anybody except St. Michael himself, and

> The table by the bed had a linen cover and a candle and a crucifix. The light was blue from Cornelia's silk lampshades. No sort of light at all, just frippery. You had to live forty years with kerosene lamps to appreciate honest electricity.

you may tell him that for me with a thank you in the bargain.

Light flashed on her closed eyelids, and a deep roaring shook her. Cornelia, is that lightning? I hear thunder. There's going to be a storm. Close all the windows. Call the children in. . . . "Mother, here we are, all of us." "Is that you, Hapsy?"

"Oh, no, I'm Lydia. We drove as fast as we could." Their faces drifted above her, drifted away. The rosary fell out of her hands and Lydia put it back. Jimmy tried to help, their hands fumbled together, and Granny closed two fingers around Jimmy's thumb. Beads wouldn't do, it must be something alive. She was so amazed her thoughts ran round and round. So, my dear Lord, this is my death and I wasn't even thinking about it. My children have come to see me die. But I can't, it's not time. Oh, I always hated surprises. I wanted to give Cornelia the amethyst set—Cornelia, you're to have the amethyst set, but Hapsy's to wear it when she wants, and, Doctor Harry, do shut up. Nobody sent for you. Oh, my dear Lord, do wait a minute. I meant to do something about the Forty Acres, Jimmy doesn't need it and Lydia will later on, with that worthless husband of hers. I meant to finish the altar cloth and send six bottles of wine to Sister Borgia for her dyspepsia. I want to send six bottles of wine to Sister Borgia, Father Connolly, now don't let me forget.

> Granny lay curled down within herself, amazed and watchful, staring at the point of light that was herself; her body was now only a deeper mass of shadow in an endless darkness and this darkness would curl around the light and swallow it up.

Cornelia's voice made short turns and tilted over and crashed. "Oh, Mother, oh, Mother, oh, Mother. . . ."

"I'm not going, Cornelia. I'm taken by surprise. I can't go."

You'll see Hapsy again. What bothered her? "I thought you'd never come." Granny made a long journey outward, looking for Hapsy. What if I don't find her? What then? Her heart sank down and down, there was no bottom to death, she couldn't come to the end of it. The blue light from Cornelia's lampshade drew into a tiny point in the center of her brain, it flickered and winked like an eye, quietly it fluttered and dwindled. Granny lay curled down within herself, amazed and watchful, staring at the point of light that was herself; her body was now only a deeper mass of shadow in an endless darkness and this darkness would curl around the light and swallow it up. God, give a sign!

For a second time there was no sign. Again no bridegroom and the priest in the house. She could not remember any other sorrow because this grief wiped them all away. Oh, no, there's nothing more cruel than this—I'll never forgive it. She stretched herself with a deep breath and blew out the light.

JOHN STEINBECK

The Chrysanthemums

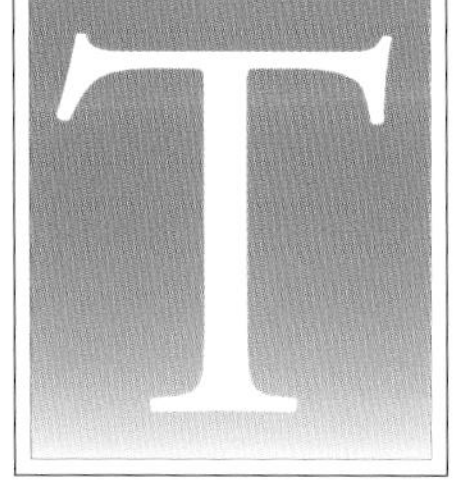

he high grey-flannel fog of winter closed off the Salinas Valley from the sky and from all the rest of the world. On every side it sat like a lid on the mountains and made of the great valley a closed pot. On the broad, level land floor the gang plows bit deep and left the black earth shining like metal where the shares had cut. On the foothill ranches across the Salinas River, the yellow stubble fields seemed to be bathed in pale cold sunshine, but there was no sunshine in the valley now in December. The thick willow scrub along the river flamed with sharp and positive yellow leaves.

It was a time of quiet and of waiting. The air was cold and tender. A light wind blew up from the southwest so that the farmers were mildly hopeful of a good rain before long; but fog and rain do not go together.

Across the river, on Henry Allen's foothill ranch there was little work to be done, for the hay was cut and stored and the orchards were plowed up to receive the rain deeply when it should come. The cattle on the higher slopes were becoming shaggy and rough-coated.

Elisa Allen, working in her flower garden, looked down across the yard and saw Henry, her husband, talking to two men in business suits. The three of them stood by the tractor shed, each man with one foot on the side of the little Fordson. They smoked cigarettes and studied the machine as they talked.

Elisa watched them for a moment and then went back to her work. She was thirty-five. Her face was lean and strong and her eyes were as clear as water. Her figure looked blocked and heavy in her gardening costume, a man's black hat pulled low down over her eyes, clod-hopper shoes, a figured print dress almost completely covered by a big corduroy apron with four big pockets to hold the snips, the trowel and scratcher, the seeds and the knife she worked with. She wore heavy leather gloves to protect her hands while she worked.

She was cutting down the old year's chrysanthemum stalks with a pair of short and powerful scissors. She looked down toward the men by the tractor shed now and then. Her face was eager and mature and handsome; even her work with the scissors was over-eager, over-powerful. The chrysanthemum stems seemed too small and easy for her energy.

She brushed a cloud of hair out of her eyes with the back of her glove, and left a smudge of earth on her cheek in doing it. Behind her stood the neat white farm house with red geraniums close-banked around it as high as the windows. It was a hard-swept looking little house, with hard-polished windows, and a clean mud-mat on the front steps.

Elisa cast another glance toward the tractor shed. The strangers were getting into their Ford coupe. She took off a glove and put her strong fingers down into the forest of new green chrysanthemum sprouts that were growing around the old roots. She spread the leaves and looked down among the close-growing stems. No aphids were there, no sowbugs or snails or cutworms. Her terrier fingers destroyed such pests before they could get started.

Elisa started at the sound of her husband's voice. He had come near quietly, and he leaned over the wire fence that protected her flower garden from cattle and dogs and chickens.

"At it again," he said. "You've got a strong new crop coming."

Elisa straightened her back and pulled on the gardening glove again. "Yes. They'll be strong this coming year." In her tone and on her face there was a little smugness.

"You've got a gift with things," Henry observed. "Some of those yellow chrysanthemums you had this year were ten inches across. I wish you'd work out in the orchard and raise some apples that big."

Her eyes sharpened. "Maybe I could do it, too. I've a gift with things, all right. My mother had it. She could stick anything in the ground and make it grow. She said it was having planters' hands that knew how to do it."

"Well, it sure works with flowers," he said.

"Henry, who were those men you were talking to?"

"Why, sure, that's what I came to tell you. They were from the Western Meat Company. I sold those thirty head of three-year-old steers. Got nearly my own price, too."

"Good," she said. "Good for you."

"And I thought," he continued, "I thought how it's Saturday afternoon, and we might go into Salinas for dinner at a restaurant, and then to a picture show—to celebrate, you see."

"Good," she repeated. "Oh, yes. That will be good."

Henry put on his joking tone. "There's fights tonight. How'd you like to go to the fights?"

"Oh, no," she said breathlessly. "No, I wouldn't like fights."

"Just fooling, Elisa. We'll go to a movie. Let's see. It's two now. I'm going to take Scotty and bring down those steers from the hill. It'll take us maybe two hours. We'll go in town about five and have dinner at the Cominos Hotel. Like that?"

"Of course I'll like it. It's good to eat away from home."

"All right, then. I'll go get up a couple of horses."

She said, "I'll have plenty of time to transplant some of these sets, I guess."

She heard her husband calling Scotty down by the barn. And a little later she saw the two men ride up the pale yellow hillside in search of the steers.

There was a little square sandy bed kept for rooting the chrysanthemums. With her trowel she turned the soil over and over, and smoothed it and patted it firm. Then she dug ten parallel trenches to receive the sets. Back at the chrysanthemum bed she pulled out the little crisp shoots, trimmed off the leaves of each one with her scissors and laid it on a small orderly pile.

A squeak of wheels and plod of hoofs came from the road. Elisa looked up. The country road ran along the dense bank of willows and cottonwoods that bordered the river, and up this road came a curious vehicle, curiously drawn. It was an old spring-wagon, with a round canvas top on it like the cover of a prairie schooner. It was drawn by an old bay horse and a little grey-and-white burro. A big stubble-bearded man sat between the cover flaps and drove the crawling team. Underneath the wagon, between the hind wheels, a lean and rangy mongrel dog walked sedately. Words were painted on the canvas in clumsy, crooked letters. "Pots, pans, knives, sisors, lawn mores. Fixed." Two rows of articles, and the triumphantly definitive "Fixed" below. The black paint had run down in little

> There was a little square sandy bed kept for rooting the chrysanthemums. With her trowel she turned the soil over and over, and smoothed it and patted it firm. Then she dug ten parallel trenches to receive the sets.

sharp points beneath each letter.

Elisa, squatting on the ground, watched to see the crazy, loose-jointed wagon pass by. But it didn't pass. It turned into the farm road in front of her house, crooked old wheels skirling and squeaking. The rangy dog darted from between the wheels and ran ahead. Instantly the two ranch shepherds flew out at him. Then all three stopped, and with stiff and quivering tails, with taut straight legs, with ambassadorial dignity, they slowly circled, sniffing daintily. The caravan pulled up to Elisa's wire fence and stopped. Now the newcomer dog, feeling outnumbered, lowered his tail and retired under the wagon with raised hackles and bared teeth.

The man on the wagon seat called out. "That's a bad dog in a fight when he gets started."

Elisa laughed. "I see he is. How soon does he generally get started?"

The man caught up her laughter and echoed it heartily. "Sometimes not for weeks and weeks," he said. He climbed stiffly down over the wheel. The horse and the donkey drooped like unwatered flowers.

Elisa saw that he was a very big man. Although his hair and beard were graying, he did not look old. His worn black suit was wrinkled and spotted with grease. The laughter had disappeared from his face and eyes the moment his laughing voice ceased. His eyes were dark, and they were full of the brooding that gets in the eyes of teamsters and of sailors. The calloused hands he rested on the wire fence were cracked, and every crack was a black line. He took off his battered hat.

"I'm off my general road, ma'am," he said. "Does this dirt road cut over across the river to the Los Angeles highway?"

The laughter had disappeared from his face and eyes the moment his laughing voice ceased. His eyes were dark, and they were full of the brooding that gets in the eyes of teamsters and of sailors.

Elisa stood up and shoved the thick scissors in her apron pocket. "Well, yes, it does, but it winds around and then fords the river. I don't think your team could pull through the sand."

He replied with some asperity, "It might surprise you what them beasts can pull through."

"When they get started?" she asked.

He smiled for a second. "Yes. When they get started."

"Well," said Elisa, "I think you'll save time if you go back to the Salinas road and pick up the highway there."

He drew a big finger down the chicken wire and made it sing. "I ain't in any hurry, ma'am. I go from Seattle to San Diego and back every year. Takes all my time. About six months each way. I aim to follow nice weather."

Elisa took off her gloves and stuffed them in the apron pocket with the scissors. She touched the under edge of her man's hat, searching for fugitive hairs. "That sounds like a nice kind of a way to live," she said.

He leaned confidentially over the fence. "Maybe you noticed the writing on my wagon. I mend pots and sharpen knives and scissors. You got any of them things to do?"

"Oh, no," she said quickly. "Nothing like that." Her eyes hardened with resistance.

"Scissors is the worst thing," he explained. "Most people just ruin scissors trying to sharpen 'em, but I know how. I got a special tool. It's a little bobbit kind of thing, and patented. But it sure does the trick."

"No. My scissors are all sharp."

"All right, then. Take a pot," he continued earnestly, "a bent pot, or a pot with a hole. I can make it like new so you don't have to buy no new ones. That's a saving for you."

> She touched the under edge of her man's hat, searching for fugitive hairs.

"No," she said shortly. "I tell you I have nothing like that for you to do."

His face fell to an exaggerated sadness. His voice took on a whining undertone. "I ain't had a thing to do today. Maybe I won't have no supper tonight. You see I'm off my regular road. I know folks on the highway clear from Seattle to San Diego. They save their things for me to sharpen up because they know I do it so good and save them money."

"I'm sorry," Elisa said irritably. "I haven't anything for you to do."

His eyes left her face and fell to searching the ground. They roamed about until they came to the chrysanthemum bed where she had been working. "What's them plants, ma'am?"

The irritation and resistance melted from Elisa's face. "Oh, those are chrysanthemums, giant whites and yellows. I raise them every year, bigger than anybody around here."

"Kind of a long-stemmed flower? Looks like a quick puff of colored smoke?" he asked.

"That's it. What a nice way to describe them."

"They smell kind of nasty till you get used to them," he said.

"It's a good bitter smell," she retorted, "not nasty at all."

He changed his tone quickly. "I like the smell myself."

"I had ten-inch blooms this year," she said.

The man leaned farther over the fence. "Look. I know a lady down the road a piece, has got the nicest garden you ever seen. Got nearly every kind of flower but no chrysanthemums. Last time I was mending a copper-bottom washtub for her (that's a hard job but I do it good), she said to me, 'If you ever run acrost some nice chrysanthemums I wish you'd try to get me a few seeds.' That's what she told me."

> She looked deep into his eyes, searchingly. Her mouth opened a little, and she seemed to be listening. "I'll try to tell you," she said. "Did you ever hear of planting hands?"

Elisa's eyes grew alert and eager. "She couldn't have known much about chrysanthemums. You can raise them from seed, but it's much easier to root the little sprouts you see there."

"Oh," he said. "I s'pose I can't take none to her, then."

"Why yes you can," Elisa cried. "I can put some in damp sand, and you can carry them right along with you. They'll take root in the pot if you keep them damp. And then she can transplant them."

"She'd sure like to have some, ma'am. You say they're nice ones?"

"Beautiful," she said. "Oh, beautiful." Her eyes shone. She tore off the battered hat and shook out her dark pretty hair. "I'll put them in a flower pot, and you can take them right with you. Come into the yard."

While the man came through the picket gate Elisa ran excitedly along the geranium-bordered path to the back of the house. And she returned carrying a big red flower pot. The gloves were forgotten now. She kneeled on the ground by the starting bed and dug up the sandy soil with her fingers and scooped it into the bright new flower pot. Then she picked up the little pile of shoots she had prepared. With her strong fingers she pressed them into the sand and tamped around them with her knuckles. The man stood over her. "I'll tell you what to do," she said. "You remember so you can tell the lady."

"Yes, I'll try to remember."

"Well, look. These will take root in about a month. Then she must set them out, about a foot apart in good rich earth like this, see?" She lifted a handful of dark soil for him to look at. "They'll grow fast and tall. Now remember this. In

July tell her to cut them down, about eight inches from the ground."

"Before they bloom?" he asked.

"Yes, before they bloom." Her face was tight with eagerness. "They'll grow right up again. About the last of September the buds will start."

She stopped and seemed perplexed. "It's the budding that takes the most care," she said hesitantly. "I don't know how to tell you." She looked deep into his eyes, searchingly. Her mouth opened a little, and she seemed to be listening. "I'll try to tell you," she said. "Did you ever hear of planting hands?"

"Can't say I have, ma'am."

"Well, I can only tell you what it feels like. It's when you're picking off the buds you don't want. Everything goes right down into your fingertips. You watch your fingers work. They do it themselves. You can feel how it is. They pick and pick the buds. They never make a mistake. They're with the plant. Do you see? Your fingers and the plant. You can feel that, right up your arm. They know. They never make a mistake. You can feel it. When you're like that you can't do anything wrong. Do you see that? Can you understand that?"

She was kneeling on the ground looking up at him. Her breast swelled passionately.

The man's eyes narrowed. He looked away self-consciously. "Maybe I know," he said. "Sometimes in the night in the wagon there—"

Elisa's voice grew husky. She broke in on him. "I've never lived as you do, but I know what you mean. When the night is dark—why, the stars are sharp-pointed, and there's quiet. Why, you rise up and up! Every pointed star gets driven into your body. It's like that. Hot and sharp and—lovely."

Kneeling there, her hand went out toward his legs in the greasy black trousers. Her hesitant fingers almost touched the cloth. Then her hand dropped to the ground. She crouched low like a fawning dog.

He said, "It's nice, just like you say. Only when you don't have no dinner, it ain't."

She stood up then, very straight, and her face was ashamed. She held the flower pot out to him and placed it gently in his arms. "Here. Put it in your wagon, on the seat, where you can watch it. Maybe I can find something for you to do."

At the back of the house she dug in the can pile and found two old and battered aluminum saucepans. She carried them back and gave them to him. "Here, maybe you can fix these."

His manner changed. He became professional. "Good as new I can fix them." At the back of his wagon he set a little anvil, and out of an oily tool box dug a small machine hammer. Elisa came through the gate to watch him while he pounded out the dents in the kettles. His mouth grew sure and knowing. At a difficult part of the work he sucked his under-lip.

"You sleep right in the wagon?" Elisa asked.

"Right in the wagon, ma'am. Rain or shine I'm dry as a cow in there."

"It must be nice," she said. "It must be very nice. I wish women could do such things."

"It ain't the right kind of a life for a woman."

Her upper lip raised a little, showing her teeth. "How do you know? How can you tell?" she said.

"I don't know, ma'am," he protested. "Of course I don't know. Now here's your kettles, done. You don't have to buy no new ones."

"How much?"

"Oh, fifty cents'll do. I keep my prices down and my work good. That's why I have all them satisfied customers up and down the highway."

Elisa brought him a fifty-cent piece from the house and dropped it in his hand. "You might be surprised to have a rival some time. I can sharpen scissors, too. And I can beat the dents out of little pots. I could show you what a woman might do."

He put his hammer back in the oily box and shoved the little anvil out of sight. "It would be a lonely life for a woman, ma'am, and a scarey life, too, with animals creeping under the wagon all night." He climbed over the single-tree, steadying himself with a hand on the burro's white rump. He settled himself in the seat, picked up the lines. "Thank you kindly, ma'am," he said. "I'll do like you told me; I'll go back and catch the Salinas road."

"Mind," she called, "if you're long in getting there, keep the sand damp."

"Sand, ma'am? . . . Sand? Oh, sure. You mean around the chrysanthemums. Sure I will." He clucked his tongue. The beasts leaned luxuriously into their collars. The mongrel dog took his place between the back wheels. The wagon turned and crawled out the entrance road and back the way it had come, along the river.

Elisa stood in front of her wire fence watching the slow progress of the caravan. Her shoulders were straight, her head thrown back, her eyes half-closed, so that the scene came vaguely into them. Her lips moved silently, forming the words "Good-bye—good-bye." Then she whispered, "That's a bright direction. There's a glowing there." The sound of her whisper startled her. She shook herself free and looked about to see whether anyone had been listening. Only the dogs had heard. They lifted their heads toward her from their sleeping in the dust, and then stretched out their chins and settled asleep again. Elisa turned and ran hurriedly into the house.

Elisa stood in front of her wire fence watching the slow progress of the caravan. Her shoulders were straight, her head thrown back, her eyes half-closed, so that the scene came vaguely into them. Her lips moved silently, forming the words "Good-bye—good-bye."

In the kitchen she reached behind the stove and felt the water tank. It was full of hot water from the noonday cooking. In the bathroom she tore off her soiled clothes and flung them into the corner. And then she scrubbed herself with a little block of pumice, legs and thighs, loins and chest and arms, until her skin was scratched and red. When she had dried herself she stood in front of a mirror in her bedroom and looked at her body. She tightened her stomach and threw out her chest. She turned and looked over her shoulder at her back.

After a while she began to dress, slowly. She put on her newest underclothing and her nicest stockings and the dress which was the symbol of her prettiness. She worked carefully on her hair, penciled her eyebrows and rouged her lips.

Before she was finished she heard the little thunder of hoofs and the shouts of Henry and his helper as they drove the red steers into the corral. She heard the gate bang shut and set herself for Henry's arrival.

His step sounded on the porch. He entered the house calling, "Elisa, where are you?"

"In my room, dressing. I'm not ready. There's hot water for your bath. Hurry up. It's getting late."

> For a second she lost her rigidity. "Henry! Don't talk like that. You didn't know what you said." She grew complete again. "I'm strong," she boasted. "I never knew before how strong."

When she heard him splashing in the tub, Elisa laid his dark suit on the bed, and shirt and socks and tie beside it. She stood his polished shoes on the floor beside the bed. Then she went to the porch and sat primly and stiffly down. She looked toward the river road where the willow-line was still yellow with frosted leaves so that under the high grey fog they seemed a thin band of sunshine. This was the only color in the grey afternoon. She sat unmoving for a long time. Her eyes blinked rarely.

Henry came banging out of the door, shoving his tie inside his vest as he came. Elisa stiffened and her face grew tight. Henry stopped short and looked at her. "Why—why, Elisa. You look so nice!"

"Nice? You think I look nice? What do you mean by 'nice'?"

Henry blundered on. "I don't know. I mean you look different, strong and happy."

"I am strong? Yes, strong. What do you mean 'strong'?"

He looked bewildered. "You're playing some kind of a game," he said helplessly. "It's a kind of a play. You look strong enough to break a calf over your knee, happy enough to eat it like a watermelon."

For a second she lost her rigidity. "Henry! Don't talk like that. You didn't know what you said." She grew complete again. "I'm strong," she boasted. "I never knew before how strong."

Henry looked down toward the tractor shed, and when he brought his eyes back to her, they were his own again. "I'll get out the car. You can put on your coat while I'm starting."

Elisa went into the house. She heard him drive to the gate and idle down his motor, and then she took a long time to put on her hat. She pulled it here and pressed it there. When Henry turned the motor off she slipped into her coat and went out.

The little roadster bounced along on the dirt road by the river, raising the birds and driving the rabbits into the brush. Two cranes flapped heavily over the willow-line and dropped into the river-bed.

Far ahead on the road Elisa saw a dark speck. She knew.

She tried not to look as they passed it, but her eyes would not obey. She whispered to herself sadly, "He might have thrown them off the road. That wouldn't have been much trouble, not very much. But he kept the pot," she explained. "He had to keep the pot. That's why he couldn't get them off the road."

The roadster turned a bend and she saw the caravan ahead. She swung full around toward her husband so she could not see the little covered wagon and the mismatched team as the car passed them.

In a moment it was over. The thing was done. She did not look back. She said loudly, to be heard above the motor, "It will be good, tonight, a good dinner."

"Now you're changed again," Henry complained. He took one hand from the wheel and patted her knee. "I ought to take you in to dinner oftener. It would be good for both of us. We get so heavy out on the ranch."

"Henry," she asked, "could we have wine at dinner?"

"Sure we could. Say! That will be fine."

She was silent for a while; then she said, "Henry, at those prize fights, do the men hurt each other very much?"

"Sometimes a little, not often. Why?"

"Well, I've read how they break noses, and blood runs down their chests. I've read how the fighting gloves get heavy and soggy with blood."

He looked around at her. "What's the matter, Elisa? I didn't know you read things like that." He brought the car to a stop, then turned to the right over the Salinas River bridge.

"Do any women ever go to the fights?" she asked.

"Oh, sure, some. What's the matter, Elisa? Do you want to go? I don't think you'd like it, but I'll take you if you really want to go."

She relaxed limply in the seat. "Oh, no. No. I don't want to go. I'm sure I don't." Her face was turned away from him. "It will be enough if we can have wine. It will be plenty." She turned up her coat collar so he could not see that she was crying weakly—like an old woman.

JAMES THURBER

The Secret Life of Walter Mitty

Peterson's
AU CHIC PARISIEN
25
Happy Cow
MILK CREAM
ART Marshall CRAFT
DELESSERT
SWISS RESTAURANT

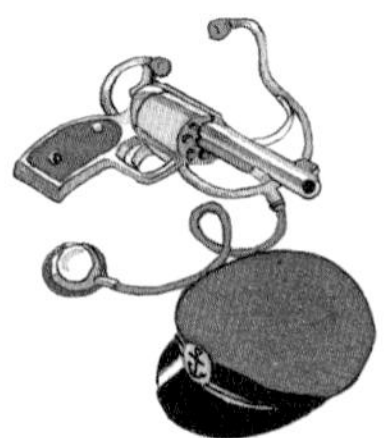

We're going through!" The commander's voice was like thin ice breaking. He wore his full-dress uniform with the heavily braided white cap pulled down rakishly over one cold gray eye. "We can't make it, sir. It's spoiling for a hurricane, if you ask me." "I'm not asking you, Lieutenant Berg," said the commander. "Throw on the power lights! Rev her up to eighty-five hundred! We're going through!" The pounding of the cylinders increased: ta-pocketa-pocketa-pocketa-*pocketa-pocketa*. The commander stared at the ice forming on the pilot window. He walked over and twisted a row of complicated dials. "Switch on number eight auxiliary!" he shouted. "Switch on number eight auxiliary!" repeated Lieutenant Berg. "Full strength in number three turret!" shouted the commander. "Full strength in number three turret!" The crew, bending to their various tasks in the huge, hurtling eight-engined Navy hydroplane, looked at each other and grinned. "The Old Man'll get us through," they said to one another. "The Old Man ain't afraid of hell!" . . .

"Not so fast! You're driving too fast!" said Mrs. Mitty. "What are you driving so fast for?"

"Hmm?" said Walter Mitty. He looked at his wife, in the seat beside him, with shocked astonishment. She seemed grossly unfamiliar, like a strange woman who had yelled at him in a crowd. "You were up to fifty-five," she said. "You know I don't like to go more than forty. You were up to fifty-five." Walter Mitty drove on toward Waterbury in silence, the roaring of the SN202 through the worst storm in twenty years of Navy flying fading in the remote, intimate airways of his mind.

"You're tensed up again," said Mrs. Mitty. "It's one of your days. I wish you'd let Dr. Renshaw look you over."

Walter Mitty stopped the car in front of the building where his wife went to have her hair done. "Remember to get those overshoes while I'm having my hair done," she said. "I don't need overshoes," said Mitty. She put her mirror back into her bag. "We've been through all that," she said, getting out of the car. "You're not a young man any longer." He raced the engine a little. "Why don't you wear your gloves? Have you lost your gloves?" Walter Mitty reached in a pocket and brought out the gloves. He put them on, but after she had turned and gone into the building and he had driven on to a red light, he took them off again. "Pick it up, brother!" snapped a cop as the light changed, and Mitty hastily pulled on his gloves and lurched ahead. He drove around the streets aimlessly for a time, and then he drove past the hospital on his way to the parking lot. . . .

"It's the millionaire banker, Wellington McMillan," said the pretty nurse. "Yes?" said Walter Mitty, removing his gloves slowly. "Who has the case?" "Dr. Renshaw and Dr. Benbow, but there are two specialists here, Dr. Remington from New York and Mr. Pritchard-Mitford from London. He flew over." A door opened down a long, cool corridor and Dr. Renshaw came out. He looked distraught and haggard. "Hello, Mitty," he said. "We're having the devil's own time with McMillan, the millionaire banker and close personal friend of Roosevelt. Obstreosis of the ductal tract. Tertiary. Wish you'd take a look at him." "Glad to," said Mitty.

In the operating room there were whispered introductions: "Dr. Remington, Dr. Mitty. Dr. Pritchard-Mitford, Dr. Mitty." "I've read your book on streptothricosis," said Pritchard-Mitford, shaking hands. "A brilliant performance, sir." "Thank you," said Walter Mitty. "Didn't know you were in the States, Mitty," grumbled Remington. "Coals to Newcastle, bringing Mitford and me up here for a tertiary." "You are very kind," said

> "Quiet, man!" said Mitty, in a low, cool voice. He sprang to the machine, which was going pocketa-pocketa-queep-pocketa-queep.

Mitty. A huge, complicated machine, connected to the operating table, with many tubes and wires, began at this moment to go pocketa-pocketa-pocketa. "The new anesthetizer is giving way!" shouted an intern. "There is no one in the East who knows how to fix it!" "Quiet, man!" said Mitty, in a low, cool voice. He sprang to the machine, which was going pocketa-pocketa-queep-pocketa-queep. He began fingering delicately a row of glistening dials. "Give me a fountain pen!" he snapped. Someone handed him a fountain pen. He pulled a faulty piston out of the machine and inserted the pen in its place. "That will hold for ten minutes," he said. "Get on with the operation." A nurse hurried over and whispered to Renshaw. Mitty saw the man turn pale. "Coreopsis has set in," said Renshaw nervously. "If you would take over, Mitty?" Mitty looked at him and at the craven figure of Benbow, who drank, and at the grave, uncertain faces of the two great specialists. "If you wish," he said. They slipped a white gown on him; he adjusted a mask and drew on thin gloves; nurses handed him shining. . .

"Back it up, Mac! Look out for that Buick!" Walter Mitty jammed on the brakes. "Wrong lane, Mac," said the parking-lot attendant, looking at Mitty closely. "Gee. Yeh," muttered Mitty. He began cautiously to back out of the lane marked "Exit Only." "Leave her sit there," said the attendant. "I'll put her away." Mitty got out of the car. "Hey, better leave the key." "Oh," said Mitty, handing the man the ignition key. The attendant vaulted into the car, backed it up with insolent skill, and put it where it belonged.

They're so damn cocky, thought Walter Mitty, walking along Main Street; they think they know everything. Once he had tried to take his chains off, outside New Milford, and he had got them wound around the axles. A man had had to come out in a wrecking car and unwind them, a young, grinning garageman. Since then Mrs. Mitty always made him drive to a garage to have the chains taken off. The next time, he thought, I'll wear my right arm in a sling; they won't grin at me then. I'll have my right arm in a sling and they'll see I couldn't possibly take the chains off myself. He kicked at the slush on the sidewalk. "Overshoes," he said to himself, and he began looking for a shoe store.

When he came out into the street again, with the overshoes in a box under his arm, Walter Mitty began to wonder what the other thing was his wife had told him to get. She had told him, twice, before they set out from their house for Waterbury. In a way he hated these weekly trips to town—he was always getting something wrong. Kleenex, he thought, Squibb's, razor blades? No. Toothpaste, toothbrush, bicarbonate, carborundum, initiative and referendum? He gave it up. But she would remember it. "Where's the what's-its-name?" she would ask. "Don't

> "I could have killed Gregory Fitzhurst at three hundred feet *with my left hand.*" Pandemonium broke loose in the courtroom. A woman's scream rose above the bedlam, and suddenly a lovely, dark-haired girl was in Walter Mitty's arms.

tell me you forgot the what's-its-name." A newsboy went by shouting something about the Waterbury trial. . . .

"Perhaps this will refresh your memory." The district attorney suddenly thrust a heavy automatic at the quiet figure on the witness stand. "Have you ever seen this before?" Walter Mitty took the gun and examined it expertly. "This is my Webley-Vickers fifty-eighty," he said calmly. An excited buzz ran around the courtroom. The judge rapped for order. "You are a crack shot with any sort of firearm, I believe?" said the district attorney, insinuatingly.

"Objection!" shouted Mitty's attorney. "We have shown that the defendant could not have fired the shot. We have shown that he wore his right arm in a sling on the night of the fourteenth of July." Walter Mitty raised his hand briefly and the bickering attorneys were stilled. "With any known make of gun," he said evenly, "I could have killed Gregory Fitzhurst at three hundred feet *with my left hand.*" Pandemonium broke loose in the courtroom. A woman's scream rose above the bedlam, and suddenly a lovely, dark-haired girl was in Walter Mitty's arms. The district attorney struck at her savagely. Without rising from his chair, Mitty let the man have it on the point of the chin. "You miserable cur!" . . .

"Puppy biscuit," said Walter Mitty. He stopped walking and the buildings of Waterbury rose up out of the misty courtroom and surrounded him again. A woman who was passing laughed. "He said 'puppy biscuit,'" she said to her companion. "That man said 'puppy biscuit' to himself." Walter Mitty hurried on. He went into an A&P, not the first one he came to but a smaller one farther up the street. "I want some biscuit for small, young dogs," he said to the clerk. "Any special brand, sir?" The greatest pistol shot in the world thought a moment. "It says 'Puppies Bark for It' on the box," said Walter Mitty.

> He gave it up. But she would remember it. "Where's the what's-its-name?" she would ask. "Don't tell me you forgot the what's-its-name."

His wife would be through at the hairdresser's in fifteen minutes, Mitty saw in looking at his watch, unless they had trouble drying it; sometimes they had trouble drying it. She didn't like to get to the hotel first; she would want him to be there waiting for her as usual. He found a big leather chair in the lobby, facing a window, and he put the overshoes and the puppy biscuit on the floor beside it. He picked up an old copy of *Liberty* and sank down into the chair. "Can Germany Conquer the World Through the Air?" Walter Mitty looked at the pictures of bombing planes and of ruined streets. . . .

"The cannonading has got the wind up in young Raleigh, sir," said the sergeant. Captain Mitty looked up at him through tousled hair. "Get him to bed," he said wearily. "With the others. I'll fly alone." "But you can't, sir," said the sergeant anxiously. "It takes two men to handle that bomber and the Archies are pounding hell out of the air. Von Richtman's circus is between here and Saulier."

"Somebody's got to get that ammunition dump," said Mitty. "I'm going over. Spot of brandy?" He poured a drink for the sergeant and one for himself. War thundered and whined around the dugout and battered at the door. There was a rending explosion, and splinters flew through the room. "A bit of a near thing," said Captain Mitty carelessly. "The box barrage is closing in," said the sergeant. "We only live once, sergeant," said Mitty, with his faint, fleeting smile. "Or do we?" He poured another brandy and tossed it off. "I never see a man could hold his brandy like you, sir," said the sergeant. "Begging your pardon, sir." Captain Mitty stood up and strapped on his huge Webley-Vickers automatic. "It's forty kilometers through hell, sir," said the sergeant. Mitty finished one last brandy. "After all," he said softly, "what isn't?" The pounding of the cannon increased; there was the rat-tat-tatting of machine guns, and from somewhere came the menacing pocketa-pocketa-pocketa of the new flamethrowers. Walter Mitty walked to the door of the dugout humming, "Auprés de Ma Blonde." He turned and waved to the sergeant. "Cheerio!" he said. . . .

At the drugstore on the corner she said, "Wait here for me. I forgot something. I won't be a minute."

Something struck his shoulder. "I've been looking all over this hotel for you," said Mrs. Mitty. "Why do you have to hide in this old chair? How did you expect me to find you?" "Things close in," said Walter Mitty vaguely. "What?" Mrs. Mitty said. "Did you get the what's-its-name? The puppy biscuit? What's in that box?" "Overshoes," said Mitty. "Couldn't you have put them on in the store?" "I was thinking," said Walter Mitty. "Does it ever occur to you that I am sometimes thinking?" She looked at him. "I'm going to take your temperature when I get you home," she said.

They went out through the revolving doors that made a faintly derisive whistling sound when you pushed them. It was two blocks to the parking lot. At the drugstore on the corner she said, "Wait here for me. I forgot something. I won't be a minute." She was more than a minute. Walter Mitty lighted a cigarette. It began to rain, rain with sleet in it. He stood up against the wall of the drugstore, smoking. . . . He put his shoulders back and his heels together. "To hell with the handkerchief," said Walter Mitty scornfully. He took one last drag on his cigarette and snapped it away. Then, with that faint, fleeting smile playing about his lips, he faced the firing squad: erect and motionless, proud and disdainful, Walter Mitty, the Undefeated, inscrutable to the last.

WALLACE STEGNER

In the Twilight

The boy stood stiffly with his hands on the bar, watching her. He heard the click of the bolt as his father threw the shell and the snip of metal as he reloaded. Then his father was running, almost as heavily as the sow, but more terribly because he was the killer and she the killed.

he boy always felt October as a twilight month. Its whole function was the preparation for winter, a getting ready, a drawing-in of the sun like a snail into its shell, a shortening and tightening against the long cold. And that year, after his father bought the sow up on the north bench and brought her in to be fattened up in the corral behind the barn, he felt obscurely the difference between the two kinds of preparation going on. The footbridge came out, was piled up in sections and planks in the loft of the barn. That would go in again next spring, as soon as the danger of the ice and floodwater was over. But the sow was not going to be back next spring. Her preparation was of a more final kind.

He had the job of carrying the swill bucket to the corral every morning, carrying a sharpened stick to poke the frantic beast away from the trough while he poured the sloppy mess of potato peelings and apple peelings and bacon rinds and sour milk and bread crusts. The sow fascinated him, though he disliked her intensely. He hated the smell of the swill, he hated the pig's lumbering, greedy rush when he appeared with the pail, he hated her pig eyes sunk in fat, he hated the rubber snout and the caked filth on her bristly hide. Still, he used to stand and watch her gobbling in the trough, and sometimes he scratched her back with the stick and felt her vast, bestial pleasure in the hunching of her spine and the deep, smacking grunts that rumbled out of her.

In a sense she was his personal enemy. She was responsible for the nasty job he had every day. She was responsible for the stink that offended him when he passed the corral. She was dirty and greedy and monstrous. But she was fascinating all the same, perhaps because all her greed worked against her, and what she ate so ravenously served death, not life. The day she broke loose, and children and dogs and women with flapping aprons headed her off from the river brush and shooed her back toward the corral, the boy and his brother, Chet, stood at the bars panting with the chase and promised her how soon she'd get hers. In just about a week now she wouldn't be causing any trouble. Chet took aim with an imaginary rifle and shot her just behind the left foreleg, and then Bruce took aim and shot her between the eyes, and they went away satisfied and somehow reconciled to the old sow, ugly and smelly and greedy and troublesome as she was, because she was as good as dead already.

In the big double bed Bruce stirred, yawned, stretched his feet down and pulled them back again quick when they touched a cold spot, opened his eyes, and looked up. The mottled ceiling above him, stained by firemen's chemicals when they had the attic fire, was a forest. He could see a bird with a big, hooked bill sitting on a tree. He yawned again, squinting his eyes, and twisted his head, and from the different angle, it was not a bird at all, but an automobile with its top down and smoke coming out behind. His eyes moved over the whole ceiling, picking out the shapes he and Chet had settled on definitely: the wildcat with one white, glaring eye; the man waving a flag; the woman with big feet and a bundle on her back. He lay picking them out, letting sleep go away from him slowly.

Downstairs he heard sounds, bumpings, the clank of a pan, and his head turned so that he could look out of the window. It was still early; the sun was barely tipping the barn roof. The folks didn't usually. . . .

Then he stabbed Chet with an elbow. "Hey! Get up. This is the morning for the pig."

Chet flailed with his arms, grumbled, and half sat up. His hair was frowsy, and he was mad. "Don't go sticking your darn elbow into me," he said. "What's the matter?"

"The pig," Bruce said. "Pa's butchering the pig this morning."

But she was fascinating all the same, perhaps because all her greed worked against her, and what she ate so ravenously served death, not life.

"Heck with the old dirty pig," Chet said, but Bruce had barely got his long black stockings on before Chet was on the edge of the bed, dressing, too. Bruce beat him downstairs by about a minute.

The kitchen was warm. The washtub and the copper boiler were on the stove, and already sent up wisps of steam. Both boys, out of habit, huddled their bottoms close to the open oven door, watching their father finish his coffee.

> He reached out and yanked a hair from Chet's head, held it between thumb and forefinger, and sliced it neatly in two with the knife. Chet watched him with one hand on his violated skull.

He seemed in high spirits, and winked at Chet. "What are you up so early for?"

"Gonna help butcher the pig."

Their mother, standing by the washstand with a couple of mush bowls in her hands, looked at them. "You just forget about the pig. Sit down and eat your breakfast. Are you washed?"

"No'm," they said. "But we want to watch."

She waved them to the washstand and set the table for them. While they ate, their father sat sharpening the butcher knife on the edge of a crock, and they watched him.

"How you gonna do it?" Bruce said. "Cut her throat?"

"Bruce!" his mother said.

"Well, is he?" Chet said. He added, "I bet it bleeds like anything," and stared at the glittering edge of the knife.

"You boys better go play in the brush, or go up to the sandhills," their mother said. "You don't want to watch a nasty, bloody mess like this is going to be. I should think you'd feel sorry for the poor old pig."

They jeered. Bruce got the vision of the throat-cutting out of his mind and punched Chet on the shoulder. "No more old slop to carry," he said.

Chet punched him back and said, "No more old ugly sow snuffing around in the manure."

"Sausages for breakfast," Bruce said.

"Pork chops for dinner," said Chet.

They giggled, and their father looked them over, laughing. "Couple of cannibals," he said. He reached out and yanked a hair from Chet's head, held it between thumb and forefinger, and sliced it neatly in two with the knife. Chet watched him with one hand on his violated skull.

"Well, I don't think they should see things like that," the mother said helplessly. "Heaven knows they kill a lot of gophers and things on the farm, but this is worse."

The father stood up. "Oh, rats," he said. "I always watched butchering when I was a kid. You want to make them so sissy they can't chop the head off a rooster?"

"I still don't think it's right," she said. "When I was little, I had to go out with a bowl and catch the blood for blood pudding. It gave me nightmares for a month after. . . ."

She stopped and turned to the stove, and Bruce saw her shoulders move as if she had had a chill. He imagined her stooping with a bowl under the pig's red, gaping throat, and the thought made him swallow twice at the mouthful he had. But a minute later his father went into the cellarway and got Chet's .22, and they crowded on his heels as he picked up the knife and went out.

"Brucie," his mother said, "don't you go!"

"Aw, heck," he said, and deliberately disobeyed her.

The morning was crisp, sunny, the air tangy with late autumn. In the far corner of the corral the sow heaved to her feet, her hindquarters still sagging loosely on the ground, and stared at them. She did not come near, and Bruce wondered why. Maybe because they didn't have a pail with them. Chet leaned on the corral bars and jeered at her.

"All right for you, old sow. This is where you get yours."

Excitement prickled in Bruce's legs. He couldn't stand still. With his hands on the top bar he jumped up and down and yelled at the ugly beast, and all his hatred of her ugliness and her vast pig appetites came out of him in shrill cries. The sow got clear up, and the father spoke sharply. "Shut up. You'll get her all excited. If you want to help, all right, but if you can't keep quiet you can go back in the house."

They fell quiet while he loaded the single-shot Remington. The sow came forward a few steps, snout wrinkling. She stopped at the edge of the manure pile, under the hole through which it was pitched from the barn, and fronted them suspiciously.

"Where you gonna shoot her?" Chet whispered.

"Head," his father whispered back. "Don't want any holes in her meat."

He leaned the gun over the rail and took aim for what seemed minutes. Then the sow moved, and he took his finger outside the trigger guard and eased up. Bruce let his breath out in a long, wispy plume, thinking: if she hadn't moved just then she'd be dead now, she'd be lying there like a chicken with its head cut off. On a day like this, with the sun just coming up and everything so bright, she'd be dead. He swallowed.

His father reached down and picked up the butcher knife, sticking it into the top bar where it would be handy. "All right now," he said. He seemed excited himself. His breath came short through his nose.

He laid the barrel over the bar again, and his cheek dropped against the stock. The sow lowered her head and snuffed at the manure, and in the instant when she was frozen there, perfectly still except for the little red, upward-peering eyes, the rifle cracked thinly, dryly, like a stick breaking.

The sow leaped straight into the air, her open mouth bursting with sound, came down still squealing to stand for a moment stiff-legged, swinging her head. Then she was running around and around the corral, faster than Bruce had ever believed she could move, around and around, ponderous, galloping, terrified, a sudden and living pain. The constant high shriek of agony, sustained at an unsustainable pitch, cut the nerves like a knife.

The boy stood stiffly with his hands on the bar, watching her. He heard the click of the bolt as his father threw the shell and the snip of metal as he reloaded. Then his father was running, almost as heavily as the sow, but more terribly because he was the killer and she the killed. The boy saw his red face, his open mouth, as he pursued the sow around the corral, trying to stop and corner her for another shot.

The squeal went on, an intolerable sound of death, and the sow charged blindly around the pen. A trickle of red ran down over her snout from between her eyes, and she went on, staggering, a death that did not want to die, a vast, greedy life hurt and dying and shrilling its pain. Even through his own terror Bruce could not miss the way she scrambled to avoid the man with the gun. She plunged up on the manure pile, was cornered there, raced down and around the bars again, and then in one magnificent running leap went clear up over the manure, through the hole, and into the barn.

> Then she was running around and around the corral, faster than Bruce had ever believed she could move, around and around, ponderous, galloping, terrified, a sudden and living pain.

"God Almighty!" the father yelled. "Head her off. *Run!*"

The two boys arrived at the barn door together, slammed the lower half shut, and peered over. The pig's wild screaming came from the cow stable, empty now. The horses in the front stalls were trembling and white-eyed, and, as Chet pushed the upper door, the nervous mare lashed out with both hind feet, and splinters flew from the board ceiling.

Their father was beside them now, looking in, the gun in his right hand. His face was so violently red that Bruce shrank away.

"Get on out behind again," the father said. "If she comes out through the hole, yell and keep her inside the fence."

He went inside, and the boys fled around behind, their eyes glued to the manure hole, their ears full of the muffled and unceasing shrilling of the wounded sow. They heard her squealing sharpen, heard the new fear in it, heard their father

Everybody was helping but him, and he lay inside like a baby because he couldn't stand the sight of blood.

shouting, and then she arched through the window again, jumping like a horse at a fence, front feet tucked up and hind legs sailing. Her feet hit the edge, and she fell rolling, but the squealing did not stop. She was up in a moment, head swinging desperately from side to side, and in that moment the father, coming around the corner, took quick aim and fired again.

The sow stood still. Her squeal went up and up and up to a cracking pitch. Her whole fat, mud-caked body quivered and began to settle, her legs spraddled as if to keep it from going down. Then the squeal trailed off to a thin whimper, the front legs buckled, the sow's snout plowed into the manure, and the father was over the fence with the knife in his hand. The stoop, the jerk of the shoulder, the rush of bright blood. . . .

"Jeez!" Chet said.

Bruce, strangling, tried to look, tried to say something to show that it had been wonderful and exciting, that it served the dirty old sow right, but he couldn't speak. His eyes, turned away from the corral, were still full of the picture of his father standing over the dead sow, towering, triumphant, the bloody knife in his hand, his back huge and broad and monstrous with power. He gulped and swallowed as a rush of salty liquid filled his mouth.

"My gosh," Chet said. "Did you see her run? Right between the eyes, and it only made her squeal and run."

Bruce turned his head further and clung to the bar. He heard Chet's voice, going away, getting dimmer. "What's the matter? You're white as a sheet."

"I am . . . not," Bruce said. He straightened his shoulders and lifted his head, but a moment later he was hanging on the corral vomiting, heaving, clinging for dear life to keep the black dots in his brain from becoming solid.

And after a minute his father's voice, still breathless and jerky with exertion. "Couldn't stand it, uh? You all right, Chet?"

Chet said he felt fine, swell. Bruce clung to the voices, hung onto them desperately, because as long as he could hear them the terror wasn't total, the black dots weren't solid. "You better get on into the house," his father said, and then raised his voice and called, "Sis!"

His mother came and held him with one arm and led him back to the house and, still frantically clinging to voices, to meanings, he heard her say, "You never should have watched it, it's horrible, I knew all the time. . . ."

There was a while when he lay on the sofa in the parlor with his eyes closed. His mother came in once to see how he felt, but the duties in the kitchen and yard were demanding, and she stayed only a minute. Listening out of his still struggle with nausea, he heard the thumpings in the kitchen, the quick footsteps, the words, and as his nausea ebbed, he wondered what was going on now. Once, when the outside door was opened, he heard the voices of boys out by the barn.

Shame made him turn over and lie face down. What he had done was sissy. Chet hadn't got sick, and the other kids out there watching now weren't sick, or they wouldn't be yelling that way. But they hadn't seen the old sow run, or heard her squeal, or seen his father stooping with the knife. . . .

His mother was out there, though, helping to get it done, and she had said from the start that she hated it. Everybody was helping but him, and he lay inside like a baby because he couldn't stand the sight of blood. What if he'd been told to catch the blood, like Ma? The thought sickened him, and he lay still.

After a while he sat up tentatively, put his feet over the edge of the sofa. He didn't seem dizzy. And he had to go out there and show them that he was as capable of watching a butchering as any of them.

He felt a queer, violent hatred for the old sow. It served her right to be shot and have her throat cut, have her insides ripped out. He would go out and get hold of her insides and pull, and everything would come out in a bundle like the insides of a fish.

He stood up. The dizziness had gone completely. Listening, he heard no sounds in the kitchen. Everybody was outside. Taking three deep breaths, the way he always did before going off the high diving board the first time in the spring, he went out to the back door.

Four boys stood in a ring around his father, who was squatting on the ground. The pig was nowhere in sight, but Bruce saw his mother bending over one of the washtubs, and he saw the rope that went up over a pulley at the corner of the barn and trailed near his father's feet. Then his father took hold of the rope and pulled, and the boys took hold and pulled too, stepping all over each other, and the sow came in sight. But not a sow any longer, not an animal, not the mud-caked, bristly-hided old brute that he had carried slop to all fall. The thing that rose up toward the pulley was clean and pink and hairless, like the carcasses in Heimie Gross's shop, and, as it swung gently on the rope that bound its hind feet, he saw the flapping, opened belly and the clean red meat inside. She hung there, turning gently half around and back again, so innocent and harmless that the boy was no longer sickened or afraid.

His father saw him come out and grinned at him, wiping his red hands on a rag. "Snapped out of it, uh? I thought you were a tough guy."

"Brucie got sick," Chet said. "When Pa cut her throat, Brucie threw up all over the corral."

"Oh, I did not!" Bruce said. He clenched his fists.

"You big liar," Chet said. "I can show you the puddle."

Not daring to look at the other boys, Bruce went over to where his mother was washing a long, whitish mess of stuff in the tubful of bloody water. She held her face to one side, out of the steam that rose from the tub, and worked at arm's length. "Feeling better now?" she said.

He nodded. Conscious of the boys behind him, knowing they must be laughing at him, shaming him, snickering, he pointed to the stuff in the tub. "What's that?"

"Intestines," she said. "They have to be cleaned to stuff sausage in." With a disgusted grimace she went back to working the long, rubbery gut through her fingers.

Bruce stood watching a minute. So sausage was stuffed into intestines. He had always loved sausage, but he could never eat it again, not ever. He couldn't eat any of the old sow. Looking over at the pink, harmless thing swinging gently by its heels, he found it hard to imagine that this was the sow. The eyes were closed, the jowly face was hairless and mild, almost comical. There was nothing to remind anyone of that violence behind the barn, until you looked right between her eyes and saw the two dark dots there, not more than a half inch apart. There were the death wounds, there was the difference. He went up and pushed the stiff front foot, and the carcass swayed. It was funny those two little dots could make all that difference. A half hour ago the old sow had got up full of life, and now she hung like a bag of grain.

"How'd they get her so clean?" he asked Chet.

"Scalded her," Chet said. "You shouldn't've got sick. You'd've seen something."

"What'd her insides look like?"

"Go look yourself," Chet said. He waved at the tub standing against the barn wall.

She hung there, turning gently half around and back again, so innocent and harmless that the boy was no longer sickened or afraid.

Slowly Bruce went closer until he could see. The bloody mess appalled him, but he had to see those insides, had to look at them carefully to keep himself reminded that it was really the old sow hanging there. If he didn't keep remembering that, if he forgot the sow and remembered only the clean, butcher-shop carcass, he might forget sometime and eat some of her, and he knew if he ever ate any of her he would die.

His father came up past him, moved him aside. "One side there," he said heartily. "One side for the working men."

He put red hands down into the tub, sorted out the liver and heart. Grinning, he made as if to throw the great, wobbly, purple liver at Bruce, and Bruce felt his stomach go weak.

"What's the matter?" his father said. "Here I thought you were a tough guy, and you go around looking peaked as a ghost."

"I *am* a tough guy!" Bruce said, but looking across at Chet, he saw the superior smile, the hands in the pockets and the shoulders insolent. "I'm not getting sick," he said, and made his white face turn fixedly toward the tub of entrails. "I'm not sick at all!" he said, and laughed.

His father looked at him queerly. "You'd better go off and sit down a while," he said finally. "You're not quite in shape yet."

> His nausea was gone, his whole mind centered on that ritual act of kicking the sow's insides around, dirtying them in the dust of the field, taking out on them his own shame and his own fear and hatred and disbelief.

"I am too in shape!" the boy screamed. He wanted to run up and plunge his hands into that red tub of guts, just to show them, but he didn't quite dare. But he stood where he was, and as he stood, the little black dots came back before his eyes, and he stood still and stared through them, fighting them down in hysterical silence. Then his father, still watching him, pulled a flat flap of insides from the tub.

"Show you something," he said to the boys. "This's one that'll surprise you."

He dipped the flap in a clean bucket of water and washed it thoroughly. Bruce, fighting off the black spots, struggling to keep the slaughterhouse smell of blood and scalded hair from turning his stomach inside out, watched with the others. When it came out of the water clean, the thing looked like a flattened bag with a tube the size of a pencil sticking out one side.

"What is it?" Chet said. "Is it her stomach?"

The father laughed. "You've seen that old sow eat, haven't you? Think she could put all that in this little bag?" He flapped it, shaking the water from the end of the tube, and then put the tube to his lips.

At the sight of his father's mouth touching the raw insides of the sow Bruce felt the blood drain from him, and the black dots streamed thicker. He shook his head violently, but they stayed. Through their thickening darkness he saw his father blow into the tube, saw the bladder swell and tighten and grow round, big as a soccer ball. The father pinched the tube, found a piece of string and tied around it, and tossed the bladder out on the ground. It bounced lightly, one side patched with adhesive dust.

His lips tight on his nausea, the blackness almost covering his sight, Bruce stared at the wavering bladder on the ground before him, the tube poking out to one side. The insides of the old sow, the red, dirty insides of the old sow he had hated and seen die. . . .

The vomit was in his very throat. He had to heave, but he couldn't. He wouldn't, with those boys around, his father there, Chet standing around with his superior hands in his pockets. The whole group of boys was staring, momentarily a little stupid, at the bladder the father had tossed out. Without thinking, in a wild leap to save himself and his nausea, Bruce sprang forward and kicked as hard as he could. It soared, and immediately all of them were after it, yelling, booting it down into the vacant lot.

Bruce broke into the running crowd again, got a chance, kicked the bladder hard and far, chased it, missed, chased again as Preacher-Kid Morrison booted it across the lot. His nausea was gone, his whole mind centered on that ritual act of kicking the sow's insides around, dirtying them in the dust of the field, taking out on them his own shame and his own fear and hatred and disbelief. And when they finally broke the bladder, far down the coulee toward school, he stood over it panting, triumphant, so full of life that he could have jumped the barn or carried the woodshed on his back.

SHIRLEY JACKSON

The Lottery

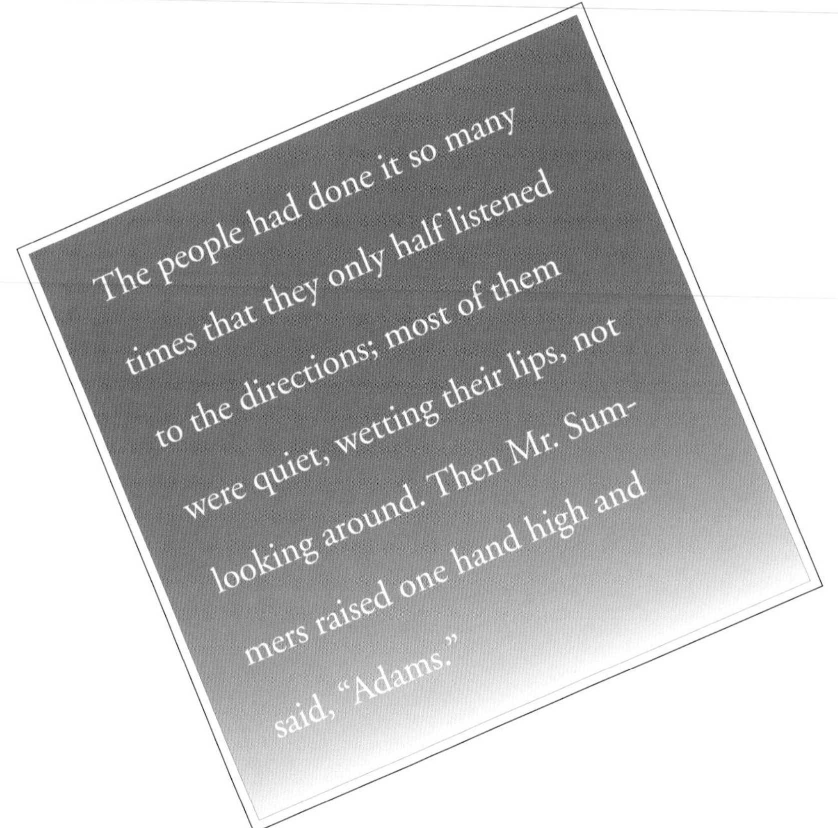

he morning of June 27th was clear and sunny, with the fresh warmth of a full-summer day; the flowers were blossoming profusely and the grass was richly green. The people of the village began to gather in the square, between the post office and the bank, around ten o'clock; in some towns there were so many people that the lottery took two days and had to be started on June 26th, but in this village, where there were only about three hundred people, the whole lottery took less than two hours, so it could begin at ten o'clock in the morning and still be through in time to allow the villagers to get home for noon dinner.

The children assembled first, of course. School was recently over for the summer, and the feeling of liberty sat uneasily on most of them; they tended to gather together quietly for a while before they broke into boisterous play. And their talk was still of the classroom and the teacher, of books and reprimands. Bobby Martin had already stuffed his pockets full of stones, and the other boys soon followed his example, selecting the smoothest and roundest stones; Bobby and Harry Jones and Dickie Delacroix—the villagers pronounced this name "Dellacroy"—eventually made a great pile of stones in one corner of the square and guarded it against the raids of the other boys. The girls stood aside, talking among themselves, looking over their shoulders at the boys, and the very small children rolled in the dust or clung to the hands of their older brothers or sisters.

Soon the men began to gather, surveying their own children, speaking of planting and rain, tractors and taxes. They stood together, away from the pile of stones in the corner, and their jokes were quiet and they smiled rather than laughed. The women, wearing faded housedresses and sweaters, came shortly after their menfolk. They greeted one another and exchanged bits of gossip as they went to join their husbands. Soon the women, standing by their husbands, began to call to their children, and the children came reluctantly, having to be called four or five times. Bobby Martin ducked under his mother's grasping hand and ran, laughing, back to the pile of stones. His father spoke up sharply, and Bobby came quickly and took his place between his father and his oldest brother.

Bobby Martin had already stuffed his pockets full of stones, and the other boys soon followed his example, selecting the smoothest and roundest ones.

The lottery was conducted—as were the square dances, the teen-age club, the Halloween program—by Mr. Summers, who had time and energy to devote to civic activities. He was a round-faced, jovial man and he ran the coal business, and people were sorry for him, because he had no children and his wife was a scold. When he arrived in the square, carrying the black wooden box, there was a murmur of conversation among the villagers, and he waved and called. "Little late today, folks." The postmaster, Mr. Graves, followed him, carrying a three-legged stool, and the stool was put in the center of the square and Mr. Summers set the black box down on it. The villagers kept their distance, leaving a space between themselves and the stool, and when Mr. Summers said, "Some of you fellows want to give me a hand?" there was a hesitation before two men, Mr. Martin and his oldest son, Baxter, came forward to hold the box steady on the stool while Mr. Summers stirred up the papers inside it.

The original paraphernalia for the lottery had been lost long ago, and the black box now resting on the stool had been put into use even before Old Man Warner, the oldest man in town, was born. Mr. Summers spoke frequently to the villagers about making a new box, but no one liked to upset even as much tradition as was represented by the black box. There was a story that the present box had been made with some pieces of the box that had preceded it, the one that had been constructed when the first people settled down to make a village here. Every year, after the lottery, Mr. Summers began talking again about a new box, but every year the subject was allowed to fade off without anything's being done. The black box grew shabbier each year; by now it was no longer completely black but splintered badly along one side to show the original wood color, and in some places faded or stained.

Mr. Martin and his oldest son, Baxter, held the black box securely on the stool until Mr. Summers had stirred the papers thoroughly with his hand. Because so much of the ritual had been forgotten or discarded, Mr. Summers had been successful in having slips of paper substituted for the chips of wood that had been used for generations. Chips of wood, Mr. Summers had argued, had been all very well when the village was tiny, but now that the population was more than three hundred and likely to keep on growing, it was necessary to use something that would fit more easily into the black box. The night before the lottery, Mr. Summers and Mr. Graves made up the slips of paper and put them in the box, and it was then taken to the safe of Mr. Summers' coal company and locked up until Mr. Summers was ready to take it to the square next morning. The rest of the year, the box was put away, sometimes one place, sometimes another; it had spent one year in Mr. Graves' barn and another year underfoot in the post office, and sometimes it was set on a shelf in the Martin grocery and left there.

There was a great deal of fussing to be done before Mr. Summers declared the lottery open. There were the lists to make up—of heads of families, heads of households in each family, members of each household in each family. There was the proper swearing-in of Mr. Summers by the postmaster, as the official of the lottery; at one time, some people remembered, there had been a recital of some sort, performed by the official of the lottery, a perfunctory,

"Clean forgot what day it was," she said to Mrs. Delacroix, who stood next to her, and they both laughed softly.

tuneless chant that had been rattled off duly each year; some people believed that the official of the lottery used to stand just so when he said or sang it, others believed that he was supposed to walk among the people, but years and years ago this part of the ritual had been allowed to lapse. There had been, also, a ritual salute, which the official of the lottery had had to use in addressing each person who came up to draw from the box, but this also had changed with time, until now it was felt necessary only for the official to speak to each person approaching. Mr. Summers was very good at all this; in his clean white shirt and blue jeans, with one hand resting carelessly on the black box, he seemed very proper and important as he talked interminably to Mr. Graves and the Martins.

Just as Mr. Summers finally left off talking and turned to the assembled villagers, Mrs. Hutchinson came hurriedly along the path to the square, her sweater thrown over her shoulders, and slid into place in the back of the crowd. "Clean forgot what day it was," she said to Mrs. Delacroix, who stood next to her, and they both laughed softly. "Thought my old man was out back stacking wood," Mrs. Hutchinson went on, "and then I looked out the window and the kids was gone, and then I remembered it was the twenty-seventh and came a-running." She dried her hands on her apron, and Mrs. Delacroix said, "You're in time, though. They're still talking away up there."

Mrs. Hutchinson craned her neck to see through the crowd and found her husband and children standing near the front. She tapped Mrs. Delacroix on the arm as a farewell and began to make her way through the crowd. The people separated good-humoredly to let her through; two or three people said, in voices just loud enough to be heard across the crowd, "Here comes your Missus, Hutchinson," and "Bill, she made it after all." Mrs. Hutchinson reached her husband, and Mr. Summers, who had been waiting, said cheerfully, "Thought we were going to have to get on without you, Tessie." Mrs. Hutchinson said, grinning, "Wouldn't have me leave m'dishes in the sink, now, would you, Joe?" and soft laughter ran through the crowd as the people stirred back into position after Mrs. Hutchinson's arrival.

"Well, now," Mr. Summers said soberly, "guess we better get started, get this over with, so's we can go back to work. Anybody ain't here?"

"Dunbar," several people said. "Dunbar, Dunbar."

Mr. Summers consulted his list. "Clyde Dunbar," he said. "That's right. He's broke his leg, hasn't he? Who's drawing for him?"

"Me, I guess," a woman said, and Mr. Summers turned to look at her. "Wife draws for her husband," Mr. Summers said. "Don't you have a grown boy to do it for you, Janey?" Although Mr. Summers and everyone else in the village knew the answer perfectly well, it was the business of the official of the lottery to ask such questions formally. Mr. Summers waited with an expression of polite interest while Mrs. Dunbar answered.

"Horace's not but sixteen yet," Mrs. Dunbar said regretfully. "Guess I gotta fill in for the old man this year."

"Right," Mr. Summers said. He made a note on the list he was holding. Then he asked, "Watson boy drawing this year?"

A tall boy in the crowd raised his hand. "Here," he said. "I'm drawing for m'mother and me." He blinked his eyes nervously and ducked his head as several voices in the crowd said things like "Good fellow, Jack," and "Glad to see your mother's got a man to do it."

"Well," Mr. Summers said, "guess that's everyone. Old Man Warner make it?"

"Here," a voice said, and Mr. Summers nodded.

A sudden hush fell on the crowd as Mr. Summers cleared his throat and looked at the list. "All ready?" he called. "Now, I'll read the names—heads of families first—and the men come up and take a paper out of the box. Keep the paper folded in your hand without looking at it until everyone has had a turn. Everything clear?"

The people had done it so many times that they only half listened to the directions; most of them were quiet, wetting their lips, not looking around. Then Mr. Summers raised one hand high and said, "Adams." A man disengaged himself from the crowd and came forward. "Hi, Steve," Mr. Summers said, and Mr. Adams said, "Hi, Joe." They grinned at one another humorlessly and nervously. Then Mr. Adams reached into the black box and took out a folded paper. He held it firmly by one corner as he turned and went hastily back to his place in the crowd, where he stood a little apart from his family, not looking down at his hand.

"Allen," Mr. Summers said. "Anderson. . . . Bentham."

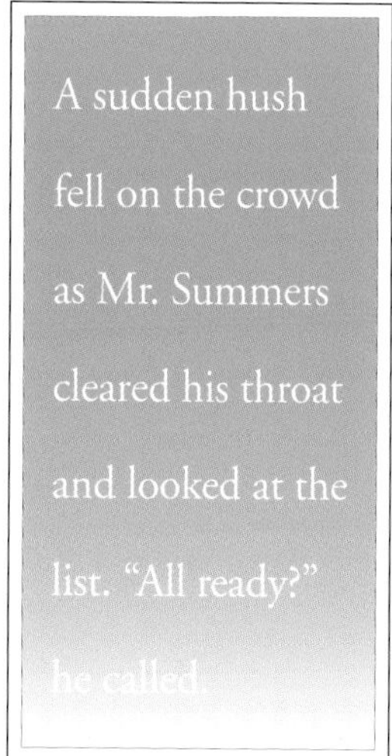

"Seems like there's no time at all between lotteries anymore," Mrs. Delacroix said to Mrs. Graves in the back row. "Seems like we got through with the last one only last week."

"Time sure goes fast," Mrs. Graves said.

"Clark. . . . Delacroix."

"There goes my old man," Mrs. Delacroix said. She held her breath while her husband went forward.

"Dunbar," Mr. Summers said, and Mrs. Dunbar went steadily to the box while one of the women said, "Go on, Janey," and another said, "There she goes."

"We're next," Mrs. Graves said. She watched while Mr. Graves came around from the side of the box, greeted Mr. Summers gravely, and selected a slip of paper from the box. By now, all through the crowd there were men holding the small folded papers in their large hands, turning them over and over nervously. Mrs. Dunbar and her two sons stood together, Mrs. Dunbar holding the slip of paper.

"Harburt. . . . Hutchinson."

"Get up there, Bill," Mrs. Hutchinson said, and the people near her laughed.

"Jones."

"They do say," Mr. Adams said to Old Man Warner, who stood next to him, "that over in the north village they're talking of giving up the lottery."

Old Man Warner snorted. "Pack of crazy fools," he said. "Listening to the young folks, nothing's good enough for *them.* Next thing you know, they'll be wanting to go back to living in caves, nobody work anymore, live *that* way for a while. Used to be a saying about 'Lottery in June, corn be heavy soon.' First thing you know, we'd all be eating stewed chickweed and acorns. There's *always* been a lottery," he added petulantly. "Bad enough to see young Joe Summers up there joking with everybody."

"Some places have already quit lotteries," Mrs. Adams said.

"Nothing but trouble in *that*," Old Man Warner said stoutly. "Pack of young fools."

"Martin." And Bobby Martin watched his father go forward. "Overdyke. . . . Percy."

"I wish they'd hurry," Mrs. Dunbar said to her older son. "I wish they'd hurry."

"They're almost through," her son said.

After that, there was a long pause, a breathless pause, until Mr. Summers, holding his slip of paper in the air, said, "All right, fellows." For a minute, no one moved, and then all the slips of paper were opened.

"You get ready to run tell Dad," Mrs. Dunbar said.

Mr. Summers called his own name and then stepped forward precisely and selected a slip from the box. Then he called, "Warner."

"Seventy-seventh year I been in the lottery," Old Man Warner said as he went through the crowd. "Seventy-seventh time."

"Watson." The tall boy came awkwardly through the crowd. Someone said, "Don't be nervous, Jack," and Mr. Summers said, "Take your time, son."

"Zanini."

After that, there was a long pause, a breathless pause, until Mr. Summers, holding his slip of paper in the air, said, "All right, fellows." For a minute, no one moved, and then all the slips of paper were opened. Suddenly, all the women began to speak at once, saying, "Who is it?" "Who's got it?" "Is it the Dunbars?" "Is it the Watsons?" Then the voices began to say, "It's Hutchinson. It's Bill," "Bill Hutchinson's got it."

"Go tell your father," Mrs. Dunbar said to her older son.

People began to look around to see the Hutchinsons. Bill Hutchinson was standing quiet, staring down at the paper in his hand. Suddenly, Tessie Hutchinson shouted to Mr. Summers. "You didn't give him time enough to take any paper he wanted. I saw you. It wasn't fair!"

"Be a good sport, Tessie," Mrs. Delacroix called, and Mrs. Graves said, "All of us took the same chance."

"Shut up, Tessie," Bill Hutchinson said.

"Well, everyone," Mr. Summers said, "that was done pretty fast, and now we've got to be hurrying a little more to get done in time." He consulted his next list. "Bill," he said, "you draw for the Hutchinson family. You got any other households in the Hutchinsons?"

"There's Don and Eva," Mrs. Hutchinson yelled. "Make them take their chance!"

"Daughters draw with their husbands' families, Tessie," Mr. Summers said gently. "You know that as well as anyone else."

"It wasn't fair," Tessie said.

"I guess not, Joe." Bill Hutchinson said regretfully. "My daughter draws with her husband's family, that's only fair. And I've got no other family except the kids."

"Then, as far as drawing for families is concerned, it's you," Mr. Summers said in explanation, "and as far as drawing for households is concerned, that's you, too. Right?"

"Right," Bill Hutchinson said.

"How many kids, Bill?" Mr. Summers asked formally.

"Three," Bill Hutchinson said. "There's Bill, Jr., and Nancy, and little Dave. And Tessie and me."

"All right, then," Mr. Summers said. "Harry, you got their tickets back?"

Mr. Graves nodded and held up the slips of paper. "Put them in the box, then," Mr. Summers directed. "Take Bill's and put it in."

"I think we ought to start over," Mrs. Hutchinson said, as quietly as she could. "I tell you it wasn't *fair*. You didn't give him time enough to choose. *Every*body saw that."

Mr. Graves had selected the five slips and put them in the box, and he dropped all the papers but those onto the ground, where the breeze caught them and lifted them off.

"Listen, everybody," Mrs. Hutchinson was saying to the people around her.

"Ready, Bill?" Mr. Summers asked, and Bill Hutchinson, with one quick glance around at his wife and children, nodded.

"Remember," Mr. Summers said, "take the slips and keep them folded until each person has taken one. Harry, you help little Dave." Mr. Graves took the hand of the little boy, who came willingly with him up to the box. "Take a paper out of the box, Davy," Mr. Summers said. Davy put his hand into the box and laughed. "Take just *one* paper," Mr. Summers said. "Harry, you hold it for him." Mr. Graves took the child's hand and removed the folded paper from the tight fist and held it while little Dave stood next to him and looked up at him wonderingly.

"Nancy next," Mr. Summers said. Nancy was twelve, and her school friends breathed heavily as she went forward, switching her skirt, and took a slip daintily from the box. "Bill, Jr.," Mr. Summers said, and Billy, his face red and his feet overlarge, nearly knocked the box over as he got a paper out. "Tessie," Mr. Summers said. She hesitated for a minute, looking around defiantly, and then set her lips and went up to the box. She snatched a paper out and held it behind her.

"Bill," Mr. Summers said, and Bill Hutchinson reached into the box and felt around, bringing his hand out at last with the slip of paper in it.

The crowd was quiet. A girl whispered, "I hope it's not Nancy," and the sound of the whisper reached the edges of the crowd.

"It's not the way it used to be," Old Man Warner said clearly. "People ain't the way they used to be."

"All right," Mr. Summers said. "Open the papers. Harry, you open little Dave's."

Mr. Graves opened the slip of paper and there was a general sigh through the crowd as he held it up and everyone could see that it was blank. Nancy and Bill, Jr. opened theirs at the same time, and both beamed and laughed, turning around to the crowd and holding their slips of paper above their heads.

> "Ready, Bill?" Mr. Summers asked, and Bill Hutchinson, with one quick glance around at his wife and children, nodded.

"Tessie," Mr. Summers said. There was a pause, and then Mr. Summers looked at Bill Hutchinson, and Bill unfolded his paper and showed it. It was blank.

"It's Tessie," Mr. Summers said, and his voice was hushed. "Show us her paper, Bill."

Bill Hutchinson went over to his wife and forced the slip of paper out of her hand. It had a black spot on it, the black spot Mr. Summers had made the night before with the heavy pencil in the coal company office. Bill Hutchinson held it up, and there was a stir in the crowd.

"All right, folks," Mr. Summers said. "Let's finish quickly."

Although the villagers had forgotten the ritual and lost the original black box, they still remembered to use stones. The pile of stones the boys had made earlier was ready; there were stones on the ground with the blowing scraps of paper that had come out of the box. Mrs. Delacroix selected a stone so large she had to pick it up with both hands and turned to Mrs. Dunbar. "Come on," she said. "Hurry up."

Mrs. Dunbar had small stones in both hands, and she said, gasping for breath, "I can't run at all. You'll have to go ahead and I'll catch up with you."

The children had stones already, and someone gave little Davy Hutchinson a few pebbles.

Tessie Hutchinson was in the center of a cleared space by now, and she held her hands out desperately as the villagers moved in on her. "It isn't fair," she said. A stone hit her on the side of the head.

Old Man Warner was saying, "Come on, come on, everyone." Steve Adams was in the front of the crowd of villagers, with Mrs. Graves beside him.

"It isn't fair, it isn't right," Mrs. Hutchinson screamed, and then they were upon her.

LANGSTON HUGHES

Thank You, M'am

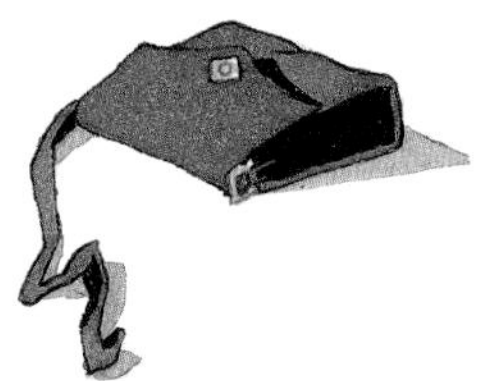

She was a large woman with a large purse that had everything in it but a hammer and nails. It had a long strap, and she carried it slung across her shoulder. It was about eleven o'clock at night, dark, and she was walking alone, when a boy ran up behind her and tried to snatch her purse. The strap broke with the sudden single tug the boy gave it from behind. But the boy's weight and the weight of the purse combined caused him to lose his balance. Instead of taking off full blast as he had hoped, the boy fell on his back on the sidewalk and his legs flew up. The large woman simply turned around and kicked him right square in his blue-jeaned sitter. Then she reached down, picked the boy up by his shirtfront, and shook him until his teeth rattled.

After that the woman said, "Pick up my pocketbook, boy, and give it here."

She still held him tightly. But she bent down enough to permit him to stoop and pick up her purse. Then she said, "Now ain't you ashamed of yourself?"

Firmly gripped by his shirtfront, the boy said, "Yes'm."

The woman said, "What did you want to do it for?"

The boy said, "I didn't aim to."

She said, "You a lie!"

By that time two or three people passed, stopped, turned to look, and some stood watching.

"If I turn you loose, will you run?" asked the woman.

"Yes'm," said the boy.

"Then I won't turn you loose," said the woman. She did not release him.

"Lady, I'm sorry," whispered the boy.

"If you think that that contact is not going to last awhile, you got another thought coming. When I get through with you, sir, you are going to remember Mrs. Luella Bates Washington Jones."

"Um-hum! Your face is dirty. I got a great mind to wash your face for you. Ain't you got nobody home to tell you to wash your face?"

"No'm," said the boy.

"Then it will get washed this evening," said the large woman, starting up the street, dragging the frightened boy behind her.

He looked as if he were fourteen or fifteen, frail and willow-wild, in tennis shoes and blue jeans.

The woman said, "You ought to be my son. I would teach you right from wrong. Least I can do right now is to wash your face. Are you hungry?"

"No'm," said the being-dragged boy. "I just want you to turn me loose."

"Was I bothering *you* when I turned that corner?" asked the woman.

"No'm."

"But you put yourself in contact with *me*," said the woman. "If you think that that contact is not going to last awhile, you got another thought coming. When I get through with you, sir, you are going to remember Mrs. Luella Bates Washington Jones."

Sweat popped out on the boy's face and he began to struggle. Mrs. Jones stopped, jerked him around in front of her, put a half nelson about his neck, and continued to drag him up the street. When she got to her door, she dragged the boy inside, down a hall, and into a large kitchenette-furnished room at the rear of the house. She switched on the light and left the door open. The boy could hear other roomers laughing and talking in the large house. Some of their doors were open, too, so he knew he and the woman were not alone. The woman still had him by the neck in the middle of her room.

She said, "What is your name?"

"Roger," answered the boy.

"Then, Roger, you go to that sink and wash your face," said the woman, whereupon she turned him loose—at last. Roger looked at the door—looked at the woman—looked at the door—*and went to the sink.*

"Let the water run until it gets warm," she said. "Here's a clean towel."

"You gonna take me to jail?" asked the boy, bending over the sink.

"Not with that face, I would not take you nowhere," said the woman. "Here I am trying to get home to cook me a bite to eat, and you snatch my pocketbook! Maybe you ain't been to your supper either, late as it be. Have you?"

"There's nobody home at my house," said the boy.

"Then we'll eat," said the woman, "I believe you're hungry—or been hungry—to try to snatch my pocketbook!"

"I want a pair of blue suede shoes," said the boy.

"Well, you didn't have to snatch *my* pocketbook to get some suede shoes," said Mrs. Luella Bates Washington Jones. "You could've asked me."

"M'am?"

The water dripping from his face, the boy looked at her. There was a long pause. A very long pause. After he had dried his face and not knowing what else to do dried it again, the boy turned around, wondering what next. The door was open. He could make a dash for it down the hall. He could run, run, run, *run*!

The woman was sitting on the daybed. After a while she said, "I were young once and I wanted things I could not get."

There was another long pause. The boy's mouth opened. Then he frowned, not knowing he frowned.

The woman said, "Um-hum! You thought I was going to say *but*, didn't you? You thought I was going to say, *but I didn't snatch people's pocketbooks*. Well, I wasn't going to say that." Pause. Silence. "I have done things, too, which I would not tell you, son—neither tell God, if He didn't

"You gonna take me to jail?" asked the boy, bending over the sink. "Not with that face, I would not take you nowhere," said the woman.

already know. Everybody's got something in common. So you set down while I fix us something to eat. You might run that comb through your hair so you will look presentable."

> "I have done things, too, which I would not tell you, son—neither tell God, if He didn't already know. Everybody's got something in common."

In another corner of the room behind a screen was a gas plate and an icebox. Mrs. Jones got up and went behind the screen. The woman did not watch the boy to see if he was going to run now, nor did she watch her purse, which she left behind her on the daybed. But the boy took care to sit on the far side of the room, away from the purse, where he thought she could easily see him out of the corner of her eye if she wanted to. He did not trust the woman *not* to trust him. And he did not want to be mistrusted now.

"Do you need somebody to go to the store," asked the boy, "maybe to get some milk or something?"

"Don't believe I do," said the woman, "unless you just want sweet milk yourself. I was going to make cocoa out of this canned milk I got here."

"That will be fine," said the boy.

She heated some lima beans and ham she had in the icebox, made the cocoa, and set the table. The woman did not ask the boy anything about where he lived, or his folks, or anything else that would embarrass him. Instead, as they ate, she told him about her job in a hotel beauty shop that stayed open late, what the work was like, and how all kinds of women came in and out, blondes, red-heads, and Spanish. Then she cut him a half of her ten-cent cake.

"Eat some more, son," she said.

When they were finished eating, she got up and said, "Now here, take this ten dollars and buy yourself some blue suede shoes. And next time, do not make the mistake of latching onto *my* pocketbook *nor nobody else's*—because shoes got by devilish ways will burn your feet. I got to get my rest now. But from here on in, son, I hope you will behave yourself."

She led him down the hall to the front door and opened it. "Goodnight! Behave yourself, boy!" she said, looking out into the street as he went down the steps.

The boy wanted to say something else other than "Thank you, m'am" to Mrs. Luella Bates Washington Jones, but although his lips moved, he couldn't even say that as he turned at the foot of the barren stoop and looked up at the large woman in the door. Then she shut the door.

"Now here, take this ten dollars and buy yourself some blue suede shoes. And next time, do not make the mistake of latching onto *my* pocketbook *nor nobody else's*—because shoes got by devilish ways will burn your feet."

RAY BRADBURY

Icarus Montgolfier Wright

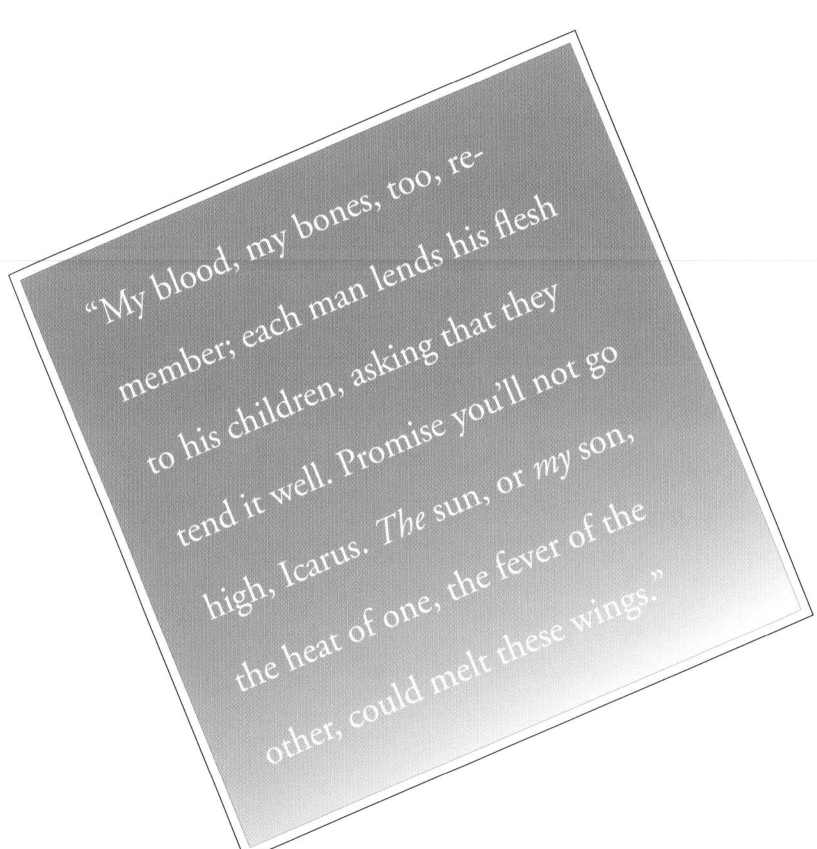

He lay on his bed and the wind blew through the window over his ears and over his half-opened mouth so it whispered to him in his dream. It was like the wind of time hollowing the Delphic caves to say what must be said of yesterday, today, tomorrow. Sometimes one voice gave a shout far off away, sometimes two, a dozen, an entire race of men cried out through his mouth, but their words were always the same:

"Look, look, we've done it!"

For suddenly he, they, one or many, were flung in the dream, and flew. The air spread in a soft warm sea where he swam, disbelieving.

"Look, look! It's done!"

But he didn't ask the world to watch, he was only shocking his senses wide to see, taste, smell, touch the air, the wind, the rising moon. He swam along in the sky. The heavy earth was gone.

But wait, he thought, wait now!

Tonight—what night is this?

The night before, of course. The night before the first flight of a rocket to the Moon. Beyond this room on the baked desert floor one hundred yards away the rocket waits for me.

Well, does it now? Is there *really* a rocket?

Hold on! he thought, and twisted, turned, sweating, eyes tight, to the wall, the fierce whisper in his teeth. Be certain-sure! You, now, who *are* you?

Me? he thought. *My* name?

Jedediah Prentiss, born 1938, college graduate 1959, licensed rocket pilot, 1971. Jedediah Prentiss . . . Jedediah Prentiss . . .

The wind whistled his name away! He grabbed for it, yelling.

Then, gone quiet, he waited for the wind to bring his name back. He waited a long while, and there was only silence, and then after a thousand heartbeats he felt motion.

The sky opened out like a soft blue flower. The Aegean Sea stirred soft white fans through a distant wine-colored surf.

In the wash of the waves on the shore, he heard his name.

Icarus.

And again in a breathing whisper.

Icarus.

Someone shook his arm and it was his father saying his name and shaking away the night. And he himself lay small, half-turned to the window and the shore below and the deep sky, feeling the first wind of morning ruffle the golden feathers bedded in amber wax lying by the side of his cot. Golden wings stirred half-alive in his father's arms, and the faint down on his own shoulders quilled trembling as he looked at these wings and beyond them to the cliff.

"Father, how's the wind?"

"Enough for me, but never enough for you . . ."

"Father, don't worry. The wings seem clumsy now, but my bones in the feathers will make them strong, my blood in the wax will make it live!"

"My blood, my bones too, remember; each man lends his flesh to his children, asking that they tend it well. Promise you'll not go high, Icarus. *The* sun or *my* son, the heat of one, the fever of the other, could melt these wings. Take care!"

And they carried the splendid golden wings into the morning and heard them whisper in their arms, whisper his name or a name or some name that blew, spun, and settled like a feather on the soft air.

Montgolfier.

His hands touched fiery rope, bright linen, stitched thread gone hot as summer. His hands fed wool and straw to a breathing flame.

Montgolfier.

And his eye soared up along the swell and sway, the oceanic tug and pull, the immensely wafted silver pear still filling with the shimmering tidal airs channeled up from the blaze. Silent as a god tilted slumbering above French countryside, this delicate linen envelope, this swelling sack of oven-baked air would soon pluck itself free. Draughting upward to blue worlds of silence, his mind and his brother's mind would sail with it, muted, serene among island clouds where uncivilized lightnings slept. Into that uncharted gulf and abyss where no birdsong or shout of man could follow, the balloon would hush itself. So cast adrift, he, Montgolfier, and all men, might hear the unmeasured breathing of God and the cathedral tread of eternity.

"Ah . . ." He moved, the crowd moved, shadowed by the warm balloon. "Everything's ready, everything's right . . ."

Right. His lips twitched in his dream. Right. Hiss, whisper, flutter, rush. Right.

From his father's hands a toy jumped to the ceiling, whirled in its own wind, suspended, while he and his brother started to see it flicker, rustle, whistle, heard it murmuring their names.

Wright.

Whispering: wind, sky, cloud, space, wing, fly . . .

"Wilbur, Orville? Look, how's *that*?"

Ah. In his sleep, his mouth sighed.

The toy helicopter hummed, bumped the ceiling, murmured eagle, raven, sparrow, robin, hawk. Whispered eagle, whispered raven, and at last, fluttering to their hands with a susurration, a wash of blowing weather from summers yet to come, with a last whir and exhalation, whispered hawk.

Dreaming, he smiled.

He saw the clouds rush down the Aegean sky.

He felt the balloon sway drunkenly, its great bulk ready for the clear running wind.

He felt the sand hiss up the Aegean shelves from the soft dunes that might save him if he, a fledgling bird, should fall. The framework struts hummed and chorded like a harp, and himself caught up in its music.

Beyond this room he felt the primed rocket glide on the desert field, its fire wings folded, its fire breath kept, head ready to speak for three billion men. In a moment he would walk and walk slowly out to that rocket.

And stand on the rim of the cliff.

> Into that uncharted gulf and abyss where no birdsong or shout of man could follow, the balloon would hush itself. So cast adrift, he, Montgolfier, and all men, might hear the unmeasured breathing of God and the cathedral tread of eternity.

Stand cool in the shadow of the warm balloon.

Stand whipped by tidal sands drummed over Kitty Hawk.

And sheathe his boy's wrists, arms, hands, fingers with golden wings in golden wax.

And touch for a final time the captured breath of man, the warm gasp of awe and wonder siphoned and sewn to lift their dreams.

And spark the gasoline engine.

And take his father's hand and wish him well with his own wings, flexed and ready, here on the precipice.

Then whirl and jump.

Then cut the cords to free the great balloon.

Then rev the motor, prop the plane on air.

And crack the switch, to fire the rocket fuse.

And together in a single leap, swim, rush, flail, jump, sail, and glide, upturned to sun, moon, stars, they would go above Atlantic, Mediterranean; over country, wilderness, city, town; in gaseous silence, riffling feather, rattle-drum frame, in

Up, yet farther up, higher, higher! A spring tide, a summer flood, an unending river of wings!

volcanic eruption, in timid, sputtering roar; in start, jar, hesitation, then steady ascension, beautifully held, wondrously transported, they would laugh and cry each his own name to himself. Or shout the names of others unborn or others long dead and blown away by the wine wind or the salt wind or the silent hush of balloon wind or the wind of chemical fire. Each feeling the bright feathers stir and bud deep-buried and thrusting to burst from their riven shoulder blades! Each leaving behind the echo of their flying, a sound to encircle, recircle the earth in the winds and speak again in other years to the sons of the sons of their sons, asleep but hearing the restless midnight sky.

Up, yet farther up, higher, higher! A spring tide, a summer flood, an unending river of wings!

A bell rang softly.

No, he whispered, I'll wake in a moment. Wait . . .

The Aegean slid away below the window, gone; the Atlantic dunes, the French countryside, dissolved down to New Mexico desert. In his room near his cot stirred no plumes in golden wax. Outside, no wind-sculpted pear, no trapdrum butterfly machine. Outside only a rocket, a combustible dream, waiting for the friction of his hand to set it off.

In the last moment of sleep someone asked his name.

Quietly, he gave the answer as he had heard it during the hours from midnight on.

"Icarus Montgolfier Wright."

He repeated it slowly so the questioner might remember the order and spelling down to the last incredible letter.

"Icarus Montgolfier Wright.

"Born: nine hundred years before Christ. Grammar school: Paris, 1783, high school, college: Kitty Hawk, 1903. Graduation from Earth to Moon: this day,

God willing, August 1, 1971. Death and burial, with luck, on Mars, summer 1999 in the Year of Our Lord."

Then he let himself drift awake.

Moments later, crossing the desert tarmac, he heard someone shouting again and again and again.

And if no one was there or if someone was there behind him, he could not tell. And whether it was one voice or many, young or old, near or very far away, rising or falling, whispering or shouting to him all three of his brave new names, he could not tell, either. He did not turn to see.

For the wind was slowly rising and he let it take hold and blow him all the rest of the way across the desert to the rocket which stood waiting there

JOHN UPDIKE

A & P

4
Peaches!
5

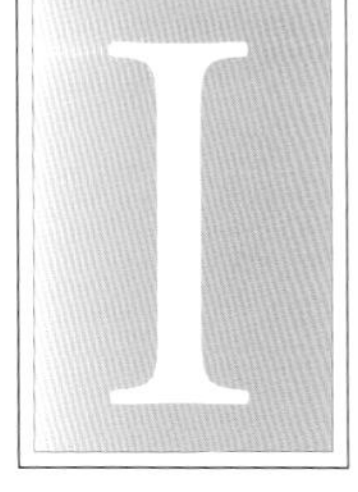

In walks these three girls in nothing but bathing suits. I'm in the third checkout slot, with my back to the door, so I don't see them until they're over by the bread. The one that caught my eye first was the one in the plaid green two-piece. She was a chunky kid, with a good tan and a sweet broad soft-looking can with those two crescents of white just under it, where the sun never seems to hit, at the top of the backs of her legs. I stood there with my hand on a box of HiHo crackers trying to remember if I rang it up or not. I ring it up again and the customer starts giving me hell. She's one of these cash-register-watchers, a witch about fifty with rouge on her cheekbones and no eyebrows, and I know it made her day to trip me up. She'd been watching cash registers for fifty years and probably never seen a mistake before.

By the time I got her feathers smoothed and her goodies into a bag—she gives me a little snort in passing, if she'd been born at the right time they would have burned her over in Salem—by the time I get her on her way the girls had circled around the bread and were coming back, without a pushcart, back my way along the counters, in the aisle between the checkouts and the Special bins. They didn't even have shoes on. There was this chunky one, with the two-piece—it was bright green and the seams on the bra were still sharp and her belly was still pretty pale so I guessed she just got it (the suit)—there was this one, with one of those chubby berry-faces, the lips all bunched together under her nose, this one, and a tall one, with black hair that hadn't quite frizzed right, and one of these sunburns right across under the eyes, and a chin that was too long—you know, the kind of girl other girls think is very "striking" and "attractive" but never quite makes it, as they very well know, which is why they like her so much—and then the third one, that wasn't quite so tall. She was the queen. She kind of led them, the other two peeking around and making their shoulders round. She didn't look around, not this queen, she just walked straight on slowly, on these long white prima-donna legs. She came down a little hard on her heels, as if she didn't walk in her bare feet that much, putting down her heels and then letting the weight move along to her toes as if she was testing the floor with every step, putting a little deliberate extra action into it. You never know for sure how girls' minds work (do you really think it's a mind in there or just a little buzz like a bee in a glass jar?) but you got the idea she had talked the other two into coming in here with her, and now she was showing them how to do it, walk slow and hold yourself straight.

> I stood there with my hand on a box of HiHo crackers trying to remember if I rang it up or not. I ring it up again and the customer starts giving me hell.

She had on a kind of dirty-pink—beige maybe, I don't know—bathing suit with a little nubble all over it and, what got me, the straps were down. They were off her shoulders looped loose around the cool tops of her arms, and I guess as a result the suit had slipped a little on her, so all around the top of the cloth there was this shining rim. If it hadn't been there you wouldn't have known there could have been anything whiter than those shoulders. With the straps pushed off, there was nothing between the top of the suit and the top of her head except just *her*, this clean bare plane of the top of her chest down from the shoulder bones like a dented sheet of metal tilted in the light. I mean, it was more than pretty.

She had sort of oaky hair that the sun and salt had bleached, done up in a bun that was unravelling, and a kind of prim face. Walking into the A & P with your straps down, I suppose it's the only kind of face you *can* have. She held her head so high her neck, coming up out of those white shoulders, looked kind of stretched, but I didn't mind. The longer her neck was, the more of her there was.

She must have felt in the corner of her eye me and over my shoulder Stokesie in the second slot watching, but she didn't tip. Not this queen. She kept her eyes moving across the racks, and stopped, and turned so slow it made my stomach rub the inside of my apron, and buzzed to the other two, who kind of huddled against her for relief, and then they all three of them went up the cat-and-dog-food-breakfast-cereal-macaroni-rice-raisins-seasonings-spreads-spaghetti-soft-drinks-crackers-and-cookies aisle. From the third slot I look straight up this aisle to the meat counter, and I watched them all the way. The fat one with the tan sort of fumbled with the cookies, but on second thought she put the package back. The sheep pushing their carts down the aisle—the girls were walking against the usual traffic (not that we have one-way signs or anything)—were pretty hilarious. You could see them, when Queenie's white shoulders dawned on them, kind of jerk, or hop, or hiccup, but their eyes snapped back to their own baskets and on they pushed. I bet you could set off dynamite in an A & P and the people would by and large keep reaching and checking oatmeal off their lists and muttering "Let me see, there was a third thing, began with A, asparagus, no, ah, yes, applesauce!" or whatever it is they do mutter. But there was no doubt, this jiggled them. A few houseslaves in pin curlers even looked around after pushing their carts past to make sure what they had seen was correct.

Stokesie's married, with two babies chalked up on his fuselage already, but as far as I can tell that's the only difference. He's twenty-two, and I was nineteen this April.

You know, it's one thing to have a girl in a bathing suit down on the beach, where what with the glare nobody can look at each other much anyway, and another thing in the cool of the A & P, under the fluorescent lights, against all those stacked packages, with her feet paddling along naked over our checkerboard green-and-cream rubber-tile floor.

"Oh Daddy," Stokesie said beside me. "I feel so faint."

"Darling," I said. "Hold me tight." Stokesie's married, with two babies chalked up on his fuselage already, but as far as I can tell that's the only difference. He's twenty-two, and I was nineteen this April.

"Is it done?" he asks, the responsible married man finding his voice. I forgot to say he thinks he's going to be manager some sunny day, maybe in 1990 when it's called the Great Alexandrov and Petrooshki Tea Company or something.

What he meant was, our town is five miles from a beach, with a big summer colony out on the Point, but we're right in the middle of town, and the women generally put on a shirt or shorts or something before they get out of the car into the street. And anyway these are usually women with six children and varicose veins mapping their legs and nobody, including them, could care less. As I say, we're right in the middle of town, and if you stand at our front doors you can see two banks and the Congregational church and the newspaper store and three real-estate offices and about twenty-seven old free-loaders tearing up Central Street because the sewer broke again. It's not as if we're on the Cape; we're north of Boston and there's people in this town haven't seen the ocean for twenty years.

The girls had reached the meat counter and were asking McMahon something. He pointed, they pointed, and they shuffled out of sight behind a pyramid of Diet Delight peaches. All that was left for us to see was old McMahon patting his mouth and looking after them sizing up their joints. Poor kids, I began to feel sorry for them, they couldn't help it.

Now here comes the sad part of the story, at least my family says it's sad but I don't think it's sad myself. The store's pretty empty, it being Thursday afternoon, so there was nothing much to do except lean on the register and wait for the girls to show up again. The whole store was like a pinball machine and I didn't know which tunnel they'd come out of. After a while they come around out of the far aisle, around the light bulbs, records at discount of the Caribbean Six or Tony Martin Sings or some such gunk you wonder they waste the wax on, sixpacks of candy bars, and plastic toys done up in cellophane that fall apart when a kid looks at them anyway. Around they come, Queenie still leading the way, and holding a little gray jar in her hand. Slots Three through Seven are unmanned and I could see her wondering between Stokes and me, but Stokesie with his usual luck draws an old party in baggy gray pants who stumbles up with four giant cans of pineapple juice (what do these bums *do* with all that pineapple juice? I've often asked myself) so the girls come to me. Queenie puts down the jar and I take it into my fingers icy cold. Kingfish Fancy Herring Snacks in Pure Sour Cream: 49¢. Now her hands are empty, not a ring or a bracelet, bare as God made them, and I wonder where the money's coming from. Still with that prim look she lifts a folded dollar bill out of

> "Girls, I don't want to argue with you. After this come in here with your shoulders covered. It's our policy." He turns his back. That's policy for you. Policy's what the kingpins want.

the hollow at the center of her nubbled pink top. The jar went heavy in my hand. Really, I thought that was so cute.

Then everybody's luck begins to run out. Lengel comes in from haggling with a truck full of cabbages on the lot and is about to scuttle into that door marked MANAGER behind which he hides all day when the girls touch his eye. Lengel's pretty dreary, teaches Sunday school and the rest, but he doesn't miss that much. He comes over and says, "Girls, this isn't the beach."

Queenie blushes, though maybe it's just a brush of sunburn I was noticing for the first time, now that she was so close. "My mother asked me to pick up a jar of herring snacks." Her voice kind of startled me, the way voices do when you see the people first, coming out so flat and dumb yet kind of tony, too, the way it ticked over "pick up" and "snacks." All of a sudden I slid right down her voice into her living room. Her father and the other men were standing around in ice-cream coats and bow ties and the women were in sandals picking up herring snacks on toothpicks off a big plate and they were all holding drinks the color of water with olives and sprigs of mint in them. When my parents have somebody over they get lemonade and if it's a real racy affair Schlitz in tall glasses with "They'll Do It Every Time" cartoons stencilled on.

"That's all right," Lengel said. "But this isn't the beach." His repeating this struck me as funny, as if it had just occurred to him, and he had been thinking all these years the A & P was a great big dune and he was the head lifeguard. He didn't like my smiling—as I say he doesn't miss much—but he concentrates on giving the girls that sad Sunday-school-superintendent stare.

Queenie's blush is no sunburn now, and the plump one in plaid, that I liked better from the back—a really sweet can—pipes up, "We weren't doing any shopping. We just came in for the one thing."

"That makes no difference," Lengel tells her, and I could see from the way his eyes went that he hadn't noticed she was wearing a two-piece before. "We want you decently dressed when you come in here."

"We *are* decent," Queenie says suddenly, her lower lip pushing, getting sore now that she remembers her place, a place from which the crowd that runs the A & P must look pretty crummy. Fancy Herring Snacks flashed in her very blue eyes.

"Girls, I don't want to argue with you. After this come in here with your shoulders covered. It's our policy." He turns his back. That's policy for you. Policy is what the kingpins want. What the others want is juvenile delinquency.

All this while, the customers had been showing up with their carts but, you know, sheep, seeing a scene, they had all bunched up on Stokesie, who shook open a paper bag as gently as peeling a peach, not wanting to miss a word. I could feel in the silence everybody getting nervous, most of all Lengel, who asks me, "Sammy, have you rung up their purchase?"

I thought and said "No" but it wasn't about that I was thinking. I go through the punches, 4, 9, GROC, TOT—it's more complicated than you think, and after you do it often enough, it begins to make a little song, that you hear words to, in my case "Hello (*bing*) there, you (*gung*) hap-py pee-pul (*splat*)"—the *splat* being the drawer flying out. I uncrease the bill, tenderly as you may imagine, it just having come from between the two smoothest scoops of vanilla I had ever known were there, and pass a half and a penny into her narrow pink palm, and nestle the herrings in a bag and twist its neck and hand it over, all the time thinking.

The girls, and who'd blame them, are in a hurry to get out, so I say "I quit"

A couple customers that had been heading for my slot begin to knock against each other, like scared pigs in a chute.

to Lengel quick enough for them to hear, hoping they'll stop and watch me, their unsuspected hero. They keep right on going, into the electric eye; the door flies open and they flicker across the lot to their car, Queenie and Plaid and Big Tall Goony-Goony (not that as raw material she was so bad), leaving me with Lengel and a kink in his eyebrow.

"Did you say something, Sammy?"

"I said I quit."

"I thought you did."

"You didn't have to embarrass them."

"It was they who were embarrassing us."

I started to say something that came out "Fiddle-de-doo." It's a saying of my grandmother's, and I know she would have been pleased.

"I don't think you know what you're saying," Lengel said.

"I know you don't," I said. "But I do." I pull the bow at the back of my apron and start shrugging it off my shoulders. A couple customers that had been heading for my slot begin to knock against each other, like scared pigs in a chute.

Lengel sighs and begins to look very patient and old and gray. He's been a friend of my parents for years. "Sammy, you don't want to do this to your Mom and Dad," he tells me. It's true, I don't. But it seems to me that once you begin a gesture it's fatal not to go through with it. I fold the apron, "Sammy" stitched in red on the pocket, and put it on the counter, and drop the bow tie on top of it. The bow tie is theirs, if you've ever wondered. "You'll feel this for the rest of your life," Lengel says, and I know that's true, too, but remembering how he made that pretty girl blush makes me so scrunchy inside I punch the No Sale tab and the machine whirs "pee-pul" and the drawer splats out. One advantage to this scene taking place in summer, I can follow this up with a clean exit, there's no fumbling around getting your coat and galoshes, I just saunter into the electric eye in my white shirt that my mother ironed the night before, and the door heaves itself open, and outside the sunshine is skating around on the asphalt.

I look around for my girls, but they're gone, of course. There wasn't anybody but some young married screaming with her children about some candy they didn't get by the door of a powder-blue Falcon station wagon. Looking back in the big windows, over the bags of peat moss and aluminum lawn furniture stacked on the pavement, I could see Lengel in my place in the slot, checking the sheep through. His face was dark gray and his back stiff, as if he'd just had an injection of iron, and my stomach kind of fell as I felt how hard the world was going to be to me hereafter.

JOYCE CAROL OATES

Where Are You Going, Where Have You Been?

To Bob Dylan

Arnold
Friend

er name was Connie. She was fifteen and she had a quick nervous giggling habit of craning her neck to glance into mirrors, or checking other people's faces to make sure her own was all right. Her mother, who noticed everything and knew everything and who hadn't much reason any longer to look at her own face, always scolded Connie about it. "Stop gawking at yourself. Who are you? You think you're so pretty?" she would say. Connie would raise her eyebrows at these familiar complaints and look right through her mother, into a shadowy vision of herself as she was right at that moment: she knew she was pretty and that was everything. Her mother had been pretty once too, if you could believe those old snapshots in the album, but now her looks were gone and that was why she was always after Connie.

"Why don't you keep your room clean like your sister? How've you got your hair fixed—what the hell stinks? Hair spray? You don't see your sister using that junk."

Her sister June was twenty-four and still lived at home. She was a secretary in the high school Connie attended, and if that wasn't bad enough—with her in the same building—she was so plain and chunky and steady that Connie had to hear her praised all the time by her mother and her mother's sisters. June did this, June did that, she saved money and helped clean the house and cooked and Connie couldn't do a thing, her mind was all filled with trashy daydreams. Their father was away at work most of the time and when he came home he wanted supper and he read the newspaper at supper and after supper he went to bed. He didn't bother talking much to them, but around his bent head Connie's mother kept picking at her until Connie wished her mother were dead and she herself were dead and it were all over. "She makes me want to throw up sometimes," she complained to her friends. She had a high, breathless, amused voice that made everything she said sound a little forced, whether it was sincere or not.

There was one good thing: June went places with girlfriends of hers, girls who were just as plain and steady as she, and so when Connie wanted to do that her mother had no objections. The father of Connie's best girlfriend drove the girls the three miles to town and left them off at a shopping plaza, so that they could walk through the stores or go to a movie, and when he came to pick them up again at eleven he never bothered to ask what they had done.

They must have been familiar sights, walking around the shopping plaza in their shorts and flat ballerina slippers that always scuffed the sidewalk, with charm bracelets jingling on their thin wrists; they would lean together to whisper and laugh secretly if someone passed by who amused or interested them. Connie had long dark blond hair that drew anyone's eye to it, and she wore part of it pulled up on her head and puffed out and the rest of it she let fall down her back. She wore a pullover jersey blouse that looked one way when she was at home and another way when she was away from home. Everything about her had two sides to it, one for home and one for anywhere that was not home: her walk that could be childlike and bobbing, or languid enough to make anyone think she was hearing music in her head, her mouth which was pale and smirking most of the time, but bright and pink on these evenings out, her laugh which was cynical and drawling at home—"Ha, ha, very funny,"—but high-pitched and nervous anywhere else, like the jingling of the charms on her bracelet.

She had a high, breathless, amused voice that made everything she said sound a little forced, whether it was sincere or not.

Sometimes they did go shopping or to a movie, but sometimes they went across the highway, ducking fast across the busy road, to a drive-in restaurant where older kids hung out. The restaurant was shaped like a big bottle, though squatter than a real bottle, and on its cap was a revolving figure of a grinning boy holding a hamburger aloft. One night in midsummer they ran across, breathless with daring, and right away someone leaned out a car window and invited them over, but it was just a boy from high school they didn't like. It made them feel good to be able to ignore him. They went up through the maze of parked and cruising cars to the bright-lit, fly-infested restaurant, their faces pleased and expectant as if they were entering a sacred building that loomed up out of the night to give them what haven and what blessing they yearned for. They sat at the counter and crossed their legs at the ankles, their thin shoulders rigid with excitement, and listened to the music that made everything so good: the music was always in the background like music at a church service; it was something to depend upon.

But all the boys fell back and dissolved into a single face that was not even a face but an idea, a feeling, mixed up with the urgent insistent pounding of the music and the humid night air of July.

A boy named Eddie came in to talk with them. He sat backward on his stool, turning himself jerkily around in semicircles and then stopping and turning back again, and after a while he asked Connie if she would like something to eat. She said she did and so she tapped her friend's arm on her way out—her friend pulled her face up into a brave droll look—and Connie said she would meet her at eleven, across the way. "I just hate to leave her like that," Connie said earnestly, but the boy said that she wouldn't be alone for long. So they went out to his car and on the way Connie couldn't help but let her eyes wander over the windshields and faces all around her, her face gleaming with a joy that had nothing to do with Eddie or even this place; it might have been the music. She drew her shoulders up and sucked in her breath with the pure pleasure of being alive, and just at that moment she happened to glance at a face just a few feet from hers. It was a boy with shaggy black hair, in a convertible jalopy painted gold. He stared at her and then his lips widened into a grin. Connie slit her eyes at him and turned away, but she couldn't help glancing back and there he was, still watching her. He wagged a finger and laughed and said, "Gonna get you, baby," and Connie turned away again without Eddie noticing anything.

She spent three hours with him, at the restaurant where they ate hamburgers and drank Cokes in wax cups that were always sweating, and then down an alley a mile or so away, and when he left her off at five to eleven only the movie house was still open at the plaza. Her girlfriend was there, talking with a boy. When Connie came up the two girls smiled at each other and Connie said, "How was the movie?" and the girl said, "*You* should know." They rode off with the girl's father, sleepy and pleased, and Connie couldn't help but look back at the darkened shopping plaza with its big empty parking lot and its signs that were faded and ghostly now, and over at the drive-in restaurant where cars were still circling tirelessly. She couldn't hear the music at this distance.

Next morning June asked her how the movie was and Connie said, "So-so."

She and that girl and occasionally another girl went out several times a week that way, and the rest of the time Connie spent around the house—it was summer vacation—getting in her mother's way and thinking, dreaming, about the boys she met. But all the boys fell back and dissolved into a single face that was not even a face but an idea, a feeling, mixed up with the urgent insistent pounding of the music and the humid night air of July. Connie's mother kept dragging her back to the daylight by finding things for her to do or saying, suddenly, 'What's this about the Pettinger girl?"

And Connie would say nervously, "Oh, her. That dope." She always drew thick clear lines between herself and such girls, and her mother was simple and kindly enough to believe it. Her mother was so simple, Connie thought, that it was maybe cruel to fool her so much. Her mother went scuffling around the house in old bedroom slippers and complained over the telephone to one sister about the other, then the other called up and the two of them complained about the third one. If June's name was mentioned her mother's tone was approving, and if Connie's name was mentioned it was disapproving. This did not really mean she disliked Connie, and actually Connie thought that her mother preferred her to June because she was prettier, but the two of them kept up a pretense of exasperation, a sense that they were tugging and struggling over something of little value to either of them. Sometimes, over coffee, they were almost friends, but something would come up—some vexation that was like a fly buzzing suddenly around their heads—and their faces went hard with contempt.

Her mother was so simple, Connie thought, that it was maybe cruel to fool her so much.

One Sunday Connie got up at eleven—none of them bothered with church—and washed her hair so that it could dry all day long, in the sun. Her parents and sister were going to a barbecue at an aunt's house and Connie said no, she wasn't interested, rolling her eyes to let her mother know just what she thought of it. "Stay home alone then," her mother said sharply. Connie sat out back in a lawn chair and watched them drive away, her father quiet and bald, hunched around so that he could back the car out, her mother with a look that was still angry and not at all softened through the windshield, and in the back seat poor old June, all dressed up as if she didn't know what a barbecue was, with all the running yelling kids and the flies. Connie sat with her eyes closed in the sun, dreaming and dazed with the warmth about her as if this were a kind of love, the caresses of love, and her mind slipped over onto thoughts of the boy she had been with the night before and how nice he had been, how sweet it always was, not the way someone like June would suppose but sweet, gentle, the way it was in movies and promised in songs; and when she opened her eyes she hardly knew where she was, the back yard ran off into weeds and a fence-like line of trees and behind it the sky was perfectly blue and still. The asbestos "ranch house" that was now three years old startled her—it looked small. She shook her head as if to get awake.

It was too hot. She went inside the house and turned on the radio to drown out the quiet. She sat on the edge of her bed, barefoot, and listened for an hour and a half to a program called XYZ Sunday Jamboree, record after record of hard, fast, shrieking songs she sang along with, interspersed by exclamations from "Bobby King": "An' look here, you girls at Napoleon's—Son and Charley want you to pay real close attention to this song coming up!"

And Connie paid close attention herself, bathed in a glow of slow-pulsed joy that seemed to rise mysteriously out of the music itself and lay languidly about the airless little room, breathed in and breathed out with each gentle rise and fall of her chest.

After a while she heard a car coming up the drive. She sat up at once, startled,

The gravel kept crunching all the way in from the road—the driveway was long—and Connie ran to the window. It was a car she didn't know. It was an open jalopy, painted a bright gold that caught the sunlight opaquely.

because it couldn't be her father so soon. The gravel kept crunching all the way in from the road—the driveway was long—and Connie ran to the window. It was a car she didn't know. It was an open jalopy, painted a bright gold that caught the sunlight opaquely. Her heart began to pound and her fingers snatched at her hair, checking it, and she whispered "Christ. Christ," wondering how bad she looked. The car came to a stop at the side door and the horn sounded four short taps, as if this were a signal Connie knew.

She went into the kitchen and approached the door slowly, then hung out the screen door, her bare toes curling down off the step. There were two boys in the car and now she recognized the driver: he had shaggy, shabby black hair that looked crazy as a wig and he was grinning at her.

"I ain't late, am I?" he said.

"Who the hell do you think you are?" Connie said.

"Toldja I'd be out, didn't I?"

"I don't even know who you are."

Connie blushed a little, because the glasses made it impossible for her to see just what this boy was looking at.

She spoke sullenly, careful to show no interest or pleasure, and he spoke in a fast, bright monotone. Connie looked past him to the other boy, taking her time. He had fair brown hair, with a lock that fell onto his forehead. His sideburns gave him a fierce, embarrassed look, but so far he hadn't even bothered to glance at her. Both boys wore sunglasses. The driver's glasses were metallic and mirrored everything in miniature.

"You wanta come for a ride?" he said.

Connie smirked and let her hair fall loose over one shoulder.

"Don'tcha like my car? New paint job," he said. "Hey."

"What?"

"You're cute."

She pretended to fidget, chasing flies away from the door.

"Don'tcha believe me, or what?" he said.

"Look, I don't even know who you are," Connie said in disgust.

"Hey, Ellie's got a radio, see. Mine broke down." He lifted his friend's arm and showed her the little transistor radio the boy was holding, and now Connie began to hear the music. It was the same program that was playing inside the house.

"Bobby King?" she said.

"I listen to him all the time. I think he's great."

"He's kind of great," Connie said reluctantly.

"Listen, that guy's *great*. He knows where the action is."

Connie blushed a little, because the glasses made it impossible for her to see just what this boy was looking at. She couldn't decide if she liked him or if he was just a jerk, and so she dawdled in the doorway and wouldn't come down or go back inside. She said, "What's all that stuff painted on your car?"

"Can'tcha read it?" He opened the door very carefully, as if he were afraid it might fall off. He slid out just as carefully, planting his feet firmly on the ground, the tiny metallic world in his glasses slowing down like gelatine hardening, and in the midst of it Connie's bright green blouse. "This here is my name, to begin with, he said. ARNOLD FRIEND was written in tarlike black letters on the side, with a drawing of a round, grinning face that reminded Connie of a pumpkin, except it wore sunglasses. "I wanta introduce myself, I'm Arnold Friend and that's my real name and I'm gonna be your friend, honey, and inside the car's Ellie Oscar, he's kinda shy." Ellie brought his transistor radio up to his shoulder and balanced it there. "Now, these numbers are a secret code, honey," Arnold Friend explained. He read off the numbers 33, 19, 17 and raised his eyebrows at her to see what she thought of that, but she didn't think much of it. The left rear fender had been smashed and around it was written, on the gleaming gold background: DONE BY CRAZY WOMAN DRIVER. Connie had to laugh at that. Arnold Friend was pleased at her laughter and looked up at her. "Around the other side's a lot more —you wanta come and see them?"

"No."

"Why not?"

"Why should I?"

"Don'tcha wanta see what's on the car? Don'tcha wanta go for a ride?"

"I don't know."

"Why not?"

"I got things to do."

"Like what?"

"Things."

He laughed as if she had said something funny. He slapped his thighs. He was standing in a strange way, leaning back against the car as if he were balancing himself. He wasn't tall, only an inch or so taller than she would be if she came down to him. Connie liked the way he was dressed, which was the way all of them dressed: tight faded jeans stuffed into black, scuffed boots, a belt that pulled his waist in and showed how lean he was, and a white pullover shirt that was a little soiled and showed the hard small muscles of his arms and shoulders. He looked as if he probably did hard work, lifting and carrying things. Even his neck looked muscular. And his face was a familiar face, somehow: the jaw and chin and cheeks slightly darkened because he hadn't shaved for a day or two, and the nose long and hawk-like, sniffing as if she were a treat he was going to gobble up and it was all a joke.

"Connie, you ain't telling the truth. This is your day set aside for a ride with me and you know it," he said, still laughing. The way he straightened and recovered from his fit of laughing showed that it had been all fake.

"How do you know what my name is?" she said suspiciously.

"It's Connie."

"Maybe and maybe not."

"I know my Connie," he said, wagging his finger. Now she remembered him even better, back at the restaurant, and her cheeks warmed at the thought of how she had sucked in her breath just at the moment she passed him—how she must have looked to him. And he had remembered her. "Ellie and I come out here especially for you," he said. "Ellie can sit in back. How about it?"

> He spoke in a simple lilting voice, exactly as if he were reciting the words to a song. His smile assured her that everything was fine.

"Where?"

"Where what?"

"Where're we going?"

He looked at her. He took off the sunglasses and she saw how pale the skin around his eyes was, like holes that were not in shadow but instead in light. His eyes were like chips of broken glass that catch the light in an amiable way. He smiled. It was as if the idea of going for a ride somewhere, to some place, was a new idea to him.

"Just for a ride, Connie sweetheart."

"I never said my name was Connie," she said.

"But I know what it is. I know your name and all about you, lots of things," Arnold Friend said. He had not moved yet but stood still leaning back against the side of his jalopy. "I took a special interest in you, such a pretty girl, and found out all about you—like I know your parents and sister are gone somewheres and I know where and how long they're going to be gone, and I know who you were with last night, and your best girlfriend's name is Betty. Right?"

He spoke in a simple lilting voice, exactly as if he were reciting the words to a song. His smile assured her that everything was fine. In the car Ellie turned up the volume on his radio and did not bother to look around at them.

"Ellie can sit in the back seat," Arnold Friend said. He indicated his friend with a casual jerk of his chin, as if Ellie did not count and she should not bother with him.

"How'd you find out all that stuff?" Connie said.

"Listen: Betty Schultz and Tony Fitch and Jimmy Pettinger and Nancy Pettinger," he said in a chant. "Raymond Stanley and Bob Hutter—"

"Do you know all those kids?"

"I know everybody."

"Look, you're kidding. You're not from around here."

"Sure."

"But—how come we never saw you before?"

"Sure you saw me before," he said. He looked down at his boots, as if he were a little offended. "You just don't remember."

"I guess I'd remember you," Connie said.

"Yeah?" He looked up at this, beaming. He was pleased. He began to mark time with the music from Ellie's radio, tapping his fists lightly together. Connie looked away from his smile to the car, which was painted so bright it almost hurt her eyes to look at it. She looked at that name, ARNOLD FRIEND. And up at the front fender was an expression that was familiar—MAN THE FLYING SAUCERS. It was an expression kids had used the year before but didn't use this year. She looked at it for a while as if the words meant something to her that she did not yet know.

"What're you thinking about? Huh?" Arnold Friend demanded. "Not worried about your hair blowing around in the car, are you?"

"No."

"Think I maybe can't drive good?"

"How do I know?"

"You're a hard girl to handle. How come?" he said. "Don't you know I'm your friend? Didn't you see me put my sign in the air when you walked by?"

"What sign?"

"My sign." And he drew an X in the air, leaning out toward her. They were maybe ten feet apart. After his hand fell back to his side the X was still in the air, almost visible. Connie let the screen door close and stood perfectly still inside it, listening to the music from her radio and the boy's blend together. She stared at Arnold Friend. He stood there so stiffly relaxed, pretending to be relaxed, with one hand idly on the door handle as if he were keeping himself up that way and had no intention of ever moving again. She recognized most things about him, the tight jeans that showed his thighs and buttocks and the greasy leather boots and the tight shirt, and even that slippery friendly smile of his, that sleepy dreamy smile that all the boys used to get across ideas they didn't want to put into words. She recognized all this and also the singsong way he talked, slightly mocking, kidding, but serious and a little melancholy, and she recognized the way he tapped one fist against the other in homage to the perpetual music behind him. But all these things did not come together.

She said suddenly, "Hey, how old are you?"

His smiled faded. She could see then that he wasn't a kid, he was much older—thirty, maybe more. At this knowledge her heart began to pound faster.

"That's a crazy thing to ask. Can'tcha see I'm your own age?"

"Like hell you are."

"Or maybe a couple years older. I'm eighteen."

"Eighteen?" she said doubtfully.

He grinned to reassure her and lines appeared at the corners of his mouth. His teeth were big and white. He grinned so broadly his eyes became slits and she saw how thick the lashes were, thick and black as if painted with a black tarlike material. Then he seemed to become embarrassed, abruptly, and looked over his shoulder at Ellie. "*Him*, he's crazy," he said. "Ain't he a riot? He's a nut, a real character." Ellie was still listening to the music. His sunglasses told nothing about what he was thinking. He wore a bright orange shirt unbuttoned halfway to show his chest, which was a pale, bluish chest and not muscular like Arnold Friend's. His shirt collar was turned up all around and the very tips of the collar pointed out past his chin as if they were protecting him. He was pressing the transistor radio up against his ear and sat there in a kind of daze, right in the sun.

"Don't you know I'm your friend? Didn't you see me put my sign in the air when you walked by?"

"He's kinda strange," Connie said.

"Hey, she says you're kinda strange! Kinda strange!" Arnold Friend cried. He pounded on the car to get Ellie's attention. Ellie turned for the first time and Connie saw with shock that he wasn't a kid either—he had a fair, hairless face, cheeks reddened slightly as if the veins grew too close to the surface of his skin, the face of a forty-year-old baby. Connie felt a wave of dizziness rise in her at this sight and she stared at him as if waiting for something to change the shock of the moment, make it all right again. Ellie's lips kept shaping words, mumbling along with the words blasting in his ear.

"Maybe you two better go away," Connie said faintly.

"What? How come?" Arnold Friend cried. "We come out here to take you for a ride. It's Sunday." He had the voice of the man on the radio now. It was the same voice, Connie thought. "Don'tcha know it's Sunday all day and honey, no matter who you were with last night today you're with Arnold Friend and don't you forget it!—Maybe you better step out here," he said, and this last was in a different voice. It was a little flatter, as if the heat was finally getting to him.

"She's too fat. I don't like them fat. I like them the way you are, honey," he said, smiling sleepily at her. They stared at each other for a while through the screen door.

"No. I got things to do."

"Hey."

"You two better leave."

"We ain't leaving until you come with us."

"Like hell I am—"

"Connie, don't fool around with me. I mean, I mean, don't fool *around*," he said, shaking his head. He laughed incredulously. He placed his sunglasses on top of his head, carefully, as if he were indeed wearing a wig, and brought the stems down behind his ears. Connie stared at him, another wave of dizziness and fear rising in her so that for a moment he wasn't even in focus but was just a blur standing there against his gold car, and she had the idea that he had driven up the driveway all right but had come from nowhere before that and belonged nowhere and that everything about him and even about the music that was so familiar to her was only half real.

"If my father comes and sees you—"

"He ain't coming. He's at a barbecue."

"How do you know that?"

"Aunt Tillie's. Right now they're—uh—they're drinking. Sitting around," he said vaguely, squinting as if he were staring all the way to town and over to Aunt Tillie's back yard. Then the vision seemed to get clear and he nodded energetically. "Yeah. Sitting around. There's your sister in a blue dress, huh? And high heels, the poor sad bitch—nothing like you, sweetheart! And your mother's helping some fat woman with the corn, they're cleaning the corn—husking the corn—"

"What fat woman?" Connie cried.

"How do I know what fat woman, I don't know every goddam fat woman in the world!" Arnold Friend laughed.

"Oh, that's Mrs. Hornsby . . . Who invited her?" Connie said. She felt a little light-headed. Her breath was coming quickly.

"She's too fat. I don't like them fat. I like them the way you are, honey," he said, smiling sleepily at her. They stared at each other for a while through the screen door. He said softly, "Now, what you're going to do is this: you're going to come out that door. You're going to sit up front with me and Ellie's going to sit in the back, the hell with Ellie, right? This isn't Ellie's date. You're my date. I'm your lover, honey."

"What? You're crazy—"

"Yes, I'm your lover. You don't know what that is but you will," he said. "I know that too. I know all about you. But look: it's real nice and you couldn't ask for nobody better than me, or more polite. I always keep my word. I'll tell you how it is. I'm always nice at first, the first time. I'll hold you so tight you won't think you have to try to get away or pretend anything because you'll know you can't. And I'll come inside you where it's all secret and you'll give in to me and you'll love me—"

"Shut up! You're crazy!" Connie said. She backed away from the door. She put her hands up against her ears as if she'd heard something terrible, something not meant for her. "People don't talk like that, you're crazy," she muttered. Her heart was almost too big now for her chest and its pumping made sweat break out all over her. She looked out to see Arnold Friend pause and then take a step toward the porch lurching. He almost fell. But, like a clever drunken man, he managed to catch his balance. He wobbled in his high boots and grabbed hold of one of the porch posts.

His whole face was a mask, she thought wildly, tanned down onto his throat but then running out as if he had plastered makeup on his face but had forgotten about his throat.

"Honey?" he said. "You still listening?"

"Get the hell out of here!"

"Be nice, honey. Listen."

"I'm going to call the police—"

He wobbled again and out of the side of his mouth came a fast spat curse, an aside not meant for her to hear. But even this "Christ!" sounded forced. Then he began to smile again. She watched this smile come, awkward as if he were smiling from inside a mask. His whole face was a mask, she thought wildly, tanned down onto his throat but then running out as if he had plastered makeup on his face but had forgotten about his throat.

"Honey—? Listen, here's how it is. I always tell the truth and I promise you this: I ain't coming in that house after you."

"You better not! I'm going to call the police if you—if you don't—"

"Honey," he said, talking right through her voice, "honey, I'm not coming in there but you are coming out here. You know why?"

She was panting. The kitchen looked like a place she had never seen before, some room she had run inside but which wasn't good enough, wasn't going to help her. The kitchen window had never had a curtain, after three years, and there were dishes in the sink for her to do—probably—and if you ran your hand across the table you'd probably feel something sticky there.

"You listening, honey? Hey?"

"—going to call the police—"

"Soon as you touch the phone I don't need to keep my promise and can come inside. You won't want that."

She rushed forward and tried to lock the door. Her fingers were shaking. "But why lock it," Arnold Friend said gently, talking right into her face. "It's just a screen door. It's just nothing." One of his boots was at a strange angle, as if his foot wasn't in it. It pointed out to the left, bent at the ankle. "I mean, anybody can break through a screen door and glass and wood and iron or anything else if he needs to, anybody at all and specially Arnold Friend. If the place got lit up with a fire, honey, you'd come runnin' out into my arms, right into my arms an' safe at home—like you knew I was your lover and'd stopped fooling around. I don't mind a nice shy girl but I don't like no fooling around." Part of those words were spoken with a slight rhythmic lilt, and Connie somehow recognized them—the echo of a song from last year, about a girl rushing into her boyfriend's arms and coming home again—

Connie stood barefoot on the linoleum floor, staring at him. "What do you want?" she whispered.

"I want you," he said.

"What?"

"Seen you that night and thought, that's the one, yes sir. I never needed to look any more."

"But my father's coming back. He's coming to get me. I had to wash my hair first—" She spoke in a dry, rapid voice, hardly raising it for him to hear.

One of his boots was at a strange angle, as if his foot wasn't in it. It pointed out to the left, bent at the ankle.

"No, your daddy is not coming and yes, you had to wash your hair and you washed it for me. It's nice and shining and all for me. I thank you, sweetheart," he said, with a mock bow, but again he almost lost his balance. He had to bend and adjust his boots. Evidently his feet did not go all the way down; the boots must have been stuffed with something so that he would seem taller. Connie stared out at him and behind him at Ellie in the car, who seemed to be looking off toward Connie's right, into nothing. This Ellie said, pulling the words out of the air one after another as if he were just discovering them, "You want me to pull out the phone?"

"Shut your mouth and keep it shut," Arnold Friend said, his face red from bending over or maybe from embarrassment because Connie had seen his boots. "This ain't none of your business."

"What—what are you doing? What do you want?" Connie said. "If I call the police they'll get you, they'll arrest you—"

"Promise was not to come in unless you touch that phone, and I'll keep that promise," he said. He resumed his erect position and tried to force his shoulders back. He sounded like a hero in a movie, declaring something important. He spoke too loudly and it was as if he were speaking to someone behind Connie. "I ain't made plans for coming in that house where I don't belong but just for you to come out to me, the way you should. Don't you know who I am?"

"You're crazy," she whispered. She backed away from the door but did not want to go into another part of the house, as if this would give him permission to come through the door. "What do you . . . You're crazy, you . . ."

"Huh? What're you saying, honey?"

Her eyes darted everywhere in the kitchen. She could not remember what it was, this room.

"This is how it is, honey: you come out and we'll drive away, have a nice ride. But if you don't come out we're gonna wait till your people come home and then they're all going to get it."

"You want that telephone pulled out?" Ellie said. He held the radio away from his ear and grimaced, as if without the radio the air was too much for him.

"I toldja shut up, Ellie," Arnold Friend said, "you're deaf, get a hearing aid, right? Fix yourself up. This little girl's no trouble and's gonna be nice to me, so Ellie keep to yourself, this ain't your date—right? Don't hem in on me. Don't hog. Don't crush. Don't bird dog. Don't trail me," he said in a rapid meaningless voice, as if he were running through all the expressions he'd learned but was no longer sure which of them was in style, then rushing on to new ones, making them up with his eyes closed. "Don't crawl under my fence, don't squeeze in my chipmunk

> He sounded like a hero in a movie, declaring something important. He spoke too loudly and it was as if he were speaking to someone behind Connie.

hole, don't sniff my glue, suck my popsicle, keep your own greasy fingers on yourself!" He shaded his eyes and peered in at Connie, who was backed against the kitchen table. "Don't mind him, honey, he's just a creep. He's a dope. Right? I'm the boy for you and like I said you come out here nice like a lady and give me your hand, and nobody else gets hurt, I mean, your nice old bald-headed daddy and your mummy and your sister in her high heels. Because listen: why bring them in this?"

"Leave me alone," Connie whispered.

"Hey, you know that old woman down the road, the one with the chickens and stuff—you know her?"

"She's dead!"

"Dead? What? You know her?" Arnold Friend said.

"She's dead—"

"Don't you like her?"

"She's dead—she's—she isn't here any more—"

"But don't you like her, I mean, you got something against her? Some grudge or something?" Then his voice dipped as if he were conscious of a rudeness. He touched the sunglasses perched up on top of his head as if to make sure they were still there. "Now you be a good girl."

"What are you going to do?"

"Just two things, or maybe three," Arnold Friend said. "But I promise it won't last long and you'll like me the way you get to like people you're close to. You will. It's all over for you here, so come on out. You don't want your people in any trouble, do you?"

She turned and bumped against a chair or something, hurting her leg, but she ran into the back room and picked up the telephone. Something roared in

"The place where you came from ain't there any more, and where you had in mind to go is canceled out."

her ear, a tiny roaring, and she was so sick with fear that she could do nothing but listen to it—the telephone was clammy and very heavy and her fingers groped down to the dial but were too weak to touch it. She began to scream into the phone, into the roaring. She cried out, she cried for her mother, she felt her breath start jerking back and forth in her lungs as if it were something Arnold Friend was stabbing her with again and again with no tenderness. A noisy sorrowful wailing rose all about her and she was locked inside it the way she was locked inside this house.

After a while she could hear again. She was sitting on the floor with her wet back against the wall.

Arnold Friend was saying from the door, "That's a good girl. Put the phone back."

She kicked the phone away from her.

"No, honey. Pick it up. Put it back right."

She picked it up and put it back. The dial tone stopped.

"That's a good girl. Now, you come outside."

She was hollow with what had been fear, but what was now just an emptiness. All that screaming had blasted it out of her. She sat, one leg cramped under her, and deep inside her brain was something like a pinpoint of light that kept going and would not let her relax. She thought, I'm not going to see my mother again. She thought, I'm not going to sleep in my bed again. Her bright green blouse was all wet.

Arnold Friend said, in a gentle-loud voice that was like a stage voice, "The place where you came from ain't there any more, and where you had in mind to go is canceled out. This place you are now—inside your daddy's house—is nothing but a cardboard box I can knock down any time. You know that and always did know it. You hear me?"

She thought, I have got to think. I have got to know what to do.

"We'll go out to a nice field, out in the country here where it smells so nice and it's sunny," Arnold Friend said. "I'll have my arms tight around you so you won't need to try to get away and I'll show you what love is like, what it does. The hell with this house! It looks solid all right," he said. He ran a fingernail down the screen and the noise did not make Connie shiver, as it would have the day before. "Now, put your hand on your heart, honey. Feel that? That feels solid too but we know better, be nice to me, be sweet like you can because what else is there for a girl like you but to be sweet and pretty and give in?—and get away before her people come back?"

She felt her pounding heart. Her hand seemed to enclose it. She thought for the first time in her life that it was nothing that was hers, that belonged to her, but just a pounding, living thing inside this body that wasn't really hers either.

"You don't want them to get hurt," Arnold Friend went on. "Now get up, honey. Get up all by yourself."

She stood.

"Now, turn this way. That's right. Come over here to me—Ellie, put that away, didn't I tell you? You dope. You miserable creepy dope," Arnold Friend said. His words were not angry but only part of an incantation. The incantation was kindly. "Now come out through the kitchen to me honey and let's see a smile, try it, you're a brave sweet little girl and now they're eating corn and hot dogs cooked to bursting over an outdoor fire, and they don't know one thing about you and never did and honey you're better than them because not a one of them would have done this for you."

Connie felt the linoleum under her feet; it was cool. She brushed her hair back out of her eyes. Arnold Friend let go of the post tentatively and opened his arms for her, his elbows pointing in toward each other and his wrists limp, to show that this was an embarrassed embrace and a little mocking, he didn't want to make her self-conscious.

She put out her hand against the screen. She watched herself push the door slowly open as if she were safe back somewhere in the other doorway, watching this body and this head of long hair moving out into the sunlight where Arnold Friend waited.

"My sweet little blue-eyed girl," he said, in a half-sung sigh that had nothing to do with her brown eyes but was taken up just the same by the vast sunlit reaches of the land behind him and on all sides of him, so much land that Connie had never seen before and did not recognize except to know that she was going to it.

ALICE WALKER

Everyday Use

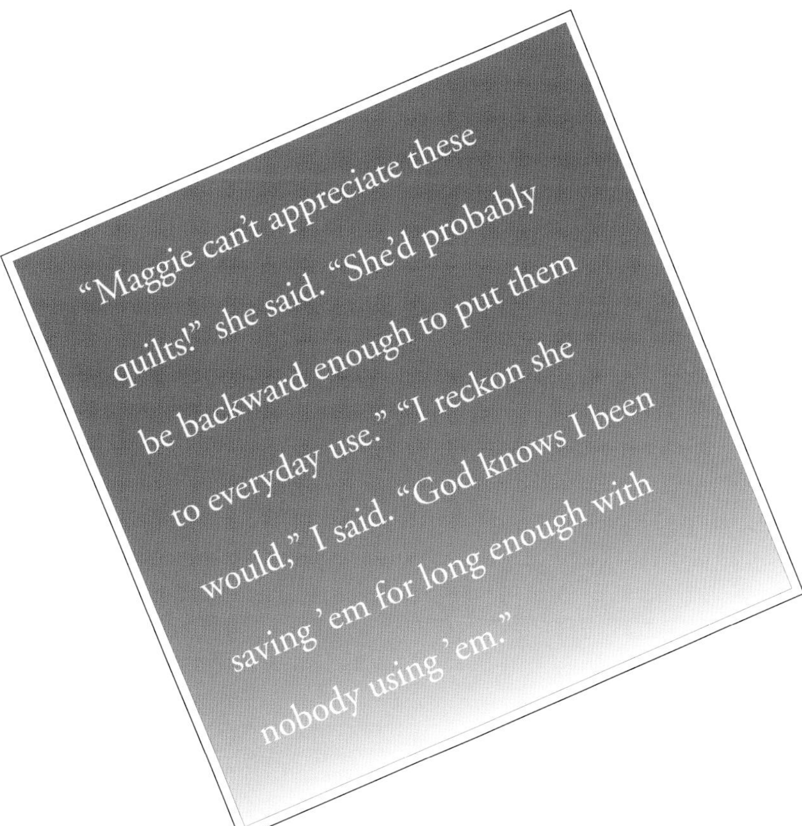

I will wait for her in the yard that Maggie and I made so clean and wavy yesterday afternoon. A yard like this is more comfortable than most people know. It is not just a yard. It is like an extended living room. When the hard clay is swept clean as a floor and the fine sand around the edges lined with tiny, irregular grooves, anyone can come and sit and look up into the elm tree and wait for the breezes that never come inside the house.

Maggie will be nervous until after her sister goes: she will stand hopelessly in corners, homely and ashamed of the burn scars down her arms and legs, eying her sister with a mixture of envy and awe. She thinks her sister has held life always in the palm of one hand, that "no" is a word the world never learned to say to her.

You've no doubt seen those TV shows where the child who has "made it" is confronted, as a surprise, by her own mother and father, tottering in weakly from backstage. (A pleasant surprise, of course: What would they do if parent and child came on the show only to curse out and insult each other?) On TV mother and child embrace and smile into each other's faces. Sometimes the mother and father weep, the child wraps them in her arms and leans across the table to tell how she would not have made it without their help. I have seen these programs.

Sometimes I dream a dream in which Dee and I are suddenly brought together on a TV program of this sort. Out of a dark and soft-seated limousine I am ushered into a bright room filled with many people. There I meet a smiling, gray, sporty man like Johnny Carson who shakes my hand and tells me what a fine girl I have. Then we are on the stage and Dee is embracing me with tears in her eyes. She pins on my dress a large orchid, even though she has told me once that she thinks orchids are tacky flowers.

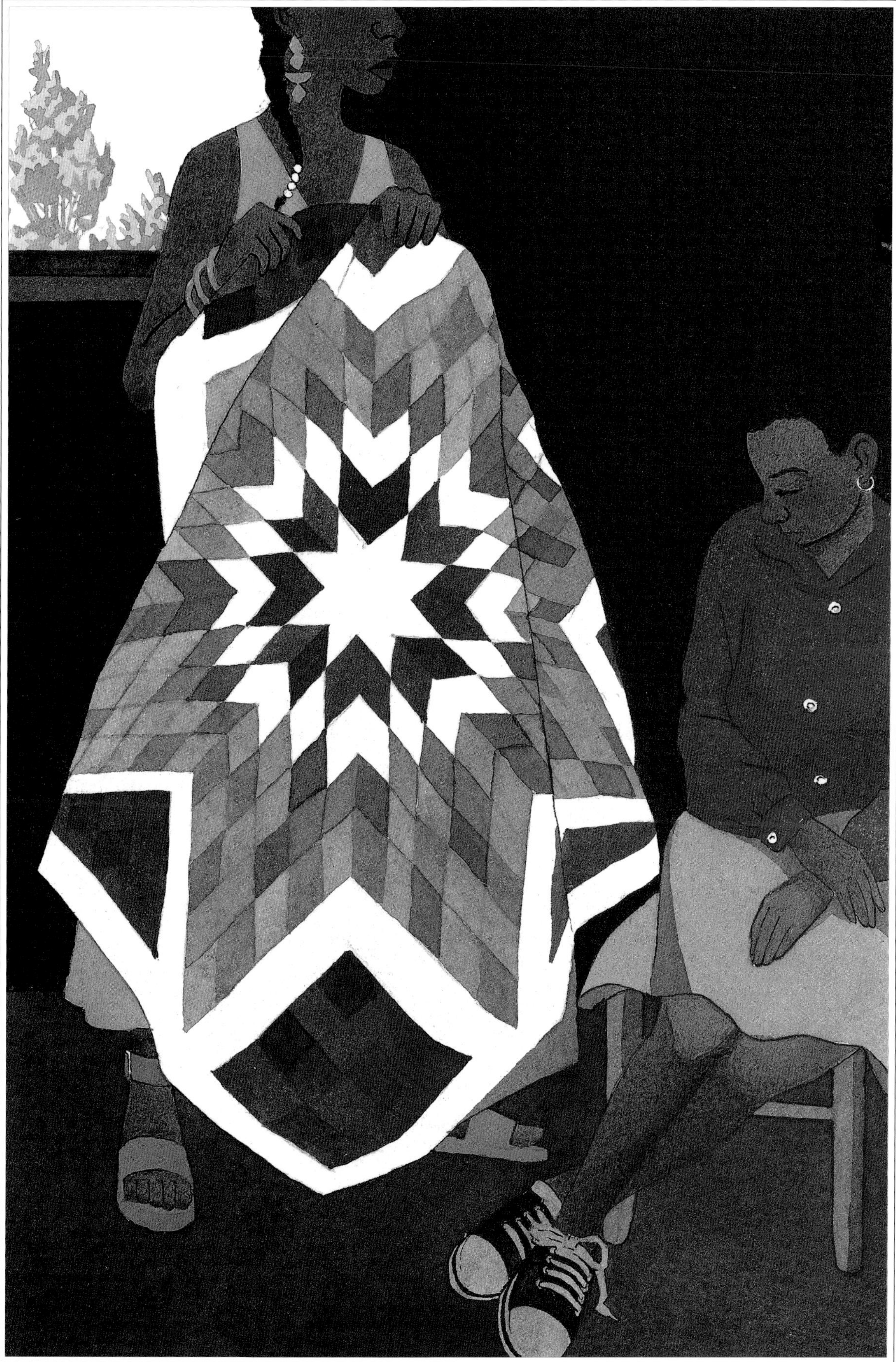

In real life I am a large, big-boned woman with rough, man-working hands. In the winter I wear flannel nightgowns to bed and overalls during the day. I can kill and clean a hog as mercilessly as a man. My fat keeps me hot in zero weather. I can work outside all day, breaking ice to get water for washing; I can eat pork liver cooked over the open fire minutes after it comes steaming from the hog. One winter I knocked a bull calf straight in the brain between the eyes with a sledge hammer and had the meat hung up to chill before nightfall. But of course all this does not show on television. I am the way my daughter would want me to be: a hundred pounds lighter, my skin like an uncooked barley pancake. My hair glistens in the hot bright lights. Johnny Carson has much to do to keep up with my quick and witty tongue.

But that is a mistake. I know even before I wake up. Who ever knew a Johnson with a quick tongue? Who can even imagine me looking a strange white man in the eye? It seems to me I have talked to them always with one foot raised in flight, with my head turned in whichever way is farthest from them. Dee, though. She would always look anyone in the eye. Hesitation was no part of her nature.

"How do I look, Mama?" Maggie says, showing just enough of her thin body enveloped in pink skirt and red blouse for me to know she's there, almost hidden by the door.

"Come out into the yard," I say.

Have you ever seen a lame animal, perhaps a dog run over by some careless person rich enough to own a car, sidle up to someone who is ignorant enough to be kind to him? That is the way my Maggie walks. She has been like this, chin on chest, eyes on ground, feet in shuffle, ever since the fire that burned the other house to the ground.

Dee is lighter than Maggie, with nicer hair and a fuller figure. She's a woman now, though sometimes I forget. How long ago was it that the other house burned? Ten, twelve years? Sometimes I can still hear the flames and feel Maggie's arms sticking to me, her hair smoking and her dress falling off her in little black papery flakes. Her eyes seemed stretched open, blazed open by the flames reflected in them. And Dee. I see her standing off under the sweet gum tree she used to dig gum out of; a look of concentration on her face as she watched the last dingy gray board of the house fall in toward the red-hot brick chimney. Why don't you do a dance around the ashes? I'd wanted to ask her. She had hated the house that much.

> Have you ever seen a lame animal, perhaps a dog run over by some careless person rich enough to own a car, sidle up to someone who is ignorant enough to be kind to him? That is the way my Maggie walks.

I used to think she hated Maggie, too. But that was before we raised the money, the church and me, to send her to Augusta to school. She used to read to us without pity; forcing words, lies, other folks' habits, whole lives upon us two, sitting trapped and ignorant underneath her voice. She washed us in a river of make-believe, burned us with a lot of knowledge we didn't necessarily need to know. Pressed us to her with the serious way she read, to shove us away at just the moment, like dimwits, we seemed about to understand.

Dee wanted nice things. A yellow organdy dress to wear to her graduation from high school; black pumps to match a green suit she'd made from an old suit somebody gave me. She was determined to stare down any disaster in her efforts. Her eyelids would not flicker for minutes at a time. Often I fought off the temptation to shake her. At sixteen she had a style of her own: and knew what style was.

I never had an education myself. After second grade the school was closed down. Don't ask me why: in 1927 colored asked fewer questions than they do now. Sometimes Maggie reads to me. She stumbles along good-naturedly but can't see well. She knows she is not bright. Like good looks and money, quickness passed her by. She will marry John Thomas (who has mossy teeth in an earnest face) and then I'll be free to sit here and I guess just sing church songs to myself. Although

I never was a good singer. Never could carry a tune. I was always better at a man's job. I used to love to milk till I was hooked in the side in '49. Cows are soothing and slow and don't bother you, unless you try to milk them the wrong way.

I have deliberately turned my back on the house. It is three rooms, just like the one that burned, except the roof is tin; they don't make shingle roofs any more. There are no real windows, just some holes cut in the sides, like the portholes in a ship, but not round and not square, with rawhide holding the shutters up on the outside. This house is in a pasture, too, like the other one. No doubt when Dee sees it she will want to tear it down. She wrote me once that no matter where we "choose" to live, she will manage to come see us. But she will never bring her friends. Maggie and I thought about this and Maggie asked me, "Mama, when did Dee ever *have* any friends?"

She had a few. Furtive boys in pink shirts hanging about on washday after school. Nervous girls who never laughed. Impressed with her they worshiped the well-turned phrase, the cute shape, the scalding humor that erupted like bubbles in lye. She read to them.

When she was courting Jimmy T she didn't have much time to pay to us, but turned all her faultfinding power on him. He flew to marry a cheap city girl from a family of ignorant flashy people. She hardly had time to recompose herself.

When she comes I will meet—but there they are!

Maggie attempts to make a dash for the house, in her shuffling way, but I stay her with my hand. "Come back here," I say. And she stops and tries to dig a well in the sand with her toe.

It is hard to see them clearly through the strong sun. But even the first glimpse of leg out of the car tells me it is Dee. Her feet were always neat-looking, as if God himself had shaped them with a certain style. From the other side of the car comes a

> She stoops down quickly and lines up picture after picture of me sitting there in front of the house with Maggie cowering behind me.

short, stocky man. Hair is all over his head a foot long and hanging from his chin like a kinky mule tail. I hear Maggie suck in her breath. "Uhnnnh," is what it sounds like. Like when you see the wriggling end of a snake just in front of your foot on the road. "Uhnnnh."

Dee next. A dress down to the ground, in this hot weather. A dress so loud it hurts my eyes. There are yellows and oranges enough to throw back the light of the sun. I feel my whole face warming from the heat waves it throws out. Earrings gold, too, and hanging down to her shoulders. Bracelets dangling and making noises when she moves her arm up to shake the folds of the dress out of her armpits. The dress is loose and flows, and as she walks closer, I like it. I hear Maggie go "Uhnnnh" again. It is her sister's hair. It stands straight up like the wool on a sheep. It is black as night and around the edges are two long pigtails that rope about like small lizards disappearing behind her ears.

"Wa-su-zo-Tean-o!" she says, coming on in that gliding way the dress makes her move. The short stocky fellow with the hair to his navel is all grinning and he follows up with "Asalamalakim, my mother and sister!" He moves to hug Maggie but she falls back, right up against the back of my chair. I feel her trembling there and when I look up I see the perspiration falling off her chin.

"Don't get up," says Dee. Since I am stout it takes something of a push. You can see me trying to move a second or two before I make it. She turns, showing white heels through her sandals, and goes back to the car. Out she peeks next with a Polaroid. She stoops down quickly and lines up picture after picture of me sitting there in front of the house with Maggie cowering behind me. She never takes a shot without making sure the house is included. When a cow comes nibbling around the edge of the yard she snaps it and me and Maggie *and* the house. Then she puts the Polaroid in the back seat of the car, and comes up and kisses me on the forehead.

Meanwhile Asalamalakim is going through motions with Maggie's hand. Maggie's hand is as limp as a fish, and probably as cold, despite the sweat, and she keeps trying to pull it back. It looks like Asalamalakim wants to shake hands but wants to do it fancy. Or maybe he don't know how people shake hands. Anyhow, he soon gives up on Maggie.

"Well," I say. "Dee."

"No, Mama," she says. "Not 'Dee,' Wangero Leewanika Kemanjo!"

"What happened to 'Dee'?" I wanted to know.

"She's dead," Wangero said. "I couldn't bear it any longer, being named after the people who oppress me."

She talked a blue streak over the sweet potatoes. Everything delighted her. Even the fact that we still used the benches her daddy made for the table when we couldn't afford to buy chairs.

"You know as well as me you was named after your aunt Dicie," I said. Dicie is my sister. She named Dee. We called her "Big Dee" after Dee was born.

"But who was *she* named after?" asked Wangero.

"I guess after Grandma Dee," I said.

"And who was she named after?" asked Wangero.

"Her mother," I said, and saw Wangero was getting tired. "That's about as far back as I can trace it," I said. Though, in fact, I probably could have carried it back beyond the Civil War through the branches.

"Well," said Asalamalakim, "there you are."

"Uhnnnh," I heard Maggie say.

"There I was not," I said, "before 'Dicie' cropped up in our family, so why should I try to trace it that far back?"

He just stood there grinning, looking down on me like somebody inspecting a Model A car. Every once in a while he and Wangero sent eye signals over my head.

"How do you pronounce this name?" I asked.

"You don't have to call me by it if you don't want to," said Wangero.

"Why shouldn't I?" I asked. "If that's what you want us to call you, we'll call you."

"I know it might sound awkward at first," said Wangero.

"I'll get used to it," I said. "Ream it out again."

Well, soon we got the name out of the way. Asalamalakim had a name twice as long and three times as hard. After I tripped over it two or three times he told me to just call him Hakim-a-barber. I wanted to ask him was he a barber, but I didn't really think he was, so I didn't ask.

"You must belong to those beef-cattle peoples down the road," I said. They said "Asalamalakim" when they met you, too, but they didn't shake hands. Always too busy: feeding the cattle, fixing the fences, putting up salt-lick shelters, throwing down hay. When the white folks poisoned some of the herd the men stayed up all night with rifles in their hands. I walked a mile and a half just to see the sight.

Hakim-a-barber said, "I accept some of their doctrines, but farming and raising cattle is not my style." (They didn't tell me, and I didn't ask, whether Wangero (Dee) had really gone and married him.)

We sat down to eat and right away he said he didn't eat collards and pork was unclean. Wangero, though, went on through the chitlins and corn bread, the greens and everything else. She talked a blue streak over the sweet potatoes. Everything delighted her. Even the fact that we still used the benches her daddy made for the table when we couldn't afford to buy chairs.

"Oh, Mama!" she cried. Then turned to Hakim-a-barber. "I never knew how lovely these benches are. You can feel the rump prints," she said, running her hands underneath her and along the bench. Then she gave a sigh and her hand closed over Grandma Dee's butter dish. "That's it!" she said. "I knew there was something I wanted to ask you if I could have." She jumped up from the table and went over in the corner where the churn stood, the milk in it clabber by now. She looked at the churn and looked at it.

"This churn top is what I need," she said. "Didn't Uncle Buddy whittle it out of a tree you all used to have?"

"Yes," I said.

"Uh huh," she said happily. "And I want the dasher, too."

"Uncle Buddy whittle that, too?" asked the barber.

Dee (Wangero) looked up at me.

"Aunt Dee's first husband whittled the dash," said Maggie so low you almost couldn't hear her. "His name was Henry, but they called him Stash."

"Maggie's brain is like an elephant's," Wangero said, laughing. "I can use the churn top as a centerpiece for the alcove table," she said, sliding a plate over the churn, "and I'll think of something artistic to do with the dasher."

When she finished wrapping the dasher the handle stuck out. I took it for a moment in my hands. You didn't even have to look close to see where hands pushing the dasher up and down to make butter had left a kind of sink in the wood. In fact, there were a lot of small sinks; you could see where thumbs and fingers had sunk into the wood. It was beautiful light yellow wood, from a tree that grew in the yard where Big Dee and Stash had lived.

After dinner Dee (Wangero) went to the trunk at the foot of my bed and started rifling through it. Maggie hung back in the kitchen over the dishpan. Out came Wangero with two quilts. They had been pieced by Grandma Dee and then Big Dee and me had hung them on the quilt frames on the front porch and quilted them. One was in the Lone Star pattern. The other was Walk Around the Mountain. In both of them were scraps of dresses Grandma Dee had worn fifty and more years ago. Bits and pieces of Grandpa Jarrell's Paisley shirts. And one teeny faded blue piece, about the size of a penny matchbox, that was from Great Grandpa Ezra's uniform that he wore in the Civil War.

"Mama," Wangero said sweet as a bird. "Can I have these old quilts?"

I heard something fall in the kitchen, and a minute later the kitchen door slammed.

"Why don't you take one or two of the others?" I asked. "These old things was just done by me and Big Dee from some tops your grandma pieced before she died."

"No," said Wangero. "I don't want those. They are stitched around the borders by machine."

"That'll make them last better," I said.

"That's not the point," said Wangero. "These are all pieces of dresses Grandma used to wear. She did all this stitching by hand. Imagine!" She held the quilts securely in her arms, stroking them.

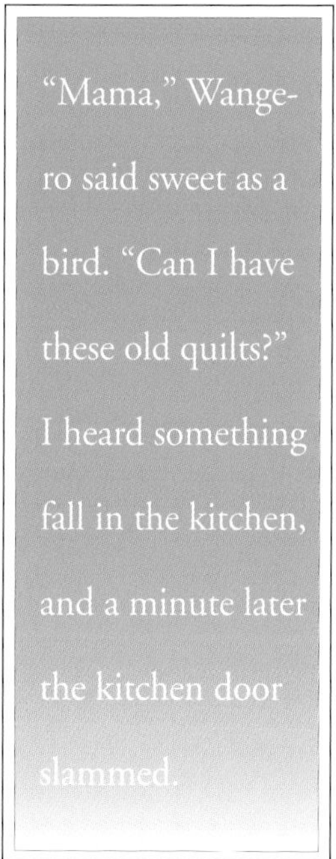

"Some of the pieces, like those lavender ones, come from old clothes her mother handed down to her," I said, moving up to touch the quilts. Dee (Wangero) moved back just enough so that I couldn't reach the quilts. They already belonged to her.

"Imagine!" she breathed again, clutching them closely to her bosom.

"The truth is," I said, "I promised to give them quilts to Maggie, for when she marries John Thomas."

She gasped like a bee had stung her.

"Maggie can't appreciate these quilts!" she said. "She'd probably be backward enough to put them to everyday use."

"I reckon she would," I said. "God knows I been saving 'em for long enough with nobody using 'em. I hope she will!" I didn't want to bring up how I had offered Dee (Wangero) a quilt when she went away to college. Then she had told me they were old-fashioned, out of style.

"But they're *priceless*!" she was saying now, furiously; for she has a temper. "Maggie would put them on the bed and in five years they'd be in rags. Less than that!"

"She can always make some more," I said. "Maggie knows how to quilt."

Dee (Wangero) looked at me with hatred. "You just will not understand. The point is these quilts, *these* quilts!"

"Well," I said, stumped. "What would *you* do with them?"

"Hang them," she said. As if that was the only thing you *could* do with quilts.

Maggie by now was standing in the door. I could almost hear the sound her feet made as they scraped over each other.

"Well," I said, stumped. "What would *you* do with them?" "Hang them," she said. As if that was the only thing you *could* do with quilts.

"She can have them, Mama," she said, like somebody used to never winning anything, or having anything reserved for her. "I can 'member Grandma Dee without the quilts."

I looked at her hard. She had filled her bottom lip with checkerberry snuff and it gave her face a kind of dopey, hangdog look. It was Grandma Dee and Big Dee who taught her how to quilt herself. She stood there with her scarred hands hidden in the folds of her skirt. She looked at her sister with something like fear but she wasn't mad at her. This was Maggie's portion. This was the way she knew God to work.

When I looked at her like that something hit me in the top of my head and ran down to the soles of my feet. Just like when I'm in church and the spirit of God touches me and I get happy and shout. I did something I never had done before: hugged Maggie to me, then dragged her on into the room, snatched the quilts out of Miss Wangero's hands and dumped them into Maggie's lap. Maggie just sat there on my bed with her mouth open.

"Take one or two of the others," I said to Dee.

But she turned without a word and went out to Hakim-a-barber.

"You just don't understand," she said, as Maggie and I came out to the car.

"What don't I understand?" I wanted to know.

"Your heritage," she said, and then she turned to Maggie, kissed her, and said,

"You ought to try to make something of yourself, too, Maggie. It's really a new day for us. But from the way you and Mama still live you'd never know it."

She put on some sunglasses that hid everything above the tip of her nose and chin.

Maggie smiled; maybe at the sunglasses. But a real smile, not scared. After we watched the car dust settle I asked Maggie to bring me a dip of snuff. And then the two of us sat there just enjoying, until it was time to go in the house and go to bed.

RICK BASS

Elk

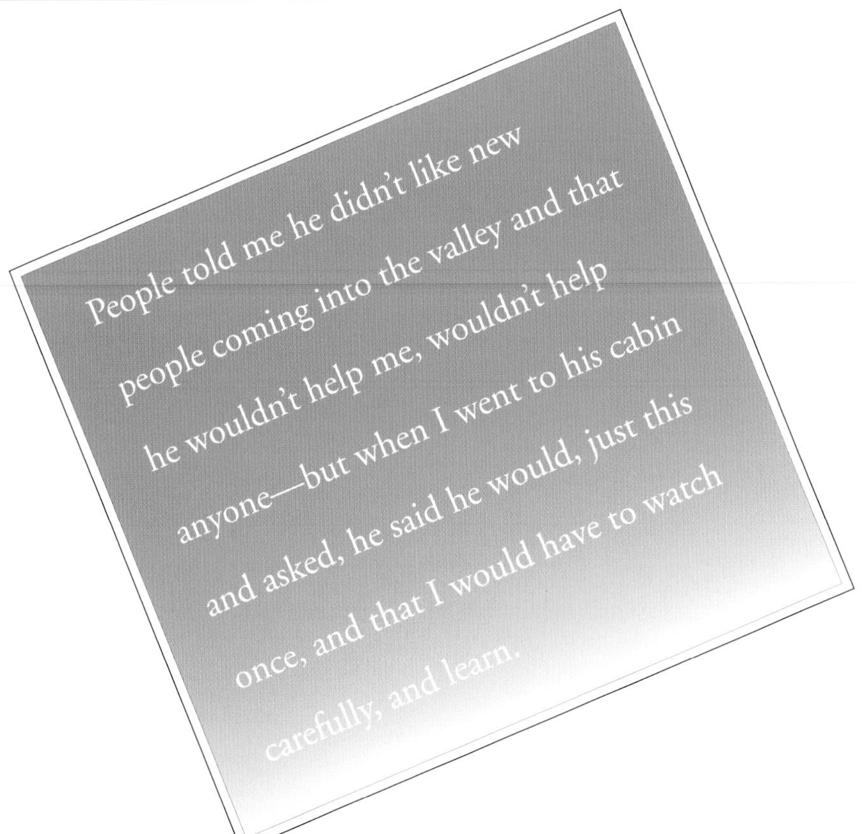

It was Matthew who killed the elk. I was only trying to learn how it was done.

My first year in the valley, I knew next to nothing, though when only a week of hunting season remained and still I had no meat, I knew enough to ask Matthew for help. People told me he didn't like new people coming into the valley and that he wouldn't help me, wouldn't help anyone—but when I went to his cabin and asked, he said he would, just this once, and that I would have to watch carefully, and learn: he would only hunt an elk for me once.

We canoed across the Yaak River and went into the wilderness. We found a bull's tracks, and followed the bull for three days, killing it on the fourth.

Afterward, Matthew built a fire in the woods next to the elk to warm us as we went to work. There was plenty of dry wood and it was easy to make a roaring fire; its flames grew almost as tall as we were, and they lit up the woods. The orange light danced against the elk's hide and against his antlers, making it seem as if he had come back to life. In his final death leap the elk had got tangled in the blowdown and now hung there, several feet off the ground. Matthew crawled underneath and began cutting. There was a rasping sound of his knife against the coarse hair and thick skin and cartilage, and from time to time he had to stop and sharpen his knife with a whetstone.

"Nothing in the world dulls a steel blade like elk hair," he said. He was doing a neat job. "I'd like a stone knife someday, black obsidian," he said. I added wood to the fire. I would not have believed that you could skin such an animal. It was surely enough meat for the coming year.

By morning we had the elk skinned and the immense antlers sawed off. Matthew had brought a small wood-handled folding saw—its blade was now ruined—and he tossed it into the fire. The bull's immense hindquarters—heavier than a man's body—were hanging from trees. So, too, were the shoulders.

We filled our packs with the loose meat—all the neck roasts, tenderloins, neck loins, and lengths of backstrap like deep-red anacondas. In lifting the hindquarters and shoulders, we became covered with blood. I was glad that the bears were already in hibernation.

The fire had sprawled and wandered through the night. Ashes and charred half-lengths of timber lay in a circle thirty feet across: a testament to what had happened here.

We roasted some of the ribs over the coals of the fire and chewed on them for a long time. We ate a whole side of the trimmings from the elk skeleton—the bones were stripped clean and gleaming when we were done—and then broke the other side in half with the hatchet. We tied the rib cages to our packs like a frame; they would help hold in place the shifting weight of the meat, which was still warm against our backs. I gathered a few stones as we were about to leave and, not knowing why, stacked them where the elk had fallen, now a pile of hooves, shins, and hair.

Matthew carried the antlers—settled them over his shoulders upside down—and with their long tips and tines furrowing the snow behind him he looked as if he were in a yoke and plowing the snow. I carried the wet hide atop my pack of meat, increasing the weight of my pack up to around a hundred and thirty pounds. Matthew said it was important to carry out the extraneous stuff first—the antlers, the hide—before our resolve weakened and we were tempted to leave them behind for the wolves.

It began to snow again. I wondered where the other elk were, if they knew that our hunt for them was over.

We stayed on the ridges. Under such a load, our steps were small and slow.

We travelled a mile, dropped our weight, then went back to where we'd left all the other meat, and carried it to the point we'd got to before—each of us carrying a hindquarter on his back, or dragging it behind like a sled.

And so we moved across the valley, slowly, as if in some eternal meat relay—continuously undoing the progress we'd made, working hours to move the whole mass only one mile, at which point we then started all over again. The winter-short days passed quickly, and we slept soundly through the nights.

The snow kept coming. We dropped off one ridge down into a creek and ascended another, and Matthew said he knew where we were. After the second or third day, the ravens appeared. They landed in front of us and strutted with outstretched wings, drawing little tracings in the snow, barking and cawing in their voices that were alternately shrill and hoarse, as if they were hurling different languages at us. Sometimes they landed behind us, darted in and pecked at whatever section of the elk we were dragging, but usually they picked at the meat fragments in the snow.

On the third day there was a moment of startling beauty. We were walking in a fog so thick that we could barely see more than a few feet in front of us. We knew to stay on the ridge. Four ravens were following us, walking behind us in their penguin strut. And then to our left, to the west, a slot appeared in the fog, a slot of pale-blue sky, and through the slot there was a shaft of gold light illuminating the forest below us. The shaft was the only thing we could see in the storm. The wind was blowing north, the direction we were going, and for a while the shaft travelled with us. As it did, it kept revealing more of the same uncut, untouched forest. The impression it made was that the uncut forest would never end. In less than a minute, the shaft had moved on—the wind was about thirty miles an hour—but the sight has stayed with me, and neither Matthew nor I said anything about it to each other, though we did stop and watch it, as if unsure of what it was we were seeing.

We ate on the elk as we travelled, but after four days I wanted bread or potatoes. I was tired of all meat.

We ate on the elk as we travelled, but after four days I wanted bread or potatoes. I was tired of all meat. I wanted an apple pie, dense with sugar, and a hot bath.

The massive antlers had sunk lower on Matthew's shoulders, and the plow they made cut deeper in the snow. Sometimes their heavy tips struck a rock beneath the snow and made a *clinking* sound. The weight of the antlers was starting to wear Matthew's skin raw, even though he had cut a small strip of hide to use as a cushion. A thin red "Y" now ran down his back, merging just below his shoulders. The furrows in the snow behind him, wide as the antlers, looked like the boundaries for a small road, a lane, and within them we sometimes spotted the tracks of the creatures that were following us: the ravens, coyotes, and wolves.

We were descending slowly, and were beginning to see the tracks of other animals again—deer, moose, and elk, though the elk tracks were those of cows and calves, not bulls.

We were down out of the high country and into the dense forest. It was growing warmer at the lower elevation, so that, rather than snow falling, there was a sleety drizzle, which was more chilling than any storm or blizzard. We came across a dropped moose antler, resting upright on the snow—we could read his tracks leading to it, and leading away from it—and the antler, upturned, was full of water and slush from the sleet. We knelt and took turns drinking from it, without disturbing it. We were almost home. One more night, and the next day. A year's worth of meat, put away safely.

The "Y" on Matthew's back widened, but he was moving stronger again. I was shivering hard by now. I was drenched. For a long time the effort of hauling and skidding the meat had been enough to keep me warm, but now that effort wasn't enough. I was cold and I needed help from the outside. My body could no longer hold off the whole mass of winter. I was without reserves.

"Do you want to stop and light a fire?" Matthew asked, watching my slowing movements, my clumsiness, my giving-upness. I nodded, still lucid enough to know that hypothermia had arrived. Matthew seemed to be a great distance away, and I felt that he was studying me, evaluating me. We were no longer partners in the hunt, brothers in the hunt—brothers in anything—and as my mind began to close down, chamber by chamber, I had the feeling that Matthew was going to let me freeze: that he had run me into the ground, had let me haul out half the elk, and now, only a day's journey from town, he was going to let winter have me. He would carry the rest of the meat out himself, leaving me to disappear beneath the snow.

He stood there waiting. I knelt and slipped out of my pack. I then lost my balance and tipped over in the snow. Not thinking clearly—not thinking at all—I searched through my pack for matches, shivering. I found them, held the small box tightly in my gloved hands, then remembered that I needed wood.

Matthew continued watching me. He had not taken his pack off—as if he had no intention of stopping here anyway—and the antlers had been with him so long that they seemed to be growing out of him. I moved off into the trees and down a slope and began indiscriminately snapping twigs and gathering branches, dropping much of what I picked up. Matthew stayed up on the hill above, watching. The rain and sleet kept coming down. He was drenched, too—there was ice on his antlers—but he seemed to have a fire and a hardness in him that I knew I didn't have.

I heaped the branches, some green and some dry, into a small pile, and began striking matches; and the sodden pile of wood would not light. I tried until I was out of matches, then rose and went back up to my pack to look for more. I was moving slowly and wanted to lie down. I had to keep going, but I knew that I wasn't going to find any more matches.

"This way," Matthew said finally, taking a cigarette lighter out of his pack. "Look at me," he said. "Watch." He walked down to the nearest dead tree, an old wind-blasted fire tree, shrouded dense with black hanging lichen. "This is what you do," he said. His words came in breaths of steam rising into the rain. He stood under the canopy of the tree's branches and moss cloak and snapped the lighter a couple of times, holding it right up against the lichen tendrils.

On the third snap the lichen caught, burned blue for a moment, then leapt into quick orange flame.

It was like something chemical—the whole tree, or the shell of lichen around it, metamorphosed into bright crackling fire: the lichen burning explosively and the sudden shock of heat, the updraft, in turn lighting the lichen above, accelerating the rush of flame as if climbing a ladder. It was a forty-foot-tall tree, and it was on fire from top to bottom in about five seconds.

"That's how you do it," Matthew said, stepping back. I had stopped shivering, my blood heated by one last squeeze of adrenaline at the sight; but now, even as I watched the flames, the chill, and then the shivering, returned.

> The rain and sleet kept coming down. He was drenched, too—there was ice on his antlers—but he seemed to have a fire and a hardness in him that I knew I didn't have.

"You'd better get on over there," he said. "They don't burn long."

I walked over to the burning tree. There was a lot of heat; the snow in all directions glistened—but I knew that the heat wasn't going to last. Flaming wisps of lichen separated from the tree and floated upward in curls before cooling and descending. By the time they landed on me, they were almost burnt out—charcoal skeletons of the lichen. A few of the tree's branches burned and crackled, but that was pretty much it; the fire was gone.

I wouldn't say I was warm, but I had stopped shivering.

"Come on," Matthew said. "Let's go find another one." He set off into the rain, the antlers behind him plowing a path.

And that was how we came out of the mountains, in that last night and the next day, moving from tree to tree—looking for the right one, properly dead—through the drizzle, from one tower of flame to the next, Matthew probing the right ones with his cigarette lighter, testing them, always choosing the right ones. That was how we walked through that night—the trees sizzling and steaming after we were done with them—and on into the gray rainy day. We were back into country that I knew well, even underneath all the snow. We were seeing the tracks of wolves, and finding some of their kills. I had stopped shivering, though we continued lighting tree torches—leaving a crooked, wandering path of them behind us.

I suspect that in twenty years I will still be able to trace our journey backward, back up the mountain from torched tree to torched tree. Some will be fallen and rotting black husks, other might still be standing. In twenty years, I'll be able to return to where it all started—that point where we first saw the elk, and then lost him, and then found him again, and killed him. From among the stones and ferns and forest, there will be a piece of charcoal, a fire-blackened rock, an antler in a tree, a rusting saw blade, even a scabbed-over set of initials, where Matthew marked his kill, although as the years go on, those initials will be harder to find, until finally you will have to know exactly where they are, and have some sort of guide, someone who has actually been there before, to show you.

We saw him because he had seen us, and was coming up the hill toward us—or, rather, toward Matthew.

The rut was on as we approached town the next day—the giant bucks chasing the does—and though we were exhausted, we could see that we had to shoot a deer.

As we drew nearer the village—the forest ripe with the scent of rut musk—we saw a swarm of antlers, dozens of bucks prowling the woods, mesmerized by sex, by creation, by the needs of the future, and we were almost home when we saw the buck we wanted.

We saw him because he had seen us, and was coming up the hill toward us—or, rather, toward Matthew. He was drawn by the sight of the giant antlers strapped to Matthew's back. We were moving through dense brush and it's possible that was all he could see, and he came forward with a strange aggression. He was wet from the rain. His antlers were black-brown, from his having lived in a dark forest, and rose three feet above his head and extended beyond the tips of his outstretched ears. It did not seem possible that he could carry such a weight on his head. Matthew dropped to his knees. The deer stopped, then came closer, still entranced by the antlers, and Matthew raised his rifle and shot the deer through the neck, now not twenty yards away.

The deer's head snapped back, and we saw a thin pattern of blood spray across the snow behind him, but the deer did not drop. Instead it whirled and ran down the hill, hard and strong.

I wondered if Matthew could ever finish anything gracefully.

We had to track it.

The snow was deep and slushy. There was little if any blood trail to follow, and the big buck's tracks merged with hundreds of others: the carnival of the rut. We stood there in the hissing, steady rain, breathing our own milky vapors.

"Fuck," Matthew said. He looked down toward the river in the direction the buck had run. He dropped his pack in the snow. The bloody "Y" on his chest was the same as the one on his back; the two together were like the delicate, perfect, world-shaped markings on the wings of some obscure tropical butterfly. I dropped my pack as well. A blood trail was beginning to form on my own back and chest.

Not to be wearing a pack after having carried one for so long gave us a feeling like flight; as if, suddenly, we could have gone for another seventy-five miles. We rested a moment, then donned our packs again. The rain and slush continued to beat down on us. We kept stopping to rest, ass-whipped. We began lighting trees again—tree after tree, following the wounded buck's tracks.

A drop of blood here; a loose hair there.

We found the buck down at the river, in a backwater slough, thrashing around in six feet of water, having broken through a skin of thawing ice as he tried to cross. We watched him for a moment as he swam in circles with only his head and the tower of antlers above the water. He was choking on his blood, coughing sprays of it across the water with each exhalation, and swallowing blood with each breath—the bullet had missed an artery, but severed a vessel—and his face was a red mask of blood.

He glared at us as he swam—a red king, defiant. It was a strange sight, those giant antlers going around and around in the small pond—like some new creature being born into the world. Matthew raised his rifle, waited for the deer to swim back around, closer to the edge of the shore.

The deer continued to watch us as it swam—head held high, drowning in

We got it out and went and got the elk and loaded it, part by part, into the canoe, until the canoe was low in the water. Dusk was coming on again and we could see a few lights across the river, the lights of town. We had been gone only two weeks but it felt like a century.

blood. Matthew shot it in the neck again, breaking it this time, and the deer stopped swimming. The antlers sank.

We sat and stared at it for a long time—watching it motionless through the refraction of water—as if expecting it to come back to life.

Another buck, following the trail of the giant's hock musk, appeared on the other side of the pond, lowered its head, trying to decipher the cone of scent that had drifted its way.

We travelled upriver to where Matthew had left the canoe. It was under a shell of snow. We got it out and went and got the elk and loaded it, part by part, into the canoe, until the canoe was low in the water. Dusk was coming on again and we could see a few lights across the river, the lights of town. We had been gone only two weeks but it felt like a century.

I stayed behind while Matthew made two crossings with the meat; then he came back for me. The rain had stopped and the sky was clearing and Matthew said we had to get the deer out now as the pond would freeze thick if we waited until the next day.

We waded out into the pond together. The water was slightly warmer than the air. Under water the deer was light, and we were able to muscle him awkwardly up to the shore. Then we dragged him over to the canoe—gutted him quickly—loaded him, and set out across one more time, riding lower than ever. Freezing seemed to be a more imminent danger than drowning, but we reached the other shore, sledded the canoe up onto the gravel, and finally we quit; abandoned the meat, hundreds of pounds of it, only a short distance from home, and ran stumbling and falling up the hill toward town.

Lights were on in the bar. We went straight in and lay down next to the big woodstove, shivering and in pain. The bartenders, Artie and Charlie, came over with blankets and hides and began helping us out of our wet clothes and wrapping the hides around us. They started heating water on the stove for baths and making hot tea for us to drink; it was the first fluid we'd had in days that was neither snow nor cold creek water, and the heat of it made us vomit the second the hot tea hit our stomachs. Artie looked at the meat we had spit up and said, "They got an elk."

STORY NOTES & BIOGRAPHICAL SUMMARIES

"The Black Cat"

First published in the August 19, 1843, edition of the *Saturday Evening Post* (then known as the *United States Saturday Post*), "The Black Cat" is one of Edgar Allan Poe's most horrific tales. Poe's decision to tell the tale from the vantage point of a murderer was unique in his day, and it brought a new perspective to storytelling, as readers could never be sure if the narrator could be trusted. Over the years, some critics have equated the first-person narrator with Poe, insisting that he wrote this story to express his own violent nature when under the influence of alcohol. Other critics, however, maintain that the narrator is simply Poe's skillful and systematic portrayal of one character's descent into madness.

"The Black Cat" was greeted with literary acclaim when it was first published in the United States. By the mid-1840s, it had been published in a Paris newspaper as well. Soon, it was discovered by French poet and critic Charles Baudelaire, who offered his own translation of the story and helped to bring Poe to the forefront of the literary scene in France.

About the Author

Born in Boston, Massachusetts, in 1809, Edgar Allan Poe was orphaned at the age of two and was raised by a prosperous merchant family. After spending less than a year at the University of Virginia, Poe published his first book of poetry before joining the army for a brief time. He then focused on writing, producing numerous short stories, poems, and literary reviews. In 1845, he published the poem "The Raven," which elevated him to a new level of fame, even as alcohol abuse and depression left him mentally unstable. In October 1849, Poe was found lying in a street, in a coma. Four days later, he died, leaving behind an indelible influence on the literary world, in which his dark and mysterious short stories laid the foundations for the modern detective tale.

"The Celebrated Jumping Frog of Calaveras County"

Based on a folktale told in the mining camps of the American West, "The Celebrated Jumping Frog of Calaveras County" was first published as "Jim Smiley and His Jumping Frog" in New York's *Saturday Press* in 1865. With its sharply drawn characters and humorous storyline about a trickster who gets tricked, the tall tale soon brought fame to its author, Mark Twain, who, at that time, was working as a journalist and miner in California's gold country.

Twain first heard the tale of the jumping frog in a barroom. He retold the story with two contrasting characters: the formal, gentlemanly narrator and Simon Wheeler, the backwoods bumpkin who gets the best of the narrator as he relates the far-fetched story of Jim Smiley. Although Twain's piece was not deemed "literary" by the standards of the day, his masterful re-creation of the American vernacular—the everyday speech of ordinary people—won it wide acclaim. In fact, Twain's contemporary James Russell Lowell called this story "the finest piece of humorous writing ever produced in America," a sentiment that Twain adopted as his own.

About the Author

Mark Twain was born in 1835 in Missouri as Samuel Langhorne Clemens. He spent his boyhood years along the Mississippi River and later served as a printer's apprentice and a steamboat pilot on the Mississippi. In 1862, he began his writing career as a reporter in Nevada, assuming the pen name "Mark Twain." During his lifetime, Twain wrote more than 30 books and hundreds of short stories and essays, publishing his masterpiece, *Adventures of Huckleberry Finn*, in 1884. By the time of his death in 1910, Twain had gained worldwide fame. His works, which depicted American life with both humor and criticism, had a profound influence on such great American authors as William Faulkner, who called him "the father of American literature."

"An Occurrence at Owl Creek Bridge"

Inspired by haunting memories of Ambrose Bierce's experiences in the Civil War, "An Occurrence at Owl Creek Bridge" took its name from a location where the author had fought as a volunteer for the Union army. The story was first published in the July 13, 1890, edition of the *San Francisco Examiner* and was included the next year as part of Bierce's first short story collection, *Tales of Soldiers and Civilians*. Reviewers across America and in England offered high praise for the stories in the collection, and after reading the book, Bierce's friend and former editor James Watkins assured the author that it was destined to "become a classic."

Over the years, "An Occurrence at Owl Creek Bridge" has received more critical attention than any of Bierce's other works of fiction and has drawn praise for its careful manipulation of time, crisp style, and rich irony. Although some scholars have criticized Bierce for deceiving his readers into thinking that the story's protagonist, Peyton Farquhar, has survived his hanging, most feel that the surprise ending is part of what makes this piece Bierce's most resonating short story.

About the Author

Born in Ohio in 1842, Ambrose Bierce experienced an unhappy childhood marked by poverty. At the age of 15, he left home, becoming a printer's apprentice before joining the Union army at the start of the Civil War in 1861. After the war, Bierce moved to San Francisco, where he began a career in journalism, eventually earning the nickname "Bitter Bierce" for his scathing articles. During his lifetime, Bierce published a number of short stories, many of which examined the futility of war. In 1881, he began publishing excerpts of *The Devil's Dictionary*, a collection of witty, sarcastic word definitions. In 1913, at the age of 71, the restless Bierce traveled as a war observer to Mexico, where he disappeared, never to be found.

"The Open Boat"

"The Open Boat" was first published in *Scribner's Magazine* in June 1897 and appeared as part of the collection *The Open Boat and Other Stories* the next year. It is one of two accounts Stephen Crane wrote of the January 1897 sinking of the SS *Commodore*, a ship carrying illegal guns to rebels in Cuba. Crane was aboard the ship on his way to report on the Cubans' struggle for independence from Spain when the vessel went down. His other account of the event was a newspaper article titled "Stephen Crane's Own Story," which described the actual sinking of the *Commodore*.

Although "The Open Boat" details the 30 hours Crane (the correspondent in the story) and his companions spent in the waters off the Florida coast, it is not simply a factual narrative. Through the story's powerful descriptions and focus on character, Crane makes larger statements about the brotherhood of men at sea and the indifference of nature to man's plight. Although the story was initially received as trivial, it is today recognized as a masterpiece of world literature.

About the Author

Born in Newark, New Jersey, in 1871, Stephen Crane was a sickly but bright child. He briefly attended college but most often skipped classes. In 1891, he dropped out and moved to New York City, where he lived in the slums, gathering information for his first novel, *Maggie: A Girl of the Streets* (1893). In 1895, Crane published the internationally acclaimed novel *The Red Badge of Courage.* Over the next five years, he continued to turn out short stories, poems, and newspaper pieces to fund his lavish home and extravagant parties. He also traveled to Greece and Cuba as a war correspondent. His travels affected his health, however, and in 1900, at the age of 28, Crane died of tuberculosis.

"Paul's Case"

First published in Willa Cather's debut short story collection, *The Troll Garden*, in 1905, and printed in *McClure's Magazine* that same year, "Paul's Case" was one of the few stories that the author allowed to be anthologized during her lifetime. Cather said that she based the story's protagonist, Paul, on a student to whom she had once taught Latin. She also incorporated her own love of Pittsburgh's Carnegie Hall and the cultural resources of New York City into her portrayal of the character.

Although "Paul's Case" received better reviews than most of the other pieces in *The Troll Garden*, the story did not win much critical acclaim when it was first published. Over the years, however, revised versions of the story appeared in other collections of Cather's short fiction, including 1920's *Youth and the Bright Medusa*. Today, it has become one of Cather's best-known stories, praised for its narrative skill as well as for the vivid portrait it paints of a young man swept up in his desire for the outward finery—the "mere stage properties"—of the artistic life he feels he was meant to lead.

About the Author

Willa Cather was born in Virginia in 1873 but moved to Nebraska with her family at the age of nine. After attending the University of Nebraska, she moved east, first to Pittsburgh, then to New York City. She spent time as a teacher and magazine editor while also writing poetry and short stories. Her first poetry collection, *April Twilights*, was published in 1903, and two years later, *The Troll Garden* appeared. In 1912, Cather's first novel, *Alexander's Bridge*, was published, and 11 years later, her novel *One of Ours* (1922) was awarded a Pulitzer Prize. By the time of her death in 1947, Cather had published a dozen novels, many of which portray the lives of ordinary men and women on America's Great Plains.

"Hills Like White Elephants"

Written during Ernest Hemingway's honeymoon with his second wife, "Hills Like White Elephants" was first published in the experimental Parisian magazine *transition* in August 1927 and appeared later that year in Hemingway's short story collection *Men Without Women*. The collection received mixed critical reviews, with writer Virginia Woolf calling Hemingway's stories "a little dry and sterile," while reviewer Dorothy Parker praised Hemingway for his ability to keep "words to their short path." Despite the disagreement among critics, the book sold 15,000 copies in 3 months—an overwhelming success for a short story collection.

Noted for his tight, direct prose, Hemingway pushed the boundaries of style with "Hills Like White Elephants" by telling it almost entirely through dialogue. To make the story even more complex, he never once refers explicitly to the subject of the conversation—whether or not the woman in the story should have an abortion. The lack of exposition in this story has caused it—and especially its ambiguous ending—to be widely debated over the years, and critics continue to search for a biographical basis for the story.

About the Author

Born in Illinois in 1899, Ernest Hemingway showed an early interest in writing. After graduating from high school in 1917, he worked briefly as a reporter before serving as an ambulance driver in World War I. After the war, Hemingway settled in Paris, where he joined other American authors in forging a new literary style characterized by spare, reportorial prose. Hemingway published his first book, *Three Stories and Ten Poems*, in 1923, and in 1929, the World War I novel *A Farewell to Arms* brought him widespread fame. In 1954, Hemingway's achievements as a novelist and short story writer were recognized with the Nobel Prize in Literature, which he was awarded for his "mastery of the art of modern narration." Seven years later, the oft-depressed author committed suicide.

"The Jilting of Granny Weatherall"

Written in 1928, "The Jilting of Granny Weatherall" was first published in the Parisian magazine *transition* in 1929. It appeared in Katherine Anne Porter's first short story collection, *Flowering Judas and Other Stories*, the next year. Although only 600 copies of the collection were printed, the critical acclaim that followed the book's publication placed Porter among America's literary elite.

With its unique stream-of-consciousness narration, "The Jilting of Granny Weatherall" has long been praised for its ability to deliver a "felt experience," as readers are taken inside the mind of Granny Weatherall during her final hours on Earth. Porter said that she based the character of Granny on several grandmother figures, including her own grandmother, with whom she lived as a child. The death of her grandmother when Porter was 11 traumatized the young girl, and this story was her vision of the shock her grandmother must have felt at confronting death. Porter may also have drawn on her own near-death experience for this story; she almost died of influenza in 1918 and saw what she called "the happy vision just before death."

About the Author

Katherine Anne Porter was born in Texas in 1890. Her mother died when Porter was two, and her father provided the girl with only one year of formal education. Married at the age of 16, Porter divorced her abusive husband at 25 and found work as an actress before becoming a reporter. In 1920, Porter traveled to Mexico, where she began writing short stories, publishing her first in 1922. Nine years later, Porter traveled to Europe, where she gathered much of the information that would later appear in her only novel, *Ship of Fools* (1962). A relentless perfectionist renowned for her original storylines and precise style, Porter won the Pulitzer Prize for Fiction in 1966. She died in 1980.

"The Chrysanthemums"

Set in California's Salinas Valley, where author John Steinbeck lived as a boy, "The Chrysanthemums" was first published in the October 1937 issue of *Harper's Magazine* and appeared the next year in Steinbeck's short story collection *The Long Valley*. With a main character some critics believe was based on Steinbeck's first wife, who, like Elisa Allen, wore "masculine clothes" and was "handsome rather than pretty," the story decries the manipulation of people's dreams for selfish gain.

Steinbeck penned "The Chrysanthemums" in early 1934, and upon completing it, he wrote a friend: "It is entirely different and is designed to strike without the reader's knowledge. I mean he reads it casually and after it is finished feels that something profound has happened to him although he does not know what nor how." Steinbeck was right in thinking that the story would have an impact on readers; it received the highest praise of all his short stories. Critic Brian Barbour proclaimed it Steinbeck's "most artistically successful story," while poet Mordecai Marcus ranked it as "one of the world's great short stories."

About the Author

Born into a middle-class California family in 1902, John Steinbeck was a shy child. He enrolled in Stanford University in 1919 but attended only sporadically and never earned a degree. In 1925, Steinbeck moved to New York, where he struggled as a freelance writer before returning to California. Steinbeck's early fiction went largely unnoticed until the 1935 publication of *Tortilla Flat* gained him sudden popularity. Soon, Steinbeck had become the foremost novelist of the Great Depression era, publishing his masterpiece, *The Grapes of Wrath*, in 1939. By the time he died in 1968, Steinbeck had become one of only five American writers to receive the Nobel Prize in Literature, which he was awarded "for his realistic as well as imaginative writings, distinguished by . . . a keen social perception."

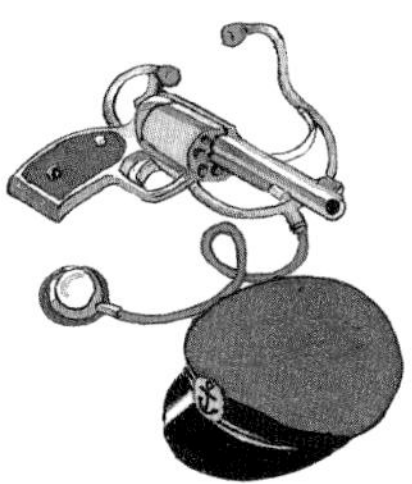

"The Secret Life of Walter Mitty"

When James Thurber's story "The Secret Life of Walter Mitty" was first published in the March 18, 1939, edition of *The New Yorker*, it met with immediate success. People everywhere could identify with the story's daydreaming hero, Walter Mitty, and Thurber said that some readers even went so far as to write and ask "how I had got to know them so well." Years later, Thurber claimed that Mitty was based on "every other man I have ever known," although friends said that the character resembled Thurber's father and brother.

Reprinted in Thurber's 1942 anthology *My World—And Welcome to It* and in *Reader's Digest* in 1943, "The Secret Life of Walter Mitty" was so popular that its terminology was soon appearing in people's everyday language. During World War II, fighter pilots often identified themselves on the radio as "Walter Mitty," and some troops used the story's term "ta-pocketa-pocketa" as a password. The British medical magazine *The Lancet* even termed extravagant daydreaming the "Walter Mitty Syndrome." Such cultural offshoots helped to ensure the story's place as one of the best-known American short stories of all time.

About the Author

Born in Ohio in 1894, James Thurber lost his left eye in an accident at the age of seven. He attended Ohio State University but left in 1918 to serve as a code clerk in Paris following World War I. Afterward, Thurber worked as a reporter before joining the staff of *The New Yorker* in 1927. Both a writer and a cartoonist, Thurber wrote and drew prolifically. Although progressing blindness eventually put an end to his drawing, Thurber continued to write, and by the time of his death in 1961, he was known as one of the greatest American humorists of the 20th century, acclaimed for what author T. S. Eliot called "a form of humor which is also a way of saying something serious."

"In the Twilight"

First published in the November 1941 issue of *Mademoiselle* and later reprinted in the short story collection *The Women on the Wall* (1950), "In the Twilight" grew out of Wallace Stegner's boyhood experiences in Saskatchewan, Canada. Although Stegner didn't necessarily share his protagonist's aversion to blood (part of his chores included beheading chickens), he could relate to the character's feelings of isolation. A small and sickly child, Stegner was often ignored by his father in favor of his stronger older brother, and he felt the failure of never living up to the "manly" ideal of the frontier, just as his protagonist Bruce does.

"In the Twilight" was one of several short stories in *The Women on the Wall* to feature Bruce, who was also the main character of Stegner's novel *The Big Rock Candy Mountain* (1943), into which many of the stories from *The Women on the Wall* were incorporated. Although Stegner initially intended for "In the Twilight" to be part of the novel, it was ultimately left out. But that has done nothing to lessen its power as one of Stegner's most compelling short stories.

About the Author

Wallace Stegner was born in Iowa in 1909 and spent his childhood in Saskatchewan and the American West. After attending the universities of Utah and Iowa, Stegner began a teaching career that included stints at both universities, as well as at Harvard, Wisconsin, and Stanford. He also wrote prolifically, publishing 31 books that ranged from biographies and histories to short story collections and novels, including the Pulitzer Prize-winning novel *Angle of Repose* (1971). Many of Stegner's works are filled with reverence for the American landscape, and the author often translated his love of nature into environmental activism. Stegner was instrumental in helping to pass the 1964 Wilderness Act, and he remained an important part of the conservation movement until his death in 1993.

"The Lottery"

Based on an idea that came to her as she pushed her daughter's stroller home from the grocery store one morning, "The Lottery" took author Shirley Jackson less than two hours to write, but the fame it brought her lasted more than a lifetime. From the moment the story was published in the June 26, 1948, issue of *The New Yorker*, it set off a sensation. Many readers were shocked and horrified by the story's violent, surprise ending and its portrayal of evil in a seemingly normal town, and hundreds of people sent angry letters to Jackson and to the magazine.

Jackson was mystified by the response the story garnered, and although she never explained exactly how she intended readers to interpret the story, she eventually wrote that her intent in "The Lottery" was to show readers "the pointless violence and general inhumanity in their own lives." Throughout her life, "The Lottery" remained Jackson's best-known work, a fact she frankly acknowledged: "I have been assured . . . , that if it had been the only story I ever wrote . . . , there would be people who would not forget my name."

About the Author

Shirley Jackson was born in San Francisco, California, in 1916 and moved to Rochester, New York, as a teenager. Interested in writing from the time she was a child, Jackson attended the University of Rochester and Syracuse University, where she wrote a number of pieces for campus publications. In 1943, Jackson began publishing short stories in *The New Yorker*, and her first novel, *The Road through the Wall*, was released in 1948. Eleven years later, she published *The Haunting of Hill House*, which is counted among the greatest horror stories of all time. By the time of her death in 1965, Jackson's works—among them short stories, novels, magazine articles, and children's books, some humorous and others horrific—had achieved wide popularity and critical acclaim.

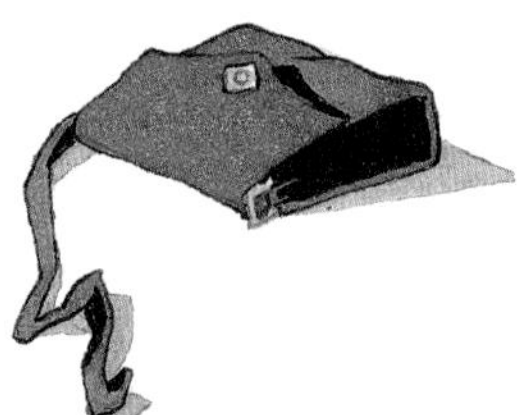

"Thank You, M'am"

Written in the spring of 1954, "Thank You, M'am" was first published on May 11, 1957, as part of Langston Hughes's weekly column in the influential black newspaper *The Chicago Defender*. It was soon reprinted in *The Langston Hughes Reader* (1958) and later also appeared in Hughes's short story collection *Something in Common and Other Stories* (1963). Hughes claimed that this story "came from a cousin's wife in Chicago having her purse snatched. But [the] rest is invention. She didn't behave so."

This brief, humorous, socially uplifting narrative represented a marked change for Hughes, whose short stories typically expressed outrage over racism. In this story, however, race is not an issue; although both characters are black, they are not in a situation unique to blacks, and their race has little to do with the story. Instead, it is their character that matters, and Hughes saw their character as that of "a good woman and a bad teenager forgiven." Although "Thank You, M'am" received little critical attention when it was first published, it soon became popular with readers, and it remains so today.

About the Author

Born in Missouri in 1902, Langston Hughes published his first poems while still in high school. After graduating, Hughes spent time in New York City, Europe, and Africa before moving to Washington, D.C., where he worked as a busboy until he was "discovered" by American poet Vachel Lindsay in 1925. The next year, he published his first book, a collection of poetry called *The Weary Blues*, and began to attend Lincoln University in Pennsylvania, from which he graduated in 1929. A prolific writer, Hughes produced more than 60 books, among them novels, short story collections, and poetry anthologies. By the time of his death in 1967, he was known as one of the leading voices of black culture in 20th-century America.

"Icarus Montgolfier Wright"

First published in the May 1956 issue of *The Magazine of Fantasy and Science Fiction*, "Icarus Montgolfier Wright" was later reprinted in Ray Bradbury's short story collection *A Medicine for Melancholy* (1959). It also appeared in *Twice 22* (1966) and *S Is for Space* (1966). Although the latter collection was intended for young readers, it was received well among all age groups, as the wonder of space and space travel sparked the imagination of people across the country during the 1960s. Soon, stories such as "Icarus Montgolfier Wright" and other space adventures had made Bradbury the unofficial spokesperson of the space age. In 1962, the story inspired an animated film, which received a 1963 Academy Award nomination for best cartoon short subject.

"Icarus Montgolfier Wright" has been referred to as "virtually a prose poem" for its unique, dreamlike rendering of the history of flight, from the waxen wings of the mythological Icarus to the launch of the world's first rocket. Although people have been to the moon and back since the publication of this story, the dream of flight continues to thrill readers half a century later.

About the Author

Born in Waukegan, Illinois, in 1920, Ray Bradbury moved with his family to Los Angeles in 1934. He began writing when he was 12 and published his first short story at 20. His first book, a short story collection called *Dark Carnival*, was published in 1947, and his famous novel *Fahrenheit 451* appeared in 1953. Although best known for his science fiction, Bradbury has also written horror, mystery, and fantasy stories. His habit of writing every day has produced more than 500 published works, among them short stories, novels, poems, and plays. In 2004, Bradbury was honored with the National Medal of Arts in recognition of "his incomparable contributions to American fiction as one of its great storytellers who . . . has illuminated the human condition."

"A & P"

First published in the July 22, 1961, edition of *The New Yorker* and reprinted in the collection *Pigeon Feathers and Other Stories* in 1962, "A & P" is John Updike's most famous short story. A brief piece with little action, "A & P" nevertheless paints a masterful picture of Sammy, the narrator, who Updike allows to relate his tale in the teenage vernacular, or everyday speech, of the 1960s. In order to draw readers into the story, Updike wrote parts of the narrative in the present tense, a technique that was rare at the time but that serves to increase the story's immediacy.

Initial reviews for "A & P" and the other stories in *Pigeon Feathers* were mixed. While some reviewers called the stories trivial, critic Arthur Mizener proclaimed that they were "a demonstration of how the most gifted writer of his generation is coming to maturity." Over the years, critics have also disagreed over whether Sammy is heroic, irresponsible, or simply naïve, but such disagreements haven't stopped readers from identifying with the narrator, which may help to explain the story's enduring popularity.

About the Author

Born in Pennsylvania in 1932, John Updike wrote his first short story when he was eight years old. After graduating from Harvard in 1954, Updike studied art in England for a year before returning to the United States, where he joined the staff of *The New Yorker* and earned the nickname "The Brilliant Young Writer." In 1957, Updike left *The New Yorker*, and the next year, he published his first book, a poetry collection called *The Carpeted Hen and Other Tame Creatures*. In the decades that followed, Updike became one of the most prolific contemporary American writers. He published numerous novels, short stories, poetry volumes, and essays, and his works, which are often set in suburban America, have met with widespread critical and popular success. He died in 2009 at age 76.

"Where Are You Going, Where Have You Been?"

Inspired by a *Life* magazine article about a murderer who killed three teenage girls in Arizona, Joyce Carol Oates's short story "Where Are You Going, Where Have You Been?" was first published in the fall 1966 issue of *Epoch* magazine and was later reprinted in her collection *The Wheel of Love* (1970). Although Oates read only part of the *Life* article because she didn't want "to be distracted by too much detail," she gleaned enough information about the murderer to incorporate his bizarre features—pancake makeup, dyed black hair, shoes stuffed with rags to make him taller—into the character of Arnold Friend.

Despite the fact that the girls in the real-life story were killed, Oates left the ending of her story unresolved. Over the years, this has led to much debate, with some critics insisting that Connie is eventually murdered and others arguing that the sequence with Arnold Friend is just a nightmare. No matter how the story is interpreted, however, the terror it produces is real, and it has made "Where Are You Going, Where Have You Been?" one of Oates's most famous works.

About the Author

Joyce Carol Oates was born into a middle-class New York family in 1938. She attended Syracuse University, publishing her first story in *Mademoiselle* magazine while still a student. After graduating in 1960, Oates earned a master of arts (MA) from the University of Wisconsin. Her first book, a short story collection called *By the North Gate*, was published in 1963. Since then, Oates has published more than 70 books, among them novels, plays, and collections of short stories, poems, and essays, and she continues to turn out new works nearly every year. Oates has also taught creative writing at Princeton University since 1978. Because her works often include elements of violence, Oates has come to be known as "The Dark Lady of American Letters."

"Everyday Use"

Often regarded as Alice Walker's best short story, "Everyday Use" was published in her 1973 collection *In Love & Trouble: Stories of Black Women*. Writing during a time in American history when African Americans were beginning to rediscover their African past, Walker used the story to emphasize the difference between a genuine understanding of heritage, as demonstrated by Maggie, and a superficial desire for the items that represent one's past simply because such items are suddenly fashionable. Although the story ends with Mama giving the quilts to Maggie, Walker apparently identified with Dee; she too had an African name—Wangero, the same name Dee takes.

With their genuine portrayal of the African American experience, "Everyday Use" and the other stories in *In Love & Trouble* received immediate acclaim. The stories were noted for their depiction of independent black women, which represented a dramatic shift from the prevailing image of the black woman as a submissive victim. Her focus on the lives of Mama, Dee, and Maggie allowed Walker to send a powerful message while at the same time achieving her own goal of revealing the "essential spirit of individual persons."

About the Author

Alice Walker was born into a poor, black Georgia family in 1944. At the age of eight, she was accidentally blinded in one eye, and the resulting disfigurement led her to retreat into the world of literature. Walker attended Spelman College in Georgia and Sarah Lawrence College in New York, graduating in 1965 and moving to Mississippi, where she was active in the civil rights movement. Her first book, a collection of poetry titled *Once*, was published in 1968. Since then, Walker has written numerous short stories, essays, and novels, including the Pulitzer Prize-winning *The Color Purple* (1982). A self-described "womanist," or black feminist, Walker's works often focus on the black woman's struggle to escape her position as what Walker once termed "the mule of the world."

"Elk"

First published in the December 1, 1997, edition of *The New Yorker*, the short story "Elk" is one of several in which Rick Bass features the majestic Yaak Valley of northwestern Montana. In fact, the story grew out of Bass's own experiences living and hunting in this remote region. A longtime nature lover, Bass moved to the valley in 1987 and spent his first years there observing the wildlife, including elk, to get the "feel and taste of the seasons," which he infused into his fiction.

Like most of Bass's short stories, "Elk" focuses on the wild world at its core, emphasizing the relationship between man and nature. It also paints a picture of human relationships, as Matthew guides the narrator out of the forest and, in the process, allows the narrator to learn about the essence of the wild—and about himself. His incredible descriptions of nature through stories such as this have earned Bass a reputation as a writer uniquely in tune with the wild, and the *Chicago Tribune* has complimented his stories as depicting "every hallmark of the natural."

About the Author

Born in Texas in 1958, Rick Bass developed an early love of the outdoors. After earning a degree in geology from Utah State University in 1979, he worked as a petroleum geologist in Mississippi for nearly a decade. In 1987, Bass and his wife moved to Montana, where he devoted himself to writing both fiction and nonfiction while also taking an active role in the movement to preserve some of America's wildest lands. Bass published his first short story collection, *The Watch*, in 1989 and his first novel, *Where the Sea Used to Be*, in 1998. Known for their magical realism and natural settings, Bass's short stories have been widely acclaimed, earning him comparisons to some of America's greatest authors, including Mark Twain and Ernest Hemingway.

PERMISSIONS

"Hills Like White Elephants" reprinted with permission of Scribner, an imprint of Simon & Schuster Adult Publishing Group, from *The Short Stories of Ernest Hemingway*. Copyright © 1927 by Charles Scribner's Sons. Copyright renewed 1955 by Ernest Hemingway.

"The Jilting of Granny Weatherall" from *Flowering Judas and Other Stories*, copyright © 1930 and renewed 1958 by Katherine Anne Porter, reprinted by permission of Harcourt, Inc.

"The Chrysanthemums," copyright © 1937, renewed © 1965 by John Steinbeck, from *The Long Valley* by John Steinbeck. Used by permission of Viking Penguin, a division of Penguin Group (USA) Inc.

"The Secret Life of Walter Mitty," copyright © 1942 by James Thurber. Copyright renewed 1970 by Rosemary A. Thurber. Reprinted by arrangement with Rosemary A. Thurber and The Barbara Hogenson Agency, Inc. All rights reserved.

"In the Twilight" from *The Collected Stories of Wallace Stegner* by Wallace Stegner, copyright © 1990 by Wallace Stegner. Used by permission of Random House, Inc.

"The Lottery" from *The Lottery* by Shirley Jackson. Copyright © 1948, 1949 by Shirley Jackson. Copyright renewed 1976, 1977 by Laurence Hyman, Barry Hyman, Mrs. Sarah Webster and Mrs. Joanne Schnurer. Reprinted by permission of Farrar, Straus and Giroux, LLC.

"Thank You, M'am" from *Short Stories* by Langston Hughes. Copyright © 1996 by Ramona Bass and Arnold Rampersad. Reprinted by permission of Hill and Wang, a division of Farrar, Straus and Giroux, LLC.

"Icarus Montgolfier Wright" reprinted by permission of Don Congdon Associates, Inc. Copyright © 1956, renewed 1984 by Ray Bradbury.

"A & P" from *Pigeon Feathers and Other Stories* by John Updike, copyright © 1962 and renewed 1990 by John Updike. Used by permission of Alfred A. Knopf, a division of Random House, Inc.

"Where Are You Going, Where Have You Been?" copyright © 1970 *Ontario Review*. Reprinted by permission of John Hawkins & Associates, Inc.

"Everyday Use" from *In Love & Trouble: Stories of Black Women*, copyright © 1973 by Alice Walker. Reprinted by permission of Harcourt, Inc.

"Elk" by Rick Bass. Originally published in *The New Yorker*, December 1997. Copyright © Rick Bass. Reprinted by permission of the author.

Special thanks to Damon White,
instructor in English at The Hotchkiss School,
for his help in selecting these stories.

Published in 2010 by Creative Editions
P.O. Box 227, Mankato, MN 56002 USA
Creative Editions is an imprint of The Creative Company.
Edited by Aaron Frisch
Designed by Rita Marshall
Text on pages 250–269 by Valerie Bodden

Printed by RR Donnelley in China
Library of Congress Cataloging-in-Publication Data
The creative collection of American short stories / illustrated by Yan Nascimbene.
ISBN 978-1-56846-202-8
1. Short stories, American. I. Nascimbene, Yan, ill. II. Series.
PS648.S5C75 2009
813'.0108—dc22 2008041479
CPSIA: 120109 PO1090

First Edition
2 4 6 8 9 7 5 3 1

QUICK FROM SCRATCH

CHICKEN

AND OTHER BIRDS

Arroz con Pollo, page 143

QUICK FROM SCRATCH

CHICKEN

AND OTHER BIRDS

American Express Publishing Corporation
New York

Editor in Chief: Judith Hill
Assistant Editors: Susan Lantzius and Laura Byrne Russell
Managing Editor: Terri Mauro
Copy Editor: Barbara A. Mateer
Wine Editor: Richard Marmet
Art Director: Nina Scerbo
Art Assistant: Leslie Andersen
Photographer: Melanie Acevedo
Food Stylist: Roscoe Betsill
Prop Stylist: Denise Canter
Illustrator: Karen Scerbo
Production Manager: Yvette Williams-Braxton

Vice President, Books and Information Services: John Stoops
Marketing Director: David Geller
Marketing/Promotion Manager: Roni Stein
Operations Manager: Doreen Camardi

Recipes Pictured on Cover: (Front) Sautéed Chicken Breasts with Fennel and Rosemary, page 21
(Back) Roast Chicken with Cranberry Apple Raisin Chutney, page 53;
Inset top: Chicken and Zucchini Couscous, page 137;
Inset bottom: Pecan-Crusted Chicken with Mustard Sauce, page 19
Page 6: *Kitchen photo:* Bill Bettencourt; *Portraits:* Christopher Dinerman

AMERICAN EXPRESS PUBLISHING CORPORATION

LIBRARY OF CONGRESS CATALOGING-IN-PUBLICATION DATA
Quick from scratch. Chicken and Other Birds.
p. cm.
Includes index.
ISBN 0-916103-35-8
1. Cookery (Chicken) 2. Quick and easy cookery. I. Food & wine (New York, N.Y.)
TX750.5.C4Q53 1997
641.6'65—dc21 96-29854
CIP

Published by American Express Publishing Corporation
1120 Avenue of the Americas, New York, New York 10036

Manufactured in the United States of America

CONTENTS

RECIPES PICTURED ABOVE: (*left to right*) pages 115, 61, 159

Perfecting a chicken dish in the FOOD & WINE Books test kitchen

Susan Lantzius trained at La Varenne École de Cuisine in Paris, worked as a chef in Portugal for a year, and then headed to New York City. There she made her mark first as head decorator at the well-known Sant Ambroeus pastry shop and next as a pastry chef, working at such top restaurants as San Domenico and Maxim's. In 1993, she turned her talents to recipe development and editorial work for FOOD & WINE Books.

Judith Hill is the editor in chief of FOOD & WINE Books, a division of American Express Publishing. Previously she was editor in chief of COOK'S Magazine, director of publications for La Varenne École de Cuisine in Paris, from which she earned a Grand Diplôme, and an English instructor for the University of Maryland International Division in Germany. Her book credits include editing cookbooks for Fredy Girardet, Jane Grigson, Michel Guérard, and Anne Willan.

Laura Byrne Russell earned a bachelor's degree in finance and worked in stock and bond sales for a few years before deciding that food is more fun. She went back to school, this time to The Culinary School at Kendall College in Illinois. After gaining experience in professional kitchens in Chicago and New York City, she came to FOOD & WINE Books, where she works as both an editor and a recipe developer.

INTRODUCTION

The amenable chicken keeps company equally well with subtle or strong ingredients; it takes on any accent—be it Tuscan, Provençal, Mexican, or Thai—with effortless facility; and it changes character from plain to posh with ease. Because of its amazing adaptability, chicken has inspired cooks the world over, including, of course, those in the FOOD & WINE Books test kitchen. Susan Lantzius and Laura Russell, our editor/cooks, have perfected Rustic Garlic Chicken (page 117), Chicken Provençale (page 35), Chicken Burritos with Black-Bean Salsa and Pepper Jack (page 163), and Chicken Pad Thai (page 133), as well as dishes influenced by a myriad of other regions, and some purely inventive combinations.

As we conceived, developed, tested, and tasted the recipes in this book, whether we were making simple Spicy Chicken Chili (page 105) or mellow, sophisticated Sautéed Chicken Breasts with Tarragon Cream Sauce (page 25), we kept repeating, "This is too easy. Chicken goes with everything." Susan and I, with our classic French training, consider chicken the veal of today, excellent just sautéed with a sprinkling of salt, pepper, and herbs to bring out its own taste and also ideal as a background for easy sauces with complex or bold flavorings. Laura dubbed the hardworking bird *cooperative chicken*. We hope that you'll find the name apt as you try the imaginative ideas here and that you'll never again think of chicken as boring.

Very nearly as flexible and available as chicken are turkey and Cornish hens. So we considered them appropriate for a book dedicated to quick yet delectable fare for busy weeknights (though many of our recipes double as lifesavers for weekend entertaining). Hence, you'll find the likes of Turkey Breast with Mustard Sage Crumbs (page 59), Turkey with Walnut Parmesan Sauce (page 47), Cornish Hens with Fruit, Walnuts, and Honey Apple Glaze (page 85), and Grilled Cornish Hens with Sun-Dried-Tomato Pesto (page 93).

We developed each of these recipes with the thought that it should be a solid main dish, needing, if anything, only the addition of a totally no-fuss accompaniment, such as a salad or bread. We included other just-as-fast menu suggestions and also suggestions for varying the ingredients according to what you can find readily in the supermarket or already in your cupboard. And, as always in the books of this series, you'll find a recommendation from Richard Marmet, president of Best Cellars, for an inexpensive everyday wine to complement each meal.

Judith Hill
Editor in Chief
FOOD & WINE Books

Before You Begin

You'll find test-kitchen tips and ideas for ingredient substitutions presented with the individual recipes throughout the book. In this opening section, we've gathered information and tips that apply to all, or at least a substantial number, of the recipes. These are the facts and opinions that we'd like you to know before you use, and to keep in mind while you use, the recipes. We hope you'll read these pages prior to cooking from the book for the first time—and have kept the section short so that you can do so with ease. The culinary information here will help make your cooking quicker, simpler, and even tastier.

RECIPES PICTURED OPPOSITE: (*top*) pages 35, 133, 25; (*center*) pages 153, 58, 143; (*bottom*) pages 167, 111, 169

Substituting Parts—or Birds

If you like white meat and the recipe calls for dark (or vice versa), or if you want to interchange Cornish hens and chicken, by all means do so. Simply increase or decrease cooking time according to the times given in our chart. These guidelines are based on chickens that weigh 3 to 3½ pounds and Cornish hens of about 1¼ pounds. The cooking times are necessarily approximate, but they'll get you close to the mark.

	INSTEAD OF	USE	COOKING METHOD	COOKING TIME
Legs				
	4 whole bone-in legs	4 bone-in individual breasts	Roast, sauté, grill Simmer	5 min. less 10 min. less
	8 bone-in thighs or drumsticks	4 bone-in individual breasts	Roast, sauté, grill Simmer	4 min. less 8 min. less
	4 boneless, skinless thighs	4 boneless, skinless breasts	Sauté, grill Simmer	4 min. less 5 min. less
	Cut-up boneless, skinless thighs	Cut-up boneless, skinless breasts	All methods	1 to 2 min. less
Breasts				
	4 bone-in individual breasts	4 whole bone-in legs	Roast, sauté, grill Simmer	5 min. more 10 min. more
	4 bone-in individual breasts	8 bone-in thighs or drumsticks	Roast, sauté, grill Simmer	4 min. more 8 min. more
	4 boneless, skinless breasts	4 boneless, skinless thighs	Sauté, grill Simmer	4 min. more 5 min. more
	Cut-up boneless, skinless breasts	Cut-up boneless, skinless thighs	All methods	1 to 2 min. more

Wings			
2 pounds wings	4 bone-in individual breasts	Roast, sauté, grill	2 to 5 min. more
2 pounds wings	8 thighs or drumsticks	Roast, sauté, grill	5 to 10 min. more
Whole or Half Chicken			
1 chicken	2 Cornish hens	Roast	15 min. less
2 chicken halves	4 Cornish-hen halves	Grill	10 min. less
Cornish Hens			
2 Cornish hens	1 chicken	Roast	15 min. more
4 Cornish-hen halves	2 chicken halves	Grill	10 min. more
Turkey			
Turkey cutlets	Chicken cutlets	Sauté, grill	Same
Turkey sausage	Chicken sausage	Sauté, grill	Same
Ground turkey	Ground chicken	Sauté, grill	Same

Essential Ingredient Information

Broth, Chicken

We tested all of the recipes in this book using canned low-sodium chicken broth. You can almost always substitute regular for low-sodium broth; just cut back on the salt in the recipe. And if you keep homemade stock in your freezer, by all means feel free to use it. We aren't suggesting that it won't work as well, only that we know the dishes taste delicious even when made with canned broth.

Butter

Our recipes don't specify whether to use salted or unsalted butter. We generally use unsalted, but in these savory dishes, it really won't make a big difference which type you use.

Coconut Milk

Coconut milk is the traditional liquid used in many Thai and Indian curries. Make sure you buy *unsweetened* canned coconut milk, not cream of coconut, which is used primarily for piña coladas. Heavy cream can be substituted in many recipes.

Garlic

The size of garlic cloves varies tremendously. When we call for one minced or chopped clove, we expect you to get about three-quarters of a teaspoon.

Mustard

When we call for mustard, we mean Dijon or grainy. We never, ever mean yellow ballpark mustard.

Nuts

Our quick pantry wouldn't be complete without several kinds of nuts. Keep in mind that nuts have a high percentage of oil and can turn rancid quickly. We store ours in the freezer to keep them fresh.

Oil

Cooking oil in these recipes refers to readily available, reasonably priced nut, seed, or vegetable oil with a high smoking point, such as peanut, sunflower, canola, safflower, or corn oil. These can be heated to about 400° before they begin to smoke, break down, and develop an unpleasant flavor.

Olives

If your store doesn't sell olives from big, open barrels, opt for the kind in jars. The canned version gives you only the slightest hint of what a real olive might taste like.

Parsley

Many of our recipes call for chopped fresh parsley. The flat-leaf variety has a stronger flavor than the curly, and we use it most of the time, but unless the type is specified, you can use either.

Pepper

- There's nothing like fresh-ground pepper. If you've been using preground, buy a pepper mill, fill it, and give it a grind. You'll never look back.
- To measure your just-ground pepper more easily, become familiar with your own mill; each produces a different amount per turn. You'll probably find that ten to fifteen grinds produces one-quarter teaspoon of pepper, and then you can count on that forever after.

Sausages, Chicken and Turkey

While testing recipes for this book, we found tremendous differences in the quality and flavor of chicken and turkey sausages. Try various kinds to find your favorite.

Tomatoes, Canned

In some recipes, we call for "crushed tomatoes in thick puree." Depending on the brand, this mix of crushed tomatoes and tomato puree may be labeled crushed tomatoes with puree, with added puree, in tomato puree, thick style, or in thick puree. You can use any of these.

Wine, Dry White

Leftover wine is ideal for cooking. It seems a shame to open a fresh bottle for just a few spoonfuls. Another solution is to keep dry vermouth on hand. You can use whatever quantity is needed; the rest will keep indefinitely.

Zest

Citrus zest—the colored part of the peel, without any of the white pith—adds tremendous flavor to many a dish. Remove the zest from the fruit using either a grater or a zester. A zester is a small, inexpensive, and extremely handy tool. It has little holes that remove just the zest in fine ribbons. A zester is quick, easy to clean, and never scrapes your knuckles.

Faster, Better, Easier
TEST-KITCHEN TIPS

Defrosting chicken

We prefer to use fresh chicken, which always has juicier meat than frozen, but everybody freezes chicken at some time or another. When you do, remember that the method of defrosting affects the texture. We tested common methods on frozen chicken quarters.

- **Micowave:** *Quickest. Good quality.* We microwaved quartered chickens on the defrost setting for twenty-two minutes. When roasted, the meat wasn't quite as juicy as fresh but was still moist. Just be sure to keep an eye on the chicken while it's defrosting; don't let it cook.
- **Refrigerator:** *Slowest. Best quality.* Defrosting chicken in the refrigerator results in juicy meat, most like that of fresh. The only problem is that you need to think ahead; quartered chickens take a good twenty-four hours to defrost.
- **Warm running water:** *Least successful.* We ran warm water over the frozen chicken quarters for forty-five minutes to defrost. When cooked, the chicken was dry and stringy. We don't recommend this method.

Measuring spoons

We've found that measuring spoons with well rounded bottoms are the most accurate. Avoid the ones that are extremely shallow; they can be off by almost 50 percent.

Don't crowd chicken when browning

To brown chicken, use a pan large enough to hold all the pieces with at least half an inch between them. We recommend a ten-inch frying pan or pot. When chicken is crowded, the heat drops, and the pieces stew rather than brown. If your pan isn't wide enough, brown the chicken in two batches.

Quick kitchen method for carving chicken

To cut up a roast chicken quickly, use primarily your hands and a pair of scissors. We like Joyce Chen scissors, which are ideally engineered with large, round handles enclosed in plastic and short, sharp blades.

- **Breasts:** Start with a knife. Cut along one side of the breast bone and then slide the knife blade along the bones, cutting the meat off the bone as you go. After that use scissors. Break the wing joint attached to the bird and cut through it so that the wing stays attached to the breast meat. Cut the breast in half crosswise. Do the same with the other breast.
- **Legs:** Bend each leg back exposing the joint. Break the joint and then cut through it and along the backbone to release the leg from the carcass. Cut it into drumstick and thigh.

Avoid cooking poultry too long

Perfectly cooked poultry is juicy, tender, and tempting. Unfortunately, once overcooked, it's tough and dry. The breast is particularly susceptible to overcooking, not to mention diced chicken or turkey.

- **Chicken breasts:** Nothing beats boneless, skinless breasts for fast cooking. So we have loads of recipes for them in this book, most of which require only ten minutes cooking time. Don't allow the breasts to overcook. Without the protection of the bone, they quickly become dry and disappointing.
- **Turkey cutlets:** Cut from the breast, these are usually about one-quarter inch thick. Cooking takes one to two minutes per side at the most (rarely longer than three minutes total). If you cook them longer, they will be dry. We know it's hard to make yourself take a cutlet out of the pan almost as soon as you put it in, but trust us, you'll be glad you did.
- **Diced poultry:** Small pieces of chicken or turkey can turn into hard little balls in a flash. Simmer or poach diced poultry at a low temperature. Never allow the liquid to boil, which would make the meat fibrous and dry.

Oven accuracy

It's not unusual for the actual temperature in your oven to vary wildly from the setting. To save your roasted and baked chickens from disaster, invest in an oven thermometer, take your oven's temperature occasionally, and adjust the setting accordingly.

Yellow-skinned chicken

Some varieties of supermarket chicken have a yellow tint to their skin, a result of the birds' feed. We find the color doesn't affect flavor, but the golden-hued poultry does seem to brown better than its fair-skinned counterpart.

Test for doneness

We think the classic method is the best way to check for doneness: Stick a small, sharp knife into the inside of the thigh. If the juices run clear, the chicken is done. If the juices are pink, continue cooking. This test applies to whole chickens, halves, and parts.

Golden-brown skin

If you're nearing the end of the roasting time and your chicken isn't quite as brown as you'd like, slide it under the broiler for the last few minutes of cooking. The skin should crisp right up.

The fastest way to peel garlic

Use a large knife to peel a garlic clove. Put the flat of the blade over the garlic and smack the blade with your fist or the heel of your hand. The clove will crack, and the skin will loosen and come off easily.

CHAPTER ONE

Sautés & Stir-Fries

PECAN-CRUSTED CHICKEN WITH MUSTARD SAUCE

Nutty sautéed chicken dipped in a creamy mustard sauce delivers nicely varied textures and flavors. Using cornstarch rather than flour makes the crust especially crisp.

WINE RECOMMENDATION The combination of the sweet pecans and the assertive mustard sauce lends itself to either a crisp sparkling wine or a stainless-steel-fermented sauvignon blanc from California.

SERVES 4

- 1 cup pecans
- 2 tablespoons cornstarch
- 1 teaspoon dried thyme
- 1 teaspoon paprika
- 1½ teaspoons salt
- Cayenne
- 1 egg
- 2 tablespoons water
- 4 boneless, skinless chicken breasts (about 1⅓ pounds in all)
- 3 tablespoons cooking oil
- 1 cup mayonnaise
- 2 tablespoons grainy or Dijon mustard
- ½ teaspoon white-wine vinegar
- ½ teaspoon sugar
- 2 tablespoons chopped fresh parsley

1. In a food processor, pulse the pecans with the cornstarch, thyme, paprika, 1¼ teaspoons of the salt, and ⅛ teaspoon cayenne until the nuts are chopped fine. Transfer the mixture to a medium bowl.

2. Whisk together the egg and the water in a small bowl. Dip each chicken breast into the egg mixture and then into the nut mixture.

3. In a large nonstick frying pan, heat the oil over moderate heat. Add the chicken to the pan and cook for 5 minutes. Turn and continue cooking until the chicken is golden brown and cooked through, 5 to 6 minutes longer.

4. Meanwhile, in a small bowl, combine the mayonnaise, mustard, vinegar, sugar, parsley, a pinch of cayenne, and the remaining ¼ teaspoon salt. Serve the chicken with the mustard dipping sauce.

MENU SUGGESTIONS

The crisp coating on the chicken invites a creamy potato gratin alongside. Green beans, perhaps sautéed in bacon fat, would taste great, too.

SAUTÉED CHICKEN BREASTS WITH FENNEL AND ROSEMARY

The Mediterranean flavors of fennel, garlic, and rosemary are perfect with chicken. The fennel and chicken are sautéed and then briefly braised in chicken broth, which becomes a tasty light sauce.

WINE RECOMMENDATION
The fennel and the rosemary will pair especially nicely with a full-bodied red wine that has a hint of sweetness, such as a Rioja from Spain.

SERVES 4

- 2 tablespoons olive oil
- 1 large fennel bulb (about 1¼ pounds), cut into ½-inch slices
- 2 teaspoons dried rosemary, crumbled
- ½ teaspoon salt
- ½ cup canned low-sodium chicken broth or homemade stock
- 4 boneless, skinless chicken breasts (about 1⅓ pounds in all)
- ¼ teaspoon fresh-ground black pepper
- 2 cloves garlic, minced
- 2 tablespoons chopped flat-leaf parsley

1. In a large nonstick frying pan, heat 1 tablespoon of the oil over moderately high heat. Add the fennel, 1 teaspoon of the rosemary, and ¼ teaspoon of the salt. Cook, stirring frequently, until the fennel is golden brown and almost done, about 12 minutes. Add the broth and bring to a boil. Cover, reduce the heat and simmer until the fennel is tender, about 3 minutes. Remove the fennel and the cooking liquid from the pan.

2. Wipe out the pan and heat the remaining 1 tablespoon oil over moderate heat. Season the chicken with the remaining ¼ teaspoon salt and ⅛ teaspoon of the pepper. Add the chicken to the pan with the remaining 1 teaspoon of rosemary and cook until brown, about 5 minutes. Turn and cook until almost done, about 3 minutes longer. Add the garlic; cook, stirring, for 30 seconds. Add the fennel and its cooking liquid and the remaining ⅛ teaspoon pepper. Bring to a simmer. Cover the pan and remove from the heat. Let steam 5 minutes. Stir in the parsley.

MENU SUGGESTIONS

Soft polenta is an appropriate accompaniment to this Italian-style dish. Mashed potatoes are another good match.

Chicken Chasseur

A French classic that never seems to go out of style, this dish combines mushrooms and chicken in a tomato and white-wine sauce. The name, literally *hunter's chicken*, harks back to a time when game birds and mushrooms from the woods were a natural autumn combination.

WINE RECOMMENDATION
This earthy dish is perfectly suited to the rustic charms of a country red wine from southwestern France. Look for a bottle from one of the various appellations in that region, such as Cahors, Madiran, or Bergerac.

SERVES 4

- 1 tablespoon cooking oil
- 4 bone-in chicken breasts (about 2¼ pounds in all)
- 1 teaspoon salt
- ½ teaspoon fresh-ground black pepper
- 1 tablespoon butter
- 1 onion, chopped
- ¾ pound mushrooms, sliced
- 2 cloves garlic, minced
- 1½ teaspoons flour
- 6 tablespoons dry vermouth or dry white wine
- ⅔ cup canned low-sodium chicken broth or homemade stock
- 1 cup canned crushed tomatoes, drained
- ¼ teaspoon dried thyme
- 2 tablespoons chopped fresh parsley

1. In a large, deep frying pan, heat the oil over moderately high heat. Season the chicken with ¼ teaspoon each of the salt and pepper and add to the pan. Cook until browned, turning, about 8 minutes in all. Remove. Pour off all but 1 tablespoon fat from the pan.

2. Add the butter to the pan and reduce the heat to moderately low. Add the onion and cook, stirring occasionally, until translucent, about 5 minutes. Raise the heat to moderately high. Add the mushrooms, garlic, and ¼ teaspoon of the salt. Cook, stirring frequently, until the vegetables are browned, about 5 minutes.

3. Add the flour and cook, stirring, for 30 seconds. Stir in the vermouth and bring back to a simmer. Stir in the broth, tomatoes, thyme, and the remaining ½ teaspoon salt. Add the chicken and any accumulated juices. Reduce the heat; simmer, covered, until the chicken is done, about 10 minutes. Stir in the parsley and the remaining ¼ teaspoon pepper.

Sautéed Chicken Breasts with Tarragon Cream Sauce

Simple sautés such as this are perfect for quick meals. The sauce has a delicate tarragon flavor; thyme would also be a good herb to try here.

WINE RECOMMENDATION
The richness of the cream sauce will contrast well with a fresh white wine from the north of Italy. Try a tocai friulano, pinot grigio, or pinot bianco from an area such as Collio or the Alto Adige.

SERVES 4

- 2 tablespoons butter
- 4 boneless, skinless chicken breasts (about 1⅓ pounds in all)
- ¾ teaspoon salt
- ¼ teaspoon fresh-ground black pepper
- 2 tablespoons chopped onion
- 1 tablespoon flour
- 1 cup dry white wine
- ½ teaspoon dried tarragon, or 1½ teaspoons chopped fresh tarragon
- ½ cup heavy cream

1. In a medium frying pan, heat the butter over moderate heat. Season the chicken with ¼ teaspoon of the salt and the pepper and add it to the pan. Cook the chicken until brown, about 5 minutes. Turn and cook until just done, 4 to 5 minutes longer. Remove the chicken from the pan and put it in a warm spot.

2. Reduce the heat to moderately low. Stir in the onion and cook until starting to soften, about 2 minutes. Sprinkle the flour over the onion and stir to combine. Increase the heat to moderate; whisk in the wine and the tarragon, and cook until the sauce starts to thicken, about 2 minutes. Stir in the cream, the remaining ½ teaspoon salt, and any accumulated chicken juices. Serve the sauce over the chicken.

Menu Suggestions

Rice along with a simple vegetable such as steamed asparagus or sautéed zucchini and carrots would round out the meal nicely.

Cornmeal-Crusted Chicken with Goat-Cheese and Sausage Stuffing

Bite through the crunchy coating and juicy meat of these chicken breasts and you'll be surprised by a soft, creamy goat-cheese center with a hint of spicy cayenne.

WINE RECOMMENDATION
There's a lot going on in this dish, from the Italian sausage to the acidic goat cheese and the crunchy cornmeal. A light, slightly chilled pinot noir from Burgundy in France or from Oregon has the fruitiness and acidity to make a perfect partner.

SERVES 4

- 5½ ounces goat cheese, crumbled
- ½ pound mild Italian sausage, casings removed, meat crumbled and cooked
- ¼ teaspoon cayenne
- ½ teaspoon salt
- 2 tablespoons chopped fresh parsley
- 4 boneless, skinless chicken breasts (about 1⅓ pounds in all)
- 1 egg
- 1 tablespoon water
- ¾ cup cornmeal
- ¼ teaspoon fresh-ground black pepper
- 3 tablespoons cooking oil

1. In a small bowl, combine the goat cheese, sausage, cayenne, ¼ teaspoon of the salt, and the parsley.

2. With a sharp knife, make an incision along the side of each chicken breast and cut into the middle, making a pocket without cutting through the edges. Fill each breast with the goat-cheese mixture and pinch the cut side of the breast together to seal in the stuffing.

3. In a small bowl, whisk the egg with the water. Mix the cornmeal with the remaining ¼ teaspoon salt and the pepper. Dip each chicken breast in the cornmeal mixture to coat lightly, then into the egg mixture, and then back in the cornmeal.

4. In a large frying pan, heat the oil over moderately high heat. Add the chicken and cook for 5 minutes. Turn and continue cooking until golden brown and cooked through, about 5 minutes longer.

Menu Suggestions

Creamy mashed potatoes and a simple green vegetable are delicious with this crisp chicken.

Potato, Mushroom, and Chicken Hash

Always a brunch favorite, hash is a hearty dinner option as well. You might top each serving with a fried egg. The yolk makes a silky sauce for every bite it touches.

WINE RECOMMENDATION
This satisfying dish will go with different drinks depending on the time of day. For brunch, try a mimosa (orange juice and sparkling wine). For dinner, serve a light, young Bordeaux from the Médoc in France.

SERVES 4

- 2 pounds boiling potatoes, peeled and cut into ¾-inch pieces
- 4 tablespoons cooking oil
- 1 onion, chopped
- 2 cloves garlic, chopped
- ½ pound mushrooms, cut into ½-inch pieces
- 1⅓ pounds boneless, skinless chicken breasts (about 4), cut into ½-inch pieces
- 1 teaspoon salt
- ¼ teaspoon fresh-ground black pepper
- ½ teaspoon dried thyme
- ¼ cup heavy cream
- 2 tablespoons chopped fresh parsley

1. Put the potatoes in a medium saucepan of salted water. Bring to a boil and simmer until almost tender, about 5 minutes. Drain.

2. In a large nonstick frying pan, heat 1 tablespoon of the oil over moderate heat. Add the onion, garlic, and mushrooms and cook, stirring occasionally, until the mushrooms are browned, about 6 minutes. Add the chicken, ½ teaspoon of the salt, the pepper, and the thyme. Sauté until the chicken is almost cooked through, 3 to 4 minutes. Remove the mixture from the pan.

3. Wipe out the frying pan and then heat the remaining 3 tablespoons oil over moderately high heat. Add the drained potatoes and let cook, without stirring, for 6 minutes. Add the remaining ½ teaspoon salt, stir the potatoes, and cook until well browned, about 4 minutes longer. Stir in the chicken and mushrooms, the cream, and the parsley. Cook until just heated through, 1 to 2 minutes longer.

Test-Kitchen Tip

This is the perfect place to use leftover cooked turkey or chicken. Just toss it in at the end with the mushrooms.

KUNG PAO CHICKEN

Quick Asian stir-fries make especially satisfying weeknight dinners. *Kung pao* is traditionally a seriously spicy dish, but we've given ours a moderate level of heat; feel free to adjust the quantity of red-pepper flakes to suit your taste. Serve with steamed rice.

WINE RECOMMENDATION
Since the chicken is salty and spicy, the drink's first job is to refresh. An aromatic white wine such as a sauvignon blanc from California or South Africa will do nicely, as will your favorite cold beer.

SERVES 4

- 1⅓ pounds boneless, skinless chicken breasts (about 4), cut into ½-inch pieces
- 5 tablespoons soy sauce
- 2 tablespoons sherry
- 1 tablespoon plus 2 teaspoons cornstarch
- 2 teaspoons sugar
- 2 tablespoons white-wine vinegar or rice vinegar
- 2 teaspoons Asian sesame oil
- ⅓ cup water
- 2 tablespoons cooking oil
- ½ cup peanuts
- 4 scallions, white bulbs and green tops cut separately into ½-inch pieces
- ¼ teaspoon dried red-pepper flakes

1. In a medium bowl, toss the chicken with 1 tablespoon of the soy sauce, 1 tablespoon of the sherry, and the 1 tablespoon cornstarch.

2. In a small bowl, combine the sugar, vinegar, sesame oil, water, and the remaining 4 tablespoons of soy sauce, 1 tablespoon of sherry, and 2 teaspoons cornstarch.

3. In a wok or large frying pan, heat 1 tablespoon of the oil over moderately high heat. Add the peanuts and stir-fry until light brown, about 30 seconds. Remove from the pan. Heat the remaining 1 tablespoon oil. Add the white part of the scallions and the red-pepper flakes to the pan and cook, stirring, for 30 seconds. Add the chicken with its marinade and cook, stirring, until almost done, 1 to 2 minutes. Add the soy-sauce mixture and the scallion tops and simmer until the chicken is just done, about 1 minute longer. Stir in the peanuts.

VARIATION

CASHEW CHICKEN

Substitute the same amount of cashews for the peanuts.

STIR-FRIED CHICKEN WITH CHINESE CABBAGE

A simple sauce of garlic, hot pepper, sherry, wine vinegar, and tomato, adds intense flavor to this quick stir-fry and it practically makes itself while the chicken and cabbage cook. Steamed rice is an ideal accompaniment.

WINE RECOMMENDATION
You need a straightforward white wine with plenty of acidity to survive the garlic, soy sauce, and hot pepper in this dish. A chenin blanc from the Loire Valley in France, particularly from Vouvray, Saumur, or Anjou, will be able to hold its own.

SERVES 4

- 1⅓ pounds boneless, skinless chicken breasts (about 4), cut into 1-inch pieces
- 1 tablespoon plus 4 teaspoons soy sauce
- 3 tablespoons dry sherry
- ¼ teaspoon cayenne
- 2 tablespoons cooking oil
- 1 onion, chopped
- 2 cloves garlic, minced
- 1 teaspoon ground coriander
- 1 tablespoon wine vinegar
- ½ head Chinese cabbage (about 1 pound), sliced
- ¾ cup drained sliced water chestnuts (from one 8-ounce can)
- 2 teaspoons tomato paste
- ¼ teaspoon dried red-pepper flakes
- 3 tablespoons water
- 3 tablespoons chopped cilantro or scallion tops
- ⅛ teaspoon salt

1. In a medium bowl, combine the chicken with the 1 tablespoon soy sauce, 1 tablespoon of the sherry, and the cayenne. Let marinate for 10 minutes.

2. In a wok or large frying pan, heat 1 tablespoon of the oil over moderately high heat. Add the chicken and cook, stirring, until almost done, 1 to 2 minutes. Remove.

3. Add the remaining 1 tablespoon oil to the pan. Add the onion, garlic, and coriander. Cook, stirring, until the onions are golden, about 4 minutes. Add the remaining 2 tablespoons sherry and the vinegar. Cook, stirring, 1 minute longer.

4. Add the cabbage, water chestnuts, the remaining 4 teaspoons soy sauce, the tomato paste, red-pepper flakes, and water and cook, stirring, for 3 minutes longer. Add the chicken and any accumulated juices, the cilantro, and the salt and cook, stirring, until the chicken is just done, 1 to 2 minutes longer.

Chicken Provençal

The flavors are bold in this French sauté with a sauce of tomatoes, garlic, rosemary, olives, and just enough anchovy paste to give the sauce depth.

WINE RECOMMENDATION
There are lots of interesting wines from the region of Provence that will be ideal with this dish. For a lighter, summer wine, look for a rosé from that region. If you prefer a red, try a Côtes de Provence.

SERVES 4

- 1 tablespoon cooking oil
- 1 chicken (about 3 to 3½ pounds), cut into eight pieces
- ¾ teaspoon salt
- ½ teaspoon fresh-ground black pepper
- 1 small onion, chopped
- 4 cloves garlic, minced
- ½ cup red wine
- 1½ cups canned crushed tomatoes with their juice
- ½ teaspoon dried rosemary
- ½ teaspoon dried thyme
- ⅓ cup black olives, such as Niçoise or Kalamata, halved and pitted
- 1 teaspoon anchovy paste

1. In a large, deep frying pan, heat the oil over moderately high heat. Season the chicken with ¼ teaspoon each of the salt and pepper and put it in the pan. Cook the chicken until browned, turning, about 8 minutes in all. Remove the chicken from the pan. Pour off all but 1 tablespoon fat from the pan.

2. Reduce the heat to moderately low. Add the onion and the garlic and cook, stirring occasionally, until the onion starts to soften, about 3 minutes. Add the wine to the pan and simmer until reduced to about ¼ cup, 1 to 2 minutes. Add the tomatoes, rosemary, thyme, olives, anchovy paste, and the remaining ½ teaspoon salt and simmer for 5 minutes.

3. Add the chicken thighs and drumsticks and any accumulated juices. Reduce the heat to low and simmer, covered, for 10 minutes. Add the breasts and cook until the chicken is just done, about 10 minutes more. Add the remaining ¼ teaspoon pepper.

Menu Suggestions

Simple roasted new potatoes or boiled green beans would be excellent with the gutsy flavors here.

Russian-Style Chicken Cutlets

So simple and so good—these cutlets are a case where the whole is greater than the sum of the parts. Ground chicken is often disappointingly dry, but here a bit of butter and cream keep the meat moist.

WINE RECOMMENDATION
The butteriness of the juicy cutlets contrasts beautifully with the racy freshness of an uncomplicated red wine. A Beaujolais from France or a merlot from Trentino in Northern Italy or will be perfect.

SERVES 4

- 2 slices good-quality white bread, crusts removed
- 1/4 cup half-and-half
- 1 pound ground chicken
- 1 egg
- 1/2 teaspoon salt
- 1/4 teaspoon fresh-ground black pepper
- 1/2 teaspoon dried dill
- 5 tablespoons butter, 3 of them at room temperature
- 1 cup dry bread crumbs
- 2 tablespoons cooking oil

1. Break the bread into pieces. In a large bowl, soak the bread in the half-and-half until the liquid is absorbed, about 2 minutes. Mix in the chicken, egg, salt, pepper, dill, and the 3 tablespoons room-temperature butter. Put in the freezer for about 10 minutes to firm up.

2. Remove the chicken mixture from the freezer; it will still be very soft. Form the mixture into four oval cutlets and coat them with the bread crumbs.

3. In a large, nonstick frying pan, heat the remaining 2 tablespoons butter and the oil over moderate heat. Cook the cutlets until golden brown and just done, 4 to 5 minutes per side.

VARIATION

Italian-Style Chicken Cutlets

Omit the dill. Use half bread crumbs, half grated Parmesan cheese to coat the cutlets.

Menu Suggestions

Sautéed mushrooms are the traditional Russian accompaniment to chicken cutlets. Beets, glazed carrots, and mashed potatoes are other excellent possibilities.

Chicken Livers with Caramelized Onions and Madeira

Rich-tasting caramelized onions combined with Madeira make a spectacular sauce for chicken livers. Serve with rice or over toast so you won't miss a single drop.

WINE RECOMMENDATION
The rich and luscious Madeira sauce is ideal with fruity, spicy grenache-based wines. A Gigondas or a Côtes-du-Rhône from the Rhône Valley in France or a bottle of grenache from California would be appropriate.

SERVES 4

- 3 tablespoons cooking oil
- 3 onions, sliced thin (about 4 cups)
- 3/4 teaspoon salt
- 1/4 teaspoon fresh-ground black pepper
- 1 1/4 pounds chicken livers, each cut in half
- 1/2 cup Madeira
- 1 hard-cooked egg, chopped
- 2 tablespoons chopped fresh parsley

1. In a large frying pan, heat 2 tablespoons of the oil over moderate heat. Add the onions, 1/2 teaspoon of the salt, and 1/8 teaspoon of the pepper. Cook, stirring frequently, until the onions are well browned, about 15 minutes. Remove the onions from the pan and put on a serving platter or individual plates.

2. In the same frying pan, heat the remaining 1 tablespoon oil over moderately high heat. Season the chicken livers with the remaining 1/4 teaspoon salt and 1/8 teaspoon pepper. Put the livers in the pan, in two batches if necessary, and cook for 2 minutes. Turn and cook until browned, about 2 minutes longer. The livers should still be pink inside. Remove the chicken livers from the pan and put them on top of the onions.

3. Return the pan to the heat and add the Madeira. Boil rapidly, scraping the bottom of the pan to dislodge any brown bits, for 1 minute. Pour the sauce over the livers and the onions. Top with the egg and parsley.

VARIATIONS

Chicken Livers with Caramelized Onions and Sherry

Use 1/2 cup of dry sherry instead of the Madeira.

Chicken Livers with Caramelized Onions and Port

Use 1/2 cup of port instead of the Madeira.

Sautéed Chicken Livers with Raisins and Pine Nuts

Sicily is the inspiration for chicken livers in a wine sauce redolent of garlic and studded with raisins and pine nuts. The livers are delicious over polenta—better yet, crisp fried polenta. Or serve them on a bed of buttered noodles or on toast.

WINE RECOMMENDATION
Try matching the savory tastes of this Sicilian-flavored dish with a rustic red wine that hails from the same region. Or serve the easy-to-find Salice Salentino from Apulia, also in Southern Italy.

SERVES 4

- 1/3 cup pine nuts
- 1/3 cup raisins
- 3/4 cup canned low-sodium chicken broth or homemade stock
- 3/4 cup dry vermouth or dry white wine
- 2 tablespoons butter
- 2 tablespoons olive oil
- 1 1/4 pounds chicken livers, each cut in half
- 1/2 teaspoon salt
- 1/4 teaspoon fresh-ground black pepper
- 4 cloves garlic, minced
- 1 1/2 teaspoons flour
- 3 tablespoons chopped flat-leaf parsley

1. Heat the oven to 350°. Toast the pine nuts in the oven until they are golden brown, about 8 minutes.

2. In a small stainless-steel saucepan, combine the raisins, broth, and vermouth. Bring to a boil and simmer until reduced to about 3/4 cup, about 8 minutes. Set aside.

3. In a large frying pan, melt 1 tablespoon of the butter with 1 tablespoon of the oil over moderately high heat. Season the livers with 1/4 teaspoon of the salt and 1/8 teaspoon of the pepper and cook, in two batches if necessary, until almost done, about 3 minutes. The livers should still be quite pink inside. Remove them from the pan.

4. Add the remaining 1 tablespoon oil and 1 tablespoon butter to the pan and reduce the heat to moderately low. Add the garlic and cook, stirring, for 30 seconds. Add the flour and cook, stirring, for 15 seconds longer. Stir in the raisin-and-vermouth mixture and the remaining 1/4 teaspoon salt and 1/8 teaspoon pepper. Bring to a simmer, scraping the bottom of the pan to dislodge any brown bits. Add the livers and any accumulated juices, the pine nuts, and the parsley and simmer until the livers are just done, about 1 minute longer.

Turkey Scaloppine with Tomatoes and Capers

Searing the turkey for two minutes and then stirring together a simple pan sauce—that's all it takes to make this Italian-inspired dish.

WINE RECOMMENDATION
An Italian wine is a natural here; a bottle of sangiovese-based Chianti from Tuscany in Italy would be perfect. Another alternative, also made from sangiovese grapes, is a Rosso di Montalcino.

SERVES 4

- 2 tablespoons cooking oil
- 4 turkey cutlets (about 1 1/4 pounds in all)
- 1/2 teaspoon salt
- 1/4 teaspoon fresh-ground black pepper
- 1/3 cup flour
- 1/3 cup dry white wine
- 1/2 cup canned low-sodium chicken broth or homemade stock
- 1/2 teaspoon dried marjoram
- 1/2 cup canned crushed tomatoes in thick puree
- 1 tablespoon butter
- 2 tablespoons capers

1. In a large nonstick frying pan, heat the oil over moderately high heat. Season the turkey with 1/4 teaspoon of the salt and the pepper. Dredge the turkey in the flour and then shake off any excess. Cook the cutlets until just done, 1 to 2 minutes per side. Remove from the pan and cover loosely with foil to keep warm.

2. Decrease the heat to moderate. Add the wine to the pan and cook, stirring to dislodge any brown bits that cling to the bottom of the pan, for 1 minute. Add the broth and marjoram and simmer for 2 minutes longer. Stir in the tomatoes, butter, and the remaining 1/4 teaspoon salt. Simmer until starting to thicken, about 4 minutes. Stir in the capers. Spoon the sauce over the scaloppine.

Menu Suggestions

Keep it simple and Italian; either sautéed spinach or spaghetti with garlic and oil would fill the bill.

TURKEY WITH BACON AND GREENS

Thin turkey cutlets are sautéed quickly and served with tender Swiss chard and a sour-cream-based sauce. Feel free to use chicken breasts instead of turkey, or spinach in place of the Swiss chard.

WINE RECOMMENDATION
This quick sauté will be great with a fairly acidic red wine, which will cut through the richness of the bacon and match the acidity of the sour cream. Look for a Beaujolais or try a grenache-based wine from California. Serve it slightly chilled.

SERVES 4

- 1½ pounds Swiss chard, long stems removed, leaves chopped and washed well
- 1 tablespoon water
- ¼ pound sliced bacon, cut into ¼-inch strips
- 1 onion, chopped
- 2 cloves garlic, chopped
- 4 turkey cutlets (about 1¼ pounds in all)
- ¾ teaspoon salt
- ¼ teaspoon fresh-ground black pepper
- ½ cup sour cream

1. Put the Swiss chard and the water in a medium pot. In a large nonstick frying pan, cook the bacon until crisp. Drain on paper towels. Pour off and reserve all but 1 tablespoon of the bacon fat, which you should leave in the pan.

2. Put the pan with the one tablespoon of fat over moderately low heat. Add the onion and cook, stirring occasionally, until translucent, about 5 minutes. Add the garlic and cook, stirring, 30 seconds longer. Add the mixture to the Swiss chard. Bring the water to a simmer, cover, and cook over low heat until the greens are wilted and tender, about 5 minutes.

3. Meanwhile, heat 2 tablespoons of the reserved bacon fat in the frying pan over moderately high heat. Season the turkey cutlets with ¼ teaspoon of the salt and the pepper. Cook until just done, 1 to 2 minutes per side. Remove the cutlets from the pan so that they don't overcook.

4. Remove the Swiss chard from the heat Stir in the sour cream and the remaining ½ teaspoon salt. Remove the greens from the pot with a slotted spoon, leaving the sauce. Divide the greens among four plates. Top each pile of chard with a turkey cutlet. Spoon some of the sauce over the top and sprinkle with the bacon.

MENU SUGGESTIONS

Since the recipe includes a vegetable, you can finish off the meal simply with steak fries or buttered orzo.

TURKEY WITH WALNUT PARMESAN SAUCE

Ground walnuts thicken this unique sauce and give it both a subtle nuttiness and an appealing creamy texture, both of which are perfect with turkey.

WINE RECOMMENDATION The walnuts will stand up to a bold red wine. Try one from the Northern Rhône in France or a California cabernet sauvignon.

SERVES 4

- 1/3 cup walnuts
- 2 tablespoons butter
- 1/2 cup chopped onion
- 2 cloves garlic, chopped
- Pinch ground cloves
- Pinch ground cinnamon
- Pinch cayenne
- 1/2 teaspoon salt
- 1 1/2 teaspoons flour
- 3/4 cup canned low-sodium chicken broth or homemade stock
- 1/2 teaspoon lemon juice
- 1 1/2 tablespoons grated Parmesan cheese
- 2 tablespoons chopped fresh parsley
- 1 tablespoon cooking oil
- 4 turkey cutlets (about 1 1/4 pounds in all)
- 1/4 teaspoon fresh-ground black pepper

1. Grind 1/4 cup of the walnuts to a powder in a food processor. In a small saucepan, melt the butter over moderately low heat. Add the onion; cook until translucent, about 5 minutes. Add the garlic and cook, stirring, 30 seconds longer. Stir in the cloves, cinnamon, cayenne, and 1/4 teaspoon of the salt. Add the flour and stir to combine. Whisk in the broth and simmer until starting to thicken, about 3 minutes. Add the ground walnuts and simmer 1 minute longer. Remove from the heat and stir in the lemon juice, Parmesan, and parsley.

2. In a large nonstick frying pan, heat the oil over moderately high heat. Season the turkey with the remaining 1/4 teaspoon salt and the pepper. Cook the turkey cutlets until just done, 1 to 2 minutes per side. Serve with the walnut sauce, sprinkling the additional nuts over the top.

MENU SUGGESTIONS

Roasted asparagus and sautéed peppers are vegetables that taste particularly good with both walnuts and Parmesan cheese.

CHAPTER TWO

Roasted, Baked & Grilled

Roast Chicken with Rosemary and Lemon

Lemon zest and rosemary placed in the cavity of the bird permeate the meat as it cooks and give a subtle Mediterranean accent to the pan juices. We call for dried rosemary, but if you have fresh, use several sprigs in place of the one tablespoon.

WINE RECOMMENDATION
A straightforward gulpable red wine will pair best with this aromatic dish. Try a Chianti from the Italian region of Tuscany.

SERVES 4

- 1 chicken (3 to 3½ pounds)
- 1 tablespoon dried rosemary
- Salt
- Fresh-ground black pepper
- 4 3-inch-long strips lemon zest
- 1 small onion, quartered
- 1 tablespoon olive oil
- 1 tablespoon plus ¼ teaspoon lemon juice
- ½ cup water

1. Heat the oven to 425°. Rub the cavity of the chicken with the dried rosemary, ¼ teaspoon salt, and ⅛ teaspoon pepper and then stuff with the strips of lemon zest and the quartered onion. Twist the wings behind the back of the chicken and tie the legs together. Put the chicken, breast-side up, in a roasting pan. Coat the chicken with the oil and sprinkle it with ¼ teaspoon of salt, ⅛ teaspoon of pepper, and the 1 tablespoon lemon juice.

2. Roast the chicken until it is just done, 50 to 60 minutes. Transfer the bird to a plate and leave to rest in a warm spot for about 10 minutes.

3. Meanwhile, pour off the fat from the roasting pan. Set the pan over moderate heat and add the water. Bring to a boil, scraping the bottom of the pan to dislodge any brown bits. Boil until reduced to approximately ¼ cup, about 4 minutes. Add any accumulated juices from the chicken along with the remaining ¼ teaspoon lemon juice and a pinch each of salt and pepper. Serve the bird with the pan juices.

Menu Suggestions

The simplicity of this chicken means that an almost endless list of accompaniments will work well with it. Among the easiest are vegetables that you can roast in a separate pan alongside the chicken, such as potatoes, squash, asparagus, or fennel. Other good choices include rice, polenta, or mashed potatoes.

Roast Chicken with Cranberry Apple Raisin Chutney

Cranberries may call the holidays to mind, but this combination tastes great any time of year. You can serve the chutney warm or at room temperature; if there's any left over, use it to light up a chicken, turkey, or ham sandwich.

WINE RECOMMENDATION
This sweet, fruit-laden dish is best with a wine that shares these characteristics, such as a slightly chilled bottle of Chinon from the Loire Valley in France or a dolcetto from Italy.

SERVES 4

- 1 chicken (3 to 3½ pounds)
- Salt
- Fresh-ground black pepper
- 4 3-inch-long strips orange zest
- 1 tablespoon olive oil
- 1 12-ounce package fresh or frozen cranberries (about 3 cups)
- 1 tart apple, such as Granny Smith, peeled, cored, and cut into ½-inch chunks
- 1 cup raisins
- ⅔ cup brown sugar
- ½ cup apple juice
- 4 teaspoons cider vinegar
- ¼ teaspoon ground ginger
- ½ cup orange juice (from about 1 orange)

1. Heat the oven to 425°. Rub the chicken cavity with ¼ teaspoon salt and ⅛ teaspoon pepper and put the orange zest inside. Twist the wings of the chicken behind the back and tie the legs together. Put the chicken, breast-side up, in a roasting pan. Coat the chicken with the oil and sprinkle with ¼ teaspoon salt and ⅛ teaspoon pepper. Roast the chicken until just done, 50 to 60 minutes.

2. Meanwhile, in a medium stainless-steel saucepan, bring the cranberries to a boil with the apple, raisins, brown sugar, apple juice, vinegar, ginger, ⅛ teaspoon salt, and ⅛ teaspoon pepper. Cover and simmer over moderate heat, stirring occasionally, until the liquid has thickened and the fruit is tender, about 15 minutes.

3. When the chicken is done, transfer the bird to a plate and leave to rest in a warm spot for about 10 minutes. Pour off the fat from the roasting pan. Set the pan over moderate heat and add the orange juice. Bring to a boil, scraping the bottom of the pan to dislodge any brown bits. Boil until reduced to approximately ¼ cup, about 4 minutes. Add any accumulated juices from the chicken and a pinch each of salt and pepper. Serve the chicken with the orange sauce and the chutney.

Roast Chicken with Maple Pepper Glaze and Sweet Potatoes

You'll look forward to cool weather just so you can make this irresistible dish. The maple pepper glaze laced with bourbon gives the chicken an extra-crisp skin and drips down to flavor the sweet potatoes as they roast alongside. To gild the lily, add one cup of pecan halves to the potatoes about ten minutes before they're done.

WINE RECOMMENDATION
With ingredients like maple syrup, bourbon, and sweet potatoes, this dish should be matched with an all-American wine. The best choice is a fruity zinfandel from California.

SERVES 4

- 2 pounds sweet potatoes (about 3), peeled and cut into 1½-inch pieces
- 2 tablespoons cooking oil
- 1 teaspoon salt
- 1¼ teaspoons fresh-ground black pepper
- 1 chicken (3 to 3½ pounds)
- 1 tablespoon butter, cut into small pieces
- 6 tablespoons pure maple syrup
- 1½ tablespoons bourbon

1. Heat the oven to 425°. In a large roasting pan, toss the sweet potatoes with 1 tablespoon of the oil, ½ teaspoon of the salt, and ¼ teaspoon of the pepper. Push them to the edges of the pan, leaving a space in the center for the chicken.

2. Rub the cavity of the chicken with ¼ teaspoon of the salt and ⅛ teaspoon of the pepper. Twist the wings behind the back and tie the legs together. Put the chicken, breast-side up, in the center of the roasting pan. Coat the chicken with the remaining tablespoon oil, sprinkle with the remaining ¼ teaspoon salt and ⅛ teaspoon of the pepper, and dot with the butter. Roast the chicken for 30 minutes.

3. Meanwhile, in a small bowl, combine the maple syrup, bourbon, and the remaining ¾ teaspoon pepper. Remove the roasting pan from the oven and stir the potatoes. Brush the chicken with about 2 tablespoons of the glaze and drizzle the potatoes with about ½ tablespoon of the glaze. Return the pan to the oven and cook, stirring the potatoes and brushing the chicken with the remaining glaze 2 more times, until the chicken and potatoes are just done, about 30 minutes longer. Transfer the bird and potatoes to a plate and leave to rest in a warm spot for about 10 minutes.

4. Meanwhile, pour off the fat from the roasting pan. Add any accumulated juices from the chicken to the liquid in the pan. Serve the chicken with the pan juices and sweet potatoes.

Roast Cornish Hens with Panzanella Stuffing

Italian bread salad is the inspiration for this simple stuffing that bakes in a dish alongside the hens until crisp and golden brown.

WINE RECOMMENDATION
This rustic, Italian-influenced recipe will go nicely with an Italian red such as a Chianti Classico. It combines fruit flavors with the acidity to stand up to the strong ingredients here.

SERVES 4

- 1 ½-pound loaf sourdough or firm country bread, cut into 1-inch cubes (about 8 cups)
- 2 Cornish hens
- 3 tablespoons olive oil
- 1 teaspoon salt
- Fresh-ground black pepper
- 1 tablespoon butter, cut into small pieces
- 2 cups drained diced canned tomatoes
- 3 cloves garlic, minced
- 6 tablespoons chopped flat-leaf parsley
- 2 teaspoons dried rosemary, crumbled, or 2 tablespoons chopped fresh rosemary

1. Set the oven at 425°. Put the bread cubes in the oven while it heats and toast them until golden brown, about 6 minutes.

2. Twist the wings of the Cornish hens behind their backs and tie the legs together. Put the hens, breast-side up, in a roasting pan. Coat the hens with 1 tablespoon of the oil; sprinkle with ¼ teaspoon of the salt and ⅛ teaspoon pepper. Dot with the butter. Roast the hens until just done, about 40 minutes.

3. Meanwhile, oil a deep 1-quart baking dish. In a large bowl, toss the tomatoes with the garlic, parsley, rosemary, the remaining ¾ teaspoon salt, and ¼ teaspoon pepper. Add the toasted bread cubes and the remaining 2 tablespoons oil and stir well to combine. Put the stuffing in the prepared baking dish and cover with a lid or with aluminum foil. Bake for 20 minutes. Remove the cover; bake until the stuffing is crisp and golden brown, about 12 minutes longer.

4. When the hens are done, transfer them to a plate and leave to rest in a warm spot for about 10 minutes. Pour off the fat from the roasting pan and add any accumulated juices from the hens. Cut the hens in half and serve with the stuffing and the pan juices.

Menu Suggestion

Only a green vegetable, perhaps broccoli rabe, is needed to complete the meal.

TURKEY BREAST WITH MUSTARD SAGE CRUMBS

Seasoned bread crumbs form an appealing brown crust on this turkey breast that tastes as good as it looks. We developed it for quick weeknight cooking, but it would make a fine holiday feast for a small group.

WINE RECOMMENDATION The mild flavors of this dish provide an opportunity to explore a full-flavored red wine. Try a bottle of easy-to-like, easy-to-drink zinfandel from California or a shiraz from Australia.

SERVES 4

- ½ cup dry bread crumbs
- 1½ teaspoons dried sage
- ¼ cup chopped fresh parsley
- 3 tablespoons melted butter
- ¾ teaspoon salt
- 1 2-pound boneless, skinless turkey breast
- ¼ teaspoon fresh-ground black pepper
- 1 tablespoon Dijon mustard

1. Heat the oven to 450°. In a small bowl, combine the bread crumbs, sage, parsley, butter, and ¼ teaspoon of the salt.

2. Season the turkey breast with the remaining ½ teaspoon salt and the pepper. Set the turkey breast in a roasting pan and then brush the top and the sides of the breast with the mustard. Pat the seasoned bread crumbs onto the mustard.

3. Roast the turkey for 20 minutes. Reduce the oven temperature to 375° and continue to roast the turkey breast until just done, 15 to 20 minutes longer. Transfer the turkey to a carving board and leave to rest in a warm spot for about 10 minutes. Cut the turkey into slices.

MENU SUGGESTIONS

A moist and creamy side dish—mashed potatoes or sweet potatoes, baked squash, or creamed corn or spinach—is the perfect foil for the turkey.

TEST-KITCHEN TIP

Sometimes boneless turkey breasts come rolled and tied like a roast. For this preparation, you'll want to unroll the breast and put it flat in the roasting pan, thereby cutting the cooking time significantly.

CHICKEN WITH WINE AND TARRAGON

Here's a delectable French classic that never seems to go out of style. The sauce takes only a few minutes to make, but if you prefer you can serve the chicken without it. Green beans are a good accompaniment.

WINE RECOMMENDATION
A full-bodied, rustic red wine from the south of France is a perfect choice for this traditional French dish. A Gigondas, Côtes-du-Rhône, or Crozes-Hermitage, each from the Rhône Valley, would be a good choice.

SERVES 4

- 3 tablespoons dry white wine or dry vermouth
- 2 teaspoons dried tarragon
- 1 chicken (3 to 3½ pounds), quartered
- 1 tablespoon olive oil
- Salt
- Fresh-ground black pepper
- 1 tablespoon butter, cut into 4 pieces
- ¼ cup water

1. Heat the oven to 375°. In a small glass or stainless-steel bowl, combine 2 tablespoons of the wine and ½ teaspoon of the dried tarragon. Set aside.

2. Coat the chicken with the olive oil and arrange the pieces, skin-side up, in a large roasting pan. Sprinkle the chicken pieces with the remaining 1 tablespoon wine and season with ¼ teaspoon salt and ⅛ teaspoon pepper. Top each piece of chicken with a piece of the butter.

3. Cook the chicken for 15 minutes and then sprinkle with the remaining 1½ teaspoons tarragon. Baste the chicken and cook until the breasts are just done, about 20 minutes longer. Remove the breasts and cook the legs until done, about 5 minutes longer. Remove the roasting pan from the oven; return the breasts to the pan.

4. Heat the broiler. Baste the chicken and then broil until the skin is golden brown, about 2 minutes. Transfer the chicken to a plate.

5. Pour off the fat from the roasting pan. Set the pan over moderate heat and add the reserved wine-and-tarragon mixture and the water. Bring to a boil, scraping the bottom of the pan to dislodge any brown bits. Boil until reduced to approximately 3 tablespoons, about 3 minutes. Add any accumulated juices from the chicken and a pinch each of salt and pepper. Spoon the sauce over the chicken.

Chicken with Port and Figs

Dried figs are poached in port to make a luscious Portuguese-inspired sauce. Ruby port provides the best color, but tawny will also taste good.

WINE RECOMMENDATION
A Portuguese red wine such as a Dão, combining soft texture with full flavor, is a geographical match. The savory sauce would also go nicely with a fruity cabernet sauvignon or merlot from either California or Australia.

SERVES 4

- 8 dried figs, tough stems removed
- 1 cup water
- ⅔ cup plus 1 tablespoon port
- 2 3-inch-long strips lemon zest
- 1 chicken (3 to 3½ pounds), quartered
- 1 tablespoon olive oil
- Salt
- Fresh-ground black pepper
- 1 tablespoon butter, cut into four pieces

1. Heat the oven to 375°. Pierce each fig three or four times with a paring knife. In a small stainless-steel saucepan, combine the figs, water, the ⅔ cup port, and the lemon zest. Bring to a boil and simmer, covered, until tender, about 30 minutes. Discard the zest and reserve the poaching liquid. Cut the figs in half.

2. Meanwhile, coat the chicken with the oil and arrange the pieces, skin-side up, in a large roasting pan. Sprinkle the chicken with the remaining 1 tablespoon port and season with ¼ teaspoon salt and ⅛ teaspoon pepper. Top each piece of chicken with a piece of the butter. Cook until the breasts are just done, about 30 minutes. Remove the breasts and continue to cook the legs until done, about 5 minutes longer. Remove the roasting pan from the oven; return the breasts to the pan.

3. Heat the broiler. Broil the chicken until the skin is golden brown, about 2 minutes. Transfer the chicken to a plate.

4. Pour off the fat from the roasting pan. Set the pan over moderate heat and add the fig-poaching liquid. Bring to a boil, scraping the bottom of the pan to dislodge any brown bits. Boil until reduced to approximately ¼ cup, about 4 minutes. Add the figs, any accumulated juices from the chicken, and a pinch each of salt and pepper. Spoon the sauce over the chicken.

Menu Suggestion

A green vegetable, such as steamed broccoli, makes a quick and easy side dish.

Spiced Chicken Breasts with Dried Apricots

A paste made of ground sesame seeds, almonds, cumin, coriander, and oregano gives both the chicken and the apricots delicious flavor.

WINE RECOMMENDATION
A red or white wine with low tannin and plenty of fruit flavor will match the sweet, tangy apricots. For a red, a pinot noir from Oregon would be a good choice; for a white, a pinot blanc from Alsace in France.

SERVES 4

- 3/4 cup dried apricots
- 1 1/2 cups water
- 1/2 cup sliced almonds
- 1/3 cup sesame seeds
- 2 tablespoons ground cumin
- 2 tablespoons ground coriander
- 2 tablespoons paprika
- 2 tablespoons dried oregano
- Salt
- 1/4 cup olive oil
- 2 tablespoons lemon juice
- 4 bone-in chicken breasts (about 2 1/4 pounds in all)

1. Heat the oven to 425°. In a small saucepan, combine the apricots and water. Bring to a boil, lower the heat, and then simmer, partially covered, for 10 minutes. Set aside.

2. Toast the almonds and sesame seeds in the oven until just beginning to brown, about 2 minutes. Transfer 1/3 cup of the almonds and 1/4 cup of the sesame seeds to a blender; pulverize with the cumin, coriander, paprika, oregano, and 1/2 teaspoon salt. Put the mixture in a small bowl; stir in the oil and lemon juice to make a paste. Stir half of the paste into the apricots and water.

3. Put the chicken breasts in a small roasting pan, skin-side up, and coat with the remaining paste. Pour the apricot mixture around the chicken. Cook in the lower third of the oven until done, 20 to 25 minutes. If the chicken seems to be browning too quickly, cover the pan with aluminum foil the last 10 minutes of cooking.

4. Transfer the chicken to a plate. Spoon the fat from the pan. Serve the chicken topped with the apricots and any pan juices. Sprinkle the remaining almonds and sesame seeds over all.

Menu Suggestions

Steamed rice is an ideal accompaniment. So are roasted potatoes cooked alongside the chicken in a separate pan.

Chicken with Banana Curry Sauce

Caribbean curries often have a mild sweetness, usually from fruit. The banana flavor here is very subtle; you needn't worry about your dinner tasting like dessert.

WINE RECOMMENDATION A completely dry wine will taste coarse and acidic with the fruity and slightly sweet flavor here. Instead, choose a white with a touch of sweetness. An off-dry California chenin blanc, gewürztraminer, or riesling will hold its own nicely.

SERVES 4

- 2 large bananas, cut into pieces
- 2 tablespoons curry powder
- 2 teaspoons ground coriander
- 1 teaspoon dry mustard
- 3 tablespoons butter
- Grated zest of 1 lime
- 4 teaspoons lime juice
- 1¼ teaspoons salt
- ½ teaspoon fresh-ground black pepper
- ¾ cup water, more if needed
- 4 bone-in chicken breasts (about 2¼ pounds in all), skin removed
- 1 tablespoon fresh chopped parsley (optional)

1. Heat the oven to 450°. In a food processor or blender, puree the bananas, curry powder, coriander, dry mustard, butter, lime zest, lime juice, salt, pepper, and ¼ cup of the water.

2. Make a few deep cuts in each chicken breast and put the breasts in a roasting pan. Pour the curry sauce over the chicken, making sure the sauce gets into the cuts. Roast in the bottom third of the oven until the chicken is just done, about 20 minutes.

3. Remove the roasting pan from the oven and remove the chicken breasts from the pan. There should be plenty of thick sauce in the bottom of the pan. Set the pan over moderate heat and whisk in the remaining ½ cup water. Continue to whisk until the sauce is heated through, adding more water if you want a thinner sauce. Serve the chicken breasts with the sauce over them. Sprinkle with parsley if you like.

Menu Suggestion

Be sure to have plenty of rice ready to catch the generous quantity of sauce.

Orange-Glazed Chicken Wings

Roll up your sleeves and dig into dinner! Orange juice and zest, soy sauce, and plenty of garlic coat these wings with fabulous flavor.

WINE RECOMMENDATION
Sweet, salty, and hot, this dish really needs a wine with good acidity, moderate alcohol, and just a touch of sweetness. Look for a low-alcohol German kabinett riesling or a semi-dry riesling from the Finger Lakes region of New York.

SERVES 4

- 1 cup fresh orange juice (from about 2 oranges)
- 2 tablespoons grated orange zest (from about 3 oranges)
- 6 cloves garlic, minced
- 1/4 cup soy sauce
- 1 tablespoon brown sugar
- 1 1/2 teaspoons salt
- 1/2 teaspoon fresh-ground black pepper
- 4 pounds chicken wings

1. Heat the oven to 400°. In a large bowl, combine the orange juice with the orange zest, garlic, soy sauce, brown sugar, salt, and pepper. Add the chicken wings and toss to coat.

2. On two large baking sheets, arrange the wings in a single layer. Reserve 1/4 cup of the orange mixture and spoon the rest of the mixture over the wings. Bake for 20 minutes. Turn the wings over and baste them with the reserved orange mixture. Cook until just done, about 10 minutes longer.

Menu Suggestions

Serve this finger food with a vegetable that you can also eat with your hands, such as strips of raw fennel or jicama.

Test-Kitchen Tip

When you grate the orange zest, remove only the orange layer of the skin, leaving the bitter white pith behind.

JERK CHICKEN

Jamaicans love this sweet-and-spicy rub on both chicken and meat. Our rub is a little less fiery than the traditional version, but if you'd like to kick the heat up a notch, just add more cayenne pepper.

WINE RECOMMENDATION
The strong flavors in this recipe will be best with a refreshing wine that combines low alcohol and good acidity. Try a slightly chilled Beaujolais from France. Or open a cold bottle of a light-bodied beer.

SERVES 4

- 3 scallions including green tops, chopped
- 2 cloves garlic, chopped
- 1 tablespoon ground allspice
- 1 tablespoon dried thyme
- 1 teaspoon cayenne
- ½ teaspoon fresh-ground black pepper
- 1¼ teaspoons salt
- 1 teaspoon grated nutmeg
- 2 tablespoons brown sugar
- ¼ teaspoon vinegar
- ¼ cup cooking oil
- 4 whole chicken legs

1. In a food processor or blender, puree all the ingredients except the chicken legs. Put the chicken in a large roasting pan and coat with the pureed mixture. Let the chicken marinate for about 30 minutes.

2. Heat the oven to 450°. Cook the chicken legs in the upper third of the oven for 15 minutes. Turn the legs over and cook until just done, about 15 minutes longer.

MENU SUGGESTIONS

Corn bread, rice and beans (or just plain rice), or corn on the cob would all taste great with this highly spiced chicken. Fried plantains are another appropriate accompaniment.

TEST-KITCHEN TIP

The longer you can marinate the chicken legs, the more the flavor will penetrate the meat. We've suggested thirty minutes, but you can marinate the chicken for up to twenty-four hours.

Baked Buffalo Chicken Wings

Most of us think of Buffalo wings as bar food, but with their accompaniment of celery sticks and creamy blue-cheese dressing, they make a fine casual meal. These wings are hot, but if you like them incendiary, pass extra Tabasco at the table.

WINE RECOMMENDATION Beer is a no-brainer with the salt, spice, and heat of this barfly classic. For a more festive alternative, serve a crisp sparkling wine; it will refresh the palate and tame the heat of the dish.

SERVES 4

- 4 pounds chicken wings
- 3 tablespoons cooking oil
- 4 cloves garlic, chopped
- 1¾ teaspoons salt
- 1½ teaspoons cayenne
- ⅔ cup mayonnaise
- ⅓ cup sour cream
- ¼ pound blue cheese, crumbled (about 1 cup)
- 2 scallions including green tops, chopped
- 5 teaspoons vinegar
- ¼ teaspoon fresh-ground black pepper
- ¼ cup ketchup
- 1 tablespoon Tabasco sauce
- 8 ribs celery, cut into sticks

1. Heat the oven to 425°. In a large bowl, combine the wings, oil, garlic, 1½ teaspoons of the salt, and the cayenne. Arrange the wings in a single layer on two large baking sheets. Bake until just done, about 25 minutes.

2. Meanwhile, in a medium glass or stainless-steel bowl, combine the mayonnaise, sour cream, blue cheese, scallions, 1 teaspoon of the vinegar, the remaining ¼ teaspoon salt, and the black pepper.

3. In a large bowl, combine the ketchup, the remaining 4 teaspoons vinegar, and the Tabasco sauce. Add the wings and toss to coat. Serve the wings with the celery sticks and blue-cheese dressing alongside.

Menu Suggestions

Pair these wings with more finger food. Corn on the cob would go nicely. Roasted potato wedges are a good alternative and can be cooked alongside the wings.

Chicken with Lemon, Oregano, and Feta Cheese

A trio of Greek flavors gives these chicken quarters Mediterranean flair. The cheese is sprinkled over the cooked chicken, which is then broiled until golden.

WINE RECOMMENDATION
This Greek-flavored dish will go nicely with a number of rustic, spicy red wines. Try finding a bottle from the Greek island of Paros or Santorini. Another alternative would be a syrah-based wine such as a Crozes-Hermitage from the northern Rhône Valley in France.

SERVES 4

- 1 chicken (3 to 3½ pounds), quartered
- 1 tablespoon olive oil
- 1½ teaspoons dried oregano
- 1 tablespoon lemon juice
- ¼ teaspoon salt
- ⅛ teaspoon fresh-ground black pepper
- 1 tablespoon butter, cut into 4 pieces
- 1½ ounces feta cheese, crumbled (about ⅓ cup)

1. Heat the oven to 375°. Coat the chicken with the oil; arrange the pieces, skin-side up, in a large roasting pan. Sprinkle the chicken with the oregano, lemon juice, salt, and pepper. Top each piece of chicken with a piece of the butter.

2. Cook the chicken until the breasts are just done, about 30 minutes. Remove the breasts and continue to cook the legs until done, about 5 minutes longer. Remove the roasting pan from the oven; return the breasts to the pan. Top the chicken pieces with the feta cheese. Press any cheese that rolls off into the pan back onto the chicken. Baste the chicken with the pan juices.

3. Heat the broiler. Broil the chicken until golden brown, about 2 minutes. Serve with the pan juices.

Menu Suggestions

Balance the tanginess of lemon and feta with a mild side dish such as orzo tossed with a little olive oil or sautéed zucchini.

Chicken Breasts with Creamy Vegetable Topping

Red bell pepper, scallion, and carrot are sautéed briefly, then mixed with cream cheese to form a bright, speckled sauce that bakes right on the chicken—simple and delicious.

WINE RECOMMENDATION
A crisp and fruity white will cut through the rich cheese and pair well with the acidity of the bell pepper and scallion. A kabinett riesling from the Mosel-Saar-Ruwer region of Germany or, if you can find it, a riesling from the Finger Lakes in New York is a good possibility.

SERVES 4

- 1 tablespoon cooking oil
- 1 red bell pepper, chopped
- 2 scallions including green tops, chopped
- 1 carrot, grated
- 8 ounces cream cheese, at room temperature
- 1 teaspoon salt
- ½ teaspoon fresh-ground black pepper
- 4 bone-in chicken breasts (about 2¼ pounds in all), skin removed

1. Heat the oven to 425°. In a medium frying pan, heat the oil over moderate heat. Add the bell pepper and cook, stirring occasionally, until starting to soften, about 3 minutes. Add the scallions and carrot and cook 2 minutes longer. Mix the vegetables with the cream cheese, ¾ teaspoon of the salt, and ¼ teaspoon of the black pepper.

2. Sprinkle the chicken breasts with the remaining ¼ teaspoons of salt and pepper. Put the breasts in a roasting pan and spread them with the vegetable cream cheese. Bake the chicken until just done, 20 to 25 minutes.

Menu Suggestions

The rich topping on the chicken leaves one wanting a simply prepared vegetable, such as steamed broccoli, asparagus, or green beans.

VARIATION

Chicken Breasts with Boursin-Cheese Sauce

Substitute a 5½-ounce package of plain or garlic-and-herb-flavored Boursin cheese for the cream cheese.

Chicken and Eggplant Parmesan

In this delicious new take on classic eggplant Parmesan, broiled eggplant is layered with fresh mozzarella, basil, and slices of chicken. If basil isn't in season, don't turn to dried basil; it has little flavor. Substitute one teaspoon dried marjoram instead, adding it to the tomato sauce with the salt.

WINE RECOMMENDATION
An Italian red wine such as a reasonably priced nebbiolo from either the Piedmont or Lombardy region has plenty of acidity and body to stand up to the rich taste of this dish.

SERVES 4

- 1 small eggplant (about 1 pound), cut into 1/4-inch rounds
- 4 tablespoons olive oil
- 1 teaspoon salt
- Fresh-ground black pepper
- 1 pound boneless, skinless chicken breasts (about 3)
- 2 cups canned crushed tomatoes in thick puree
- 1/2 pound fresh mozzarella, cut into thin slices
- 1/3 cup grated Parmesan cheese
- 1/4 cup lightly packed basil leaves

1. Heat the broiler. Arrange the eggplant in a single layer on a large baking sheet. Coat both sides of the eggplant with 2 1/2 tablespoons of the oil and sprinkle with 1/2 teaspoon of the salt and 1/4 teaspoon pepper. Broil, turning once, until browned, about 5 minutes per side. Turn off the broiler and heat the oven to 425°.

2. In a large nonstick frying pan, heat 1 tablespoon of the oil over moderately high heat. Season the chicken with 1/4 teaspoon of the salt and 1/8 teaspoon pepper and add to the pan. Partially cook the chicken for 2 minutes per side and remove from the pan. When cool enough to handle, cut the chicken crosswise into 1/4-inch slices.

3. Oil an 8-inch square baking dish. Put one third of the eggplant in a single layer in the dish. Top with half of the chicken, half of the tomatoes, half of the mozzarella, one third of the Parmesan, half of the basil, and the remaining 1/4 teaspoon of salt. Repeat with another third of the eggplant, the remaining chicken, tomatoes, and mozzarella, another third of the Parmesan, and the remaining basil. Top with the remaining eggplant and sprinkle with the remaining cheese. Drizzle with the remaining 1/2 tablespoon oil. Bake for 20 minutes and let sit for 5 minutes before cutting.

Chicken and Brussels Sprouts over White-Bean and Rosemary Puree

A drizzle of pan juices ties everything together to make a complete meal that's welcome during the winter. Cannellini, one of our favorite canned beans, make a quick, delicious puree.

WINE RECOMMENDATION
Pair this Mediterranean-inspired dish with a full-flavored red from France. Try one from the southern Rhône Valley such as a Châteauneuf-du-Pape or a Côtes-du-Rhône.

SERVES 4

- 3/4 pound Brussels sprouts, cut in half from top to stem
- 4 tablespoons olive oil
- Salt
- Fresh-ground black pepper
- 4 chicken thighs
- 4 chicken drumsticks
- 2 cloves garlic, minced
- 1 teaspoon dried rosemary, crumbled, or 1 tablespoon chopped fresh rosemary
- 4 cups drained and rinsed white beans, preferably cannellini (from two 19-ounce cans)
- 1/2 cup water
- 2 tablespoons chopped flat-leaf parsley

1. Heat the oven to 450°. In a medium bowl, toss the Brussels sprouts with 1 tablespoon of the oil, 1/4 teaspoon of salt, and 1/4 of teaspoon pepper. Set aside.

2. Put the chicken pieces in a large roasting pan and toss with 1 tablespoon of oil, 1/4 teaspoon salt, and 1/4 teaspoon pepper. Arrange the chicken pieces about 1 inch apart, skin-side up, and roast for 25 minutes. Add the Brussels sprouts and continue cooking until the chicken and sprouts are done, about 12 minutes longer. Transfer them to plate and leave to rest in a warm spot for about 5 minutes.

3. Meanwhile, in a medium saucepan, heat the remaining 2 tablespoons oil, the garlic, and the rosemary over low heat, stirring, for 3 minutes. Raise the heat to moderate and add the beans, 1/4 cup of the water, 1/4 teaspoon salt, and 1/8 teaspoon pepper. Cook, mashing the beans to a coarse puree, until hot, about 5 minutes. Stir in the parsley.

4. Pour off the fat from the roasting pan. Set the pan over moderate heat and add the remaining 1/4 cup water. Bring to a boil, scraping the bottom of the pan to dislodge any brown bits. Boil until reduced to 1/4 cup, about 4 minutes. Add any accumulated juices from the chicken and a pinch each of salt and pepper. Spoon the white-bean puree onto plates and top with the chicken, the Brussels sprouts, and then the pan juices.

Cornish Hens with Scallion Butter and Lime

The typical Mexican combination of cumin and lime works beautifully with Cornish hens. Scallion butter both moistens the cooked birds and adds an extra fillip of flavor.

WINE RECOMMENDATION A number of hearty red wines would be nice with the straightforward, rustic flavors here. Look for a Corbières from the south of France, a zinfandel from California, or a Rosso di Montalcino from Tuscany in Italy.

SERVES 4

- 4 tablespoons butter, at room temperature
- 1 teaspoon dried oregano
- 1 teaspoon cumin
- ½ teaspoon salt
- Fresh-ground black pepper
- 2 Cornish hens (about 1¼ pounds each), halved
- 1 scallion including green top, chopped
- Lime wedges, for serving

1. Heat the oven to 450°. In a small bowl, combine 2 tablespoons of the butter with the oregano, cumin, ¼ teaspoon of the salt, and ¼ teaspoon pepper.

2. Rub the mixture over the skin of the hens and arrange them, skin-side up, on a baking sheet. Roast in the upper third of the oven until golden and cooked through, about 20 minutes.

3. Meanwhile, combine the remaining 2 tablespoons butter with the scallion, the remaining ¼ teaspoon salt, and ⅛ teaspoon pepper. When the hens are roasted, top with the scallion butter. Serve with lime wedges.

Menu Suggestions

You could roast new potatoes right alongside the hens with almost no effort. Sautéed bell peppers would complete the meal.

VARIATION

Cornish Hens with Herb Butter and Lime

Mix one tablespoon chopped fresh herbs, such as chives, parsley, and/or oregano, with the butter in place of the scallions.

Cornish Hens with Fruit, Walnuts, and Honey Apple Glaze

Dried fruits, fresh apples, and nuts make a delightful dressing for these roasted Cornish hens. The dish seems perfect for a chilly fall evening, but it can certainly be served any time of the year.

WINE RECOMMENDATION
The fruits and nuts in this dish will pair well with the rich texture and flavor of a Tokay Pinot Gris, a white from Alsace in France. A red wine with plenty of fruit flavor, such as a grenache from California, would be another good match.

SERVES 4

- 2 tart apples, such as Granny Smith, peeled, cored, and diced
- 2/3 cup dried apricots, cut into thin slices
- 2/3 cup raisins
- 1 cup walnuts, chopped
- 1/4 teaspoon cinnamon
- 2 tablespoons melted butter
- 1/4 cup apple juice
- 2 tablespoons honey
- 1/4 teaspoon dried thyme
- 1/2 teaspoon salt
- 2 Cornish hens (about 1 1/4 pounds each), halved
- 1/4 teaspoon fresh-ground black pepper

1. Heat the oven to 425°. In a roasting pan, combine the apples, apricots, raisins, walnuts, cinnamon, and butter. Spread the mixture over the bottom of the pan.

2. In a small bowl, combine the apple juice, honey, thyme, and 1/4 teaspoon of the salt to make a glaze. Sprinkle the Cornish hens with the remaining 1/4 teaspoon salt and the pepper and set them breast-side down on top of the fruit-and-nut mixture. Brush the hens with some of the glaze and then cook for 10 minutes.

3. Remove the roasting pan from the oven. Stir the fruit-and-nut mixture and turn the hens over. Brush them with more of the glaze, return the pan to the oven, and cook until just done, about 15 minutes longer. Glaze the hens one final time and serve them with the fruit-and-nut dressing.

Menu Suggestions

Earthy wild rice or bulgar pilaf will balance the sweet fruit dressing here.

Grilled Chicken Breasts with Grapefruit Glaze

Simply prepared yet special, these chicken breasts are grilled and basted with a bitter, tart, and sweet glaze.

WINE RECOMMENDATION
The crisp acidity, effervescence, and moderate alcohol level of a brut Champagne from France or a sparkling wine from California will be perfect with the smokey taste here and with the high acidity of the grapefruit juice.

SERVES 4

- 2 cloves garlic, minced
- 1 teaspoon grapefruit zest (from about ½ grapefruit)
- ½ cup grapefruit juice (from 1 grapefruit)
- 1 tablespoon cooking oil
- 2 tablespoons honey
- ½ teaspoon salt
- ¼ teaspoon fresh-ground black pepper
- 4 bone-in chicken breasts (about 2¼ pounds in all)

1. Light the grill. In a small bowl, combine the garlic, grapefruit zest, grapefruit juice, oil, honey, salt, and pepper.

2. Grill the chicken breasts over moderately high heat, brushing frequently with the glaze, for 8 minutes. Turn and cook, brushing with more glaze, until the chicken is just done, 10 to 12 minutes longer. Remove.

3. In a small stainless-steel saucepan, bring the remaining glaze to a boil. Boil for about 1 minute, remove from the heat, and pour over the grilled chicken.

Menu Suggestions

Since the chicken breasts don't have a lot of sauce, serve a juicy vegetable such as grilled or sautéed summer squash or zucchini alongside.

VARIATION

Grilled Chicken Breasts with Citrus Glaze

Use a combination of citrus juices, such as orange, lemon, or lime, instead of all or part of the grapefruit juice.

Grilled Chicken with Spicy Brazilian Tomato and Coconut Sauce

Redolent of ginger and jalapeños, the tomato sauce is a lively addition to plain grilled chicken. If you like less heat, use only one jalapeño.

WINE RECOMMENDATION This spicy dish will demolish any subtlety in a wine. Go for something straightforward and gulpable: a fresh white wine such as a pinot bianco from northern Italy, a slightly chilled red such as Beaujolais from France, or a beer.

SERVES 4

- 4 tablespoons cooking oil
- 3 cloves garlic, minced
- 1 chicken (3 to 3½ pounds), quartered
- ¾ teaspoon salt
- Fresh-ground black pepper
- 1 onion, chopped
- 1 tablespoon minced fresh ginger
- 2 jalapeño peppers, seeds and ribs removed, minced
- 1¼ cups canned crushed tomatoes in thick puree
- 1 cup canned unsweetened coconut milk
- 2 tablespoons chopped cilantro or parsley

1. Light the grill. In a shallow dish, combine 3 tablespoons of the oil with two-thirds of the minced garlic. Coat the chicken with half of the garlic oil and season with ¼ teaspoon of the salt and ⅛ teaspoon pepper. Grill the chicken over moderately high heat, basting with the remaining garlic oil, until just done, about 10 minutes per side for the breasts, 13 for the legs.

2. Meanwhile, in a medium saucepan, heat the remaining 1 tablespoon oil over moderately low heat. Add the onion and cook, stirring occasionally, until translucent, about 5 minutes. Add the remaining garlic, the ginger, and the jalapeños, and cook, stirring, for 1 minute longer. Add the tomatoes, the coconut milk, the remaining ½ teaspoon salt, and a pinch of pepper. Bring to a simmer and cook, stirring occasionally, until thickened, about 5 minutes. Stir in the cilantro and serve with the chicken.

Menu Suggestions

Rice and beans or refried beans are typical Brazilian side dishes that taste especially good with chicken.

Grilled Tandoori Chicken

Flavored by a yogurt and spice paste with ginger, cumin, and coriander, this chicken tastes almost as good as if it were cooked in a tandoor oven. Like Indian cooks, we remove the chicken skin and score the flesh so that the spice paste penetrates.

WINE RECOMMENDATION Spicy dishes such as this pair best with wines with low alcohol, high acidity, and a touch of fruitiness. Try an off-dry riesling from Oregon, California, or New York State.

SERVES 4

- 1 chicken (3 to 3½ pounds), cut into 8 pieces and skin removed
- 3 tablespoons lemon juice
- 1½ tablespoons water
- 1½ teaspoons salt
- ¼ teaspoon ground turmeric
- ½ cup plain yogurt
- 2 large garlic cloves, chopped
- 1 tablespoon chopped fresh ginger
- 1¼ teaspoons ground coriander
- ¾ teaspoon ground cumin
- ⅛ teaspoon cayenne
- 3 tablespoons cooking oil

1. Light the grill. Using a sharp knife, cut shallow incisions in the chicken pieces at about ½-inch intervals. In a large, glass dish or stainless-steel pan, combine the lemon juice, water, salt, and turmeric. Add the chicken pieces and turn to coat. Let the chicken pieces marinate for 5 minutes.

2. Meanwhile, in a small bowl, combine the yogurt, garlic, ginger, coriander, cumin, and cayenne. Add to the chicken and lemon mixture; turn to coat. Let marinate for 10 minutes.

3. Grill the chicken over moderately high heat, basting with oil, for 10 minutes. Turn and cook, basting with the remaining oil, until just done, about 10 minutes longer for the breasts, 12 for the thighs and drumsticks.

Menu Suggestions

Indian flatbread, such as naan, is the traditional accompaniment to tandoori. You can grill store-bought naan or other flatbread, such as pita or lavash. In summer, the sweetness of grilled corn on the cob makes a nice balance to the spiciness of the chicken. Another option is eggplant, a favorite vegetable in India, sliced and grilled.

Grilled Cornish Hens with Sun-Dried-Tomato Pesto

Since the tomato pesto here is made in a processor or blender, you have to make more than the small quantity needed. Use leftover pesto later in the week on grilled vegetables or fish. It's also a delicious addition to sandwiches, not to mention pasta.

WINE RECOMMENDATION
For this grilled dish, with its smoke, salt, and acidity (from tomatoes), choose a wine that's simple and refreshing. Among the many options are Italian red wines with good acidity such as Chianti Classico or dolcetto.

SERVES 4

- 2/3 cup reconstituted sun-dried tomatoes, or sun-dried tomatoes packed in oil, drained
- 2 cloves garlic, chopped
- 3 tablespoons grated Parmesan cheese
- 3/4 teaspoon salt
- 1/4 teaspoon fresh-ground black pepper
- 1 tablespoon lemon juice
- 1/2 cup olive oil
- 2 Cornish hens (about 1 1/4 pounds each), halved

1. Light the grill. In a food processor or blender, mince the tomatoes and garlic with the Parmesan, salt, pepper, and lemon juice. With the machine running, add the oil in a thin stream and continue whirring until the ingredients are well mixed.

2. With your fingers, loosen the skin from the breast meat of each hen, leaving the skin around the edge attached. For each half hen, spread 1 tablespoon of pesto under the skin and 1 tablespoon over it. Cook the hens over moderate heat, skin-side down, for 12 minutes. Turn the hens and cook until just done, about 12 minutes longer.

Menu Suggestions

Creamy polenta topped with a dollop of the extra pesto will be perfect with the hens. Also, since the grill is already hot, you might throw on some vegetables—peppers, zucchini, asparagus.

Reconstituting Sun-Dried Tomatoes

In a small pan, bring enough water to a boil to cover the dried tomatoes. Add the tomatoes, then remove from the heat and let them steep in the hot water for about 5 minutes. Drain.

Grilled Cornish Hens with Rice and Sicilian Butter

The traditional combination of olives, anchovies, and oranges shows up here in a flavored butter that adds a special richness and intensity to hens hot off the grill. Make a double batch and keep the extra in your freezer to use at a moment's notice.

WINE RECOMMENDATION
The saltiness of olives and anchovies can make the wrong wine appear coarse and too alcoholic. A rosé is the perfect choice. If you can find one from Sicily, buy it. If not, pick a bottle from Navarre in Spain or from the south of France.

SERVES 4

- 8 tablespoons butter, at room temperature
- 1⁄3 cup black olives, such as Kalamata, halved and pitted
- 2 teaspoons anchovy paste
- 1 tablespoon grated orange zest (from about 1 navel orange)
- 2 teaspoons orange juice
- 2 cloves garlic, minced
- 1⁄4 teaspoon fresh-ground black pepper
- 2 Cornish hens (about 1 1⁄4 pounds each), halved
- 2 tablespoons cooking oil
- Boiled or steamed rice, for serving

1. Light the grill. In a food processor, puree the butter and olives with the anchovy paste, orange zest, orange juice, garlic, and pepper. With a rubber spatula, scrape the butter into a small bowl and refrigerate.

2. Rub the hens with oil and cook over moderate heat for 12 minutes. Turn and cook until just done, about 12 minutes longer.

3. Remove the hens from the grill and serve with the rice. Top each serving with 2 tablespoons of the flavored butter, letting the butter melt over both the hen and the rice.

Menu Suggestions

You might grill some eggplant slices and drizzle them with balsamic vinegar to go with these hens. Sautéed broccoli rabe with garlic and a sprinkling of Parmesan would also match the Italian mood.

Grilled Asian Cornish Hens with Asparagus and Portobello Mushrooms

Though marinated only briefly with lime juice, garlic, ginger, and soy sauce, the Cornish hens and vegetables nevertheless have a deliciously intense flavor.

WINE RECOMMENDATION
An acidic, assertively flavored white wine, such as a sauvignon blanc from Australia or South Africa, is great with the asparagus and the bold flavors of the soy sauce and lime juice.

SERVES 4

- 6 tablespoons soy sauce
- ¼ cup lime juice (from about 2 limes)
- ¼ cup cooking oil
- 4 cloves garlic, minced
- 1 teaspoon ground ginger
- ½ teaspoon fresh-ground black pepper
- ¼ teaspoon salt
- 2 Cornish hens (about 1¼ pounds each), halved
- 1 pound asparagus
- ⅔ pound portobello mushrooms, stems removed, caps cut into ¼-inch slices, or 6 ounces sliced portobello mushrooms

1. Light the grill. In a small glass or stainless-steel bowl, combine the soy sauce, lime juice, oil, garlic, ginger, pepper, and salt. Put the hens into two large glass dishes. Pour ½ cup of the marinade over them and turn to coat. Let marinate, turning once, for 10 minutes.

2. Cook the hens over moderate heat for 12 minutes. Turn and cook until just done, about 12 minutes longer.

3. Meanwhile, snap off and discard the tough ends of the asparagus. In a medium bowl, toss the asparagus spears with 2 tablespoons of the remaining marinade and grill for about 12 minutes, turning once.

4. In the same bowl, toss the mushrooms with the remaining 2 tablespoons marinade and grill for about 5 minutes per side. Serve the hens with the asparagus and mushrooms alongside.

Menu Suggestions

Make your whole dinner outdoors by adding new potatoes or sweet-potato wedges to the grill.

CHAPTER THREE

Soups, Stews, Curries & Other Braised Dishes

Thai Chicken and Coconut Soup with Noodles

With its seductive flavors of coconut, lime, ginger, and cilantro, this Thai soup is quickly becoming a favorite across the country. Our version includes enough chicken and noodles to make it a main course. If you like, turn up the heat with more cayenne.

WINE RECOMMENDATION
The spices and the coconut milk will be best accompanied by a wine with a hint of sweetness. Try a chenin blanc from California or a demi-sec version of Vouvray (also made from the chenin blanc grape).

SERVES 4

- 1½ tablespoons cooking oil
- 1 small onion, chopped
- 4 cloves garlic, minced
- 1½ teaspoons ground coriander
- ½ teaspoon ground ginger
- ¼ teaspoon fresh-ground black pepper
- ⅛ teaspoon cayenne
- 1 quart canned low-sodium chicken broth or homemade stock
- 2 cups canned unsweetened coconut milk
- 5 teaspoons Asian fish sauce (nam pla or nuoc mam)* or soy sauce
- 1¾ teaspoons salt
- 2 3-inch-long strips lime zest
- ½ pound egg fettuccine
- 1 pound boneless, skinless chicken breasts (about 3), cut into ¼-inch slices
- 2 tablespoons lime juice
- 3 tablespoons chopped cilantro (optional)

*Available at Asian markets and some supermarkets

1. In a large pot, heat the cooking oil over moderately low heat. Add the onion and cook, stirring occasionally, until it is translucent, about 5 minutes. Add the garlic, coriander, ginger, black pepper, and cayenne; cook, stirring, for 30 seconds.

2. Add the broth, coconut milk, fish sauce, salt, and lime zest. Bring to a simmer, stirring occasionally. Reduce the heat and simmer, partially covered, for 10 minutes.

3. Meanwhile, in a large pot of boiling, salted water, cook the fettuccine until just done, about 12 minutes. Drain.

4. Add the chicken to the soup and simmer until just done, about 1½ minutes. Remove the pot from the heat and stir in the fettuccine, lime juice, and cilantro, if using. Serve the soup in bowls with a fork and spoon.

Kale and Potato Soup with Turkey Sausage

The traditional Portuguese kale and potato soup inspired this delicious country-style dish. It's especially welcome in the winter months when kale is at its peak.

WINE RECOMMENDATION
An aromatic, acidic white wine such as a sauvignon blanc is always a great choice for leafy greens. But the heartiness of this country soup can also work well with a full-bodied Portuguese red wine such as a Dão.

SERVES 4

- 1 tablespoon cooking oil
- 1 pound turkey or chicken sausage
- 1 onion, chopped
- 4 cloves garlic, cut into thin slices
- 1 quart water
- 2 cups canned low-sodium chicken broth or homemade stock
- 1½ teaspoons salt
- 1½ pound boiling potatoes, peeled and cut into ¼-inch pieces
- Pinch dried red-pepper flakes
- 1 pound kale, stems removed, leaves shredded
- ¼ teaspoon fresh-ground black pepper

1. In a large pot, heat the oil over moderately low heat. Add the sausage and cook, turning, until browned, about 10 minutes. Remove the sausage from the pot and, when it is cool enough to handle, cut it into slices. Pour off all but 1 tablespoon fat from the pan.

2. Add the onion and cook, stirring occasionally, until it is translucent, about 5 minutes. Add the garlic to the pan and cook, stirring, for 1 minute longer.

3. Add the water, broth, and salt and bring the soup to a boil. Add the sausage, potatoes, and red-pepper flakes and bring back to a simmer. Cook, partially covered, for 2 minutes. Add the kale and bring the soup back to a simmer. Cook, partially covered, until the potatoes and kale are tender, about 6 minutes longer. Add the black pepper.

Menu Suggestions

An interesting bread completes this meal with aplomb. Try corn bread or tomato-topped Italian focaccia. A good crusty loaf of white bread will do fine, too.

Spicy Chicken Chili

Serving this spicy stew is a surefire way to please everyone at the table. Leftover turkey or chicken can be substituted for the chicken thighs.

WINE RECOMMENDATION
A red wine with plenty of acidity is best suited to the spice and heat here. Look for a sangiovese from California or a dolcetto from the Piedmont region of Italy.

SERVES 4

- 2 tablespoons cooking oil
- 1 onion, chopped
- 2 cloves garlic, minced
- 1 pound skinless chicken thighs (about 4), cut into thin strips
- 4 teaspoons chili powder
- 1 tablespoon ground cumin
- 2 teaspoons dried oregano
- 1 teaspoon salt
- 2 jalapeño peppers, seeds and ribs removed, chopped
- 1½ cups canned crushed tomatoes with their juice
- 2½ cups canned low-sodium chicken broth or homemade stock
- 1⅔ cups drained and rinsed pinto beans (from one 15-ounce can)
- 1⅔ cups drained and rinsed black beans (from one 15-ounce can)
- ½ teaspoon fresh-ground black pepper
- ⅓ cup chopped cilantro (optional)

1. In a large saucepan, heat the oil over moderately low heat. Add the onion and garlic; cook until they start to soften, about 3 minutes.

2. Increase the heat to moderate and stir in the chicken strips. Cook until they are no longer pink, about 2 minutes. Stir in the chili powder, cumin, oregano, and salt. Add the jalapeños, the tomatoes with their juice, and the broth. Bring to a boil, reduce the heat, cover, and simmer for 15 minutes.

3. Uncover the saucepan and stir in the beans and black pepper. Simmer until the chili is thickened, about 15 minutes longer. Serve topped with the cilantro.

Menu Suggestions

Wedges of corn bread are always a good complement to chili. Or serve the chili over macaroni or rice.

Groundnut Stew

Peanut butter and okra flavor and thicken this tasty African stew. You can substitute green beans for the okra, if you like; the consistency of the sauce won't be quite the same, but it will still be thick enough to cling to the chicken.

WINE RECOMMENDATION A simple, fruity red wine such as a Beaujolais (or, if it's December through March, a Beaujolais Nouveau) will make a lively companion to the peanut butter in this stew.

SERVES 4

- 2 tablespoons cooking oil, more if needed
- 1 chicken (3 to 3½ pounds), cut into 8 pieces
- 1¾ teaspoons salt
- ½ teaspoon fresh-ground black pepper
- 1 onion, chopped
- 2 tablespoons tomato paste
- 1 cup canned crushed tomatoes, drained
- ¼ teaspoon cayenne
- 2¾ cups water
- ½ cup creamy peanut butter
- 1 10-ounce package frozen sliced okra

1. In a large pot, heat the oil over moderately high heat. Season the chicken pieces with ¼ teaspoon each of the salt and black pepper. Cook until browned, turning, about 8 minutes in all. Remove. Pour off all but 1 tablespoon fat from the pot.

2. Reduce the heat to moderately low. Add the onion to the pot and cook, stirring occasionally, until starting to soften, about 3 minutes. Stir in the tomato paste and then the tomatoes and cayenne. Return the chicken legs and thighs to the pot and stir in 2 cups of the water. Bring to a simmer and cook, partially covered, for 10 minutes.

3. Whisk together the peanut butter and the remaining ¾ cup water until smooth. Add this mixture to the stew along with the chicken breasts and wings, the okra and the remaining 1½ teaspoons of salt and ¼ of teaspoon black pepper. Cook, partially covered, until the okra is just done, about 10 minutes.

Menu Suggestions

Serve the stew with rice or egg noodles to capture every drop of the distinctive sauce.

Chicken Stew with Cider and Parsnips

Carrots, parsnips, and chicken simmer in a sauce of apple cider and chicken broth, making a delicious and homey stew—perfect for a chilly fall evening.

WINE RECOMMENDATION A "comfort" wine will make this dish even more satisfying. A rustic red from the south of France, such as a Cahors or Minervois, is a good possibility.

SERVES 4

- 2 tablespoons cooking oil
- 4 chicken thighs
- 4 chicken drumsticks
- ¾ teaspoon salt
- ¼ teaspoon fresh-ground black pepper
- 1 tablespoon flour
- 1 cup apple cider
- 1½ cups canned low-sodium chicken broth or homemade stock
- 1 onion, cut into thin slices
- 1 pound parsnips, cut into 1-inch pieces
- 2 carrots, cut into 1-inch pieces
- ½ teaspoon dried thyme

1. Heat the oven to 400°. In a large pot or Dutch oven, heat the oil over moderately high heat. Season the chicken thighs and drumsticks with ¼ teaspoon of the salt and the pepper. Cook the chicken until browned, turning, about 8 minutes in all. Remove. Pour off all but 1 tablespoon of the fat from the pot.

2. Reduce the heat to moderate and stir in the flour. Whisk in the cider and the broth and bring to a simmer, scraping the bottom of the pot to dislodge any brown bits. Add the onion, parsnips, carrots, thyme, and the remaining ½ teaspoon of salt. Simmer, partially covered, for 10 minutes.

3. Return the chicken to the pot. Bring the stew back to a simmer, cover, and put in the preheated oven until the chicken is done and the vegetables are tender, about 15 minutes.

Menu Suggestions

Simple boiled potatoes, egg noodles, or rice would be perfect for catching the stew's extra sauce.

Indian-Spiced Chicken and Spinach

The flavor of this dish is rich, fragrant, and mellow—not hot. You can make the sauce ahead of time and simmer the chicken in it just before serving.

WINE RECOMMENDATION
An off-dry chenin blanc from California or a chenin-blanc-based French Vouvray (look for a demi-sec) will be lovely with the aromatic cream sauce. The acidity of these wines and their melon and apricot notes are perfect foils for the exotic stew.

SERVES 4

- 2 tablespoons cooking oil
- 1 onion, chopped
- 3 cloves garlic, chopped
- 1 tablespoon chopped fresh ginger
- 1 tablespoon ground cumin
- 1 tablespoon ground coriander
- ½ teaspoon turmeric
- ½ teaspoon paprika
- 1½ teaspoons salt
- 2 jalapeño peppers, seeds and ribs removed, minced
- ½ cup canned crushed tomatoes, drained
- ½ cup heavy cream
- 1 cinnamon stick
- 1½ cups water
- 2 10-ounce packages frozen chopped spinach, thawed
- 4 boneless, skinless chicken breasts (about 1⅓ pounds in all), cut into 3 pieces each

1. In a large frying pan, heat the oil over moderately low heat. Add the onion and cook until starting to soften, about 3 minutes. Add the garlic and ginger and cook, stirring occasionally, for 2 minutes longer. Stir in the cumin, coriander, turmeric, paprika, and 1 teaspoon of the salt. Cook until the spices are fragrant, about 1 minute, and then stir in the jalapeños and tomatoes. Add the cream, cinnamon stick, and water. Squeeze the spinach to remove excess liquid and add the spinach to the pan. Bring to a simmer. Cover the pan, reduce the heat, and simmer for 5 minutes.

2. Stir in the chicken and the remaining ½ teaspoon salt, cover, and simmer the stew until just done, about 10 minutes. Remove the cinnamon stick before serving.

Menu Suggestions

Indian basmati rice would be an ideal accompaniment here, but plain white rice will work well, too.

Massaman Curry

So many curries are made throughout the world that it's hard to pick favorites. But this dish, based on a Thai and Muslim combination including potatoes, peanuts, and five-spice powder, must be one of the best.

WINE RECOMMENDATION
For this bold curry, bursting with heat, spice, and sweetness, a fresh, aromatic white that won't get pushed around—a chenin blanc from the Loire Valley in France or from California, for example, or a sauvignon blanc from New Zealand—is a good match.

SERVES 4

- 1 tablespoon cooking oil
- 1 onion, chopped
- 2 cloves garlic, minced
- 1 teaspoon chopped fresh ginger
- 1 teaspoon Chinese five-spice powder
- 1 teaspoon ground cumin
- 1/4 teaspoon cayenne
- 1/4 teaspoon turmeric
- 1 teaspoon salt
- 1 cup canned low-sodium chicken broth or homemade stock
- 1/2 cup canned unsweetened coconut milk or heavy cream
- 1/2 pound boiling potatoes (about 2), peeled and cut into 1/2-inch pieces
- 1 1/3 pounds boneless, skinless chicken breasts (about 4), cut into 1/2-inch pieces
- 1/2 cup chopped peanuts
- 1/2 pound plum tomatoes (about 4), cut into wedges
- 3 tablespoons chopped cilantro

1. In a large saucepan, heat the oil over moderately low heat. Add the onion and cook, stirring occasionally, until it is translucent, about 5 minutes. Add the garlic, ginger, five-spice powder, cumin, cayenne, turmeric, and 1/2 teaspoon of the salt. Stir until fragrant, about 1 minute. Whisk in the broth and then the coconut milk; bring to a simmer. Stir in the potatoes, cover, and cook over low heat until they are almost tender, about 12 minutes.

2. Add the chicken to the sauce, cover, and simmer for 5 minutes. Stir in the peanuts, tomatoes, cilantro, and the remaining 1/2 teaspoon salt. Turn the heat off, cover, and let steam until the chicken is just done, about 2 minutes longer.

Menu Suggestion

For this curry, steamed white rice is the only accompaniment you need.

Spiced Chicken Legs with Apricots and Raisins

Fruity and peppery, this exotic dish will perk up your midweek menu. Yet it's no more trouble than the simplest chicken recipe in your repertoire.

WINE RECOMMENDATION
The sweetness here will be nicely mirrored by an off-dry, aromatic white wine, such as a chenin blanc, riesling, or gewürztraminer from California.

SERVES 4

- 2 tablespoons cooking oil
- 4 chicken thighs
- 4 chicken drumsticks
- 1¾ teaspoons salt
- ½ teaspoon fresh-ground black pepper
- 1 onion, chopped
- 3 cloves garlic, chopped
- 1¼ cups canned low-sodium chicken broth or homemade stock
- ¼ teaspoon allspice
- ¼ teaspoon red-pepper flakes
- ⅔ cup dried apricots, quartered
- ¼ cup dark or golden raisins
- ¼ cup chopped fresh parsley

1. In a large, deep frying pan, heat the oil over moderately high heat. Season the chicken thighs and drumsticks with ¼ teaspoon each of the salt and pepper. Cook the chicken until browned, turning, about 8 minutes in all. Remove. Pour off all but 1 tablespoon of the fat from the pan.

2. Reduce the heat to moderately low. Add the onion and garlic to the pan; cook, stirring occasionally, until the onion starts to soften, about 3 minutes. Add the broth, the remaining 1½ teaspoons salt and ¼ teaspoon black pepper, the allspice, and the red-pepper flakes. Add the chicken, apricots, and raisins. Bring to a simmer, reduce the heat, and simmer the chicken, partially covered, until just done, about 20 minutes. Serve topped with the parsley.

Menu Suggestion

Couscous is a natural with this Moroccan-inspired dish.

Rustic Garlic Chicken

Yes, *three* heads of garlic. You don't have to peel the cloves first. They soften during cooking and take on a subtle sweetness. Each person squeezes the garlic out of its skin onto the plate to eat with the chicken.

WINE RECOMMENDATION
This simple Gallic dish will work well with a rustic red wine from the south of France. Look for lesser-known, good-value bottles from Corbières or Minervois, or a more serious, tannic wine from Cahors.

SERVES 4

- 2 tablespoons cooking oil
- 1 chicken (about 3 to 3½ pounds), cut into 8 pieces
- 1 teaspoon salt
- ¼ teaspoon fresh-ground black pepper
- 3 heads garlic, cloves separated
- 2 tablespoons flour
- 1 cup dry white wine
- 1 cup canned low-sodium chicken broth or homemade stock
- 2 tablespoons butter
- 2 tablespoons chopped fresh parsley

1. Heat the oven to 400°. In a Dutch oven, heat the oil over moderately high heat. Sprinkle the chicken with ½ teaspoon of the salt and the pepper. Cook the chicken until well browned, turning, about 8 minutes in all, and remove from the pot. Reduce the heat to moderate, add the garlic, and sauté until it is starting to brown, about 3 minutes. Sprinkle the flour over the garlic and stir until combined. Return the chicken to the pot, cover, and bake for 15 minutes.

2. Remove the pot from the oven and put it on a burner. Remove the chicken pieces from the pot. Over moderately high heat, whisk in the wine and simmer for 1 minute. Whisk in the broth and the remaining ½ teaspoon salt and simmer until starting to thicken, about 3 minutes. Turn the heat off, whisk in the butter, and pour the sauce over the chicken. Sprinkle with the parsley.

Menu Suggestions

There's plenty of luscious, garlicky sauce here. Take advantage of it with mashed potatoes, egg noodles, or rice.

CHICKEN GOULASH

Fragrant with paprika and brimming with flavor, this Hungarian classic continues to please. Our quick version loses none of the original appeal.

WINE RECOMMENDATION
With this dish, it's natural to experiment with one of the increasing number of reds imported from Hungary. Try Egri Bikavér or a varietal such as a merlot or a cabernet sauvignon.

SERVES 4

- 1 tablespoon cooking oil
- 8 chicken thighs
- 1½ teaspoons salt
- 1 onion, chopped
- 2 carrots, cut into ¼-inch slices
- 2 ribs celery, cut into ¼-inch slices
- 2 cloves garlic, minced
- 2 tablespoons paprika
- 1 tablespoon flour
- ⅛ teaspoon cayenne
- 1½ cups canned low-sodium chicken broth or homemade stock
- 1½ cups canned crushed tomatoes in thick puree
- ¼ teaspoon dried thyme
- 1 bay leaf
- 2 tablespoons chopped fresh parsley
- ¼ teaspoon fresh-ground black pepper

1. In a large, heavy pot, heat the oil over moderately high heat. Season the chicken with ¼ teaspoon of the salt and add it to the pan. Cook the chicken until browned, turning, about 8 minutes in all. Remove. Pour off all but 1 tablespoon fat from the pan.

2. Add the onion, carrots, celery, and garlic to the pan. Reduce the heat to moderate and cook, stirring occasionally, until the onion is translucent, about 5 minutes.

3. Reduce the heat to moderately low and add the paprika, flour, and cayenne to the pan. Cook, stirring, for 30 seconds. Stir in the broth, tomatoes, the remaining 1¼ teaspoons salt, the thyme, and the bay leaf. Add the chicken and bring to a simmer. Reduce the heat and simmer, partially covered, until the chicken is done, about 20 minutes. Remove the bay leaf and add the parsley and black pepper.

MENU SUGGESTIONS

Serve the goulash with spaetzle, buttered noodles, or boiled or mashed potatoes.

Chicken and Cavatelli

So comforting and yummy, this dish reminds us of Grandma's chicken and dumplings. In fact, you can substitute frozen dumplings for the cavatelli.

WINE RECOMMENDATION
Because this dish has no bold or assertive flavors to compete with the wine, options are unlimited: red or white, full-flavored or light-bodied. Three good choices would be a merlot or a chardonnay from California or a Meursault (also made from chardonnay) from France.

SERVES 4

- 5 cups canned low-sodium chicken broth or homemade stock
- 1 bay leaf
- 1 onion, cut into thin slices
- 2 ribs celery, cut into ½-inch pieces
- 3 carrots, cut into ½-inch pieces
- 1 teaspoon dried sage
- 1½ teaspoons salt
- ¼ teaspoon fresh-ground black pepper
- 4 bone-in chicken breasts (about 2¼ pounds in all)
- ¾ pound frozen cavatelli, egg noodles, or dumplings
- 2 tablespoons butter, softened
- 2 tablespoons flour

1. In a large pot, bring the broth, bay leaf, onion, celery, and carrots to a simmer. Simmer for 5 minutes. Add the sage, salt, pepper, and chicken breasts and simmer, partially covered, until just done, about 25 minutes. Turn the chicken breasts a few times during cooking.

2. Meanwhile, in a large pot of boiling, salted water, cook the cavatelli until just done, about 10 minutes. Drain.

3. In a small bowl, stir the butter and flour together to form a paste. Remove the bay leaf from the pot, push the chicken to the side and then whisk the butter mixture into the liquid. Simmer until thickened, 1 to 2 minutes. Stir in the cooked cavatelli and simmer until just heated through.

Frozen Pasta

Several brands of frozen cavatelli, flat egg noodles, and gnocchi are available in supermarkets. Unlike dried pasta, these products have an appealing doughy chew that we find just right with this type of saucy stew. Cook the frozen pasta separately according to package directions, drain, and then stir into the pot with the chicken.

Chicken Thighs with Lentils, Chorizo, and Red Pepper

Reminiscent of cassoulet—the glorious goose, sausage, and bean casserole from southwestern France—this dish is quicker, easier, and bound to become a winter favorite. If you like, use a green bell pepper in place of the red.

WINE RECOMMENDATION
The chorizo, pepper, and lentils pair well with a full-flavored, bold red wine. Two possibilities from France: a red from the Médoc, in Bordeaux, or a Châteauneuf-du-Pape from the southern Rhône Valley.

SERVES 4

- 1⅔ cups lentils (about ⅔ pound)
- 3 cups water
- 1 teaspoon salt
- ¼ teaspoon dried thyme
- 1 bay leaf
- 2 tablespoons cooking oil
- ½ pound dried chorizo or salami, casings removed, cut into ⅛-inch slices
- 1 onion, chopped
- 2 cloves garlic, minced
- 1 red bell pepper, cut into 1-inch pieces
- 4 chicken thighs
- ¼ teaspoon fresh-ground black pepper
- ⅔ cup canned low-sodium chicken broth or homemade stock
- 2 tablespoons lemon juice
- 2 tablespoons chopped fresh parsley

1. In a large saucepan, bring the lentils, water, ¾ teaspoon of the salt, the thyme, and bay leaf to a boil over moderately high heat. Reduce the heat. Simmer, covered, until the lentils are tender but not falling apart, about 25 minutes.

2. Meanwhile, in a large frying pan, heat 1 tablespoon of the oil over moderate heat. Add the chorizo and cook, stirring occasionally, until browned, about 5 minutes. Pour off all but 2 tablespoons of the fat from the pan. Reduce the heat to moderately low and add the onion, garlic, and bell pepper. Cook, stirring occasionally, until the onion is translucent, about 5 minutes. Add the onion mixture to the simmering lentils.

3. Heat the remaining tablespoon of oil in the pan over moderate heat. Season the chicken with the remaining ¼ teaspoon salt and the black pepper and add it to the pan. Cook the chicken, turning, until brown, about 12 minutes in all. Pour off all the fat from the pan. Add the broth, reduce the heat and simmer, covered, until the chicken is just done, about 15 minutes. Add the pan juices from the chicken to the lentils along with the lemon juice and the parsley. Top with the chicken and let sit, covered, for 5 minutes.

CHAPTER FOUR

Pasta & Grains

Chicken Breasts with Orzo, Carrots, Dill, and Avgolemono Sauce

Avgolemono sauce, a Greek contribution to the world's cuisine, is a delicate blend of chicken broth, dill, and lemon, thickened lightly with egg. In the spring, asparagus would substitute beautifully for the carrots.

WINE RECOMMENDATION Lemon and dill will work best with a full-flavored white wine with decent acidity. Try one from the southern part of Burgundy such as a Mâcon or Pouilly-Fuissé (both made from chardonnay grapes).

SERVES 4

- 2 tablespoons olive oil
- 4 boneless, skinless chicken breasts (about 1⅓ pounds in all)
- Salt and fresh-ground black pepper
- 1¼ cups canned low-sodium chicken broth or homemade stock
- 1 teaspoon dried dill
- 1½ cups orzo
- 4 carrots, quartered and cut into 2-inch lengths
- 2 eggs
- 2 tablespoons lemon juice

1. In a large stainless-steel frying pan, heat 1 tablespoon of oil over moderate heat. Season the chicken breasts with ¼ teaspoon salt and ⅛ teaspoon pepper and add to the pan. Cook until browned, about 5 minutes. Turn the chicken; add the broth, dill, and 1¼ teaspoons salt. Bring to a simmer, reduce the heat, and simmer, partially covered, until the chicken is just done, about 4 minutes. Remove the chicken and cover lightly with aluminum foil to keep warm. Set aside the pan with the broth.

2. Meanwhile, in a large pot of boiling, salted water, cook the orzo for 6 minutes. Add the carrots and continue cooking until the orzo and carrots are just done, about 6 minutes longer. Drain and toss with the remaining 1 tablespoon oil and ⅛ teaspoon each salt and pepper.

3. In a medium glass or stainless-steel bowl, beat the eggs, lemon juice, and ⅛ teaspoon of pepper until frothy. Bring the chicken broth back to a simmer and add to the eggs in a thin stream, whisking. Pour the mixture back into the pan and whisk over the lowest possible heat until the sauce begins to thicken, about 3 minutes. Do not let the sauce come to a simmer, or it may curdle. Put the orzo and carrots on plates and top with the chicken and sauce.

ORECCHIETTE WITH CHICKEN, CARAMELIZED ONIONS, AND BLUE CHEESE

The sweetness of the onions contrasts perfectly with the saltiness of the cheese in this exciting dish. Orecchiette (little ears) is a thick and satisfying pasta that we adore, but, if you like, you can use shells or bow ties instead.

WINE RECOMMENDATION
The onions and cheese drive the wine choice for this dish. A lighter red wine from the Piedmont region of Italy, such as one based on the barbera or dolcetto grapes, has the weight and acidity to stand up to the sweet and salty flavors.

SERVES 4

- 1 tablespoon butter
- 3 tablespoons olive oil
- 2 onions, quartered and cut into thin slices
- 1 teaspoon salt
- 1⅓ pounds boneless, skinless chicken breasts (about 4)
- ¼ teaspoon fresh-ground black pepper
- ¾ teaspoon dried rosemary, crumbled, or 2 teaspoons chopped fresh rosemary
- 1 clove garlic, minced
- ½ pound orecchiette
- 2 ounces blue cheese, crumbled (about ½ cup)

1. In a large nonstick frying pan, melt the butter with 2 tablespoons of oil over moderately high heat. Add the onions and ½ teaspoon of the salt and cook, stirring frequently, until well browned, about 25 minutes. Remove.

2. Add the remaining 1 tablespoon oil to the pan and reduce the heat to moderate. Season the chicken with ¼ teaspoon of the salt and ⅛ teaspoon of the pepper and add to the pan along with the rosemary. Cook the chicken until brown, about 5 minutes. Turn and cook until almost done, about 3 minutes longer. Add the garlic. Cook, stirring, for 30 seconds. Cover the pan, remove from the heat, and let steam for 5 minutes. Cut the chicken into ¼-inch slices.

3. Meanwhile, in a large pot of boiling, salted water, cook the orecchiette until just done, about 15 minutes. Reserve about ¼ cup of the pasta water. Drain the pasta and toss with 2 tablespoons of the pasta water, the onions, the chicken with pan juices, the blue cheese, and the remaining ¼ teaspoon salt and ⅛ teaspoon pepper. If the pasta seems dry, add more of the reserved pasta water.

FUSILLI WITH SPICY CHICKEN SAUSAGE, TOMATO, AND RICOTTA CHEESE

Hearty and comforting, this pasta makes a great meal for a cold winter evening. If you like, replace the hot sausages with mild ones, or use turkey sausage instead.

WINE RECOMMENDATION
The acidity of the tomato and spiciness of the sausage are best suited to a red wine with soft tannin and good acidity. Try a sangiovese from Tuscany such as Chianti Classico or Rosso di Montalcino or look for a version from California.

SERVES 4

- 1 tablespoon olive oil
- 1 pound hot chicken sausages
- 1 onion, chopped
- 2 cloves garlic, chopped
- 1/4 cup dry white wine
- 1 1/2 cups canned crushed tomatoes in thick puree
- 1/4 cup water
- 1/4 teaspoon dried rosemary, crumbled
- Pinch dried red-pepper flakes
- 1/2 teaspoon salt
- 3 tablespoons chopped flat-leaf parsley
- 1/2 pound fusilli
- 3/4 cup ricotta cheese

1. In a large, deep frying pan, heat the oil over moderate heat. Add the sausage and cook, turning, until browned and cooked through, about 10 minutes. Remove the sausage and, when it is cool enough to handle, cut it into 1/4-inch slices. Pour off all but 1 tablespoon fat from the pan.

2. Reduce the heat to moderately low. Add the onion to the pan and cook, stirring occasionally, until translucent, about 5 minutes. Add the garlic and cook 30 seconds longer.

3. Add the wine and bring to a simmer. Add the sausage, tomatoes, water, rosemary, red-pepper flakes, and 1/4 teaspoon of the salt and bring to a simmer. Cook, stirring occasionally, for 10 minutes. Stir in the parsley.

4. Meanwhile, in a large pot of boiling, salted water, cook the fusilli until just done, about 13 minutes. Drain and toss with the sauce, the ricotta, and the remaining 1/4 teaspoon salt.

Chicken Pad Thai

Our version of *pad thai*, the satisfying rice-noodle dish from Thailand, is made with chicken, tofu, bean sprouts, and, in place of hard-to-find rice noodles, linguine. The fish sauce is available at Asian markets and keeps forever. If you like, you can use a mixture of soy sauce and oyster sauce instead. Lime wedges make a nice final touch.

WINE RECOMMENDATION
Anything more than a straightforward white with some residual sugar would be pointless with the forceful flavors of the *pad thai*. A riesling from California or Australia will be fine.

SERVES 4

- 1 pound boneless, skinless chicken breasts (about 3), cut into 1-inch cubes
- 5 tablespoons plus 1 teaspoon Asian fish sauce
- ½ pound firm tofu, cut into ¼-inch cubes
- 1 cup water
- 2 tablespoons lime juice
- 1½ teaspoons rice-wine vinegar
- 3½ tablespoons sugar
- ¾ teaspoon salt
- ¼ teaspoon cayenne
- ¾ pound linguine
- 3 tablespoons cooking oil
- 4 cloves garlic, chopped
- ⅔ cup salted peanuts, chopped fine
- 2 cups bean sprouts
- ½ cup lightly packed cilantro leaves

1. In a small bowl, combine the chicken and ½ teaspoon of the fish sauce. In another bowl, combine the tofu with another ½ teaspoon of the fish sauce. In a medium glass or stainless-steel bowl, combine the remaining 5 tablespoons fish sauce with the water, 1½ tablespoons of the lime juice, the vinegar, sugar, salt, and cayenne.

2. In a pot of boiling, salted water, cook the linguine until done, about 12 minutes. Drain.

3. Meanwhile, in a wok or large frying pan, heat 1 tablespoon of the oil over moderately high heat. Add the chicken and cook, stirring, until just done, 3 to 4 minutes. Remove. Put another tablespoon of oil in the pan. Add the tofu and cook, stirring, for 2 minutes. Remove. Put the remaining 1 tablespoon oil in the pan, add the garlic and cook, stirring, for 30 seconds.

4. Add the pasta and the fish-sauce mixture. Cook, stirring, until nearly all the liquid is absorbed, about 3 minutes. Stir in the chicken, tofu, and ⅓ cup peanuts. Remove from the heat. Stir in the remaining ½ tablespoon lime juice, the bean sprouts, and half the cilantro. Top with the remaining peanuts and cilantro.

Fettuccine with Turkey and Brandied Mushrooms

A hint of brandy flavors the sautéed mushrooms. You might use port or sherry. For a special treat, try an assortment of wild mushrooms.

WINE RECOMMENDATION
A rich, oaky chardonnay will be ideal with the brandy and cream here. Good possibilities are those produced in Washington State, California, and Australia.

SERVES 4

- 1 tablespoon cooking oil
- 1 pound turkey cutlets (about 3)
- 1¼ teaspoons salt
- ½ teaspoon fresh-ground black pepper
- 2 tablespoons butter
- 2 scallions, white bulbs and green tops chopped separately
- 1 pound mushrooms, cut into thin slices
- ⅓ cup brandy
- 1 cup canned low-sodium chicken broth or homemade stock
- ½ pound fettuccine
- ¼ cup heavy cream
- 2 tablespoons chopped fresh parsley

1. In a large nonstick frying pan, heat the oil over moderately high heat. Season the turkey cutlets with ¼ teaspoon each of the salt and pepper. Cook the cutlets until they are almost done, about 1 minute per side. Remove the cutlets from the pan, let cool, and then cut them into thin strips.

2. Melt the butter in the same pan over moderate heat. Add the white part of the scallions, the mushrooms, ½ teaspoon of the salt, and the remaining ¼ teaspoon pepper. Cook, stirring occasionally, until the mushrooms let off their liquid and it evaporates, about 5 minutes. Add the brandy and cook until almost no liquid remains in the pan, about 2 minutes more. Add ½ cup of broth and simmer until almost completely evaporated, about 4 minutes.

3. In a large pot of boiling, salted water, cook the fettuccine until almost done, about 7 minutes. Drain the pasta and then add it to the mushrooms. Add the remaining ½ cup broth, the cream, the scallion tops, the remaining ½ teaspoon salt, and the turkey strips. Simmer until the turkey is just done, about 1 minute longer. Top with the parsley.

Menu Suggestion

A simple side dish of boiled or sautéed green beans is all that's needed.

CHICKEN AND ZUCCHINI COUSCOUS

A version of the North African classic, this recipe combines chicken, chickpeas, and zucchini in a cumin-spiced tomato broth. Traditionally chicken is braised in a special pot with a top compartment for steaming the couscous, but you can cook couscous, available at most supermarkets, in a saucepan in a matter of minutes.

WINE RECOMMENDATION
The aromatic spices in this dish are best with an assertive, flavorful wine; color is almost secondary. For a red, try a wine from the indigenous South African grape, pinotage. For white, try a Tokay Pinot Gris from Alsace in France.

SERVES 4

- 1 tablespoon olive oil
- 1 chicken (3 to 3½ pounds), cut into 8 pieces
- 1½ teaspoons salt
- 1 onion, chopped
- 4 cloves garlic, chopped
- 1 tablespoon chopped fresh ginger
- ½ teaspoon paprika
- ¾ teaspoon ground cumin
- ½ teaspoon dried oregano
- ¼ teaspoon cayenne
- ¼ teaspoon ground turmeric
- 1½ cups canned low-sodium chicken broth or homemade stock
- 1 cup canned crushed tomatoes in thick puree
- 1 cup canned chickpeas, drained and rinsed
- 1 zucchini, cut into ¼-inch slices
- 3 tablespoons chopped fresh parsley
- 1 tablespoon lemon juice
- 4 cups cooked couscous

1. In a large pot, heat the oil over moderately high heat. Season the chicken pieces with ¼ teaspoon of the salt and add them to the pot. Cook, turning, until browned, about 8 minutes in all. Remove. Pour off all but 1 tablespoon fat from the pot.

2. Reduce the heat to moderately low. Add the onion to the pot and cook, stirring occasionally, until translucent, about 5 minutes. Add the garlic, ginger, paprika, cumin, oregano, cayenne, and turmeric and cook, stirring, for 30 seconds.

3. Add the broth, tomatoes, and the remaining 1¼ teaspoons of salt, scraping the bottom of the pot to dislodge any browned bits. Add the chicken thighs and drumsticks. Bring to a simmer and cook, covered, for 10 minutes. Add the chicken breasts with any accumulated juices, the chickpeas, and the zucchini and bring back to a simmer. Cook, covered, until the chicken and zucchini are just done, about 12 minutes longer. Add the parsley and lemon juice and serve over the couscous.

Mushroom and Chicken Risotto

If you're using canned chicken broth to make risotto, be sure it's *low-sodium*. The broth reduces at the same time that it's cooking into the rice, and regular canned broth would become much too salty.

WINE RECOMMENDATION
The mushrooms and Parmesan in this dish will go beautifully with one of the lighter red Burgundies, which have fruitiness, earthiness, and firm acidity.

SERVES 4

- 2 tablespoons butter
- 1/2 pound mushrooms, cut into thin slices
- 2/3 pound boneless, skinless chicken breasts (about 2), cut into 1/2-inch pieces
- 1 teaspoon salt
- 1/4 teaspoon fresh-ground black pepper
- 5 1/2 cups canned low-sodium chicken broth or homemade stock, more if needed
- 1 tablespoon cooking oil
- 1/2 cup chopped onion
- 1 1/2 cups arborio rice
- 1/2 cup dry white wine
- 1/2 cup grated Parmesan cheese, plus more for serving
- 2 tablespoons chopped fresh parsley

1. In a large pot, heat the butter over moderate heat. Add the mushrooms. Cook, stirring frequently, until the mushrooms are browned, about 5 minutes. Add the chicken, 1/4 teaspoon of the salt, and the pepper. Cook until the chicken is just done, 3 to 4 minutes. Remove the mixture from the pan. In a medium saucepan, bring the broth to a simmer.

2. In the large pot, heat the oil over moderately low heat. Add the onion and cook, stirring occasionally, until translucent, about 5 minutes. Add the rice and stir until it begins to turn opaque, about 2 minutes.

3. Add the wine and the remaining 3/4 teaspoon salt to the rice. Cook, stirring frequently, until all of the wine has been absorbed. Add about 1/2 cup of the simmering broth and cook, stirring frequently, until it has been absorbed. The rice and broth should bubble gently; adjust the heat as needed. Continue cooking the rice, adding broth 1/2 cup at a time and allowing the rice to absorb it before adding the next 1/2 cup. Cook the rice in this way until tender, 25 to 30 minutes in all. The broth that hasn't been absorbed should be thickened by the starch from the rice. You may not need to use all the liquid, or you may need more broth or some water.

4. Stir in the chicken and mushrooms, the Parmesan, and the parsley and heat through. Serve the risotto with additional Parmesan.

Risotto with Smoked Turkey, Leeks, and Mascarpone

The mascarpone gives this risotto its delectable creaminess. If you like, you can make a close substitute with two ounces of cream cheese, at room temperature, and seven ounces of heavy cream. Whir them in a blender just until smooth; don't blend the mixture too long or it may curdle. Also, you can use a large onion in place of the leeks.

WINE RECOMMENDATION
Go for an Italian white wine with good body and acidity to offset the creaminess here. Look for an Arneis from the Piedmont region or pinot grigios from the regions of Alto Adige or Collio.

SERVES 4

- 5 cups canned low-sodium chicken broth or homemade stock, more if needed
- 1 cup water, more if needed
- 3 tablespoons olive oil
- 1½ pounds leeks (about 3), white and light-green parts only, cut crosswise into thin slices and washed well
- 2 cups arborio rice
- ½ cup dry white wine
- 2 teaspoons salt
- 1 6-ounce piece smoked turkey, cut into ¼-inch dice
- 1 cup mascarpone cheese
- ¼ teaspoon fresh-ground black pepper

1. In a medium saucepan, bring the broth and water to a simmer.

2. In a large pot, heat the oil over moderately low heat. Add the leeks and cook, stirring occasionally, until translucent, about 10 minutes. Add the rice and stir until it begins to turn opaque, about 2 minutes.

3. Add the wine and salt to the rice and cook, stirring frequently, until all of the wine has been absorbed.

4. Add about ½ cup of the simmering broth to the rice and cook, stirring frequently, until the broth has been completely absorbed. The rice and broth should bubble gently; adjust the heat as needed. Continue cooking the rice, adding the broth ½ cup at a time and allowing the rice to absorb the stock before adding the next ½ cup. Cook the rice in this way until tender, 25 to 30 minutes in all. The broth that hasn't been absorbed should be thickened by the starch from the rice. You may not need to use all of the liquid, or you may need to add more broth or water. Add the turkey, cheese, and pepper.

Arroz con Pollo

Here's a perfect all-in-one meal—the chicken, rice, and vegetables simmer together, enhancing each other and giving the cook a break.

WINE RECOMMENDATION This traditional Spanish favorite will work well with any smooth, full-flavored red, such as a merlot or zinfandel from California or a Rioja from Spain.

SERVES 4

- 1 tablespoon olive oil
- 4 chicken thighs
- 4 chicken drumsticks
- 2 teaspoons salt
- ½ teaspoon fresh-ground black pepper
- 2 ounces smoked ham, cut into ¼-inch dice
- 1 small onion, chopped
- 2 cloves garlic, minced
- 1 red bell pepper, chopped
- 1 green bell pepper, chopped
- 1¾ cups canned tomatoes, drained and chopped
- 1 tablespoon tomato paste
- 2 cups canned low-sodium chicken broth or homemade stock
- 1 cup rice, preferably long-grain
- 2 tablespoons chopped fresh parsley

1. In a large, deep frying pan, heat the oil over moderately high heat. Season the chicken with ¼ teaspoon each of the salt and pepper. Cook the chicken, turning, until well browned, about 8 minutes in all. Remove. Pour off all but 2 tablespoons of the fat from the pan.

2. Reduce the heat to moderately low. Add the ham, onion, and garlic to the pan and cook, stirring occasionally, until the onion starts to soften, about 2 minutes. Add the bell peppers and cook, stirring occasionally, until they start to soften, about 3 minutes longer.

3. Add the tomatoes, tomato paste, broth, and the remaining 1¾ teaspoons salt and ¼ teaspoon of the pepper and bring to a simmer. Stir in the rice and add the chicken in an even layer. Simmer, partially covered, over moderately low heat until the chicken and rice are just done, 20 to 25 minutes. Sprinkle with parsley.

Chicken with Rice and Beans

Three favorite Latin-American ingredients combine here to make one hearty and delicious dish that's welcome any time of year. We recommend Goya canned black beans, which hold up during cooking better than other brands do.

WINE RECOMMENDATION
A fruity red wine such as a merlot is best with this classic dish. If you can, try to find a bottle from a producer in Argentina or Chile, or open your favorite California merlot.

SERVES 4

- 1 tablespoon cooking oil
- 4 chicken thighs
- 4 chicken drumsticks
- 1¾ teaspoons salt
- ¼ teaspoon fresh-ground black pepper
- 1 onion, chopped fine
- 2 cloves garlic, minced
- 1 cup canned crushed tomatoes
- ½ cup bottled pimientos, drained
- 1⅔ cups drained and rinsed black beans (from one 15-ounce can)
- 1 cup rice, preferably medium-grain
- 1¾ cups water
- 2 tablespoons chopped fresh parsley
- ⅛ teaspoon cayenne
- 4 lime wedges (optional)

1. In a large, deep frying pan, heat the oil over moderately high heat. Season the chicken with ¼ teaspoon of the salt and the pepper and add to the pan. Cook, turning, until well browned, about 8 minutes in all. Remove. Pour off all but 1 tablespoon of the fat from the pan.

2. Add the onion to the pan and reduce the heat to moderately low. Cook, stirring occasionally, until translucent, about 5 minutes. Add the garlic and cook, stirring, for 30 seconds longer. Add the tomatoes and pimientos, scraping the bottom of the pan to dislodge any brown bits. Stir in the beans, rice, water, parsley, the remaining 1½ teaspoons of salt, and the cayenne, and arrange the chicken on top in an even layer.

3. Bring to a boil and simmer until all the water is absorbed, about 12 minutes. Turn the drumsticks and reduce the heat to very low. Cover and cook until the chicken and rice are just done, about 15 minutes longer. Serve with the lime wedges, if using.

Turkey Sausage with Cheddar-Cheese Grits and Tomato Sauce

Creamy, cheesy grits capture the juices from the fresh tomatoes, making a perfect foil for the sausage links. Chicken sausage also works well in this homey combination.

WINE RECOMMENDATION A simple, refreshing white wine is a nice contrast to the rich cheddar flavor of the grits. Try a pinot bianco from the Veneto region of Italy or a pinot blanc from Alsace in France.

SERVES 4

3½ cups water
1 teaspoon salt
¾ cup old-fashioned grits
¼ pound cheddar cheese, grated
1 tablespoon cooking oil
1 pound turkey sausages
1½ pounds tomatoes, chopped (about 2 cups)
¼ teaspoon fresh-ground black pepper
2 tablespoons chopped fresh parsley

1. In a medium saucepan, bring the water and ¾ teaspoon salt to a boil. Add the grits in a slow stream, whisking. Reduce the heat, cover, and simmer, stirring frequently with a wooden spoon, until the grits are very thick, about 20 minutes. Remove the saucepan from the heat and stir in the cheese.

2. Meanwhile, in a medium, nonstick frying pan, heat the oil over moderately low heat. Add the sausages and cook until they are just done, about 15 minutes. Remove the sausages from the pan. Add the tomatoes, the remaining ¼ teaspoon salt, and the pepper to the pan. Cook until the tomatoes are just heated through, 1 to 2 minutes. Stir in the parsley.

3. Serve the grits topped with the sausages and the tomato sauce.

Menu Suggestions

Vegetables such as okra, lima beans, or cooked greens would be perfectly in keeping with the Southern theme.

CHAPTER FIVE

Salads & Sandwiches

Grilled Chicken and Vegetable Salad with Lemon and Pepper Vinaigrette

Cool mixed greens topped with hot grilled chicken, carrots, and shiitake mushrooms make a great light meal. You can also let the grilled vegetables and chicken cool and serve them at room temperature.

WINE RECOMMENDATION
Look for a wine that has plenty of acidity to stand up to the vinaigrette. In the warmer months, a white such as a California sauvignon blanc or an Italian pinot grigio will taste best. If you prefer a red wine, try a gamay or pinot noir from California.

SERVES 4

- 1/3 cup plus 3 tablespoons olive oil
- 1 teaspoon dried thyme
- 1 pound boneless, skinless chicken breasts (about 3)
- 1 teaspoon salt
- 3/4 teaspoon fresh-ground black pepper
- 1/4 pound shiitake mushrooms, stems removed
- 4 carrots, cut diagonally into 1/4-inch slices
- 1/2 teaspoon Dijon mustard
- 4 teaspoons lemon juice
- 2 heads leaf lettuce, torn into bite-size pieces (about 3 quarts)
- 2 scallions including green tops, chopped

1. Light the grill. In a small bowl, combine the 3 tablespoons oil and the thyme. Coat the chicken with about 1 tablespoon of the thyme oil and sprinkle with 1/4 teaspoon of the salt and 1/8 teaspoon of the pepper. Grill the chicken over moderately high heat until just done, about 4 minutes per side. Remove and let rest for 5 minutes, and cut diagonally into 1/4-inch pieces.

2. In a medium bowl, toss the mushrooms and carrots with the remaining thyme oil, 1/4 teaspoon of the salt, and 1/8 teaspoon of the pepper. Grill the vegetables over moderately high heat, turning, until just done, about 4 minutes per side for the carrots and 6 minutes per side for the mushrooms.

3. In a small glass or stainless-steel bowl, whisk together the mustard, lemon juice, and the remaining 1/2 teaspoon salt and 1/2 teaspoon pepper. Whisk in the remaining 1/3 cup oil.

4. In a large bowl, combine the lettuce, half of the scallions, and all but 2 tablespoons of the vinaigrette. Mound onto plates. Top with the vegetables and chicken. Drizzle the remaining vinaigrette over the chicken and top with the remaining scallions.

Vietnamese Chicken Salad

Bold flavors star in this Vietnamese salad—acidic lime juice, hot pepper, salty soy sauce, and cooling herbs. The combination of mint and cilantro is typical and refreshing, but you can use only one herb, or leave them both out completely if you prefer.

WINE RECOMMENDATION
A lively, acidic white wine that has no oak flavor will be best with the spices and greens in this dish. Try a sauvignon blanc from South Africa or Australia or a pinot grigio from Italy.

SERVES 4

- 1⅓ pounds boneless, skinless chicken breasts (about 4)
- 1 cup canned low-sodium chicken broth or homemade stock
- 4 scallions including green tops, chopped
- ½ teaspoon salt
- 1¼ pounds green cabbage (about ½ head), shredded (about 4 cups)
- 3 carrots, grated
- 6 tablespoons chopped fresh mint and/or cilantro (optional)
- ¼ cup lime juice (from about 2 limes)
- ¼ cup soy sauce or Asian fish sauce (nam pla or nuoc mam)*
- 4 teaspoons sugar
- ¼ teaspoon dried red-pepper flakes
- ¼ cup chopped peanuts

*Available at Asian markets and some supermarkets

1. Cut each chicken breast into five diagonal strips. In a medium saucepan, combine the broth, ¼ of the scallions, and ¼ teaspoon of the salt. Bring to a simmer, add the chicken, stir, and cover the pan. Cook over low heat for 5 minutes. Turn the heat off and let the chicken steam for 5 minutes. Remove the chicken from the pan and shred it.

2. In a large bowl, combine the shredded chicken, the remaining scallions, the cabbage, carrots, and 4 tablespoons of the herbs, if using. In a small glass or stainless-steel bowl, whisk together the lime juice, soy sauce, sugar, red-pepper flakes, and the remaining ¼ teaspoon salt. Toss the salad with the dressing. Sprinkle with the remaining 2 tablespoons chopped herbs and the peanuts.

Menu Suggestions

This crunchy, Asian-flavored salad will taste even more refreshing served with tropical fruit, such as pineapple, mango, papaya, or star fruit.

Spinach Salad with Smoked Chicken, Apple, Walnuts, and Bacon

Celebrate autumn's apple season with this delicious and substantial salad. We call for the thick-sliced, smoked chicken now available in the meat department of supermarkets. Of course, you can always use smoked turkey from the deli counter instead. If you like a more pronounced sweet-and-sour flavor, use another teaspoon of vinegar.

WINE RECOMMENDATION
This substantial fall salad, with its hearty flavors, will taste great with a Beaujolais or, for something off the beaten path, a fruity pinotage from South Africa. In either case, chill the bottle for fifteen minutes or so before serving.

SERVES 4

- 3/4 cup walnuts, chopped
- 1/4 pound sliced bacon
- 2 tablespoons red-wine vinegar
- 1 teaspoon Dijon mustard
- 3/4 teaspoon salt
- 1/4 teaspoon fresh-ground black pepper
- 1/3 cup cooking oil
- 2/3 pound smoked and sliced boneless chicken breast
- 1 pound spinach, stems removed, leaves washed (about 9 cups)
- 1 small red onion, chopped fine
- 1 tart apple, such as Granny Smith, peeled, cored, and cut into 1/2-inch pieces

1. Heat the oven to 350°. Toast the walnuts until golden brown, about 8 minutes. Let cool.

2. In a large frying pan, cook the bacon until it is crisp. Drain the bacon on paper towels and then crumble it.

3. In a small glass or stainless-steel bowl, whisk the vinegar with the mustard, salt, and pepper. Whisk in the oil.

4. In a large bowl, combine 2 tablespoons of the dressing with the chicken. Let sit for about 5 minutes so that the chicken absorbs the dressing. Add the walnuts, bacon, spinach, onion, apple, and the remaining dressing and toss.

Menu Suggestions

Hot garlic bread, served either plain or with a little Parmesan cheese, goes well with all the flavors here.

Sesame Chicken Salad

Sesame sauce bathes layers of chicken, cucumber, and noodles in this satisfying main-course salad. Assemble the salad just before serving, or the cucumbers will release liquid, turn limp, and make the sauce watery.

WINE RECOMMENDATION
The bold flavors of the salad will be complemented by the acidity and slight sweetness of a German kabinett riesling from the Mosel-Saar-Ruwer.

SERVES 4

- 1/4 pound vermicelli
- 1 cup plus 3 tablespoons canned low-sodium chicken broth or homemade stock
- 3 scallions including green tops, cut into 1/4-inch slices
- 1/4 teaspoon salt
- 1 1/3 pounds boneless, skinless chicken breasts (about 4)
- 1 tablespoon chopped fresh ginger
- 4 cloves garlic, chopped
- 2 tablespoons tahini (sesame-seed paste)
- 1 tablespoon Asian sesame oil
- 2 teaspoons sugar
- 2 1/2 tablespoons cooking oil
- 1/8 teaspoon dried red-pepper flakes
- 3 tablespoons soy sauce
- 1/2 teaspoon fresh-ground black pepper
- 2 cucumbers, halved lengthwise, peeled, and seeded

1. In a pot of boiling, salted water, cook the vermicelli until just done, about 9 minutes. Drain. Rinse with cold water; drain thoroughly.

2. In a medium saucepan, combine the 1 cup broth, one third of the scallions, and the salt. Bring to a simmer, add the chicken, stir, and cover the pan. Simmer for 5 minutes. Turn the heat off and let the chicken steam for 5 minutes. Remove the chicken from the saucepan and shred it.

3. In a blender, puree the remaining 3 tablespoons broth, the ginger, garlic, tahini, sesame oil, sugar, cooking oil, red-pepper flakes, soy sauce, and pepper. Put the cucumber halves cut-side down and slice them lengthwise into thin strips.

4. To serve, put the vermicelli on plates or in bowls. Scatter each serving with a layer of cucumber strips and then top with the shredded chicken. Pour the sesame sauce over the chicken and sprinkle with the remaining scallions.

Moroccan Chicken and Potato Salad with Olives

A savory lemon dressing with cumin, paprika, ginger, and oregano gives this salad an exotic flavor. Serve the salad warm or at room temperature.

WINE RECOMMENDATION
This dish would be wonderful with a well-chilled bottle of rosé, which will refresh the palate without interfering with the salad's flavors. Look for a bottle from Bandol, Cassis, or elsewhere in the South of France.

SERVES 4

- 1½ pounds boiling potatoes (about 5)
- 1½ tablespoons lemon juice
- 1 teaspoon ground cumin
- 1 teaspoon paprika
- 1 teaspoon salt
- Fresh-ground black pepper
- ¼ teaspoon ground ginger
- ¼ teaspoon dried oregano
- 7 tablespoons olive oil
- 1 pound boneless, skinless chicken breasts (about 3)
- ½ red onion, chopped fine
- ⅓ cup black olives, such as Kalamata, halved and pitted
- ½ cup chopped flat-leaf parsley

1. Put the potatoes in a medium saucepan with salted water to cover and bring to a boil. Reduce the heat and cook at a gentle boil until tender, about 25 minutes. Drain the potatoes. When they are cool enough to handle, peel the potatoes and cut into ¼-inch slices.

2. Meanwhile, in a small glass or stainless-steel bowl, whisk together the lemon juice, cumin, paprika, ¾ teaspoon of the salt, ¼ teaspoon pepper, the ginger, and the oregano. Whisk in 6 tablespoons of the oil.

3. Heat a grill pan or a heavy frying pan over moderate heat. For the grill pan, coat the chicken with the remaining 1 tablespoon oil; sprinkle with the remaining ¼ teaspoon salt and ⅛ teaspoon pepper. Cook the chicken for 5 minutes. Turn and cook until browned and just done, about 4 minutes longer. Remove, and when cool enough to handle, cut the chicken into ¼-inch slices. For the frying pan, heat the oil in the pan and then season, cook, and slice the chicken in the same way.

4. In a large bowl, combine the warm potatoes with half of the dressing. Add the chicken, onion, olives, parsley, and the remaining dressing and toss.

Southwestern Tortilla Salad

This Tex-Mex favorite comes together in minutes. You'll be surprised by how quick and easy it is to make your own refried beans—and how much better they taste than the ready-made variety.

WINE RECOMMENDATION The forceful flavor of cheddar cheese and the saltiness of the olives will go very nicely with a crisp and lively sauvignon blanc from California.

SERVES 4

- 8 taco shells
- 5½ tablespoons cooking oil
- 2 cups drained and rinsed kidney beans (from one 19-ounce can)
- ⅓ cup tomato salsa
- ¾ teaspoon salt
- 1½ tablespoons wine vinegar
- ¾ teaspoon Dijon mustard
- ¼ teaspoon fresh-ground black pepper
- ¼ teaspoon chili powder
- ¼ cup chopped cilantro (optional)
- 1 head romaine lettuce, shredded
- 2 large tomatoes, chopped
- 1 avocado, cut into thin slices
- ¼ pound cheddar cheese, grated (about 1 cup)
- 1 roasted chicken, bones and skin removed, meat shredded (about 1 pound meat)
- ⅓ cup black olives, such as Kalamata, halved and pitted

1. Heat the oven to 350°. Put the taco shells on a baking sheet and bake them until crisp, about 8 minutes. Break each one in half.

2. In a medium saucepan, heat 1 tablespoon of the oil over moderate heat. Add the beans, salsa, and ¼ teaspoon of the salt. Cook, mashing with a potato masher, for about 5 minutes.

3. In a small glass or stainless-steel bowl, whisk together the vinegar, mustard, pepper, chili powder, and the remaining ½ teaspoon salt. Add the remaining 4½ tablespoons oil, whisking. Add the cilantro.

4. To serve, spread one side of the taco-shell halves with the refried beans and put four on each plate. Top with layers of the lettuce, tomatoes, avocado, cheese, chicken, and olives. Pour the dressing over the salads.

CHICKEN BURRITOS WITH BLACK-BEAN SALSA AND PEPPER JACK

Pepper Jack cheese looks innocent enough but adds a nice kick to these burritos. If you prefer a milder taste, use regular Jack instead.

WINE RECOMMENDATION
With the heat from the cheese, stay away from any serious, high-alcohol, low-acid wines. Try a white from a cooler growing area such as a riesling from the Finger Lakes region of New York or any white from the Alto Adige region of Italy. A cold beer is a great alternative.

SERVES 4

- 1⅔ cups drained and rinsed black beans (from one 15-ounce can)
- 2 scallions including green tops, chopped
- 1 tablespoon lemon or lime juice
- ¼ teaspoon ground cumin
- ½ teaspoon salt
- 1⅓ pounds boneless, skinless chicken breasts (about 4)
- ¼ teaspoon chili powder
- ¼ teaspoon fresh-ground black pepper
- ½ pound pepper Jack cheese, grated
- 4 large (9-inch) flour tortillas

1. Light the grill or heat the broiler. In a small glass or stainless-steel bowl, combine the beans, scallions, lemon juice, cumin, and ¼ teaspoon of the salt.

2. Rub the chicken breasts with the chili powder, pepper, and the remaining ¼ teaspoon salt. Cook the chicken over moderate heat for 5 minutes. Turn and cook until brown and just done, 4 to 5 minutes longer. Remove, let the chicken rest for a few minutes, and then slice.

3. Heat the oven to 350°. Put one quarter of the cheese in a line near one edge of each tortilla. Top the cheese with one quarter of the black-bean salsa and then with one quarter of the chicken slices. Roll up the burritos and wrap each one in foil. Bake them until the cheese melts, about 15 minutes.

DO-AHEAD TIP

You can assemble the burritos ahead of time and bake them just before serving. If they've been in the refrigerator, add about five minutes to the baking time.

MENU SUGGESTIONS

Embellish your burritos with sour cream or salsa, if you like. Sliced tomatoes or rice would make good side dishes.

Chicken and Feta Tostadas

A Mexican classic with a Greek twist, these tostadas appeal to children of all ages. If you can't buy roasted chicken ready-made, use leftover chicken or cook some according to whichever of the methods on pages 180 to 181 seems easiest to you. Serve one burrito-size tortilla or two of the smaller ones per person.

WINE RECOMMENDATION
The saltiness of the feta cheese and olives and the tartness of the tomatoes will pair well with the crisp acidity in a sauvignon blanc from either the Loire Valley or a northern region of Italy such as Collio or Veneto.

SERVES 4

- ¾ pound plum tomatoes, chopped
- ½ cup black olives, such as Kalamata, pitted and chopped
- ¼ cup chopped fresh parsley
- 1 roasted chicken, bones and skin removed, meat shredded (about 1 pound boneless meat)
- ½ teaspoon salt
- ½ teaspoon fresh-ground black pepper
- 2 tablespoons red-wine vinegar
- 3 tablespoons cooking oil, plus more for brushing tortillas
- 8 small or 4 large flour tortillas
- ½ pound feta cheese, crumbled (about 2 cups)

1. Heat the oven to 450°. In a large glass or stainless-steel bowl, combine the tomatoes, olives, parsley, chicken, salt, pepper, vinegar, and the 3 tablespoons oil.

2. Brush the tortillas on both sides with oil and then put on baking sheets, overlapping if necessary. Bake the tortillas until starting to brown, 2 to 3 minutes. Turn the tortillas and brown the other side, 2 to 3 minutes longer.

3. Remove the baking sheets from the oven and top each tortilla with an equal amount of the feta cheese. Return the baking sheets to the oven; cook until the cheese is just melting, 1 to 2 minutes longer. Top the tortillas with the chicken mixture.

Menu Suggestions

A fruit salad would be an easy and complementary accompaniment.

BEAUJOLAIS

CHICKEN SOUVLAKI

Grilled chicken on pita with tomatoes, onions, and *tzatziki*, a yogurt and cucumber sauce, makes a cool yet satisfying warm-weather supper. Souvlaki is often rolled to eat in your hand as a snack, but this more substantial version is served on a plate with a knife and fork. If you like, accompany the souvlaki with lemon wedges. When using wooden skewers, soak them first in water for at least ten minutes, or they'll smoke during cooking.

WINE RECOMMENDATION
This traditional Greek preparation goes with a number of choices to suit the occasion and your taste. Look for a very fruity red such as a Beaujolais, a sparkling wine from California, or a sauvignon blanc from northern Italy.

SERVES 4

- 2 cups plain yogurt
- 1 cucumber, halved lengthwise, peeled, seeded, and grated
- 1¼ teaspoons salt
- 1 clove garlic, minced
- Fresh-ground black pepper
- ¼ teaspoon dried dill
- 2 tablespoons olive oil
- 1½ teaspoons lemon juice
- 1 tablespoon dried oregano
- 1⅓ pounds boneless, skinless chicken breasts (about 4), cut into 1-inch cubes
- 4 pocketless pitas
- 6 tablespoons butter, at room temperature
- 1 small onion, cut into thin wedges
- 2 tomatoes, cut into thin wedges
- ⅓ cup black olives, such as Kalamata, halved and pitted

1. Put the yogurt in a strainer lined with cheesecloth, a coffee filter, or a paper towel and set it over a bowl. Let drain in the refrigerator for 15 minutes. In a medium glass or stainless-steel bowl, combine the cucumber with 1 teaspoon of the salt; let sit for about 15 minutes. Squeeze the cucumber to remove the liquid. Put the cucumber back in the bowl and stir in the drained yogurt, the garlic, ⅛ teaspoon of pepper, and the dill.

2. Light the grill or heat the broiler. In a small glass or stainless-steel bowl, combine the oil, lemon juice, oregano, the remaining ¼ teaspoon of salt, and ¼ teaspoon of pepper. Toss the chicken cubes in the oil mixture and thread them onto skewers. Grill the chicken over high heat or broil, turning once, until done, about 5 minutes in all. Transfer the chicken to a plate.

3. Spread both sides of the pitas with the butter and grill or broil, turning once, until golden, about 4 minutes in all. Cut into quarters.

4. To serve, put the pitas on plates and top with the onion, tomatoes, and chicken skewers with any accumulated juices. Serve with the *tzatziki* and olives.

Spicy Pita Pockets with Chicken, Lentils, and Tahini Sauce

Here's something great to do with roasted chicken from the deli—a Middle Eastern sandwich chock-full of spicy lentils, bulgar, lettuce, tomato, and tahini sauce. Two pockets per person is enough to make a meal. If you like, serve extra Tabasco sauce at the table. You can find tahini (sesame-seed paste) in most supermarkets.

WINE RECOMMENDATION
You need a straightforward wine that won't compete but will be gulpable enough to prepare the palate for the next hot bite. Try a chenin blanc or a white zinfandel from California.

SERVES 4

- 1 cup dried lentils
- ½ onion, cut in half
- 2¾ cups plus 6 tablespoons water
- 1 tablespoon olive oil
- 2½ teaspoons salt
- 1 bay leaf
- ½ cup coarse bulgar
- 1½ teaspoons Tabasco sauce
- ½ cup tahini
- 2 cloves garlic, minced
- 5 teaspoons lemon juice
- 1 cup plain yogurt
- 8 pitas
- 1 roasted chicken, bones and skin removed, meat shredded
- 2 large tomatoes, chopped
- 1 head romaine lettuce, shredded

1. Heat the oven to 350°. In a medium saucepan, combine the lentils, onion, the 2¾ cups water, the oil, 1 teaspoon of the salt, and the bay leaf. Bring to a boil; simmer, partially covered, for 15 minutes. Stir in the bulgar and continue cooking, partially covered, stirring occasionally, until the lentils and bulgar are just done, about 12 more minutes. Remove from the heat, stir in the Tabasco sauce, and let sit, partially covered, for 5 minutes. Remove the onion and the bay leaf.

2. Meanwhile, in a medium glass or stainless-steel bowl, whisk together the tahini, the remaining 6 tablespoons water, the garlic, the lemon juice, the remaining 1½ teaspoons salt, and the yogurt.

3. Wrap the pitas in aluminum foil and warm them in the oven, about 10 minutes.

4. Cut the top third off of each pita. Spoon ¼ cup of the lentil mixture into each pita. Divide half the chicken and tomatoes among the pitas and drizzle each with 1 tablespoon of the sauce. Top with half the lettuce. Repeat. Serve with the remaining sauce.

Chicken Pan Bagnat

Literally *bathed bread* in the ancient dialect of Provence, *pan bagnat* delivers meat, bread, and salad all in one handful. You both brush the bread with oil and let the finished rolls sit for a few minutes to allow the dressing to permeate the bread and bathe it with flavor.

WINE RECOMMENDATION
The south-of-France flavor of this sandwich is perfect with the delicate, herbal notes found in many rosés from Provence. Bottles from the Coteaux du Varois, Cassis, or Bandol would all be good possibilities.

SERVES 4

- 1 tablespoon lemon juice
- 2 teaspoons chopped fresh thyme, or ¾ teaspoon dried thyme
- ¾ teaspoon salt
- ¾ teaspoon fresh-ground black pepper
- ⅓ cup plus 2 tablespoons olive oil
- 4 large, crusty rolls, cut in half
- 1 large clove garlic, cut in half
- 8 large, crisp lettuce leaves, such as Boston
- 2 large tomatoes, sliced thin
- 1 roasted chicken, bones and skin removed, meat shredded
- 2 hard-cooked eggs, sliced
- 1 red onion, sliced thin
- 1 green bell pepper, sliced thin
- ⅓ cup black olives, such as Kalamata, halved and pitted
- 8 anchovy fillets (optional)

1. In a small glass or stainless-steel bowl, whisk together the lemon juice, thyme, ½ teaspoon each of the salt and pepper. Whisk in the ⅓ cup of oil.

2. Remove the soft centers of the rolls, leaving a ½-inch shell. Rub the garlic on the inside of each and brush with the 2 tablespoons oil.

3. Top the bottoms of the rolls with the lettuce. Layer with half the tomato slices and the chicken; sprinkle with ⅛ teaspoon each of salt and pepper. Top with half the slices of egg, onion, and bell pepper, and half the olives, and then drizzle with half the dressing. Repeat with the remaining tomato, chicken, ⅛ teaspoon each salt and pepper, egg, onion, bell pepper, olives, and dressing. Top with the anchovies, if using. Cover with the tops of the rolls. If you have time, wrap each roll tightly in aluminum foil; let sit for 10 minutes. Otherwise, press down on the rolls firmly so that the dressing moistens the bread.

Menu Suggestions

You really don't need anything with this, but roasted potato wedges would be nice.

TURKEY BURGERS

The focaccia adds to the Italian flavor of these juicy burgers. However, bread selections are endless—toasted country bread, onion rolls, or whatever you like.

WINE RECOMMENDATION
This meaty sandwich should be paired with a fresh, full-flavored red, perhaps one made from the versatile, food-friendly barbera grape. Several are imported from Italy's Piedmont region.

SERVES 4

- 1½ pounds ground turkey
- ¼ cup dry bread crumbs
- ¼ cup grated Parmesan cheese
- ¼ cup chopped fresh parsley
- 2 scallions including green tops, chopped
- Salt
- ¼ teaspoon fresh-ground black pepper
- 2 tablespoons milk
- 1 egg, beaten to mix
- 2 tablespoons cooking oil
- ¼ pound provolone cheese, sliced
- ½ cup mayonnaise
- 3 tablespoons pesto, store-bought or homemade
- 1 10-inch round or 8-by-10-inch rectangle of focaccia
- ½ pound tomatoes, sliced

1. In a medium bowl, combine the ground turkey, bread crumbs, Parmesan cheese, parsley, scallions, ¾ teaspoon salt, the pepper, milk, and egg. Form the mixture into four patties, each about 1-inch thick.

2. In a large nonstick frying pan, heat the oil over moderate heat. Add the turkey burgers and cook for 5 minutes. Turn and then top each burger with the provolone cheese. Cook until just done, about 6 minutes longer.

3. Meanwhile, in a small bowl, combine the mayonnaise and the pesto. Cut the focaccia into quarters. Cut each piece in half horizontally. Spread the cut surfaces of each piece with the pesto mayonnaise.

4. Top the bottoms of the focaccia with the turkey burgers and then the tomato slices. Sprinkle the tomato with a pinch of salt. Cover with the top piece of focaccia.

MENU SUGGESTIONS

Burgers go best with other finger food—oven-roasted potato wedges and raw carrot or fennel sticks, for example.

SMOKED TURKEY AND SLAW ON COUNTRY TOAST

A simple slaw complements deli turkey in this tempting sandwich. Experiment with different breads, such as toasted sourdough, rye, or pita.

WINE RECOMMENDATION
Serve a simple, flavorful wine, such as a barrel-fermented sauvignon blanc from California or a a pinot blanc from Alsace in France.

SERVES 4

- 2 tablespoons wine vinegar
- 1 pound red cabbage (about 1/3 head), shredded (about 1 quart)
- 2 carrots, grated
- 1/2 cup mayonnaise
- 1/4 teaspoon ground cumin
- 1/4 teaspoon paprika
- 1/4 teaspoon salt
- 1/4 teaspoon fresh-ground black pepper
- 8 thick slices from 1 large round loaf of country bread
- 1 pound smoked turkey, sliced thin
- 1 pound tomatoes, sliced

1. In a medium stainless-steel saucepan, heat the vinegar over moderate heat. Add the red cabbage and toss until it is starting to wilt, 1 to 2 minutes. Transfer the cabbage to a medium glass or stainless-steel bowl and toss with the carrots, mayonnaise, cumin, paprika, salt, and pepper.

2. Heat the broiler. Put the bread on a baking sheet and broil, turning once, until crisp on the outside but still slightly soft in the center, about 3 minutes in all. Sandwich the turkey, sliced tomato, and slaw between pieces of toast.

MENU SUGGESTIONS

Sandwiches need simple, no-fuss companions, such as oven fries, chips, or fruit salad.

VARIATIONS

Embellish the slaw as you like. Chopped scallions, grated jicama, or thin slices of green pepper all make good additions.

Multiply Your Options

Look to this section for practical help in deciding what ingredients to keep on hand, choosing the easiest way to cook your chicken, and planning how to serve it. Among the useful guides, you'll find ideas for making salads and simply sauced dishes and, for those times when you can't think what to do with the remainders of a roast chicken or turkey, a list of recipes in which you can include leftovers.

RECIPES PICTURED OPPOSITE: *(top)* pages 63, 47, 23; *(center)* pages 155, 41, 157; *(bottom)* pages 147, 131, 171

The Quick Pantry

If you keep basic staples on hand, you can cut shopping to a minimum. Then you'll only have to make one short stop to pick up the fresh vegetables and poultry you need to complete the recipe.

CUPBOARD

- apple cider or juice
- apricots, dried
- beans, canned: black, chickpeas, kidney, white
- bread crumbs
- bulgar
- chicken broth, low-sodium
- coconut milk, unsweetened
- couscous
- figs, dried
- garlic
- grits, old-fashioned
- honey
- lentils
- maple syrup
- oil: cooking, olive
- onions
- pasta, dried: various shapes
- peanut butter
- pimiento
- potatoes
- raisins
- rice: arborio, long or medium grain
- soy sauce
- Tabasco sauce
- taco shells
- tomatoes: canned, paste, sun-dried
- vinegar: balsamic, red- or white-wine, rice-wine

SPICE SHELF

- allspice
- bay leaves
- cayenne
- chili powder
- cinnamon
- cloves
- coriander, ground and seeds
- cumin
- curry powder
- dill
- five-spice powder
- ginger
- marjoram
- mustard, dry
- nutmeg
- oregano
- paprika
- red-pepper flakes
- rosemary
- sage
- sesame seeds
- tarragon
- thyme
- turmeric

LIQUOR CABINET

- bourbon
- brandy
- port
- sherry
- vermouth, dry white
- wine: dry white, red

FREEZER

- bacon
- frozen vegetables: Brussels sprouts, okra, spinach
- nuts: peanuts, pecans, pine nuts, walnuts
- pasta

REFRIGERATOR

- anchovy paste
- apples
- butter
- capers
- cheese: Parmesan
- cream
- eggs
- fish sauce, Asian
- ginger, fresh
- jalapeño peppers
- ketchup
- lemons
- limes
- mayonnaise
- mustard: Dijon or grainy
- olives: black, green
- oranges
- parsley
- pesto
- salsa
- scallions
- sesame oil, Asian
- sour cream
- tahini
- yogurt, plain

LEFTOVERS

You can use leftover chicken or turkey in any of the recipes listed here. Substitute either one for the poultry called for in the ingredient list and add the meat when the dish is almost finished so that it just reheats rather than overcooks.

Sautés and Stir-Fries:

Baked and Grilled:

Soups, Curries, and Other Braised Dishes:

Pasta and Grains:

Salads and Sandwiches:

Basic Chicken-Cooking Methods

Some of our recipes call for store-bought roast chicken. If you'd rather cook your own, use any of the following methods. You'll find these recipes handy not only when you need cooked meat but when you want to serve plain chicken, embellish it with a pan sauce or compound butter, or make chicken salad (see pages 182 and 183).

ROASTED WHOLE CHICKEN

- 1 chicken (3 to 3½ pounds)
- ½ teaspoon salt
- ¼ teaspoon fresh-ground black pepper
- 1 tablespoon cooking oil

Heat the oven to 425°. Rub the bird inside and out with the salt and pepper. Twist the wings behind the back; tie the legs together. Put the chicken, breast-side up, in a roasting pan. Coat the chicken with the oil. Roast the chicken until done, about 55 minutes. Let the bird rest at least 10 minutes before cutting.

INDIVIDUAL SERVINGS

These recipes render about one pound of chicken meat. If you are serving individual pieces to four people, increase the number of thighs from six to eight, or replace the thighs with four whole legs. Add a few more minutes cooking time if you use legs.

BONE-IN BREASTS OR THIGHS

BAKED

- 4 bone-in chicken breasts or 6 thighs
- 1 tablespoon cooking oil
- ¼ teaspoon salt
- ⅛ teaspoon fresh-ground black pepper

Heat the oven to 400°. Coat the chicken with the oil; season with the salt and pepper. Put the chicken, skin-side up, in a roasting pan. Bake until just done, about 25 minutes for the breasts and 30 minutes for the thighs.

GRILLED

- 4 bone-in chicken breasts or 6 thighs
- 3 tablespoons cooking oil
- ¼ teaspoon salt
- ⅛ teaspoon fresh-ground black pepper

Light the grill. Coat the chicken with 1 tablespoon of the oil and season with the salt and pepper. Grill over moderately high heat, basting with the remaining 2 tablespoons oil, until just done, about 10 minutes per side for breasts and 12 per side for thighs.

POACHED

2 cups canned low-sodium chicken broth or homemade stock

1/2 teaspoon salt

4 bone-in chicken breasts or 6 thighs

In a large frying pan, combine the broth and salt and bring to a simmer. Add the chicken in a single layer and simmer, covered, for 10 minutes for breasts, 15 for thighs. Remove the pan from the heat. Let the chicken steam until just done, about 5 minutes, and remove from the broth. Strain the flavorful broth for later use.

BONELESS, SKINLESS BREASTS OR THIGHS

SAUTÉED

1 tablespoon cooking oil

4 boneless, skinless chicken breasts, or 6 boneless, skinless thighs

1/4 teaspoon salt

1/8 teaspoon fresh-ground black pepper

In a large nonstick frying pan, heat the oil over moderate heat. Season the chicken with the salt and pepper, add to the pan, and cook until brown, about 5 minutes. Turn and cook until almost done, about 3 minutes longer for breasts and 5 for thighs. Cover the pan, remove from the heat, and let steam 5 minutes.

GRILLED

4 boneless, skinless chicken breasts, or 6 boneless, skinless thighs

3 tablespoons cooking oil

1/4 teaspoon salt

1/8 teaspoon fresh-ground black pepper

Light the grill. Coat the chicken with 1 tablespoon of the oil and season with the salt and pepper. Grill the chicken over moderately high heat, basting with the remaining 2 tablespoons oil, until just done, about 5 minutes per side for breasts and 7 minutes per side for thighs.

POACHED

2 cups canned low-sodium chicken broth or homemade stock

1/2 teaspoon salt

4 boneless, skinless chicken breasts, or 6 boneless, skinless thighs

In a large frying pan, combine the broth and salt and bring to a simmer. Add the chicken in a single layer and simmer, covered, for 5 minutes for breasts, 10 for thighs. Remove the pan from the heat, let the chicken steam for 5 minutes longer, and remove from the broth. Strain the flavorful broth for later use.

Infinite Possibilities

PAN SAUCES

An easy way to make a quick meal is to sauté your favorite chicken parts and finish them off with a simple pan sauce. The technique is easy; just adapt it to what you like and have on hand.

1. ***SAUTÉ*** chicken in a little oil or a combination of oil and butter. Remove chicken from the pan.

2. ***ADD*** aromatic vegetables and cook until starting to soften. For a simpler sauce, skip this step.

   TRY: 2 to 4 tablespoons chopped onion, shallot, scallion, celery, pepper, carrot, or 1 clove chopped garlic.

3. ***DEGLAZE*** the pan with a flavorful liquid or combination of liquids: Bring to a boil, scraping the bottom of the pan to dislodge any browned bits. Boil until reduced to half the original quantity.

   TRY: ½ to 1 cup chicken or vegetable stock, red or white wine, vermouth, Madeira, or cider.

4. ***THICKEN*** the sauce. Add a thickening ingredient and simmer for 2 minutes. (Optional.)

   TRY: ¼ to ½ cup cream, half-and-half, or tomato puree or 1½ teaspoons tomato paste, or whisk in 1 to 2 tablespoons butter until just incorporated and remove from the heat before completely melted.

5. ***SEASON*** the sauce with salt, pepper, and your flavoring(s) of choice.

   TRY: chopped fresh herbs, capers, Dijon mustard, sun-dried tomatoes, or a few drops of citrus juice.

SAMPLE COMBINATIONS

French

1. Sauté the chicken.
2. Add shallot.
3. Deglaze with vermouth and chicken stock.
4. Thicken with butter.
5. Season with chopped tarragon.

Italian

1. Sauté the chicken.
2. Add garlic.
3. Deglaze with red wine.
4. Thicken with tomato puree.
5. Season with capers and chopped basil.

Southwestern

1. Sauté the chicken.
2. Add red bell pepper.
3. Deglaze with chicken stock.
4. Thicken with half-and-half.
5. Season with chopped cilantro and a little lime juice.

Compound Butters

Compound butters melt to make the simplest of sauces for grilled, baked, broiled, or sautéed chicken (see pages 180 to 181). Start with softened butter and stir in any of the following, or almost anything else you like; you can also use a food processor to combine. Season with salt and pepper. Use the butter immediately or make it ahead, roll it into a log, freeze it, and cut off slices as you need them to top hot chicken.

- Parsley and lemon juice
- Pine nuts, basil, and sun-dried tomatoes
- Lemon zest and crushed black peppercorns
- Soy sauce and chopped scallion
- Capers and anchovy paste
- Pecans and maple syrup
- Orange zest and cayenne pepper
- Tarragon
- Chipotle chiles, lime juice, and cilantro
- Calvados and walnuts
- Olives and crushed fennel seed
- Garlic and sage
- Red wine and roasted red pepper
- Basil and mint

Chicken Salads

Don't ignore chicken salad as a basic of the quick-dinner repertoire. Serve warm or at room temperature with raw vegetables or on bread. Use leftover chicken, store-bought roasted chicken, or chicken just cooked by one of our easy Basic Cooking Methods (see pages 180 to 181) and add one of the possibilities below—or ingredients of your choice.

For creamy chicken salad, mix cooked, cut-up chicken with mayonnaise, sour cream, yogurt, or a combination of these. Season with salt and pepper to taste. If you like, add:

- Parmesan cheese and lemon juice
- Dijon mustard and dill
- Pesto and cherry tomatoes
- Watercress and cucumber
- Fennel and walnuts
- Avocado, cayenne, and lime juice
- Red onion and tarragon

For a lighter chicken salad, toss the meat with a vinaigrette made from three or four parts oil to one part vinegar and seasoned with salt and pepper. If you like, add:

- Green beans and scallions
- Bean sprouts, carrots, and sesame oil
- Bell pepper and oregano
- Artichoke hearts and lemon juice
- Radicchio and sun-dried tomatoes
- Smoked mozzarella and asparagus
- Pear and a touch of curry powder

INDEX

Page numbers in **boldface** indicate photographs ❦ indicates wine recommendations

C

D

E

F

G

N

O

P

R

S

T

Z